WORDS IN PRAISE

"Skillfully plotted and with vividly drawn characters, *The Golden Dice* is suspenseful, exciting, romantic drama . . ."

Sherry Jones, author, *Four Sisters, All Queens*

"There aren't many novels of the Roman world that provide such a comprehensive picture, which should give *The Golden Dice* an appeal to a variety of readers."

Sarah Johnson, reviews editor for the *Historical Novels Review*

"Storrs gives us two new third-person female viewpoint characters: Pinna, the prostitute, and Semni, the flighty young servant. These characters add complexity to the plot—indeed it is hard to imagine the story without them—and give us a portrait of women at war."

Elizabeth Jane, *Historical Novels Review*

Runner-up, 2013 Sharp Writ Book Awards for General Fiction

THE
GOLDEN
DICE

ALSO BY ELISABETH STORRS

The Wedding Shroud
Call to Juno (to be published April 2016)

THE
GOLDEN
DICE

— A Tale of Ancient Rome —

ELISABETH STORRS

LAKE UNION
PUBLISHING

Published by Lake Union Publishing, Seattle

www.apub.com

Amazon, the Amazon logo, and Lake Union Publishing are trademarks of Amazon.com, Inc., or its affiliates.

ISBN-13: 9781477828564
ISBN-10: 1477828567

Cover design by Mumtaz Mustafa
Cover image © Elisabeth Storrs
Map © Elisabeth Storrs

Library of Congress Control Number: 2014919197

Printed in the United States of America

To Beth, John, and Jacqui

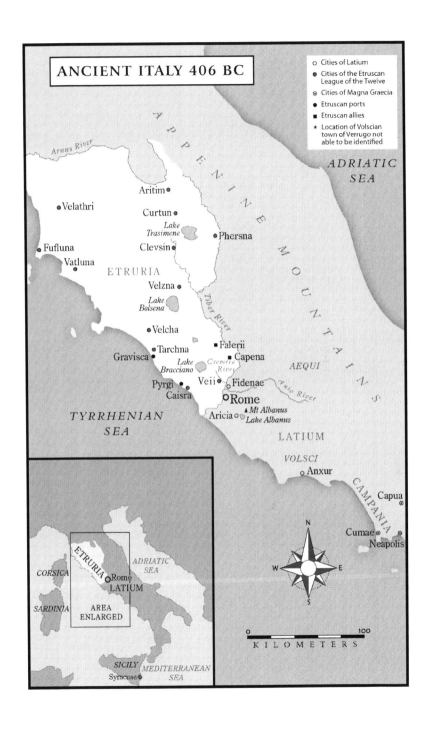

ANCIENT ITALY 406 BC

○ Cities of Latium
◉ Cities of the Etruscan League of the Twelve
⊙ Cities of Magna Graecia
● Etruscan ports
■ Etruscan allies
★ Location of Volscian town of Verrugo not able to be identified

Arnus River

A P P E N I N E

ADRIATIC SEA

•Velathri

•Aritim

•Curtun

Lake Trasimene

•Phersna

•Fufluna

•Clevsin

•Vatluna

E T R U R I A

•Velzna

M O U N T A I N S

Lake Bolsena

Tiber River

•Velcha

■ Falerii

•Tarchna

•Capena

Gravisca•

Lake Bracciano

Cremera River

AEQUI

Veii•

Pyrgi•

•Fidenae

Caisra•

○Rome

Anio River

TYRRHENIAN SEA

Aricia○

▲ Mt Albanus
◡ Lake Albanus

LATIUM

VOLSCI

○Anxur

CAMPANIA

Capua
◉

Cumae◉

Neapolis◉

CORSICA

ETRURIA

ADRIATIC SEA

Rome○

LATIUM

SARDINIA

AREA ENLARGED

N
W   E
S

SICILY

MEDITERRANEAN SEA

Syracuse◉

0 ——————— 100
K I L O M E T E R S

CAST

Veii

Caecilia (Aemilia Caeciliana): Born in Rome, Mastarna's wife (nickname Bellatrix and Cilla)

Vel *Mastarna* Senior: Etruscan nobleman, Caecilia's husband

Semni: A potter, servant in Mastarna's house

Arruns: Mastarna's Phoenician bodyguard

Artile Mastarna: Soothsayer, Mastarna's brother

Tarchon Mastarna: Adopted son of Mastarna

Ramutha Tetnies: Caecilia's friend

Cytheris: Caecilia's handmaid

Aricia: Cytheris' daughter, nursemaid

Tas (Vel Mastarna Junior): Caecilia and Mastarna's firstborn son

Larce Mastarna: Caecilia and Mastarna's second son

Arnth Mastarna: Caecilia and Mastarna's youngest son

Kurvenas: King (lucumo) of Veii, Mastarna's rival

Vipinas: Chief magistrate (zilath) of Veii

Sethre Kurvenas: Son of Kurvenas

Caile: Grandson of Vipinas

Lusinies: A general

Thia (Larthia) Mastarna: Caecilia and Mastarna's daughter

Perca: Junior nursemaid

Velthur: Semni's husband

Metli Tetnies: Ramutha's daughter
Aule Porsenna: Zilath of Tarchna, Mastarna's father-in-law
Tulumnes: Former king of Veii, Kurvenas's cousin
Seianta: Mastarna's first wife
Thefarie Ulthes: Ramutha's husband, Mastarna's friend
Arnth *Ulthes:* Murdered zilath of Veii, Mastarna's friend

Rome

Pinna (Lollia): A prostitute
Marcus Furius *Camillus:* Patrician consular general
Marcus Aemilius Mamercus Junior: Aemilius's son, Caecilia's
    cousin
Appius Claudius *Drusus:* Friend of Marcus, Caecilia's former
    admirer
Marcus *Aemilius* Mamercus Senior: Caecilia's uncle and adopted
    father
Genucius: Plebeian consular general
Calvus: Plebeian people's tribune
Sergius: Patrician consular general
Verginius: Patrician consular general
Fusca: Pinna's mother
Lollius: Pinna's father

Italicized names are used more commonly than full titles.

The Gods

Nortia/Fortuna: Goddess of Fate
Uni/Juno: Goddess of marriage/mothers/children, queen of the
    gods, wife of Tinia/Jupiter
Tinia/Jupiter: King of the gods, husband of Uni/Juno
Turan/Venus: Goddess of love

Aita: God of the Afterworld (his worshippers follow the Calu Death Cult)

Fufluns/Dionysus: God of wine and regeneration (his worshippers follow the Pacha Cult)

Mater Matuta: Goddess of the dawn

Mars: Roman god of war

Vesta: Roman goddess of hearth, home, and family

Menerva/Minerva: Goddess of wisdom, arts, war, and commerce

THE PROMISE

ONE

———

He smelled of leather, horse, and beeswax polish, the bronze of his armor cold against her despite her heavy woolen cloak. When he kissed her, though, hard and hungrily, his mouth and tongue were warm despite chill lips and cheeks.

"You need to take this off," she said, as she always did, pressing against the corselet, needing the feel of his body.

"Don't worry, I plan to," he replied, as he always did, then laughed and kissed her.

She could not move away from him, arms tightening around his waist, not trusting that he had returned, that another year had passed and he had not been killed.

For there were only two seasons now: war and winter.

Before this, it had been summer that made Caecilia smile with its lazy heat and languid evenings. But after seven years of conflict, she welcomed the hint of ice in the north wind and the bare stripped branches of trees ready to bear the burden of snow. Short days and long darkness no longer seemed oppressive because, in winter, her husband would come home.

Another long, clear note of the war trumpets sounded. Still holding Mastarna close, Caecilia turned her head to scan the tumult around her, glad the horns did not herald a charge but instead a return, as line after line of soldiers entered through the massive Menerva Gates of the Etruscan city of Veii.

The vast town square and wide avenues seethed with the color of the massed crowd, and timber- and terra-cotta-clad houses and temples were gaudy with garlands and ribbons. As the army marched into the forum a surge of people breached its formation, military discipline forgotten as wives and children hastened to kiss husbands and fathers while mothers and older men embraced sons.

Amid the throng, fine, long-legged warhorses shifted and whinnied as they were held fast, steam rising from their hides in the coldness of the afternoon, hot breath snorting from their nostrils. Adding to the clamor were laughter and merry tunes from double pipe, castanet, and timbrel, interrupted by snatches of sobbing, the lament of women whose men had not returned: a tragic counterpoint to celebration.

Caecilia could not ignore their sorrow. Even in her happiness a tight knot of apprehension remained, the voice that told her this reunion was due to respite in conflict, not its resolution. She chided herself not to sour the sweetness of Mastarna's return with the anticipation of his inevitable departure.

There was a rhythm to the fighting.

When the war season began with the lengthening of days and the greening of fields, the Veientanes would ride out to meet the Romans, who were assaulting Veii with a dogged vengeance. A vengeance sought in the name of Aemilia Caeciliana. A vengeance sought against her.

For seven years Caecilia had watched the Romans, who were once her people, hew pickets and planks and stakes from Veientane woodland to build stockades and siege engines to surround her adopted city, hindering trade, blocking supplies, and raiding farmlands until, by bright autumn and the falling of leaves, Veii's patience would falter as it waited for winter and the enemy to retreat. Each city pausing. Licking its wounds. For Roman bellies need to be fed, too. Roman crops need to be sown: barley and pulses and wheat. Roman families need to embrace their men, and Roman generals need to be elected.

Mastarna's cheek, heavy with bristle, brushed against hers, his own apprehension hinted in his deep, low voice, a voice whose timbre always stirred her. "And the baby?"

Smiling, she broke from him and searched for two women who stood jostled by those celebrating around them. Both were grinning as they observed husband and wife. The stout, wiry-haired maid called Cytheris gripped one hand each of two small boys while the nursemaid, Aricia, stepped forward on command and handed a swaddled bundle to her mistress.

"Another son," Caecilia said proudly.

Mastarna took the babe with the confidence of a man practiced in such a task. Even so, the mother wondered at the sight of a warrior cradling soft tininess against the hard contours of his corselet.

Exchanging his nurse's warmth for the cold comfort of his father's armor didn't please the child. His protests were loud and strident. Unperturbed, Mastarna chuckled, planting a kiss upon the baby's head as he hugged Caecilia once again. "Thank you. I could have no better wife."

"Nor I a better husband." She reclaimed the bawling baby, who settled immediately at her touch.

"Now where are those other sons of mine?" Mastarna turned to face his older children. Wide-eyed and wary of the scarred, metal-clad giant who had returned into their lives, the boys were speechless.

Mastarna's thigh-high greaves grated as he crouched down beside them. "Don't tell me you've forgotten me?"

The older boy was solemn, bowing in greeting. "Of course I know who you are, Apa. Hail, General Vel Mastarna!"

"Hail, my son," said his father with equal seriousness before placing his leather-lined bronze helmet upon the boy, engulfing him. The child pulled it back, tilting his head so he could spy the world through the slits between nose and cheek pieces, both hands held firmly on either side to bear the weight.

Seeing his brother gaining such favor, the two-year-old forgot his awe of the warrior. He hastened from behind Cytheris's skirts, bounding over to wrest the trophy from the other. "Give me, Tas, give me!"

The five-year-old turned away, raising the bright-blue crested helmet firmly out of reach, not prepared to surrender his prize. "Go away, Larce. Apa gave it to me."

Mastarna laughed and lifted his younger son onto his hip. The boy's startled expression changed to one of glee as he caught sight of the curved sword strapped to his father's side. "Look, Ati," he shrieked at his mother, gripping the hilt. "Sword! Sword!" Despite his struggling to remove the weapon from its sheath it remained secure.

"Hello, Caecilia."

A soldier stood beside her with open arms. It took a moment to recognize the bearded man as Tarchon. Mastarna's other son. Adopted. Little older than she was. The thought was sobering. In spring she would be twenty-six.

There was no sign of the effeminate youth she once knew. He was a man now, boasting battle scars. What warrior did not, after so many years of war? Nevertheless, his fine face was unscathed, its beautiful symmetry incongruous against the blatant masculinity of bronze.

"Thank the gods you have been spared." She hugged him.

Tarchon returned the embrace, cautious of the bundle of boy squeezed between them.

"Thank the gods also that you bore my brother safely." He touched the baby's cheek gently with one finger and was rewarded with a smile. It was no surprise. Tarchon pleased everyone—everyone except his father.

"He has your big, round Roman eyes, but I won't hold that against him."

Caecilia frowned, glancing at the sloe-eyed Etruscans around her. She doubted they'd ever forgive her for being a daughter of Rome. "Yes, but others might."

Tarchon kissed her cheek. "I'm only teasing. Besides, all here respect you now."

Before she could reply, Mastarna interrupted. "Isn't it time I named my new son?" He swung Larce to the ground. The boy immediately grasped his leg, demanding to be returned to the heights. Cytheris quickly drew him away.

Caecilia nodded. Ever since her son was born she'd been anxious to perform the ceremony. After all, the child was two months old and rightly should have been claimed within nine days of his birth. There was always an undercurrent of concern within her. What if Mastarna did not return? Would the right of this boy to take his father's name be questioned? What would become of her, no longer Roman but never Etruscan, if her husband should die?

"What name have you chosen?"

"Arnth. After Arnth Ulthes, our great friend."

Mastarna searched her face. "Are you sure?"

"Very sure. It is a strong name, given in honor of a noble man."

"He would be pleased that you wish to remember him." He stroked her hair. "Now let me claim him."

Despite her desire for the rite to be performed, Caecilia hesitated at the thought of placing the child at his father's feet. The crowd around them was unruly and she was afraid that the horses could trample the baby.

Then she noticed Arruns, Mastarna's guard—head shaven, the snake tattoo upon his face adding, as always, a rugged menace to him. Without needing an order he cleared a space around the family, holding the reins of his master's horse tight.

Laying the baby on the cobblestones, Caecilia anxiously watched as Mastarna lifted him above his head.

"All present here bear witness that this boy is my son. His name shall be Arnth of the House of Mastarna. Child of my loins and that of Aemilia Caeciliana's—known to all as Caecilia."

Unlike Larce, the infant did not enjoy being raised in the air, screaming with a fierceness at odds with his size. Mastarna hastily lowered him, holding him close, before taking a gold amulet necklace from Caecilia and placing it around the little boy's neck.

"May this bulla protect you forever from the evil eye. May all the great and almighty gods watch over you!"

Caecilia took the sobbing baby from his father, soothing him once again. As she did so, she noticed that the crowd around them had quieted. She tensed, holding her breath, aware their stares were reserved for her, their silence signaling resentment of her as much as respect for Mastarna.

And she knew why that must be.

Seven years ago, in a glade beside a river between two cities, she had made a choice to forsake her home. A choice Rome claimed provoked a war. And she had questioned that decision many times. Not because she did not love her husband but because his people did not love her.

She knew what to do today, though. Had done it before. She slowly held Arnth out to the crowd. "I give my son to this city. Another man-child to bear arms for Veii. Another warrior for you who have become my people."

There was no response at first, their gaze wavering from her to the baby and then to the warrior.

Then cheering erupted. "Hail, Arnth of the House of Mastarna! Hail, General Vel Mastarna!"

Relief filled her, reassured in that moment to know that, even if the Veientanes hated her, she was safe as long as they revered her husband.

TWO

Caecilia signaled the slave boy to draw the heavy red curtain of the bedchamber closed, sorry it was too cold to leave it open so that she could view the garden. Then she ordered him and the other slave who was lighting the candelabras to leave.

Mastarna pulled her to him. She laughed. "You need a bath!"

"Do you want to wait that long?"

Shaking her head, she began unbuckling the straps of his cuirass, staggering slightly at the weight as she helped him to remove it and its kilt of heavy linen strips. Then, faster now, loosening the armbands before kneeling to help him off with his greaves. Both let the armor clatter to the floor. Both stripped with equal haste. Then Mastarna lifted her onto the high, wide bed to kiss her, all of her, cheeks and nose and throat, breasts and belly and toes, before parting her soft white thighs and ending the lovers' long wait.

Afterward, they lay nestled together in a room made cozy despite the fug of smoke pooling under the high ceiling above the wall vents. The leopard painted on the wall peered out of its laurel grove, swallows flitting over its head, a constant companion guarding them for all these years.

Caecilia stroked the long scar across Mastarna's chest and stomach, then the one that ran from nose to lip. His arms were crisscrossed with old wounds also. "I can't see any fresh ones."

"Only scrapes and grazes this time. I managed to avoid a Roman sword point. I must be getting careful in my old age."

"Or maybe you've finally learned some skills."

He laughed and pulled the coverlet of red, green, and blue plaid from her. "Let me see if you have changed."

Caecilia protested at the rush of cold air and pulled the counterpane up again, but Mastarna stopped her. "Let me look at you," he repeated, gently running his hand over her hips and belly, tracing the silver web of lines upon her skin.

Caecilia clasped his hand, aware of how she was aging, how bearing her babies, however beloved, had robbed her body of tautness. "Don't, they're ugly."

Mastarna kissed the delicate marks. "You should be proud of them. They are proof you are a mother and have borne more pain than any I might face. Was your labor very terrible?"

This time he let her draw the quilt close around them. She always forgot the agony once it was over. Holding a baby to her breast healed her.

"I wish that one day you'll be there to see me give birth, Vel. I prayed every day before Arnth was born that you would come home."

Mastarna was silent for a time. "One day," he murmured. "One day."

Caecilia regretted speaking. She knew he wanted to be there, and it was no use wishing for what was not fated. She should be rejoicing that the gods gave Vel the chance to hold their children at all.

And how she loved them, her winter-seeded sons. Loved their touch: the soft dimpled fingers of Arnth reaching up to touch her mouth as she kissed them, or tugging at her earrings; Larce measuring the small span of his two-year-old palm against hers, his thumb and fingers tiny. And then there was her firstborn, Vel Mastarna Junior. So quiet and earnest they had nicknamed him "Tas," the silent one. Believing himself too grown-up to need his mother, until darkness came and he would clasp her hand, pretending it was she who needed comfort.

Mastarna shifted to sit on the edge of the bed. "Let's bathe before the feast. I'm looking forward to soaking in hot water."

Caecilia lingered under the bedclothes, studying him. His nose was battered and his face lined: features of a man who had suffered both inside and outside. And although his dark sloe eyes could be hard, they always softened when he gazed at his family.

Seeing how the skin of his body was smooth compared to the heavy afternoon bristle upon his chin, she smiled. It always surprised her how the Veientanes took their barbers on campaign. Not to mention the enormous retinue of other servants to cater to their every need. As if they could not leave luxury behind for even one moment. Fine clothes and furniture and utensils. Musicians and dancers and poets alongside blacksmiths and bow-makers. And, of course, seers and priests to ensure the gods' intentions could be divined and their favor secured. "However do you find time to shave or pluck your body while at war?" she teased.

"So you would have me as hairy as a bear like some Roman soldier?" He rubbed his chin. "Although I'm considering growing my beard."

Kneeling behind him, Caecilia slipped her arms around his waist, laying her cheek against the broadness of his back. "Don't you dare!"

He laughed. "I suppose you're right. It's a rare woman who likes her skin scraped."

Caecilia was glad he could not see her expression. For there were other kinds of slaves included among the camp followers: concubines and harlots. It always tormented her that Vel might find fidelity too onerous in the long months of fighting. "As long as it's only my cheek you scratch."

Smiling, Mastarna turned and pulled her onto his lap. "And have you taken a lover yet? All these young slave boys at your disposal."

She pushed against him. "How could you even suggest it?"

He was serious now, his dark, almond-shaped eyes somber, an edge to his voice. "Then you should not suspect me either."

Ashamed, she looked down.

He raised her chin between thumb and forefinger to make her face him. "I wish you could see yourself as I do. Then you could never doubt me, Bellatrix." He traced a line between her breasts, then examined the pendant around her neck. "Remember why I gave this to you? To remind you that you are brave."

The locket was an amulet he'd given her when they'd first married. It had become a love token that she treasured. The huntress Atlenta was depicted upon it, a mortal who'd also fallen in love with a husband she'd been decreed to wed. Caecilia had only learned of her story after she came to Veii. She fingered the charm. Vel claimed she was like the mythical girl—a warrioress, a bellatrix—but she doubted she deserved such a nickname.

She encircled his neck. "Forgive me for being foolish?"

He laid her back upon the soft mattress, nuzzling her neck. "I already have."

THREE

The flames ripped along the wood as the torch was set to the pitch, the fire consuming the thick oxhide sides of the siege towers, wooden struts burning, acrid black smoke billowing.

After a long year of deprivation the Veientanes gathered on every side of the city, the sound of their shrieking saturating the air. Escaping the prison of their homes they streamed down the roads sloping from the plateau. Beneath a wintry sun, they traversed woodland and stream to reach the Roman fortifications to set them afire. There they hacked at the vestiges of war left behind by their enemy to fuel the blaze: dismantling wheeled shelters and mantlets, stripping stockades of stakes, and wrenching pickets from trenches.

Now as night fell, Caecilia and Mastarna watched their rampage from the heights of the citadel. A line of bonfires stretched around the walls, a circle of liberation, some mere pinpricks twinkling in the distance, others nearer that were roaring, fierce and bright. Directly across from the acropolis was the greatest conflagration. Like a malignant boil on the skin of the city, the main

Roman camp sat on the rise beyond the dark strip of river. In the darkness, its fences and guard posts glowed deep red.

Observing this unleashing of hatred, Caecilia leaned the back of her head against Vel's chest as he stood behind her, the familiar scent of his sandalwood perfume and the circle of his arms making her feel safe. She felt her relief that she was not among the Etruscans, then silently scolded herself for thinking of them by that name. It was what the Romans called them. The people of Veii referred to themselves as the Rasenna, and Veii was only one of many cities in which they dwelt. Rome considered itself mighty, but in truth it was a township compared to such a metropolis as Veii. This did not stop its onslaught. Valor and persistence had brought many of its larger enemies down.

Caecilia shivered a little from both cold and disquiet. Mastarna drew his tebenna cloak around them, its heavy folds covering the yellow of her fine woolen mantle. She had learned not to speak to him of her fears. How she was anxious that the brittle respect paid to her by his people would one day crack.

There was another reason why she did not want to mingle with the Rasenna. She knew that over this long day retaliation had merged with religious fervor. The pyres were raging, the fires hot enough to cause cheeks to flush and muscles to loosen, and the Veientanes were drinking strong, unwatered wine laced with freedom. The Winter Feast of the god Fufluns had begun.

The beat of drums and the weird rising moan of the bullroarers heralded the commencement of the ceremony. Led by horse-tailed satyrs and wild-eyed maenads, the wine god's followers donned grotesque masks of stag, boar, or goat. Frenzy followed as copious drafts of vinegary wine were consumed. Then, desiring revelation, the believers stripped and rutted before the fires, seeking to attain oneness with the divine, worshipping the potency of the sacred phallus, believing the power of coitus was a challenge to death.

Once, long ago, drugged and despairing, Caecilia had been drawn into such rituals. The visions she saw that night still haunted her, confirming she could never worship Fufluns. She may have forsaken Rome but she could not desert its gods. Yet she did not condemn the Veientanes's dedication to the deity. With their enemy besieging them for so long, the promise of rebirth and regeneration was compelling. And, over time, familiarity with such rites had beveled the edges of her disapproval.

Hearing the music and ecstatic cries from below the acropolis, she covered Mastarna's hands with her own as he clasped her waist. Some aristocrats like Tarchon had already descended into the woods to seek epiphany with commoners and slaves alike. At least she was reassured that Vel would not indulge in the revels. He knew she could not bear him seeking rapture with other women, and so he always stayed by her side at these festivals, his devotion to Fufluns remaining private. Both had come to tolerate each other's beliefs.

The wine god must have been pleased because the night was mild and starlit. Mild enough for the zilath, Vipinas, the chief magistrate of Veii, to order a pavilion with banqueting klines to be set up beside a giant bonfire in front of the palace. The lord and lady principes dined together, draped luxuriantly across the deep-cushioned couches. Ribbons entwined with ivy had been wound around statues and steles in the forum, trailing cheerfulness, encouraging a belief that all was as it should be. Symbols of Fufluns were ever present: pinecones piled as decorations, leopards engraved on footstools and furniture. Musicians wandered between the divans, the strains of cithara and double flute a sweet antidote to the months of privation. With swirling skirts, dancers lifted their arms to the night sky in praise.

Caecilia turned and laid her cheek on Mastarna's shoulder. Tall as she was, she could watch the banqueting principes while resting there. The feast was well in progress. Naked slave boys, chosen for their beauty, hastened to pour a fine vintage into double-handled goblets. No sour wine would do for the high councillors and their wives when toasting the wine god.

She gazed at the noblewomen, beautiful in their finery, as they shared the divans with their husbands. Robed in vivid chitons, the women had dressed their hair elaborately with amber and glass diadems, and golden torques graced their necks. Caecilia smiled, delighted that she was clothed and adorned in this way, too. In many ways she was no longer an outsider. She gave thanks to Juno every day that she had found independence here, giving audience to tenants in the absence of her husband, and acting as patron to artisans famed for their fine ceramics. Observing how the ladies laughed and drank and conversed with the men also lifted her spirits. There would have been no such freedoms if she'd remained in Rome, only the confines of atrium and bedroom, the company of women, and sullen obedience to the men of her family. Rome and Veii lay only twelve miles apart across the Tiber, but they were different worlds.

She wrapped her arms around Vel and squeezed him.

He laughed. "Why the hug?"

"I'm just glad you are with me again. Glad that I live here."

He kissed her brow. "So am I. But much as I would love to stay here holding you, Bellatrix, I think it's time we returned to the feast."

Caecilia reluctantly agreed, but as she slipped her arms from around him she knocked a small dice box from the sinus fold of his tebenna.

"You see," he said, retrieving the golden canister, "I've been careful not to lose my luck charms."

He spilled two golden dice onto her palm from the box. Each had the symbols of numbers carved upon them rather than dots. They were worn around the edges from constant use. Given her husband's love of gambling this was no surprise. "There will be complaints if you try these old things at the gaming tables tonight," she teased. "You can barely read the markings."

Mastarna reclaimed the tesserae. "You know I never play with them anymore. But I keep them as my link to you when I am far from home. Without these, we might never have been reunited."

Caecilia pressed against him again. The last time she rolled the dice she had asked the goddess of Fate to give her a sign, and she had returned home to Vel. But it worried her that he had suffered because of her return. Her husband would never become the zilath of the Veientanes. Not while he had a Roman for a wife. Instead he was always sent to campaign in the north instead of leading the assault on the main Roman camp. Yet Vel never vented his frustration upon her. Never blamed her for the halter placed upon his ambition. He was resigned to being a great commander who had been given the worst command. She raised her head to meet his gaze. "Do you ever regret marrying me again?"

He cupped her chin with his hand and kissed her. "I sent for you, remember? The divine Nortia brought you back to me for a reason."

As she hugged him again she noticed they were no longer alone. The zilath, Vipinas, had joined them at the citadel wall.

"As usual the supplies you have brought are most welcome, Vel Mastarna."

Breaking from their embrace, her husband bowed. "I think it's the amphorae of wine that is most appreciated. It's thirst that's being sated tonight, not hunger."

The lean old man smiled, his false gold-and-ivory front teeth glinting. It was a rare sight. The chief magistrate doled out his mirth as frugally as he did the grain rations. "There is no doubting the people always wait anxiously for your return. Without your success in thwarting the blockades and protecting farmland, the city would be facing famine now."

She was pleased to hear the compliment. It was good that her husband was acknowledged. Due to his achievements, bullock trains had trundled through the gates all day to disgorge their cargoes to a rejoicing population. And tomorrow wagons laden with goods would travel on a network of roads to other cities. Barges would again wend their way along rivers. Soon ships with Veientane cargoes would sail to foreign ports of which Caecilia had only dreamed.

A woman's mock shriek accompanied by male laughter distracted Caecilia's attention. The aristocratic principes on the klines were toasting the wine god.

Mastarna ignored the merriment. "Our cause was helped when Camillus failed to draw the lot to lead the campaign against us. How foolish Rome is to waste their best consular general in fighting the Volscians in the south."

"Yes, but it's to our advantage if the Romans send him and their remaining generals to fight their neighbors," replied Vipinas. "Better to keep most of their forces busy attacking other Latin tribes. At least there are only two of their armies sitting upon our threshold."

Mastarna pointed to the massive tufa walls below them. "I see that their ramp nearly reached us."

Vipinas paused, glancing at Caecilia before continuing. "General Aemilius was effective enough. Romans are none too pretty when you see them at close quarters. It reminded us, too, that we can't be complacent."

Caecilia offered no comment, having finally learned to think before she spoke. Even though her opinion as a woman would not be disdained, her ancestry was best glossed over. For General Aemilius was both her adopted father and her uncle. The last time she'd seen him he'd been furious at how she'd changed from Roman maiden to Rasennan wife. How humiliated he must be that she remarried Vel after he had formally arranged their divorce. To

Aemilius she had forsaken her people, betrayed her clan, and shamed her family. Hearing Camillus's name also stirred feelings. She hated that general as much as he despised her. When she'd first been offered as a treaty bride he'd assured her he would protect her while she lived among the foe. Instead he'd been prepared to sacrifice her in the name of war.

Mastarna squeezed her hand in reassurance. She returned the pressure, grateful that he sensed her unease. Once again she gave silent thanks that he had given her a second chance to leave Rome behind.

"As long as the Romans keep electing different consular generals every year," he said, "there's always a good chance they will make no headway."

"Different generals, different strategies," agreed Vipinas, coughing. "And none of them have succeeded."

Caecilia nodded, aware that another aristocrat had approached. She glanced at Vel, sensing he would not welcome the intrusion.

Vipinas greeted the nobleman. "Ah, here is Kurvenas. You should congratulate him, Mastarna. It was his troops that repelled Aemilius so ably this year."

Kurvenas bowed to the chief magistrate, then curtly acknowledged Mastarna and Caecilia.

Caecilia knew how little regard Vel had for this man. He bristled and nodded briefly in return. She heard the click of the dice within the golden box as Mastarna fingered it beneath his cloak. He always did this without thinking when aggravated or uncertain. A tell she alone knew about him.

Kurvenas's hair, longer than most Rasennan men, gleamed with unguents. He rubbed the scar that creased his short clipped beard. There was a polish to his bulk and height, so different to the rawness that emanated from her husband's scarred face and powerful body. "Honors should also go to Vel Mastarna," he said. "Once again, he has valiantly guarded the vulnerable north."

Mastarna did not acknowledge the praise. Kurvenas's popularity irked him. Persuasive in his counsel, the aristocrat concentrated on being everybody's friend. Caecilia suspected, though, that such affability veiled rancor against those who opposed him. Yet she could not deny his prowess as a commander or that he was liked as much as Vel by his men.

Ignoring his rival, Mastarna offered his forearm to her. "Isn't it time we rejoined the banquet?"

Zilath Vipinas laid his hand upon Mastarna's shoulder. "I'm afraid we need to discuss the upcoming election first. Our meal can wait." He turned to Caecilia. "If you wish, you may return to your divan."

Mastarna slid his arm around her. "Your tone is ominous. I think, perhaps, that she should stay."

Kurvenas and Vipinas exchanged glances, causing husband and wife to exchange their own. Caecilia had never known these men to be allies.

"Let's be frank, then." Kurvenas's smile was broad, his tone even. "The time has come to dispense with annual elections. Veii is weakened by them. As is Rome. Winter should be spent planning how we are to defeat our foe, not arguing among us who should lead the city."

Mastarna's fingers tightened on Caecilia's waist. "Our chief magistrates can retain office for more than one year so we don't face the same problem as the Romans. As a result our defense tactics have remained consistent and successful. So what are you proposing? Elect a lucumo king instead? Be governed by a man until he dies? Has your memory grown so poor that you've forgotten what happened last time a monarch was proclaimed? Tulumnes was corrupted by power!"

Skin pale, Vipinas flushed, coughing again. "See reason. I know you must find it strange that I support such a change, but our resources could be put to better use than always voting every winter. Let's elect a sovereign and concentrate on war alone."

Mastarna's bass voice resounded across the square, causing the diners to stop and stare. Turning from Kurvenas, he concentrated solely on the older man. "King Tulumnes had Arnth Ulthes—a zilath just like you—assassinated in order to take control. And Tulumnes insulted you, your clan also." Mastarna pointed at Kurvenas. "And that tyrant was this man's cousin. How can you support his kin?"

Vipinas put up his hands as though to fend off a blow. "Calm down. We must put those personal enmities behind us for the sake of Veii. I doubt anyone would be foolish enough to rule like Tulumnes."

"So who do you suggest should be this lucumo king?" Mastarna stabbed his finger in Kurvenas's direction again. "Him? His family members have always considered themselves more royal than others. They have no respect for our government. Choose him and you will have a despot, one who will triumph as he tramples over our people."

Unruffled, Kurvenas brushed off a few stray hairs that had settled upon his cloak, his gaze traversing Caecilia from head to foot. "I think your judgment is clouded."

His smugness was a goad. Mastarna stepped toward him. "Are you questioning my loyalty to this city?"

Kurvenas continued to smile, unfazed by his opponent's proximity. "Of course not, it's just that you might have some qualms about the new strategy I have put to the High Council."

Mastarna frowned. "And what scheme would that be?"

The aristocrat returned his attention to Caecilia. "Why, to conquer Rome, of course."

She stiffened, then breathed deeply, trying to control her shock and muster her thoughts. Until now she could abide Veientanes

killing Romans to defend themselves. But could she stand by and
watch the city of her birth and her family attacked?

Mastarna also tensed. "You're deluded! The only chance Veii
has of assailing Rome is if we gain the support of the League of the
Twelve Rasennan cities. Support that will never be forthcoming.
The congress despises kings. Besides, Tulumnes insulted them and
was expelled like a dog as a result. If your plan is to attack Rome's
citadel without such an alliance, you will weaken Veii instead."

Again Kurvenas remained calm, but moved a step back from
Mastarna as a precaution. "See, my Lord Zilath, I told you he
would not want to storm her city."

The argument had caused others to leave the bonfire and
gather—a circle of querying faces. One in particular stood ashen-
faced. Thefarie Ulthes. Younger brother of the zilath poisoned
at Tulumnes's behest. Normally Thefarie's wide grin and throaty
chuckle infected others, provoking good humor even in the
reluctant. Tonight he remained solemn and soundless. His wife,
though, could not restrain herself. Ramutha Tetnies quaked as
she accosted Vipinas. "How could you? How could you? To elect
a sovereign is to dishonor Clan Ulthes!"

Caecilia could see Kurvenas flinch. Most Veientane men
esteemed their wives, valuing their opinions. The way he glared
at Ramutha showed Caecilia that he was more a Roman than
Rasennan husband. His wife was absent tonight. Instead he'd
brought his courtesan. Ignoring Ramutha, he addressed the principes around him. "All of you know that I am not like my cousin
Tulumnes. And we do not need a woman's hysteria to distort my
motives. I mean no offense to the House of Ulthes but we have had
seven years of siege. Rome must be attacked. And a king should
lead us."

Suddenly Thefarie found his voice, volume making up for his
earlier silence. And just like his wife, he reserved his anger for

Vipinas. "How can you countenance this? I thought you were a friend of my family."

The old man straightened his shoulders, which set him coughing again. "I am no one's enemy." He struggled to gain breath. "Nor are the tribal leaders of the High Council."

The sick feeling within Caecilia deepened as she realized the matter must have already been decided. How quickly the euphoria of reunion had disappeared. Heady elation replaced by the feeling of life careening out of control.

Mastarna gave a sour laugh. "Oh, now I see. While I've been away Kurvenas hasn't just been campaigning against the Romans."

Before either man could respond another nobleman interrupted, his head as bald as his beard was thick. Lusinies was grizzled, the tip of his nose missing, his ears fibrous from years of wearing a helmet. "It's not just Kurvenas who sees the sense in ceasing annual elections, Mastarna. You and Thefarie would be outnumbered in any vote. All four of the six high councillors favor a monarch. And we think that man should be Kurvenas."

Ramutha's jaw dropped. "And when was this decided? When was your little conspiracy concocted? Did you sharpen your knives while Thefarie was risking his life defending the north with Mastarna?"

Caecilia marveled at her friend. Ramutha was elegant in her fury. Normally the expression in her kohl-rimmed eyes was of amusement. Now it was harsh, her straight brow furrowed. Her lapis earrings jiggled amid waves of light-brown hair as she shook in indignation; her tapered fingers clenched the gold chain baldrics that crossed her breasts. Although diminutive, this woman had a heart as fierce as any of these soldiers.

Thefarie put his hand on her shoulder to calm her as he again faced Vipinas. "Then if there is to be a king, it must be you."

The zilath shook his head, wheezing. "I'm nearly seventy and I am ill. We must choose a man who can lead us for many years."

Caecilia studied the old man's waxen face. He had grown more gaunt over the past year. His false teeth seemed too large in a shrunken mouth.

Ramutha shrugged her husband away to stand closer to the zilath. "You're not just weak from illness and age."

Caecilia gasped. Her friend was letting anger overcome prudence. And having learned the hard way the damage that could be wrought through rashness, she knew such emotion needed to be curbed. She moved to Ramutha and placed her arm around her. Her friend's body thrummed with nerves and rage. "Hush," she murmured, "before it's too late."

For a moment she thought the noblewoman would continue her rant and smash old alliances, but instead Ramutha steadied herself before she spoke again. "Then Mastarna should be elected. He is the greatest general among you."

Earlier the other aristocrats had been quiet due to surprise; now it was from discomfort.

Mastarna shook his head. "I would never seek such an office." There was disgust in his voice, his face, his eyes. "We'd be mad to tether ourselves to one man. And what if Rome is conquered? Then our ruler would hold enormous power. We may well be unable to control a king who becomes an oppressor."

Cries from the revelers in the city below edged into the quiet that followed. Their joy was at odds with the gloom that had fallen over the principes. When one of the logs in the bonfire collapsed and crashed within the flames, everyone was startled.

From the darkness a man wearing a sheepskin cloak and pointed hat emerged, a curved staff in one hand. It was Lord Artile, chief priest of Veii—the man Caecilia loathed most in the world. To see him was to feel afresh the sting of his spite.

Mastarna grimaced. "Don't tell me you have consulted my charlatan brother for guidance?"

Before Vipinas opened his mouth, Lusinies spoke. "You are unwise to denigrate him, Mastarna. Your brother is the greatest seer in Veii. Lord Artile has asked the gods what path we should follow. As our most skilled haruspex, he has divined the future from the liver of a ram."

The sense of her world unraveling spread as Caecilia remembered another prophecy. Artile had confirmed that the gods favored a monarch then also. Tulumnes. A ruler who threatened her with death and mutilation, prompting her to flee back to Rome.

The haruspex smoothed the arch of one eyebrow slowly. "The portent was clear. The gods wish Veii to choose a lucumo."

Caecilia tugged Mastarna's cloak, trying to warn him not to be reckless. He ignored her, slowly and deliberately turning his back on his brother. A dangerous insult. "Very well, place your faith in this priest. Elect your king. But know that I will never swear loyalty to him."

The defiance finally provoked Kurvenas to temper. "That is treason!"

Vipinas sighed. "There isn't time for this, Mastarna. It will be you who will cause our people to suffer if you plunge us into internal conflict. Do you think anyone would be prepared to follow you if you incite clansmen to fight one another as well as the Romans?"

Mastarna hesitated, and Caecilia knew the zilath's words stirred memories of a promise made to his murdered friend. Arnth Ulthes had also warned her husband never to risk civil war. She touched Vel's arm, making him glance down at her. For the second time that night she counseled caution. "It's no use. Remember Ulthes's advice. He would not want Rasenna to fight Rasenna."

He scanned her face, weighing her words, then sighed. "Very well. For the sake of concord I will lead my army in the name of a sovereign. But without the League of the Twelve's support I won't help Veii attack Rome."

Kurvenas snorted and once again eyed Caecilia up and down as if ogling a whore. "So speaks a man who keeps a Roman in his bed."

Mastarna took a step toward him again, but before he could seize his opponent, she moved between the men, her heart thumping, restraint forgotten.

Facing the aristocrats, she once again took a deep breath to quell her nerves. Even so, she was surprised to find her voice was calm. "All know here that there is no going back for me. And I risk death as surely as you do should the enemy breach our walls. So if anyone here doubts my allegiance I will return to Rome tomorrow and meet a traitor's death."

All avoided her gaze. No one spoke.

Trying not to show she was trembling, Caecilia held out her hand for Mastarna to escort her from the square. Thefarie and Ramutha followed. After a few steps Mastarna bent and growled, "That was foolish! What if someone had challenged you?"

Her own temper flared, not needing a reminder she'd been rash. "I don't know, but you're the one who taught me to gamble."

Mastarna halted briefly as though to rebuke her again. Then he grunted acknowledgment and placed his arm around her shoulders.

Caecilia glanced back at the gathering as they walked away. Kurvenas, rather than Vipinas, was calling to the others to resume their feasting. At such cajoling, Lusinies slapped the future monarch on the back. The assembled principes drifted after them, their sober mood growing lighter.

The flames of the ring of fires around the city seared the darkness. The song of the Veientanes caressed the air.

FOUR

In the dark chill before daybreak she woke before she heard the baby crying, her breasts tight, the sheet crusted from leaking milk.

Mastarna reached for her in the cocoon of their bed but Aricia was already calling for permission to enter, holding a squawking Arnth. A slave boy followed, wheeling a freshly stoked brazier.

The infant settled quickly at the teat, noisy in his guzzling. Caecilia loosened the clean swaddling so that she could feel the baby's skin next to hers. Mastarna lay on his side, propping his head against one hand as he studied his wife and son. "He is greedy, Bellatrix."

"Just like his father."

He smiled, offering his fingers to the child. Arnth ignored him until, hunger easing, he clasped the calloused thumb with a tiny fist, smiling around his mother's breast.

"You should retain a wet nurse." He broke from the boy's grasp to run his hand along his wife's arm. "Then you might quicken before I leave again."

Caecilia frowned, drawing her woolen shawl about her, knowing that a woman who holds a babe to her breast rarely falls with child. Her chances of conceiving were always limited to those winters when she was not suckling. Yet she did not want another woman to feed her son. It was unbearable to think of surrendering the tenderness, the gentle tug at her nipple, the drowsy warmth nestled against her. A nearness that her own mother had denied her. And Arnth was not yet one season old. Her body needed respite. "Aren't three healthy sons enough?"

Mastarna bent over and blew noisily on Arnth's back. The infant gurgled. "But if we let this chance go by there might not be a next time, Bellatrix." He sat up and put his arm around her, Arnth content between them. "Besides, what better place to brave the cold than under the bedcovers."

"Don't joke. I could not bear it if you were killed."

"I don't need to leave Veii to be knifed."

She scanned his face. Dark circles under his eyes. When they had returned home from the Winter Feast he had remained silent, brooding. She knew better than to probe the wound. Both had slept fitfully.

"Ati! Ati!"

The edge of the bedchamber's curtain was thrown back and Larce rushed in. He clambered onto the footstool, eager to greet them.

Mastarna reached down and placed his hand under his son's bottom, scooping him up so that the boy landed with a thump onto the deep mattress. There was a rush of giggles. Regaining his balance, Larce scrambled down onto the footstool. "Again, Apa! Again!"

As Mastarna duly complied, Tas entered. Solemn, the older boy climbed up to kiss his mother before greeting his father. He made no attempt to join in the play, and instead sat at the end of the bed observing his raucous brother.

"And how is the heir to the House of Mastarna this morning?"

"Well, Apa." Tas pointed to the wide purple scar that slanted across the warrior's chest. "Does that hurt?"

Mastarna peered down at the puckered flesh. "This scratch? No. What you need to remember is to cause your foe greater hurt."

Caecilia raised her eyebrows. Knowing the story behind the injury, she was unimpressed with such bravado. Vel was lucky to have survived the attack that caused it.

She noticed Tas glance down at his knees. They were badly grazed from where he'd fallen clumsily in some childish game. There had been tears. Brief and angry. She had chided him for weeping, telling him that young soldiers do not cry.

Raising Arnth to her shoulder, Caecilia rubbed his back to burp him. The baby's skin was smooth and flawless. She knew every inch of it, checked constantly to see if there were any blemishes. She had done the same with Tas and Larce when they were infants. And then, as they grew bolder, she could not keep tally anymore of their scrapes and bruises, could not protect them as they took first steps and began exploring. She knew she must discourage tears, and that a brave face was expected to be shown, yet the thought that one day her sons might bear wounds like their father caused a sudden sadness. She leaned her cheek against Arnth, her lips brushing the soft down on his head.

"Did a Roman do that to you?" Tas was persistent in his questioning.

"No, it was a Syracusan pirate. But I don't plan to let any Roman have such satisfaction."

Expression grave, the boy turned to Caecilia. His eyes had a somber beauty. Honey-colored like hers. Feline eyes, not just because of their shape. There was something distant in them.

"But I am half a Roman because of Ati, aren't I? Does that mean you must hate me?"

Caecilia studied her oldest son, surprised that he had grown from one who merely listened to one who understood.

"Come and sit here." Mastarna leaned forward, drawing the boy onto his lap.

Larce protested at having to share the space so Caecilia called him to her. He came reluctantly, but once she tickled him under his arm he planted a kiss first on her cheek and then on Arnth's head before snuggling in beside them.

"Of course I don't hate you, Tas," said Mastarna. "Your mother has a Veientane heart, a Veientane soul. And so do you."

Her son looked at her for reassurance. Caecilia nodded. Although she knew that her desire to be wholly Rasennan was not enough. There was a residue of Roman in her she doubted could ever be washed away.

Tas perched upon Mastarna like a cat deigning to bestow favor. So different from Larce's puppyish fawning. "Tell me the story, Apa. I like the story."

Mastarna smiled. "Very well, but you must help Arruns clean my armor in payment."

"That sounds fair," replied Tas, formal and earnest as usual.

Mastarna settled into the familiar account. "Before the war began Ati was married to me to seal a treaty between our two cities. For, you see, Rome and Veii had been at peace for twenty years. Both wanted the truce to continue so that Veientane traders could pass through Roman land, and Roman bellies could be filled with Veientane corn."

"But then a mean man became the king of Veii," said Tas, showing he appreciated that a good yarn needed a villain.

"Yes, a man called Tulumnes seized control by poisoning the wise and just Zilath Ulthes. He declared himself lucumo and threatened to kill your mother unless I helped him wage war on Rome."

Larce dared to pipe up. "What's a 'cumo?"

Caecilia stroked the two-year-old's hair. "Lucumo is the title that the Rasenna give our kings."

"Don't interrupt, Larce!" Tas was impatient to resume the story. "But then Ati ran away from the bad lucumo, didn't she?"

Caecilia smiled, thinking how well her oldest son knew the story. Time would ingrain it in him and his brothers. As they learned it by rote, soon the tale would grow fabulous, a legend created. "Yes. Tarchon helped me escape to Rome so your father didn't have to worry about King Tulumnes hurting me."

"But you defeated him, didn't you, Apa?"

Mastarna shook his head. "Not alone. Tulumnes was a coward—cruel and selfish. He offended the leaders of the League of the Twelve, who didn't like monarchs. And then he ran away when the principes of Veii rose up against him."

"But the Romans still wanted to fight, didn't they?"

"Yes," added Caecilia. "Wolves had taken power in Rome by then."

The boy frowned. "Had they eaten all the people?"

She smiled. "No, I mean men who were as hungry as wolves. Generals decided that Rome needed Veii's land for their citizens, so they declared war."

"But they said the war was your fault, Ati. Didn't they?"

Caecilia nodded, trying to keep her voice even. Bitterness always welled inside her when she thought of the day war was declared. Camillus planned to attack Veii whether she was Tulumnes's hostage or not. Her escape home was seen as a nuisance. And her defection an excuse to rally the Roman people against an old foe. "Yes, Tas. They said I betrayed them because I wanted to be with Apa. They are seeking vengeance against me, but they would have attacked Veii even if I'd stayed behind."

Tas paused as though digesting the information, then reached over his father to the table beside the bed. Retrieving Mastarna's small golden box, he rattled the dice within it. "And Apa gave you these to ask a goddess what she wanted you to do." The boy scattered the two gilded tesserae onto the coverlet. Larce immediately tried to grab them. Mastarna deftly collected them, denying both sons possession.

"Yes," he said, handing the dice to his wife. "I sent Arruns to give these to Ati so she could ask divine Nortia if she wished your mother to come back to me." He raised his eyes to Caecilia. "And she did."

She rubbed the dice between her fingers, remembering their smoothness as she'd held them in her hand, heavy with potential, on that summer's afternoon. Remembered, too, how they seemed to tumble forever as she rolled them upon the dusty road, waiting for an answer. She closed her eyes briefly. Now she was beholden to the goddess Nortia forever.

The touch of Larce's hand prizing the tesserae released her from the memory. She surrendered them to him.

"And you were married again," said Tas, ignoring that his brother had claimed the dice.

"Yes, Bellatrix returned to Veii and once again became my wife."

"Why do you call her a bellatrix?"

"Because she is a warrioress."

"Girls can't be soldiers!"

"No, but they can be as brave as any hoplite, as courageous as any horseman. And your mother can be fierce. Don't try to cross her!"

The seriousness with which Tas nodded made both parents laugh.

"And then Ati had me," he said, once again intent on the tale.

"Me too!" Larce stood up unsteadily on the soft mattress before putting his head down and somersaulting over the quilt.

Mastarna grabbed him, tickling the boy's tummy and making him squeal. Then he tried to do the same to his older son.

"Don't!" Tas yelled, body rigid. "I'm not a baby. I'm not a baby!"

The boy's flare of anger was startling.

"Be quiet!" Mastarna's roar silenced the tantrum.

Tas lowered his head, his bottom lip trembling. "Sorry, Apa."

"You will be a man soon enough," said Mastarna, still gruff. "And no one will think less of you for enjoying foolery. Even soldiers like to jest."

By now the chamber had grown lighter but the mood within the bedroom had darkened. At the boom of their father's deep voice, Larce was tearful and Arnth began to mewl.

Mastarna cast aside the coverlet and sat upon the edge of the bed. "Time to rise. I need to train with Arruns."

Caecilia beckoned Aricia to come forward from the corner where she'd been quietly waiting. She handed the whimpering baby to the nursemaid, then also rose from the bed and lifted Larce to the floor.

Cytheris entered, hastening to the ornately carved linen chest to await direction as to which gown her mistress wished to wear. Arruns also appeared, holding a pitcher of hot water and a razor to shave his master's stubble. The routine of the day had begun, the servants who peopled their lives bustling around them.

Tas climbed down to stand next to the guard, studying the blue tattooed serpent biting into the man's face, before declaring, "Apa said I should help you clean his armor."

If the freedman was surprised or annoyed by this news, he gave no sign.

"After training, Tas," Mastarna growled. "Now go and get dressed."

As the children padded after Aricia, a breeze crept into the room, the charcoal in the brazier flaring. Caecilia shivered and drew her shawl around her, wishing Tas had kept his temper and that Mastarna would enjoy a day of rest.

"Do you really need to practice war today, Vel?"

Mastarna seated himself on a stool and directed Arruns to shave him. "I'm over two score years, Bellatrix. Youth doesn't oil my limbs anymore. If I slacken for even a day my body stiffens and my muscles ache."

There was quiet for a time, the only sound that of the scrape of razor against bristles and the sweep of a brush along Caecilia's hair.

"Our son's bouts of anger have not improved," Mastarna finally said. "He is a strange one, that one."

"He is still young and will grow out of such childishness soon enough." She hoped she spoke the truth. Tas was like a drum stretched too tightly. The slightest touch could start a resonance humming. His lack of control worried her. And it worried her, too, that he had learned the failing from her.

Face cleanly shaven, Mastarna stood while Arruns lifted his master's breastplate from the wall. The cuirass was embossed with dozens of minute figures portraying tales from the Trojan War. Caecilia knew that Tas would relish the task of burnishing the armor not only for the honor of serving his father but also for the chance to touch the heroes. "Vel, we need to talk about Kurvenas."

Mastarna didn't respond other than to command Arruns to fetch his greaves.

"Vel?"

"Later. Now I just want to exercise."

His closed look warned her not to press further. She moved to affix the protective linen strips that hung from the shoulders of the muscle cuirass.

Unlike her son, Caecilia gained no pleasure from the subject decorating her husband's cuirass. Helen caused a siege that lasted ten years and was despised by the peoples of two cities. The similarity of her own story to the Greek girl's always disturbed her. Until now, Tas had been enchanted by the tales of Achilles and Ajax, Odysseus and Hector. This morning her son had been enthralled by his parents' story also. One day, though, he might not think his mother valiant. One day he might see her as a traitoress who started a never-ending war.

FIVE

The youths were not yet old enough to boast beards, their faces retaining the soft edges of boyhood, wisps of down tracing the line of cheek and jaw, pimples upon nose and chin. Their expressions were tense, readying themselves for the initiation ceremony they were about to undergo.

Sitting bareback upon fine, long-legged horses, they drew into formation on the edge of the arena. Concentration was essential if they were to hold the animals to the line as the horses tossed and dipped their heads, manes of chestnut or bay shiny from grooming.

As Caecilia waited for these noble sons to perform, she hoped the excitement of the ritual would bring some respite from the grief that had followed from the Winter Feast. Fervid worshippers had turned into anguished mourners trudging to cemeteries outside the city. Lamenting women led funeral processions, their keening loud and poignant. The roads were clogged with two-wheeled wagons as relatives bore their dead loved ones to reopened tombs, resting places of grief and veneration. This time the pall of smoke that hung in the air was not from a fiery ring of celebration but funeral pyres.

For a year the Romans had besieged the City of the Dead as well as the living, depriving passage to the necropolises outside the sacred boundary. At last the remains of those who'd fallen both far away and near to home could be reunited with their forebears. Resentment was not buried, though. Layers of bitterness had accumulated, crammed as densely as ashes into an urn.

Today was gray-skied but the chill was forgotten as aristocratic clansmen crowded together in wooden stands. Nine days had been laid aside for celebrating funeral games, and another nine for private mourning by families. The dead would be remembered. Ancestral heroes would be honored. Praise and sacrifice would be made.

During the games, athletes would vie for trophies while charioteers sent their teams hurtling around the tracks. On this first day, though, the Troy Game held everyone's attention.

Caecilia realized that eventually her sons would be impatient to complete this rite of passage. She thought especially of Tas. He was already keen to leave childhood behind while she, a selfish mother, wished all three boys would remain dewy-eyed with plump, dimpled fingers.

As grooms handed each youth their weapons, she noticed how the recruits could not hide their nerves, swallowing hard as they clenched spears with whitened knuckles. Their horses nickered and snorted, pawing the ground.

For some, their breastplates and shields, greaves and armbands, bore no dents or marks, the metal shiny in untried newness. Others wore inherited bronze cleansed of battle gore and burnished brightly, the panoply of a fallen father or slaughtered brother who no longer needed its protection. A warrior legacy to be passed from generation to generation.

One youth was composed, lance and shield held steady, his steed calm under soft hands and loose reins. Sethre Kurvenas, the son of the man Mastarna despised. Caecilia could not deny he was handsome, although there was an arrogance about him, a common trait among his family.

Beside Sethre was a youth with ruddy cheeks and red, full lips. Caecilia thought him too sweet-faced to become a soldier as he struggled to balance both massive shield and tasseled reins in one hand. He was Caile, grandson of Vipinas. The zilath doted on him as he was the only family the old man had left.

Caecilia could not help thinking how young these recruits were, their eyes mimicking the fierceness of a warrior without knowing the savagery that nurtured such harshness. Come the war season, they would soon learn.

A horn sounded. A single note, strident and martial. The crowd fell silent at the signal. The grooms assisted each youth to draw on crested helmets.

Sethre commanded his horse forward with the briefest touch of his heels. He had been chosen to lead the rite. The sons of the noble houses of Veii would follow him in a ceremony that would grant them the right to fight for city, tribe, and clan.

To the beat of a drum and mellow notes of an aulos, Sethre rode his horse around the ring with a slow, clipped precision. To Caecilia it was as though the animal relished the task, head tucked close to a boastful chest, crest arched, strong legs prancing in time to the music. The rider guided his mount in ever-diminishing circles, each volte tighter, demanding more skill with the shortening of the circuit. Then, at the center, Sethre stopped. Pulling upon the bit gently, he coaxed the stallion to balance itself onto its hocks and then raise its forelegs to display belly to sheath. The horse seemed to revel in the chance to show off its strength, rearing for seconds in the pose.

Caecilia saw that the maneuver had left traces in the sawdust. The hoofprints marked out a perfect spiral, creating the labyrinth called the City of Troy. It was a maze the initiates would enter as boys and emerge from as men.

The crowd erupted in applause.

Caecilia glanced across to where Kurvenas sat gazing upon his only son with total absorption. Although she distrusted the man she could not begrudge him his pleasure. If it were Tas who'd completed the intricate pattern through the poised and silent command of his horse, she too would be sitting puffed with pride.

She clapped loudly. "The boy has talent."

"We'll see," grunted Mastarna. "Drawing the City of Troy is easy. Weaving one through horseflesh and armor is the true test. Let's see if the lad can keep his seat while avoiding the others' spears."

"You are harsh."

Mastarna's expression and voice remained stony. "Why? At least these cadets have had the chance to practice for hours to prove themselves this day. They'll face more peril on the battlefield. The enemy won't tell them in advance which way they are going to charge."

Caecilia turned her attention back to the ring, conscious of the truth of his words. There was danger in playing the Troy Game. Last year a boy had been killed. And the year before, three were crippled. She scanned the line of riders, nervous for them.

Beside her, Ramutha reached over and twined her fingers through hers. Her palm was sweaty, her face white. "Pray for them. That is all we can do."

Caecilia frowned when she noticed her friend's pallor. "Are you ill?"

Ramutha hesitated, then shook her head. "No, Mele, just worried for them."

Caecilia granted her friend a brief smile on being called "Mele." The nickname, "honeyed one," pleased her. It also reminded her that, with this woman's friendship, the lonely girl from Rome could now gossip and giggle with a peer for the first time in her life. Secrets were shared. Comfort offered. And, with her influence,

Ramutha had convinced most of the Veientane ladies to accept Caecilia as well.

Thefarie sat next to his wife. His face was lined with fatigue. Both he and Mastarna had been campaigning over the last few days to convince the other high councillors to change their minds. All had remained firm. And so, after the period of bereavement had ended, an election would be held and Kurvenas would be crowned. Caecilia was steeling herself to cope with Mastarna's temper once his rival was in power.

A rapid drumbeat signaled the horsemen to begin. Caecilia watched in anticipation.

The sons of the principes rode their horses with a rhythmic gait around the outline of the spiral, then formed a line beside Sethre. Their backs were straight, their thighs gripping their steeds' sides to give greater purchase to bear the weight of their spear and shield. Yet their lower legs swung loose and their torsos were supple, their posture flexible.

The horses had been chosen for their spirit and noble bearing: tall withers, fleshy double-backs, and rounded barrels to aid riders to remain mounted in combat. High necks and crests, small ears, gleaming eyes, and flaring nostrils—for beauty and for fierceness. All were stallions, unpredictable and prideful, biting and kicking at each other as they jostled for position.

Although the youths had broken in their horses, their control over them was still precarious. A sudden lowering of a maned head or unexpected bucking and rearing could unseat them just as swiftly as an enemy lance. Today, though, the heirs of Veii must prove they were the masters.

Sethre had already established this. The smooth bit in his horse's mouth proclaimed that he had tamed it completely. Both beast and boy understood each other without pain and pulling. No spurring on, no whipping was needed—just touch and voice and balance—and the desire of both to show their skill.

Vipinas's grandson struggled to steady his stallion, yanking at a cruel bit fashioned with heavy disk and spikes. Caecilia felt sorry for the beast. It whinnied with hurt, straining at the reins.

Caecilia glanced at the zilath. His brow was furrowed as he watched the youth's awkward handling of the horse. She prayed that if Caile fell all he would suffer was bruises rather than a broken neck.

Sethre's shout startled her back to watching as he ordered his colleagues to commence.

The pace of the horses grew faster as they once again circled the spiral: trot to canter, canter to gallop, until suddenly, with an ear-splitting yell from their leader, half the boys wheeled around and, with lances leveled, charged.

The Troy Game had begun.

Missing by a hairsbreadth, both teams pulled up, turned, then charged again. Hooves thudded in rhythm, spraying sawdust. The crowd hooted and shouted, urging them on.

Crisscrossing and whirling, the cadets wound between each other. Each nimble turn and pelting stride demanded perfection lest bodies of both beast and boy clash, fall, and be trampled, the mock skirmish ending in bloodshed instead of triumph.

Sitting forward, Caecilia clutched Vel's arm, her heartbeat sharp. Watching the surge and retreat, she held her breath at the speed and nearness of their passes. And yet she soon became enthralled, absorbed in the conquering of a maze of motion and danger, the defiance of the god of death.

Dynamic yet agile, Sethre took command with the demeanor of one who had the makings of an officer. Caecilia found it difficult to drag her attention from him.

Vipinas's grandson had managed to handle his horse throughout, but as he wheeled his stallion around for the next pass, he clipped his leader's horse. Sethre steadied his mount, swerving to avoid another collision while retaining a grip on spear and shield.

Caile's steed shied and reared. Unbalanced, the youth slid to the side and dropped both his weapons so he could cling to the horse's mane.

Caecilia half rose in her seat, her cry of concern added to the crowd's. Mastarna edged forward in his seat, expression tense. "Come on, boy, come on," she heard him murmur.

Ramutha covered her face with one hand and clutched Caecilia's sleeve with the other. "Grant mercy," she repeated over and over.

Vipinas was standing, working his false teeth against his gums, bright spots of color on his pale cheeks.

The spectators yelled encouragement to Caile. Summoning a strength and tenacity that surprised her, he finally dragged himself back onto the animal's back, then rejoined his team. Caecilia touched Ramutha. "You can look now. He has righted himself."

Her friend continued to hold her hand over her eyes. "I'm not watching again until this has ended."

Caecilia frowned, wondering why Ramutha was so anxious. It was not as though Caile was one of her family.

The riders slowed, completing a final maneuver. The rhythm returned to steady hoofbeats until, re-forming into one line, the youths held their stallions trotting on the spot.

Then stillness.

The cheering was deafening. Caecilia joined the clamor, rejoicing that these young men had survived and that life had vanquished death. The boys who had conquered the labyrinth of the City of Troy were now reborn as men.

Helmets removed, sweat streaming down flushed faces, chests heaving with exertion, the new warriors let out a whoop of joy. Then, raising their spears, they turned and saluted the zilath.

Vipinas returned their greeting, his relief patent, a glint of gold in his ivory-toothed smile. His grandson had faltered, recovered, and survived. The shield and spear that remained scattered across the sawdust was a reminder, though, of how narrowly Caile had escaped both death and shame.

Laughing now, Ramutha stood and applauded. Thefarie remained seated, smiling at his wife's exuberance.

Some of the spectators began chanting Sethre's name. Enjoying the adulation, the youth rode a lap round the arena. Caecilia thought him haughty as he hailed his admirers. And yet when he halted his horse before Kurvenas, his look was uncertain, as though seeking paternal approval. There was no doubt that he had received it. The father grinned at his son with adoration.

Kurvenas's smile reminded her of those her Uncle Aemilius bestowed upon her cousin Marcus. With it came a heavy expectation. Fame and glory in combat. Ambition and success in politics. She guessed Sethre would feel a similar pressure. The acclaim he'd gained today was yet a beginning.

She wondered if Marcus had begun his steady progression up the Honored Way to high office. He was now of an age to become a lesser magistrate in Rome. Last time she'd seen him he'd won an oak leaf crown in battle—a high honor for one so young. Had he won other awards? As a war hero he was bound to be elected. And yet she remembered a time when he was wrought with doubts that he could be so courageous. She was his confidante then. His enemy now. It was painful to think about the rift.

She returned her attention to the conquerors of the Troy Game. From the youths' exhilaration it was clear that both recruits and horses were now kin. These sons of the tribes of Veii were a brotherhood forged together. She was saddened, too. For this test of horsemanship was not the true initiation. In spring, the young Rasennan soldiers would attain manhood through bloodshed: warrior against warrior, warhorse against warhorse.

She turned to Mastarna. He was lost in concentration, ignoring the hubbub around him as he studied Kurvenas. The princip was laughing with the grizzled Lord Lusinies, accepting his congratulations over Sethre's success.

Caecilia touched her husband's hand. It took a moment to gain his attention. "Imagine if it was one of our sons who rode so well, Vel. You would be boasting, too."

Mastarna scrutinized Sethre and frowned. "That lad is acting as though he is a clan hero when he is yet to be blooded. His swagger tells me that he thinks himself heir to the crown just as his father believes he was born to be king."

Caecilia thought her husband unfair. Sethre deserved only praise today. It was not his fault that Kurvenas had sired him. Yet she knew that Mastarna's mood and mind would not be improved by her challenging him in front of their friends. She hooked her arm through his, trying to cajole him from his gloom. "I hear there is going to be a footrace next. Will you place a wager?"

He shook his head and returned to observing the zilath and high councillors. She heard the click of the golden dice in their box as he fingered it under his cloak.

Caecilia chose to ignore his ill humor and chatted with Ramutha instead. Outwardly calm, inwardly churning. It had been days now and Vel had still not discussed Kurvenas's coup or Vipinas's changing loyalties. Each time she broached the subject he would make excuses. Instead he seemed to be avoiding her, gambling heavily each night, the thrill of risking his wealth a way to vent his frustration. There had been no counsel sought as they lay under the plaid quilt of their bed, no confidences shared as they sat at the table.

Another blast of the horn. The new warriors prepared to leave the arena. As she watched the riders form a line, she realized Mastarna was no longer preoccupied with Kurvenas but studying her. She smiled but he remained solemn.

Disconcerted, she reached for his hand. "What is it, Vel? Have I displeased you?"

He turned away and clapped for the departing horsemen. "Of course not," he said. "Must there be a reason for a man to gaze upon his wife?"

Caecilia joined in the applause, a pulse flickering in one of her temples. A sharp worry was rising within her. His distance reminded her of when they'd first wed. But they had been strangers then. Now love, not diplomacy, united them.

She glanced at him, wishing he'd turn and smile. His attention remained intent on the arena, his expression grave.

SIX

When Lord Artile, the chief haruspex, entered the arena, Caecilia knew there would be no more entertainment. No more laughing at acrobats racing to reach the top of greased poles, climbing and sliding in turn. No more delighting at a juggler throwing disks into a vase on the head of a girl wreathed in a sheer skirt, her body goose-pimpled in the cold.

All week Caecilia had enjoyed watching athletes jumping with weights in both hands or hurling javelin or discus. Runners had strived to be the fleetest while wrestlers competed to be champions. Now she steeled herself to watch a different kind of contest. On the final day of the funeral games the welfare of those journeying to the Beyond needed to be addressed. For Aita, god of the Afterworld, demanded satisfaction. Today the dead would be revitalized by the spilling of human blood.

When she'd first traveled to Veii, Caecilia had marveled at the complexity of its religion. Here she found seers who could commune with the deities, foretelling the future by reading the livers of beasts, or deciphering divine will through lightning and thunder. Compared to such science, Roman augury seemed primitive.

And while her city expected its people to learn its articles of faith through recitation, the Rasenna boasted a codex of beliefs, a set of sacred books that held the secrets of fate, prophecy, and the afterlife.

Fufluns's promise of rebirth was life-affirming. Caecilia understood why the revelers worshipped that god through the Pacha Cult, even though she did not wish to seek such an epiphany. But the Calu Death Cult of Aita was a dark side of the Veientanes that still shocked her. She could not fathom how a people who valued art, music, and beauty could follow a creed that demanded a man be sacrificed.

A hush spread over the crowd as Lord Artile lifted his curved staff. Sweeping the lituus in a circle, he carved a sacred boundary in space. The arena had now become holy.

Caecilia hated him. Hated the sight of his fringed sheepskin cloak and long tunic, and how his peculiar priest's hat spiraled to a point. She still felt ashamed that she'd once fallen under his influence. When she was a vulnerable and frightened bride plunged into an alien world, it had been easy for Artile to stoke her fears and gull her into seeking salvation through an addiction to a potion. She shivered, remembering her observance of the unrelenting rituals required to convince Aita to favor her.

For the journey to join the ancestors was perilous. Demons guarded the gates of the Beyond, and monsters threatened safe passage. But if enough prayers were chanted, and enough blood was shed, the god of death might transform a devotee into a lesser god. Under Artile's guidance, Caecilia had strived to become one of the Blessed, until she witnessed the terrible offering needed to become immortal.

The crowd had become noisy again, impatient for the rite to begin. Raising his arms, Lord Artile silenced them. When he intoned a prayer, his voice was so deep Caecilia thought it must surely resonate in Aita's realm as well as in the heavens.

Edging nearer to Mastarna, she closed her eyes, summoning courage to endure the ceremony ahead. He put his arm around her, knowing her reluctance to watch. But she would not fail him. It was a test of her loyalty to Veii. She would hide her abhorrence and show respect.

Necks craned, the audience peered toward the entrance to the ring. In the stillness, the creaking wheels of an approaching cart seemed too loud.

The odor of death was strong. The faint sweet sickness of it. Caecilia fumbled to find a kerchief to hold to her nose but the cloth was scant barrier to the stink. She flinched at the sight of the wagon's noisome cargo. As many as twenty men were lashed together on its tray. They were naked, smeared with excrement, and their ankles and wrists were chafed from struggling against the ropes binding them. Some were already stiffened corpses, deadweight strapped to their companions. The eyes of the survivors were dark and empty. Roman soldiers.

Her stomach heaved. The presence of the cadavers was a new layer of cruelty. Trying not to inhale, she scanned the row of men to check if her cousin Marcus was among them. Drusus also. The boy who'd once loved her. Relief coursed through her at their absence. And then she prayed she would not recognize anyone else with whom she'd shared meals and thanksgiving. The Roman gods had truly forsaken these warriors.

The living men were cut loose, the dead left in the wagon. The prisoners remained propped against each other, weak from hunger and beatings. It was as though they were reluctant to be separated despite the severing of their bonds.

The baying and barking of hounds could be heard growing nearer and nearer until, snarling and straining, a pack of dogs appeared. They were held in check by a terrible master, their leads wrapped around his wrists and fists. The man was known as the

Phersu. As the servant of Aita, the murders he committed today would be sacred.

The crowd rose as one, cheering. Caecilia tensed at the sight of the holy executioner in his high, stiffened conical hat. He wore a false black beard attached to a scarlet mask, its mouth frozen in a rictus. His chest, arms, and legs were massive. As he pulled the curs away from the captives, she glimpsed his manhood beneath his short black-and-white kilt.

Lord Artile once again commanded quiet. Obedient, the throng settled. Then, at the haruspex's order, slaves scurried to pull bags over the victims' heads before handing them clubs and gingerly backing away.

The last expression Caecilia saw on each Roman's face varied: some cringed in terror and confusion, others murmured fraught prayers. A few showed boldness, soldiers to the end. They immediately grasped and swung their bludgeons but, blinded by the burlap sacks, their attack was futile. Their weapons swiped through air.

She turned away. "I can't watch this."

Mastarna reached for her hand and squeezed her fingers. "Keep looking, Bellatrix. Be brave."

She swallowed hard, the taste of bile burning her throat. She wished he would relent and let her leave. Or at least let her shut her eyes. And yet she knew he was right. As a child she'd been taught that fortitude was a virtue. Now she needed to heed the lesson. She could not afford to offend the Veientanes.

The crowd, hysterical, zealous, began the familiar chant: "Phersu! Phersu! Phersu!"

Despite the noise of the tumult, Caecilia heard Ramutha moan beside her.

She was hunched over, hand pressed to her mouth, her complexion ashen. Thefarie seemed not to notice his wife's distress, intent on watching the Phersu hunt down his quarry. Caecilia slipped her hand from Vel's and leaned over to rub her friend's back. "What's the matter?"

"I don't think I can stay here."

Caecilia frowned. Ramutha was an ardent devotee of the Calu Death Cult. Why was she squeamish today? She had never shown discomfort at the slaughter before.

"The stench," said the noblewoman, gagging. "I'm going to be sick."

Thefarie finally dragged his attention from the spectacle. He patted Ramutha on the shoulder halfheartedly. Caecilia sensed he was torn between the need to care for his wife and his desire to watch the sacrifice.

She took Ramutha by the hand and stood. "Come, then."

Thefarie nodded his thanks, clearly relieved he did not have to miss the performance. Mastarna checked her. "Where are you going?"

"Ramutha is ill. I need to take her outside."

The women struggled past the rows of spectators, weathering dark looks for momentarily blocking views. Yet they did not succeed in escaping before the hounds were let loose. The screams of the doomed men rent the air as the dogs leaped upon them. Some of the Romans managed to make contact, their clubs thudding upon the animals' heads or flanks. Most were felled and mauled quickly, while others dropped their weapons and fled, only to be hunted down.

Caecilia quickened her pace, dragging her friend after her. As soon as they reached the open space behind the stands Ramutha sank to her knees to retch. The smell of vomit triggered Caecilia's own nausea. Bile once again surged into her throat but she controlled the urge to be sick.

Cytheris appeared, Ramutha's handmaid following close behind. Caecilia bade both to fetch some water as she crouched beside her friend.

Another roar. Caecilia put her hands over her ears. It was of little help. The screams of the prey could not be muffled. She told herself that these Romans were the enemy. After all, if she'd been captured, there would be no mercy. All Rome would relish witnessing her execution. Even so, tears pricked her eyes knowing the carnage the Phersu and his hounds were wreaking.

Ramutha sat back on her haunches and wiped her mouth with the edge of her mantle. "Come, Mele, you should be used to this by now."

Another shout echoed from the ring but no more cries from the hunted. The killing had been swift. Caecilia thought it a melancholy blessing. In other years, it had taken over an hour for all to succumb: throats torn out, their flesh savaged.

She helped Ramutha to her feet. "I will never get used to it. It's loathsome. And it was worse today. Twice the usual number of victims. And some were already dead when brought into the arena."

"But the sacrifice is sacred." The Veientane brushed dirt from her skirt, her tone matter-of-fact. "Blood must be shed. Aita demands it."

Caecilia noticed Ramutha's face was still white, the red carmine on her lips stark against her paleness. The kohl that rimmed her eyes and darkened her lashes was smudged. "Then why your revulsion today? Was it just the stench of the corpses? Or did you eat some spoiled food that made you queasy?"

To her surprise, Ramutha blushed. "If only it were that simple."

It took some moments before Caecilia understood, remembering how Ramutha had declined to eat while watching the events each morning, then craved figs and walnuts the rest of the day. And now it made sense why she had taken to wearing flowing robes instead of tight-fitted chitons. "You're with child? Why, that's wonderful!"

She tried to embrace her but Ramutha fended her off. "Don't. It's nothing to celebrate. The baby is not Thefarie's."

Caecilia's eyes widened. "May Juno have mercy!"

"Be quiet," Ramutha urged, "someone will hear you. It's not easy to take precautions. Silphion is most effective but supplies of the plant are hard to come by while there is a blockade. I had to use it sparingly." Her laugh was rueful. "Too sparingly, it seems."

Caecilia continued to struggle with the news. "Are you sure it's not his?"

Ramutha unwrapped the lilac mantle twisted around her waist then smoothed her hand across her chiton to reveal a gentle curve. Soon costly fabrics and loose gowns would not hide her secret. "Very. Four moons have waxed and waned since my last flux. Thefarie was campaigning in the north with Mastarna all war season. I've only warmed his bed since his recent return. There is no way I can present him with a chubby-limbed newborn and claim the child came early." She twined the mantle around herself again. "And with the city under siege I'm not free to retreat to our country villa and appear a year later as though I had never quickened."

Her friend's acceptance of her predicament was alarming. Caecilia clutched her arm. "How can you be so calm! When Thefarie finds out he could kill you."

Ramutha patted Caecilia's hand as though she were a child. "Don't be foolish. We aren't in Rome. Husbands can't execute their wives for adultery and go unpunished."

Caecilia relaxed her grip, relieved once again for the difference between Rome and Veii. And yet she still wrestled with the infidelity. "I don't understand. Why did you cheat on Thefarie? Don't you love him?"

The sound of the crowd was now of babbling conversation. Exchanging opinions, claiming winnings from wagers, expressing disappointment that the ritual was over.

Ramutha gestured toward the arena. "The ceremony is finished. Our husbands will be wondering what's happened to us."

"Please answer me."

She sighed. "Do I love him? No. But he is a good man, and a fair enough lover. He doesn't beat me either for my indiscretions. He knows a woman can't be expected to go for months without a man. And I know he indulges himself with camp whores as does Mastarna."

Caecilia pursed her lips, sensing her friend was trying to avoid further queries with mischief. "Vel is faithful."

Ramutha cocked her head to one side. "That's what he tells you. Are you sure?"

"Very."

The Veientane primped the ringlets framing her cheeks, and checked the snood that covered the rest of her abundant hair. "Anyway, Thefarie and I have an understanding."

Caecilia put her hands on her hips. "I hardly think he'll 'understand' you bearing another man's child."

Ramutha's eyes narrowed. "Don't be so judgmental. Besides, Thefarie's courtesan has borne him a daughter. And I've caught him more than once dallying with the maids. I don't see why I can't use a slave or freedman for my own pleasure every now and then."

Caecilia stared at her, wondering why she was drawn to this woman who was so different from any she had known in Rome. Roman virtues were never drummed into Ramutha. Such lessons could not be easily forgotten. Her friend always relished shocking her as she would a country cousin. Her teasing was always softened by smiles, though. It was hard to dislike her. Yet the revelation she'd lain with a man of low status was disturbing, so too the realization that she had more than one lover. "Please tell me you're not carrying a servant's child!"

Ramutha gestured to her to lower her voice. "Don't fret. The child is a princip."

Caecilia chewed her lower lip. The potential for scandal had now doubled. She glanced around for eavesdroppers. "And did you ever consider using your remaining supply of silphion to end this?"

Ramutha straightened. "I want this child. Besides, it is too late for that now."

The response was almost defiant. Caecilia was even more puzzled. "So just who is the father?"

Ramutha hesitated, glancing around her. "Caile."

Caecilia groaned. "The zilath's grandson! Why, he rode in the Troy Game. By the gods, he would be no more than seventeen!"

The Veientane grinned slyly. "Ah, but young boys are insatiable. You should try one."

Caecilia recalled how Caile had struggled to control his horse, then imagined him grappling with Ramutha instead. She shook her head again, disapproval doubling. Ramutha was thirty. Yet she knew of even older matrons who harbored affection for youthful vigor. Downy cheeks and slim physiques held allure for some Veientane ladies. There was a reason Rasennan men had skill in bed. Many had gained their education from experienced women. She doubted, though, that Vipinas would appreciate Ramutha schooling his grandson. "At least tell me this infatuation is over."

Ramutha concentrated on rearranging the woolen tassel hanging from her shoulder, a symbol of her nobility. And yet, as far as Caecilia was concerned, her friend had betrayed both her class and her husband.

"Yes, it's finished between us."

The chill in the air had grown sharper, a breeze rising. Caecilia wrapped her cloak around herself. "So when do you plan to tell Thefarie?"

Ramutha twisted her string of turquoise beads around her fingers. "Not yet. While he's preoccupied with Kurvenas attaining royal office I don't want to add to his worries. And there is already too much friction between him and Vipinas."

Caecilia realized her friend was not so brazen after all. And she was relieved to hear she was concerned about her husband. "So you do care for him."

"Of course I do! No man likes to be made a cuckold." She rearranged her mantle again, ensuring it was draped elegantly. "It won't be easy either if the child is a boy. After giving him two girls, he will be none too pleased if I bear a son to another man."

Once again, Caecilia was unnerved at her friend's coolness about the consequences that must surely follow. "But aren't you afraid he'll divorce you? What will happen to you then? And the baby?"

There was a tinge of cynicism in Ramutha's voice. "Thefarie might want to cut ties with me but not with my fortune. My father has funded him for too long. As for the babe, I keep telling you, Mele, this isn't Rome. I can declare the infant as one of my bloodline. I don't need my husband to claim it, nor the Vipinas family for that matter. The child will belong to Clan Tetnies. My clan."

Caecilia stared at her. Even after eight years, Veii could amaze her. She was always in awe of the rights of Rasennan women. Hearing her friend could claim a child in her own name was astounding.

Ramutha smiled. "Oh, Mele, it's not like you to be speechless." Then her almond-shaped eyes softened. "Besides, I want this baby. I can weather censure as long as I nurse Caile's child."

Caecilia's wonder turned to dismay. It was disastrous enough that the youth was to become a father, but to continue the affair? "But you said it was over between you!"

"I know, Mele." Ramutha hugged her, laying her cheek upon her shoulder. Her charm and warmth was disarming as ever. "But I can't stop thinking about him. I love him."

Caecilia groaned, shaking her. "This is madness."

Ramutha steepled her fingers in supplication. "Please, Mele, promise me you'll keep quiet for the moment—about the baby, and about Caile."

Caecilia hesitated, uncomfortable with conspiracy. "You know I don't like keeping secrets from Vel." She touched the swell of her friend's belly. "And you will not be able to keep this hidden much longer."

"Please! At least until this sham election is over." She cupped Caecilia's cheek. Her fingers were icy. It was no wonder. Snowflakes were drifting and swirling around them.

With the change in the weather, the food vendors hastily covered their firepots, shouting to people to buy their remaining nuts and sweetmeats as the spectators spilled from the stands.

Cytheris struggled through the crowd to reach the two ladies. The Greek woman was not prepared to be shooed away. "Mistress, you need to come now. I've called for the carriage for you and the master."

Ramutha gripped both of Caecilia's hands, voice beseeching. "Please, Mele."

Sighing, she relented. "Very well—but as soon as the election is over you must speak up."

The Veientane kissed her. "Thank you, thank you."

Cytheris clucked in disapproval as she watched Ramutha hasten to find her husband. "Another cuckoo in a rich man's nest," she said, stamping her feet to warm them.

As always, Caecilia marveled at the handmaid's ability to guess what was unspoken. "How did you know?"

"Easily enough. Lady Ramutha's maid is a dreadful gossip."

"And you aren't, I suppose." Caecilia was less impressed with her servant's intuition.

Cytheris chuckled. "As long as the rumors aren't about me."

The crowd was thickening, their heightened mood descending into irritation. Thrown into the eddy of departure, they bumped against one another. The wealthy were escorted to their carriages, and the less privileged began a long walk home in the snow. Caecilia moved out of the flow, seeking shelter under one of the stands while she waited for Mastarna.

Cytheris took hold of her mistress's elbow. "Best stay away, my lady."

"Why?"

"Prostitutes and slave boys are conducting business under that one." The maid sniffed. "There could be gamblers too, playing with too much wine and bad temper. It's not safe."

Caecilia recalled the muted voices and noisy bumps sometimes heard from beneath the benches while watching the games: competition in plain sight within the arena, debauchery glimpsed between gaps in floorboards.

As Caecilia moved away, the leather flap covering the frame of the nearest stand was flung back and a man exited from the gloom. It did not surprise her that it was Tarchon. Mastarna's adopted son had a taste for pretty boys and wagers. This didn't overly concern her, but his failure to marry did. She accepted he preferred those of his own sex, but nevertheless wished he would take himself a wife. At least the pretense would satisfy society. And Mastarna. Even if it was unlikely any child would be born from such a union.

Tarchon did not give her his usual lazy smile, instead glanced back over his shoulder before taking her elbow. "Don't you have sense enough to get out of the wind?"

Another occupant of the stand emerged from the dimness. Sethre Kurvenas drew his tebenna over his head with a shiver. This time Caecilia was surprised. It seemed Caile was not the only one gaining experience. She wondered if the general would be proud of his son seeking this type of initiation.

With an antipathy inherited from his father, Sethre ignored her as he sauntered away, as haughty and arrogant as he had been in the Troy Game. He barely acknowledged Tarchon either, nodding curtly.

Before she could catch sight of any other denizens beneath the stand, Tarchon led her toward the carriage. "Where is Mastarna?"

She scanned the crowd. "He should be here somewhere."

Her husband finally broke from the current of people. "Are you all right?" He replaced Tarchon at her side. "What was the matter with Ramutha? She doesn't usually have qualms at watching the Phersu."

Caecilia hesitated. "Nothing. A weak stomach. Can we go now? I'm cold."

The lie was small but covered a large secret. She instantly felt guilty. It had been a long time since she'd been untruthful with her husband. Yet if she told him he would be honor-bound to inform Thefarie. And it would only add to both men's concerns. It was better to wait for Ramutha to make her confession.

Mastarna surveyed the whores' den before turning to his son with a knowing look. "It's not like you to miss the sacrifice. But I guess your lust won over worship."

The questioning of his piety sparked a terse response from Tarchon. He was as devout in observing the Calu Cult as he was in indulging his vices. Caecilia, too, thought it strange he would choose to miss the ceremony.

"At least I won't be damned for being an unbeliever."

Mastarna glowered. "I've never hidden my lack of belief in the death cult." He gestured toward the stand. "You have sunk lower than I thought if you need to seek satisfaction in such a makeshift brothel."

Tarchon reddened but squared his shoulders. Over the last year the tension between them had worsened. Even though Tarchon had proved himself in combat he had yet to impress his father. It disappointed her that Mastarna could not put aside his prejudices against his son's past failings. "Stop it, you two." She tugged at her husband's arm. "Please, Vel, can we go?"

Mastarna continued to bristle but acceded to her wishes. Despite his bluster, Tarchon seemed relieved at her intervention. As they walked away, the father could not help one last retort. "You should be careful, Tarchon. Otherwise you'll be remembered for dying from pox instead of battle wounds. And for bringing shame upon our House."

SEVEN

Carriages and litters clogged the road, the traffic extending for a mile outside the Menerva Gates. Those who did not have the luxury of transport trudged beside them, heads bent to bear the brunt of falling snow. Oxen fouled the whitened ground as they waited uncomplaining in their traces. Their owners were not so patient, tempers flaring, cursing the standstill, the glow of wine waning as good humor was blown away by freezing wind.

Mastarna soon grew irritated at being cooped up in the confines of the carriage. "It would be faster walking."

He stepped out when the snowfall ceased and the wind eased. Caecilia, legs cramped, decided to join him. She breathed in the crispness, delighting in the fresh snow coating the ground away from the road. Soon the commoners were staring at the principes who had decided to get their boots wet, no doubt thinking them foolish for swapping coziness for chill.

Caecilia surveyed the bleak winter landscape. Once the woods had been dense with shimmering summer green, or the autumn blanket of russet and purple. Harvested for its timber by the

Romans, the forest was growing sparser and sparser, raw stumps instead of the stark silhouettes of winter.

Dotted along the landscape lay the remnants of forts, picket trenches, and siege engines, which had fueled the bonfires of the Winter Feast. Their blackened struts were skeletal against a bellicose sky. The prospect of the enemies repeating the routine of construction and destruction was now an expectation. Caecilia hoped that Rome might see sense. Grow weary of it.

Husband and wife walked in silence. After a time they reached the scorched hulk of the enormous siege tower that lay in front of the city. The war engine stood halfway along an earthen ramp. Despite the weather, slaves were laboring to dismantle the slope, their burden doubled now that they needed to shovel snow before using picks to dig out frozen dirt and rubble.

The Romans had erected the tower on the plain throughout last spring, tier upon tier, higher and higher. Each level housed archers ready to spew quarrels of arrows through slits in the wooden walls. Pregnant with danger, the massive machine had then been wheeled up the ramp to try to bring it abreast with the top of Veii's walls. If not for Kurvenas's troops thwarting its progress, the Romans may well have slid gangplanks across and overrun the city.

Today, the seared hunk of timber was inert and useless. Nevertheless, its proximity was evidence of the considerable advance made by General Aemilius that year. Her uncle's doggedness had been disturbing. Caecilia often wondered if it was Veii alone he wanted to destroy. She knew that she might be dead to him, but did he wish to be the one to end her life?

The thickness of the cows' hides stretched taut and nailed to the tower's frame had protected the structure from being totally consumed by fire. A faint stink of singed hair wafted in the air. Despite this, there was a kind of beauty to the wreck, the snow softening its contours as it stood in a patchwork of colors, half scorched, half unscathed. Was Marcus one of the officers who ordered its erection? Did he, too, wish her dead?

"It could have been my cousin in the arena today."

Mastarna paused beside one giant wheel of the ruined tower. "But it wasn't. And I wouldn't let him be a victim if he'd been taken."

"I'll never understand why there have to be any victims at all!"

"You know why, Bellatrix. The Calu Cult is part of our religion. People are scared. They face death from Romans in this world, and then the torments of demons in the Beyond. Why wouldn't they seek salvation?"

"I don't believe killing humans can help make you immortal. No matter what priests like Artile say."

Mastarna cracked off a piece of burned wood. "Neither do I, but my brother and his colleagues peddle dread. What do you expect me to do? His power grows greater with each year the war continues." He crumbled the charred chunk, letting it trickle through his fingers, leaving a scattering of charcoal upon the white.

"It went too far this time. Dead men lashed to the living? It was more than a holy rite; it was vengeance."

He broke off another piece of wood and flung it toward the forest. His tone was deliberate. Each word clipped. "I've seen worse in battle."

She studied his face. The scar that ran from nose to lip, the shadow stippling his jaw line, his eyes that could be flinty. It scared her to think what deeds Vel performed in combat. There was a coldness to him. Expected of him.

"But this wasn't a battle." Stubbornness had always been her flaw.

"You must not expect pity for prisoners of war," he snapped. "Especially when they could have been the very men who killed those whose funerals we attended."

"But blinded men brought down like hinds in a hunt? I can't bear it."

Mastarna placed his hands on her shoulders. "And do you think Roman soldiers are always honorable, Bellatrix? I've seen their savagery in the aftermath of combat. They would rape and torture our women and children if they breached Veii's walls. There is good reason why we're fighting so fiercely to protect this city."

She fell silent, knowing he would not lie about the ruthlessness of Rome. Yet her lack of response seemed to provoke him.

"And they are no better with the soldiers they defeat," he continued. "They defile the dead, mutilate the wounded. Your people can be as merciless as the Rasenna. And they are relentless. How much longer do you think we can endure this constant siege? Our farmlands are ravaged. We must wait until winter to replenish our corn supplies. It's no wonder Kurvenas wants to destroy Rome. Or that other high councillors believe there is merit in such a tactic."

Caecilia was stunned. Finally he had broken his silence. All this time she thought his surliness was because he was railing against his peers. Now she realized he'd been reluctant to tell her that he believed Veii should march on Rome.

She shrugged him away, clenching her fingers. "What are you saying, Vel? That Kurvenas is right? That Rome should be razed? You refer to the Romans as my people when I thought you considered me Rasennan! You know I've always believed Veientanes should defend themselves. But this talk of conquering Rome is different. And there is danger in the strategy. What happens if Veii fails?"

He raked his fingers through his hair. "Can't you see I'm torn over this? And worried about challenging you? I'm exhausted from weighing advantage and disadvantage."

She stared at him, still angry he had kept this from her. Did he no longer trust her?

Mastarna reached for her but she tensed at his touch. He stiffened at the rebuff.

Needing to be alone, she ducked into the hulk of the blackened tower. It was gloomy inside, the acrid smell from the scorched pelts stronger. Mastarna remained outside with a familiar brooding look.

She gazed up through the inside of the structure. The fire had eaten holes through the floors and ceilings of each of the four tiers. The rungs of the ladders leading between them were half burned away. She could see where the blaze had spurted upward, the charred tessellations marking the lick of the flames. She remembered watching the Romans erect it as she stood at the ramparts upon the plateau. It had taken her some time to pluck up the nerve to observe the faces of her besiegers. But when she recognized one of the soldiers laboring behind a wheeled shelter, she'd hastily looked away, the sense of being alien filling her. Where did she belong? Was she truly a traitor when all she wanted was peace?

She fingered the iron amulet on her wrist with its Aemilian crest. Marcus had given it to her long ago. It linked her to him and to her clan even now. Could she stand by and watch the city of her birth and her tribe annihilated? No matter how much she wished she could feel nothing, the fact remained she would never shuck off her ties to Rome. Even though Marcus was now her enemy, she could not bear to see him harmed. Not when he was the only person there whom she loved. And Drusus? She would not want her former admirer dead either.

There was a flurry of snowflakes. The line of traffic crawled along, darkness creeping. No sun to make shadows.

Seeing the snow settling on Mastarna's head and shoulders, she stepped forward and extended her hand to him, this man she loved but whom she should have hated.

Mastarna hugged her. "Please, let's not argue. I'm sorry I upset you."

She drew away from him, searching his face. He wore no armor today other than that he used to guard his emotions. "Do you really think Kurvenas should launch an assault?"

He sighed. "Nothing is clear. There is value in his scheme but he is foolish if he thinks he can attack Rome without the support of the League of the Twelve. And they will never agree if we are led by a lucumo instead of a zilath. Not after King Tulumnes antagonized them."

She slid her arms around him beneath his tebenna cloak and leaned against his chest, the wool of his tunic soft against her cheek. "So you don't regret wedding a Roman? Our marriage has made it so difficult for you."

Vel pressed his lips to her forehead. "Of course not. I've told you before, Nortia brought you back to me for a reason."

"And can Veii not sue for peace?"

"On Roman terms? Never."

"So it will continue."

"Unless other foes distract to the south and east of them—the Volscians, the Aequi. The Latin tribes are always threatening Rome."

"But General Camillus has just succeeded in routing the Volscians!"

He stroked her cheek. "Then we must hope the Romans turn upon themselves. Patrician against plebeian. General against general. It has happened before."

"But not here."

"No, that is why I won't oppose Kurvenas becoming the lucumo. I won't weaken Veii from within."

She smoothed her hand along his chest. "Please promise me you will never agree to his plan. It's too perilous without the assistance of the Twelve."

"I promise," he said, but his voice was too quiet.

She gripped the edges of his tebenna. "Because I could not bear that, Vel. Not just because of Marcus. There is no guarantee of success. Veii might be defeated in the attempt."

"Hush." He took both her hands in his, bringing them to his lips, kissing each in turn. "I promise." His tone was firmer.

A snowflake settled on her cloak. She looked up to see a column of snow tumbling from a gap in the roof of the tower. They moved farther beneath the unburned section, accepting they would have to wait a little longer to make their way home. The heavy falling flakes outside blurred their vision to the line of oxen and donkeys.

"The snow is early this year," she said. "Winter will be bleaker if trade is hampered by frozen roads and rivers."

Mastarna did not reply.

"It will make the ground hard for plowing," she continued. "Seeds may wither before taking root. There was once peace for twenty years when Rome was preoccupied with feeding itself instead of fighting. Perhaps that will happen again."

"Perhaps." He leaned against a beam, unconcerned that a coating of ash marked his cloak. Caecilia stood with her back resting against him, drawing his arms around her waist. "Veii is impregnable, isn't it? With its high citadel, walls, and encircling rivers?"

"True," he murmured, wrapping his tebenna around them both. "We are heavily fortified. None have succeeded in taking the city before."

"So maybe this spring, the Romans will accept it is fruitless to prolong this war."

"Perhaps. We should never give up hope."

Her teeth were chattering, her feet freezing within her fine ankle boots. She rubbed her hands together, aware that the comfort in his voice was familiar. It was the one with which she soothed Tas to sleep after a nightmare, reassuring him that the monsters will have disappeared when he closed his eyes.

THE WINTER CAMPAIGN

EIGHT

Rome, Winter, 399 BC

Pinna was a night moth. A tomb whore surviving outside the city wall of Rome. Hiding in the darkness. Drawn to the light but knowing it brought danger. Destined to live a life that was sorrowful and brief.

For her, winter brought a special cruelty. The wind was bitter and the cold seeped from the earth to chill the marrow. Her clothes were sodden, fingers icy and painful from chilblains, lips blue and ringed with sores.

She worked as a hired mourner also. She could not afford to spurn the chance to earn money at the funerals of patricians in the daylight or well-off plebeians in the night. She did not care whether it was noble or common ash that landed upon her skin, as long as she could support herself and Fusca, her poor sad mother. Although neither job ever paid enough to quell the hunger pangs for long or allow her to escape to a world where her skin was not tinged gray or her clothes dyed darkly.

Tonight she welcomed the chance to lament the death of a wealthy plebeian. She did not mind caking her hair in ashes or wearing sackcloth when it meant that, for a few hours, she could warm herself beside the flames of a burning bier. Hovering close to the fire, she tried to ignore how it roasted the pale anointed body, the unguents a macabre seasoning to dead flesh. Yet when the flames seized a pocket of fat or worried at sinew she winced at how it popped and sizzled. Covering her nose and mouth could not block the stench or taste of cooking viscera saturating the smoke.

And it was with bitterness that she watched the women of the family douse the embers, knowing that cold would soon creep into her bones again just as heat had cracked and charred the corpse's. Resentful that honey and oil would be used to steep the ashes rather than feed a shivering girl. Aggrieved also that the sacrificial sow would only be consumed among the family once the deceased's portion was burned upon the pyre.

Wintertime was always busy for a hired mourner. All those dead soldiers. Dead heroes. Yet, although she might be paid to mourn for a fallen warrior, the men she serviced were not rich enough to ever wield weapons. Poor men, slaves, and bondsmen spent their paltry wages to use her. The lowlife of Rome could not afford to be choosy. The lee of a doorway of a rich man's tomb was cover enough for her to give a hand to a needy man or kneel before him.

After the family of the dead man departed to inter the remains, Pinna steeled herself, knowing she had yet to earn enough that night. Holding aloft a feeble lantern to attract customers, she formed a tiny shrine with pebbles and a stub of candle, leaving a paltry offering to Mater Matuta, the goddess of dawn. She renewed her contract daily with the deity, promising she would revere her if she raised her to a brothel whore so she could enjoy shelter while bearing the weight of men upon her. She did not forget to flatter the Shades of the Dead either as she worked among them, calling them good, as all do.

Hunched against the wall outside the city's sacred boundary, Pinna hoped the oil in her lantern would last the night. At least little Lacerta brought her comfort. The tiny lizard kept on a string around her neck scampered beneath her tunic and the crevice between her breasts. It was her only friend, gaining warmth and food even though fidelity was at the end of a tether. It shared space with the fascinum charm Pinna wore to ward off ghouls and flesh-eating witches who squabbled with phantoms in the darkness.

This tiny phallus was not potent enough, though, to protect her from the urgent hunger and mean souls of her clients. Both men and specters could make her blood quiver and raise goose bumps upon her skin.

When lightning flared she could not bring herself to continue plying her trade. The fear of being seared by a storm bolt struck her with terror. As thunder erupted, she ran through the rows of tombs toward home, the wind blowing out her lamp.

As the storm lit the Campus Martius she huddled for a moment outside a crypt of the Claudian clan. The tomb was built from marble with a boar's crest emblazoned upon it, as impressive as the history of this family. Hoping to gain shelter, she edged toward its entrance only to find a light within. Crouching inside were two young men, the fineness of their woolen cloaks and the cut of their tunics declaring they were noblemen, not grave robbers.

As she hid beside the opening, curiosity overcame fear. Inside, a lantern was propped on a shelf, which housed a line of urns as though their ashy occupants were on parade. One man, lean and angular, was absorbed in writing upon a beaten sheet of lead, his auburn hair common to a descendant of the Sabines. The other watched him, the lines of his face somber with concentration, the bridge of his nose scarred, the skin puckered at the corner of his eye.

Around her, shadows stained surfaces from gray to pitch. Pinna could see the russet-haired man was inscribing a message, laboring over the task as would a schoolboy with stylus and wax tablet. There was anger in the strokes as he gripped the pen. Her eyes widened. What he was doing was forbidden. And she knew why he had to be careful. Casting a curse was a serious business. Carving damnation upon a lead defixio sheet needed precision if a guarantee of harm was to be achieved.

"It's finished, Marcus. Now I'll add it to the others so that he will be thrice cursed." He turned to the wall of the crypt where two other defixios had already been nailed.

His friend was frowning as he examined the two aging leaden sheets spiked to the brickwork. "When did you write these?"

The patrician's reply was bitter. "The first one on the night he wed her. The second, a year later, when she chose to return to the Veientane and this war began."

Marcus grimaced, squeezing his friend's shoulder. "I'm ashamed of what she did to you, Drusus. Ashamed also of how Caecilia disgraced the Aemilian family and dishonored our clan. Choosing Veii over Rome. Him over you."

Drusus picked up the defixio. "She also insulted the Claudians when she spurned me. The Etruscan may have corrupted her but she's a degenerate, too. She is dead to me and should suffer when her husband is destroyed. I pray this curse comes true."

Marcus placed his hand over his friend's. "But are you sure you want to do this? Curse a man? The penalty is death if this is discovered."

The Claudian slid his hand away and brandished the leaden sheet. "It's not a citizen but an enemy of Rome I seek to doom. And don't worry. If I ever get the chance I will relish killing him. In the meantime, why not invoke evil spirits to plague a foe?"

Marcus prized the defixio from his friend's fingers. "Then let me read it aloud. They say a hex is stronger that way. If he is to be condemned then let it be done with vehemence."

His voice was earnest, steady, the words chilling. "I consecrate Vel Mastarna to damnation. May his mind and soul be tormented, his body twisted and shattered, and his head cut off. And if he has, or shall have, any money or inheritance, may they be lost, and his entire House be stricken with disaster and destruction."

Drusus smiled as he listened to this relegation of an enemy to darkness. "Then you think it is enough?"

Marcus nodded as he handed Drusus the sheet. "Yes, it is enough. It is no small thing to wish such a fate upon a man."

It had begun to rain, making Pinna creep farther inside. She shivered. It was not a Roman name but it was a Roman curse. Brutal and annihilating. And she understood the reason, and why Marcus Aemilius would disown his cousin. Vel Mastarna and Aemilia Caeciliana. Their names would be linked forever. An enemy and a traitoress.

Their wedding day was one that Pinna would remember always, but for a very different reason, because it was on that summer's day, at the age of eleven, that she became a whore.

Unlike others, she did not watch the wedding procession wind its way through the crowded streets, nor did she spy the groom's caravan departing the next day on its journey to Veii. Although she heard later that both were solemn proceedings since many felt sorry that Aemilia Caeciliana was being married to an enemy to seal a truce. But not Pinna. She felt too sorry for herself. Pinna did not see them because she needed to take advantage of the crowd. A state occasion was good for business.

At eleven she was too young to be a wife. Not too young, though, to remain a virgin. The stonemason's son who picked his ears and tasted of stone dust claimed that prize in an awkward coupling. It had made Pinna wonder why women would seek a repetition unless they were paid. Until she slept with a customer and knew that no amount of bronze would ever be enough.

Her first was a fat oaf who hummed before, during, and after. A thin little whine that set her teeth on edge, a tuneless melody to accompany his groping. At least the next was quick on a day that seemed to last forever as one man after another taught her what was expected of a harlot. And over the years she had borne the same and worse. But not Aemilia Caeciliana. In that time she fell in love with a foe and started a war.

Marcus placed his hand on Drusus's back. "Forget Caecilia. Think instead of how we will tear down Veii's wall."

Drusus shrugged him away. "Only if Camillus is given the chance to lead an assault! I'm sick of lesser generals commanding us at Veii. And now we will have to wait another year for him to be given the chance to be elected as one of the six consular generals."

The muscles in Marcus's shoulders tensed. "Don't forget my father is one of those 'lesser' men. I am proud of serving under him. He gained more ground this year than any other commander."

Drusus flushed crimson as he stammered: "I meant no offense. General Aemilius is a fine man. I've learned much from him. But neither he nor any other of our leaders have taken Veii. It's time Camillus is given the task." Suddenly his voice no longer faltered. "You have to admit there is fire in him. Look how he succeeded against the Volscians this year."

Marcus smiled. "I agree. He has the power to lead men to victory. It would be a privilege to be under his command," he continued. "But it is unlikely that would ever happen. My father would never approve."

A sheet of lightning pierced the inner darkness, cutting short any reminiscences. Marcus drew his cloak around him. "It's time to leave. Nail the curse to the wall and let us be gone."

Drusus shook his head. "You go. I want to stay a little longer."

Worried Marcus would discover her as he left, Pinna stepped back outside, flattening herself against the shadows of the tomb wall. She smiled to see the Aemilian shiver from more than cold as he quickened his step to dodge any tortured spirits that might detain him.

The rain was steady, the water trickling down the back of her neck to mingle with the ash on her skin. She was quaking, too. A layer of sackcloth did little to ward off the cold. Thunder grumbled, encouraging her once again to take up her position within the crypt. Drawn to watch.

Drusus had taken another sheet of lead from his cloak. His list of enemies must indeed have been long. Growing bolder, she crept closer, peering over to his handiwork. The words were cut deep with the force of frustration and, surprisingly, for an educated man, his lettering was crude.

This time tears flowed as he wrote. This time his fingers trembled as he held the stylus. She was confused at how determined he was to use the defixios. Rich young officers were expected to defeat their enemies in battle, not by calling on dark fate to stab them in the back.

Intent on his task, he did not notice her. His tongue was pushed into one cheek as though he had eaten a slice of apple. A frown split his brow, his eyelashes stuck with wetness. A snail's trail of clear snot was smeared along the top of his lip where he had wiped his nose.

Pinna wondered who could cause a soldier to weep even as he damned them, but as Drusus read his sentence aloud, one finger painstakingly tracing the words, she was stunned. It was no curse but an enchantment.

"May Aemilia Caeciliana burn with dreams. Let her feel aflame for Drusus so that she may know love, and Drusus peace."

He must have heard her surprise. He lifted his head, voice wavering and his neck tensing as though the hair was rising on his skin. "Who's there?"

Too frightened to speak she turned to flee, but the man crossed the gap between them in one stride and dragged her into the lantern light. He was lean, raw-boned, and strong, filling the cramped space in the low-ceilinged chamber. Realizing a mere night moth was observing him rather than a Shade, his arrogance emerged. "You little slut, how long have you been listening?"

She was filled with a familiar sense of dread, sensing there was an edge to this man, a tinge of violence, a need for power—even over a night moth of eighteen.

Humoring them sometimes averted the pain. The highborn did not seek out tomb whores, but she suspected that under his fine woolen weave this one's prick and needs would be the same. "It's more exciting when you know a lemur spirit is watching." She took his hand and rubbed it along the damp skin of her breasts while lifting the hemline of her tunic.

Lacerta darted across his fingers. Startled, Drusus shoved the girl away. "Get out! I can smell your last customer upon you."

"Please, my lord, I'm afraid of the lightning."

He raised the lamp higher to scan her. Pinna studied him, too—his tear-stained face, his reddened nose. Thinking her no threat, he pushed her away. "Leave!" He picked up the mallet, centering the nailhead to hammer in both sheets. "Go back to fucking the city's scum."

Pinna should have known better, should have obeyed meekly as she'd done all her life. Yet his words stirred her ire. Contempt taught her by her family for the haughtiness of patricians. This man was dismissing her when it was he who should be ridiculed. There had never been time or money enough to indulge her in learning, but even though she could not read, she had heard treason spoken plainly.

"I may be a night moth but I do not pine after a traitor. You're a fool to declare your love for Aemilia Caeciliana. What would Rome think if it knew you would betray it for that bitch?"

He clipped her jaw, felling her, his fury exploding; a long pent-up wrath transcribed within a curse and now transferred to force.

Pinna did not cry nor sob nor wail. She was paid to do that at other people's funerals. There was nothing left within her to lament her own pain. She cowered before him, waiting for the next blow, knowing that some men cannot stop at one as though an odd number was a bad omen. When he raised his hand again he knocked the spell to the floor. Realizing in one brief moment of brightness that it could save her, Pinna scrabbled to retrieve it, running out into the downpour, the needles slicing through her clothes.

The soldier blundered after her but the graveyard was hers. She knew where to hide.

"Night moth, stop! Give that to me. It's not what you think."

Her mother had taught her their trade, but Pinna had learned business opportunity from experience. Patricians always talked of honor. A commodity that was affordable when a man wasn't starving. They detested being shamed. She perched upon one of the tombs, taunting Drusus as she held the leaden sheet high above her. "Hit me again and I will nail this to the speakers' platform. Word will soon spread that a Claudian is lovesick for a betrayer. That he needs magic to overcome his foe."

"Come down, I won't hurt you," he shouted, his beard and hair dripping, his robes sodden as he swiped at her feet with one arm. She shuffled back, alarmed at his height. She'd not realized how tall he was as he'd crouched over his inscription.

"Do you think that, because I'm a whore, I'm stupid?" She prayed he would not manage to drag her down and beat her, and to her relief he stopped his pursuit. Drusus leaned his head against the wall, shoulders slumping, letting the rain smash upon his face.

Pinna slipped the defixio into her tunic to let Lacerta guard it. The pain of the welt upon her chin and cheek smarted. Unsure if she was being foolish, she slid down beside him. She was embarrassed for him, uncomfortable at seeing a warrior display such emotion. Felt sorry, briefly, that an enemy could cause a soldier this type of wound.

Fumbling at his clothes, he pulled out a purse and shook two weights onto her palm. "Please, you must tell no one about this."

Pinna stared at the bronze with the boars stamped upon them. She'd never seen so much wealth in her life. The currency this patrician had tumbled into her hands was life-changing, not small change.

At that moment the rain ceased, a few patters of errant drops hitting them as the wind swept through the graveyard. Then all was still, dripping, puddles forming.

The night moth stared at him, then retrieved the defixio from her clothes. He snatched it from her, drying it with his sleeve.

"Don't cross me." He straightened his shoulders, confidence regained. "Or I will find you and kill you."

His threat was pointless. With the bronze now hers, Pinna didn't care about the strips of lead that weighed heavy in both his hand and mind.

As she watched the nobleman thread his way back through the sepulchres to the Claudian tomb, Pinna did not try to follow. She knew what he would do. How he would clench the mallet, knuckles whitening, and hammer both desire and curse into the brickwork with one long iron nail—to remain there forever potent and terrible, guarded by ghosts.

NINE

The tub of melted snow was freezing but Pinna needed a bath. She'd not had one for months and the daily washing of arms, face, and legs in the murky rainwater from the communal well made little headway on her filthy skin. She had collected the snow from the Campus Martius, determined to be clean when she stood before the city magistrate. Teeth chattering, she scrubbed until her skin was red and her lips were blue. The sweet-smelling oil was a treat, though, as she combed out the tangles and clumps of ash from her hair, shedding lice and nits and knots until it gleamed.

Next she slipped a new tunic over her head and began wrapping a length of colored cloth around her that would mark her as a registered whore. A toga. It was the cloak of a male citizen but she was far from that in status. Far also from being a decent woman, entitled to wear a stola and palla shawl. Pinna did not mind. She had long ago lost the chance to shield her face in modesty when walking through the streets of Rome. She was just pleased to wear any robes that were not sackcloth. The sandals that she donned, though, seemed cumbersome on calloused feet that had trod barefoot for years.

As she fingered the moss-green woolen cloak, she noticed her nails were still black from grime. She glanced over to a sleeping form in the corner of the room. "I know, I know, Mama. It's not a market day. It could be unlucky to cut them, but I can't go before the magistrate with dirty fingers."

There was no answer and Pinna began to trim them, starting with a forefinger so as not to invoke ill fortune. To be doubly sure she was protected from the evil eye, she tied a shell of Venus around her neck together with her tiny wooden fascinum. Lacerta furiously darted over her fingers as though irritated she must share her space with so many luck charms.

"Shh," she murmured to the lizard. "Soon we shall be warm within our new home," but she could hear the tremor in her voice, the hint of apprehension. Her prayers had been answered by the lovelorn soldier, but it was frightening to make the journey into a fresh life. She had grown used to the slums of the Esquiline and the tombs of the Campus—her home and her workplace. "At least I'll have customers who are better behaved," she whispered, but remembering the sting of Drusus's blow, she knew that it was just a wish.

The woman in the corner of the room moaned quietly. Pinna knelt beside her, but Fusca's eyes had closed once more. "Rest, Mama. I will be back soon."

Heading toward the Forum, she passed by the doorway of a lupanaria, a den of so-called she wolves, for the prostitutes of the city were considered dangerous and venal. Yet Pinna doubted these women would be any less vulnerable than night moths.

In daylight the brothel looked no different than any other house, but at night Pinna knew the pimps would be drumming up business outside and customers would lurk in the street waiting their turn. The prospect of working in such an establishment now seemed daunting. She did not think she could summon up courage to speak to one of the lenos. Instead she would try and find customers herself to bring back to her new lodgings. Faced with such a prospect she suddenly felt very much alone.

As she passed through the markets, Pinna's nerves at meeting the official mingled with excitement as she realized that she could buy some festive treats along the way. The Saturnalia was due to be held soon, the festival where Saturn, god of sowing, would be praised and Juno Lucina would bid light to outlast the dark. For the first time she would be able to eat sweets and spoil her mother with gifts. For the first time they would have something to celebrate—no more graveyards, no more grave clothes.

The Street of Perfumes was crowded. It used to be called the Tuscan Way, but with Rome at war against the Etruscans, the name had been changed to one much sweeter. As she browsed the shopfronts, she absorbed the competing aromas of orris and anise, rose and lily, together with the musky odors from the cattle market nearby.

Pinna knew this artery well. In the past she was not above testing her skill as a cutpurse there. Amid the bustle of vendors and noise from the barkers it had always been easy for her to find victims as they paused at the booksellers or were distracted by purchasing incense and oils. Out of habit, she went to pinch some pretty candles before remembering she could pay for them now.

To her surprise the shopkeepers and passersby did not snub her despite her telltale toga. When she bought honeycomb and chestnuts at the fruit market the upright citizens and traders seemed unconcerned who was walking among them, although a few women hissed at her, less forgiving than their husbands and sons.

Houses and shops crowded the edges of the Forum. Pinna wondered where she could rent a room, determined to find one with a humble hearth shrine in a better area. She scanned the great hills of Rome. The wealthy Palatine and holy Capitoline loomed above her. On the roof of the great temple that crowned the sacred mount, the Great and Mighty Jupiter galloped his chariot toward her. He seemed ready to trample her not because she had transgressed but because he did not notice one so unworthy.

The city magistrate was a busy man; dispensing corn and water to the citizens of Rome was onerous, as was policing prostitution. Yet ensuring the supply of both was essential—whores were as necessary as temples, streets, and drains. The time caller had shouted the hour twice before the magistrate was ready to see Pinna. She twisted the amulets around her neck and whispered to Lacerta as she entered.

It unnerved her that the man had a cast in one eye, and she was unsure which she should focus upon. It did not really matter, though; both were beady and set too close together.

The patrician scanned her from head to toe, tapping his bony fingers upon one skinny knee. At his feet a clerk sat scribbling down decisions, dry points of commerce reduced to scratches in wax tablets. When she stated her business the scribe unrolled an enormous scroll of crackling papyrus. A list stretched across it—a roll of hundreds of whores, their names never to be erased. It reminded her that Rome would never forget who she was and always would be. For a moment Pinna felt an ache within her. What if she managed to live to be as old as forty? What would it be like to try to satisfy men then? Mocked and pathetic, begging for favors from men as desperate as she was.

"What is your name?" The magistrate was imperious.

"Lollia, daughter of Gnaeus Lollius, my lord."

"And your working name?"

Pinna blinked, wondering how to answer him. She did not want to be known by her nickname. It was special to her. All her life she had loved her patient, quiet mother as surely as she was wary of her father. Her mother had called her "Feather," her "Little Wing," as though she hoped one day Pinna could fly away from hardship.

Not that Lollius ever had the chance to register his daughter. A girl's existence was only officially recorded on her wedding day. How humiliating it would have been for him that she was finally noted not as a citizen but as a whore.

"Lollia, I'll just be known as Lollia." She handed the clerk the amount of one client's fee by way of payment.

The scribe scratched her name on the roll of she wolves.

The night moth was no more.

TEN

Moving into the hubbub Pinna noticed a crowd was heading toward the sanctuary of the Lapis Niger in the Comitium. Curious, she followed them, wondering what was drawing them to the assembly area. Pinna had seen politicians declaiming before in this part of the Forum. She'd soon learned to appreciate the various orators for the opportunity they gave her to glean fertile pickings from an audience immersed in rhetoric. There was value in distinguishing those who could keep the crowd's attention from those who wasted their breath in speaking; spellbound citizens never noticed a thief's nimble fingers. More than once, she'd been thankful that Romans loved to argue, loved to claim injustice, and, most of all, loved speeches. She had not cared what was being debated. It was always the same complaint: the elite claimed the commoners were plotting to bring down Rome, and the plebeians demanded the patricians grant them high office, land, and spoils.

Until this winter's day such inequities were of little interest to her. Caring about possessing rights was for those who had enough to want more. But today was different. Warmly clothed and with belly full, Pinna decided to listen to the orations. Nevertheless she was daunted by the sanctity of the surroundings: Vulcan's enormous shrine, the sacred fig tree, and the sanctuary with its holy black cippus stone and engraved pillar. The stone lions that stood vigil over King Romulus's grave also warned that they protected consecrated ground.

Three patricians passed by the altar and wellhead, and climbed the stairs to the stone speakers' platform. One was clumsily draped in the purple-edged cloak of a senator, and even from a distance Pinna could see his fat bushy eyebrows were furrowed into a rigid line of gray. The other two boasted dazzling white togas signifying they were candidates in the upcoming elections. Their servants must have labored for hours to whiten the cloth with chalk.

The shallow tiered amphitheater in the Comitium was already packed with men, the crowd spilling beyond its confines. Pinna was conscious the onlookers in front of her would not welcome a woman in this male domain. She clambered onto a canopy of a shop and then its roof tiles, cursing the hindrance of her own cumbersome toga. Below her, a couple of citizens stood talking loudly at the far fringes of the throng. Their skin was thick with scars, telling her they were veterans. Making herself comfortable on her perch, she strained to eavesdrop on their conversation. And from their derision, it was clear the two patrician candidates swathed in pristine white would be hard-pressed to sway this audience of common men.

"That pompous ass, Sergius, is still feuding with Verginius, you know," sniffed one, his nostrils red, raw from blowing his nose.

His companion nodded, picking teeth, which were rimed with green scum. "Yes, he's as short on brains as he is on stature, but Verginius is just as stubborn. I wouldn't vote for either of them."

"Or want to serve under them if they end up being consular generals," replied the other, wiping his snot away with the back of his hand.

Pinna looked across to the two politicians on the curved dais. The squat, swarthy Sergius stood remote from his colleague, keeping his shoulder turned to the silver-haired Verginius. However, both men were equally disdainful as they weathered catcalls from the assembly.

Finally the senator with the fearsome eyebrows raised his arms to call the crowd to attention. Runny Nose nudged his friend's arm. "What's Marcus Aemilius Mamercus doing up there? He's retiring from office as consular general. He can't stand again for another year. Don't say we have to listen to 'has-beens' as well as 'would-bes.'"

Pinna concentrated on the speaker. His name was familiar. Was this the father of Marcus, the soldier who'd huddled together with Drusus in the tomb? And was he truly a general? He was far from imposing as he struggled to hitch his toga onto one shoulder.

"Men of Rome! Listen to me!" Despite his paunchy appearance, General Aemilius's voice was hard-edged enough to cut through the din. The crowd settled, readying for an afternoon of oratory.

"Veii stands fast despite our efforts these past seven years," he said, thumping his fist into his palm. "Each spring we labor at building forts and ramps around that city. Then winter comes. Our defense works are abandoned and when we return they have been destroyed." He paused, taking a breath as though summoning courage. "And so it is time to establish permanent quarters! It is time for us to return immediately! Rome must suffer the hardship of fighting in winter if our enemy is to fall."

There was a lull, then the crowd erupted into a chorus of boos. To Pinna's surprise, Aemilius didn't cower from such hostility but squared his shoulders, showing the bearing of a commander despite his disheveled robes. In comparison, the immaculately clad Sergius and Verginius shifted nervously behind him.

Out of the commotion, another man stepped onto the dais. Mouth set in a hard, grim line, he planted his feet apart, arms folded across his chest, back straight as a spear. At the sight of him, the assembly calmed.

"Ah, here is Calvus," said Runny Nose. "Let's see if he's worth his salt as a people's tribune and tells this patrician the madness of such a plan."

Pinna observed the representative of the common man. His garb appeared costly although he lacked the right to wear senatorial robes. It took riches to gain office, whether plebeian or patrician. From the scowl on his face, Pinna also suspected Calvus enjoyed clothing himself in indignation.

"Fine words, but we all know that Rome needs to feed its troops," he boomed. "Soldiers are also farmers. If they fight throughout winter there will be no crops to reap come spring."

This time Aemilius successfully hitched his cloak higher onto his shoulder as he glowered at Calvus. "The state pays soldiers while they are on campaign. A salary that was never paid before this siege began. Remember that Rome covers annual costs but men do not serve throughout four seasons. It is time they worked for their entire wage."

The people's tribune turned to the assembly, accentuating incredulity by staggering back in a mocking manner before bellowing, "A wage that is only paid by taxing us! And even then it is not enough to pay debts accrued while away at war."

Calvus's defiance started a deluge of heckling. Pinna edged back on the roof. The politician seemed to enjoy riling the crowd. She could feel outrage welling and spreading.

Aemilius listened to the jeers with a scornful expression, but Sergius and Verginius both scouted around as though mindful they might need an escape route should the mob charge the speakers' platform.

"You promised we'd beat the Veientanes in a year," yelled Green Teeth. "Soon we'll all end up as bondsmen."

"We'll be shivering inside goatskin tents while the Veientane pricks are lying cozy in their beds!" Runny Nose's voice cracked as he shouted.

Pinna scanned the citizens below her. For the most part they were veterans who'd returned from fighting the Veientanes and Volscians and Aequi. Weary men who'd not seen their parents, wives, and children for almost a year. Tired men, resentful of having set out in March only to return to the iciness of a Roman November to heft the yoke upon their shoulders, plant seeds of beans and barley, and lay down the vintage from their grapevines.

Seven years ago Rome's legions marched to conquer Veii. All thought the fighting would be over in one war season. All believed that warriors would march from home that summer and deliver the groaning granaries of the Veientanes by winter, once again satisfied at defeating another enemy who coveted the seven hills.

Hearing Aemilius's words stirred memories within her. The haughty nobleman spoke of a soldier's wage but such compensation was too little for her father. A salary did not help him to escape bondage.

Lollius had been proud to own a plot of land. Half an acre that qualified him to fight. A meager square of soil that yielded a small harvest, enough to feed his family and some to sell.

Her father's hands were large. Larger than any that Pinna had seen. Broad-palmed, the length between seam, knuckles, and tips enormous. They were farmer's hands, skin crusted and ingrained with dirt. Soldier's hands—scarred, finger pads and palms calloused. When he was in a temper, which was often, Pinna and her mother would feel their hard edge.

His kit was propped beside the hearth fire on a frayed rug in one corner of their home. It lacked greaves and corselet but boasted an oxhide helmet as well as a spear and sword that looked as though they should have long ago been melted into plowshares. There was a shield, too. It was battered but its bronze and leather strapping was polished, scoured clean of blood and brains and bowels. His armor declared him entitled to serve as a hoplite of the third class. A duty and a privilege.

Even though she was only a child, Pinna understood that disappointment was a companion to her father's pride. His wife had only borne a daughter. A girl's hands could never wield his weapons. In time, though, they grew strong enough to lift his tools.

Lollius soon became more soldier than farmer, forced to leave the harvest to his women through summers that grew ever hotter and where no rain fell. The heat bathed wife and daughter in sweat, withering the crops and denying their goat and geese any water.

Praying to Mater Matuta to grant a fruitful harvest was of no use. And paying a war tax to fund his own salary both galled him and bled Lollius dry. And so to tide his family over while he was fighting the Volscians, he made a contract with his patron. On one side of the scales were weights of copper, on the other his oath to forfeit his freedom should his liabilities not be discharged.

Pinna remembered rising before dawn to do men's work, leaving her to perform her usual chores after dusk. Soon her palms were blistered, her face burned, her ten-year-old body growing lean. She would cry from weariness, but her mother continued with bleak determination, knowing their debts were growing even if their crops were not. Soon she needed to borrow more for seed and fodder and food, until Lollius returned that last bitter winter to find them eating gruel, his animals sold, his land barren, and his patrician creditor at his door.

"I will find the money to free you," her mother had promised as Lollius was fettered in chains.

"Feed yourself and Pinna instead." He was unable to meet their eyes as he was led away to bondage, dragging the weight of those heavy irons, shuffling his feet, his shoulders slumped.

Pinna could not let him go. She clutched at one of his large hands with its wrist scraped raw from struggling. She squeezed his fingers, wanting his toughness to be transferred to her, but they were limp and he did not bid her farewell.

Remembering her loss, Pinna joined in the taunting. She was overcome with hatred for Aemilius. He may not have been the nobleman who ruined her father but he was just the same, just as cruel.

Calvus held up his hands. The clamor died away. "Perhaps the patricians want the common man to be away in winter for another reason. After all, the elections are to be held in a few weeks. If a man is absent from Rome he cannot vote. Isn't it enough that the aristocracy denies us a chance to govern? Now they want to prevent us from voting at all. I say no to a winter campaign. I say no to any levy of troops!"

Pinna nodded as she listened to the plebeian with the upright stance and righteous demeanor. This man may have been excluded from being a senator, magistrate, or consul, but he did hold power. Power that he wielded as smugly as any highborn. As one of the ten people's tribunes he could indeed veto any law that was proposed, any edict the Senate declared.

The portly Aemilius waggled one finger at him like an irascible tutor. "You're talking mutiny while you should be swearing fealty."

Once again the throng howled. A few stray missiles were thrown. Pinna could smell their sweat and fury. Fearing a riot could break out she glanced around her, wondering if she could escape across the rooftops instead of having to brave the crush of incensed citizens. Others must have been thinking the same as they scrambled to higher ground. Soon there was a gallery of observers balanced atop the terra-cotta roof tiles of buildings lining the Forum.

From the corner of her eye, Pinna saw a man stride from the steps of the nearby Senate House and ascend the platform.

He bowed to the others. Calvus stiffly responded but Aemilius scowled, as did Sergius and Verginius. Pinna wondered why the three patricians were annoyed by the newcomer. After all, it was another of their class.

Green Teeth tugged at Runny Nose. "It's Marcus Furius Camillus. I fought under him this year at Anxur. He is a true warrior, a leader worth following. It's a pity he can't be elected general two years in a row."

Amid the tumult the consular general stood silent. Those in the front ceased their shouting as they began to notice his stillness. The quiet spread outward like ripples on a pond.

Pinna could not take her eyes from him. His clothes were the same as those worn by any other nobleman but, unlike Aemilius, who was adjusting his rumpled cloak to hide his potbelly, there was a grace to how his toga was draped. His hair and beard were neatly trimmed, emphasizing the angles of his face. He looked slightly older than two score years. No younger or older than any of her customers. Pinna sensed he would be more at home in armor, his athletic body welcoming the definition of corselet, greaves, and armbands. For the first time in her life, she found herself wanting to know how broad a man's chest was, how flat his belly, whether his arms were strong under the layers of tunic and toga.

And then he spoke. His voice was measured and soft, yet in the silence pervading the Forum, all could hear it. He pointed to the front of the platform. Nailed into the brickwork for all to read were the Twelve Tables, the laws of Rome. Beneath them were a number of light rectangular patches where bronze plaques containing the terms of treaties had once been fastened. None remained. Their city was at war with all its neighbors.

"Soldiers of Rome, do you trust the Veientanes?"

Murmurs spread.

The general stared into the eyes of each of the citizens in front of him, then raised his gaze to slowly scan row after row until he reached the rim. Then upward to survey the people sitting atop shops and temples. It was as though he was looking directly at her. Pinna felt as important as the veterans and citizens in front of her.

"For twenty years the treaty with Veii was skewered to this platform until Aemilia Caeciliana betrayed our people."

Pinna felt all eyes swivel to Aemilius. The older man tensed and hoisted his cloak over his shoulder yet again. Being the adopted father and uncle of a traitoress was a dangerous thing. Yet despite the scandal, he had prevailed. He'd already led two assaults against Veii. No one could question Aemilius's loyalty to Rome. No one would dare.

"For twenty years we were at peace," Camillus repeated, drawing attention back to him. "Don't forget, however, that before this our cities fought many wars. And why? Because the Veientanes cannot be trusted! They have long coveted our salt mines and raided our farmlands. One of their kings treacherously murdered our envoys. And now they wish to plunder our land, rape our women, and kill our children."

His voice was growing louder, his words falling into a rhythm, stirring her and all around her. The name of the traitoress was whispered also, making Pinna wonder again how this woman could have forsaken her people, sacrificed her virtue, and surrendered her birthright.

"If we don't act quickly Veii will convince the Etruscan League to rise against us. It gives our enemy comfort to hear us bickering. It's time for noblemen and commoners to unite!"

As the general strode the platform, Pinna noticed that he limped slightly. Suddenly he crouched down, hailing those he knew, naming them as only a commander who loved his men could know them, praising each one for past valor, urging them to be brave again. "I have fought with you and seen your daring. Do not tell me now that you fear the cold. Do not cry that you wish to be home instead of fighting."

He stood and swept his arm in an arc. "You hunt in winter, eager to bring down boar or buck. It is time to hunt Veientanes instead! It's time to show them that we can endure! Raise the siege and do so all year round. Trap them and, in time, thirst and hunger will stalk them and defeat them. Our enemies must learn that Rome fights its wars until it gains victory."

His eyes remained on the throng. "Remember, if we don't show Veii what kind of men we are, all Etruria will ensnare us and force us to defend our city walls. And then there will be no need to cry that we cannot plow our land—because we will have no land to plow!"

He thrust his fist skyward. "So forget winter cold and weariness, forget summer heat and homesickness, but never forget that you fight for the glory of Rome!"

Cheering erupted. Camillus had asked them to ignore the cold. In the heat of his speech, she had indeed forgotten the winter chill. Now she understood why Drusus and Marcus had spoken of him with admiration at the cemetery that night. Now she understood why they wanted to follow him.

The general slid his arm around Calvus's shoulders, drawing him forward to face the group of senators who were gathered on the Curia Senate House steps, a solid block of purple and white. He waited for the welter of spectators to calm, and the assembly once again settled into a still expanse of citizens clad in homespun. "The time has also come for Romans to accept that a man of the people must be given the chance to be elected one of the six consular generals. It's time a plebeian led the siege to the gates of Veii!"

Pinna smiled. It would seem that she was not the only one to recognize an opportunity. Camillus was as wily as he was eloquent. If Calvus was elected he would hardly encourage any of his fellow tribunes to veto a levy that he himself might command.

"Remember also," the general continued, "it is no use coveting Veientane land. Let's take it so that it might be shared by all—both commoner and nobleman."

Enveloped in noise, Pinna felt as though she had gone deaf and that her ears would ring for hours once the racket stopped. She studied the stunned faces of the patricians around the Forum. One of their own was supporting the election of a commoner for the first time in the history of Rome. One of their own was daring to offer these veterans land acquired in war.

Calvus stood speechless as Camillus clapped him on the back. Aemilius's shock was no less palpable. The two patrician candidates looked horrified. Sergius had forgotten to remain aloof from his rival, instead whispering in Verginius's ear, both men's glares fixed on Camillus. Neither man wanted to be among the first patricians to share the military tribunate with a plebeian.

Pinna knew she should be wary. After all, Camillus was still asking the soldiers of Rome to suffer. He was still expecting them to risk bondage. And yet she could feel the fervor rise within her as the veterans around her surged with blood desire to conquer Veii and claim the spoils.

She climbed back down to the ground. For one foolish minute she felt she was a citizen. An urge to squeeze through the crowd rushed through her. She wanted to touch the general, to see his features clearly. Then she checked herself, knowing she risked being kicked and hit for being a prostitute. Instead, with her back pressed against a shop's wall, she made do with a glimpse of him as he was borne aloft on the shoulders of his admirers as they flowed into the Forum shouting again and again, "Camillus! Camillus! Camillus!"

ELEVEN

The sun was setting. The crowd had dispersed as well as the politicians. As the street vendors closed their stalls, Pinna hastened back to the Esquiline, anxious to be home.

As she moved closer to the city wall she saw streetwalkers emerging from their haunts to loiter beside temple walls or shadowy arches. These women stayed awake all night. Night moths, unregistered whores who serviced their customers amid rat droppings and the stench from the great public drain. The harlots had marked their territories, keeping a working distance between them as men furtively approached, seeking hand or mouth, ass or cunni, for a sum.

She called to the harlots, watching in amusement how many did not recognize her with her clean face, unstained clothes, and anointed hair. Some wished her well, others ignored her. Either way, she had left their world behind.

Reaching home, Pinna knelt beside Fusca, who still lay upon the pallet. "Mama, I'm sorry I'm so late."

As she lit a candle she noticed how her mother's pupils were wide despite the sudden flare of light. The woman's eyes moved hectically in her partly frozen face while her head bobbed in agitation as she shied away from her daughter, shrieking, "Ghoul! Ghoul!"

The girl tried to place a hand on Fusca's shoulder but this only caused her to scream louder. Pinna gripped her mother's wrist to stop her from attacking her.

"Hush, Mama, hush. It's me. I've brought you a treat."

Pinna held out the honeycomb. Fusca stared at it, her breathing slowing, her shoulders relaxing. As she let the girl drip the sweetness onto her tongue, she awkwardly held it with her one good hand, sucking at it like a babe at the breast.

The smell of fresh urine lingered over the usual staleness within the room. Pinna had left her for too long. Stripping and wiping her clean, she was sorry to hear her whimpering because of her aching joints.

"Soon"—Pinna unwrapped her toga and wound it around Fusca instead—"we shall have a hearth, which Vesta will make burn bright. You'll see, Mama. We'll have a true home where Janus will guard our door."

Stroking her mother's cheek, Pinna avoided touching the pustules on the woman's face.

Combing her hair was fruitless. It was so matted Pinna would have to shave it. She sighed to remember how, before her mother's hair turned gray from ash and sadness, it was shiny and black just as her name described.

Fusca had always been the strong one. A small woman, she'd never seemed diminished before the taller or the greater. She was stronger than Pinna's father, withstanding his moods and shouldering his burdens. When he bellowed, Pinna always scurried for safety but Fusca would stand silent, waiting for the abuse to subside before obeying him as a good wife must. Sometimes he would forget the law and beat her anyway, but at other times such acquiescence made him grumpily accede to her, somehow uncomfortable that his unreasonableness had been heeded.

When her husband was made a bondsman, Fusca sold his land and animals, weapons and tools, but it had not been enough. Lollius's patron and protector was now his owner. He had become a citizen without rights, a man without a soul, his life and labor forfeited until the debt was paid. But there was no means left to do so.

Desperate, wretched, and starving, Fusca found that men who had once paid her respect as Lollius's wife instead paid to poke her, taking her secretly in the byways and lanes around the farmland that had once been hers.

The Great City was enormous, noisy, and fearsome, but there Fusca found men who were prepared to pay a higher fee. Men whose lives weren't linked to the rhythm of the land, who weren't qualified to serve. Men who did not know her name as they grunted and grasped her.

Pinna would wait for her in one of the dank caves outside the wall of the Esquiline Hill where they first lived, too terrified to venture out amid the rotting corpses of criminals, slaves, and babies, and of being haunted by any lemures, those spirits trapped between the world of the living and the dead.

And it had taken more than Pinna being a cutpurse or keening for dead men for the pair to escape from the caves to the slums. She, too, had needed to become a night moth, although Fusca wept as though she would never stop at asking her daughter to join her.

"Father has cursed me," Fusca said, when her womb and joints began to ache. "He has cursed me for failing him," she whispered, when she realized she could not escape the pox. Pinna soothed her, not believing her, telling her that it was not true—until the day Fusca accused her of being a demon and word was sent that Lollius had died.

At least tonight Fusca was smiling as she crunched the sticky sweet, wiping her mouth with the back of her hand, the honey smeared across grubby skin.

Pinna stared at the woman with her swollen limbs, and covered with lesions. She felt as alone as when she'd lain with her first customer, praying that he would not hurt her. She needed her mother to guide her, to protect her as she once had, to love her again and stand beside her as she started their new life. She tenderly wiped the nectar from the woman's chin. "It tastes good, doesn't it?"

Fusca paused in devouring the honeycomb and peered at her daughter. "Is that you, Mother?" Her words were slurred.

"No. I'm not Grandma," said Pinna, her voice catching. "I'm Feather, your Little Wing."

Fusca did not heed her. She clasped Pinna's hand, her cry plangent: "Mother! Mother! I need you so."

TWELVE

Veii, Autumn, 398 BC

At times Semni felt as though she was no more than a kiln, a furnace to form the infant inside her with her body's heat.

Wiping sweat from her forehead, she waited for one of the slaves to heave aside the stone cover of the enormous oven. It was not just the force of the fire that made her perspire. She was always hot now. Hot and weary. Her fecund body a burden. Once again the baby gained her attention, pressing its limbs against the walls of her womb. Sliding her hand beneath her heavy leather apron she rubbed her belly, the navel protruding, and cursed the small being within.

Heat blasted the air as the door was opened. Semni shielded her face from the roaring fierceness. The slave slid the tray of dried pots onto the shelf inside. The door was slammed shut. The firing began.

She had worked all morning on the pieces. Bucchero wine jugs. Not coiled but fashioned on the wheel. Stamps of maenads and satyrs dancing on their sides. Expensive. Destined to grace rich men's tables.

Semni sat down once again to her work. Her hands were caked. Using the back of her wrist, she pushed away strands escaping from the tenuous knot that held back her thick hair. She liked the steady pace to creation, the kick to start the flywheel, the stone blurring with speed as she centered the clay, slurry coating hands and splashing forearms as she hollowed the lump and raised it, contours swelling and tapering in the spinning. Later she would burnish the surface, rubbing a polished stone across the texture, friction forming smoothness, her arms strong from practice. Finally applying the coating of moist slip, which would give the pottery its color.

Inside the workshop it was always stifling. The temperature soared from the heat of the kilns in the internal courtyard. The chill of the autumn morning did not permeate the walls. Most of the potters worked bare-chested in loincloths, skin streaked with sweat and clay, feet dusty.

Before Semni had grown large, the men had enjoyed flirting with her, although none were foolish enough to do so when her husband was looking. They would ogle her as she labored, spying through the sides of her apron how the sweat made her thin shift cling to deep cleavage, nipples, curved hips, and rounded buttocks. How she hitched the fabric high to reveal firm pliant thighs parted around the wheel. She would flash them sly sloe-eyed smiles and dimples, the warm pink tip of her tongue peeking from a full-lipped mouth, hinting at how it could be put to better use.

And with some she had done more than flirted. Enjoying the power she had to arouse both jealousy and their manhood. She had a body made for lusting but now, gravid and swollen-limbed, she gained no attention. Forbidden territory, no longer alluring. The men who had been prepared to cuckold her husband were not so keen to do so when he was to be a father.

Not that the old goat, Velthur, was likely to be the sire. His sixty years had robbed him of his vigor. She did not complain. At least this limited their coupling. He rarely hardened unless using a switch on her before eventually being able to finish with a different type of rod. She doubted that he was virile enough to seed a child.

Instead, Semni believed that the infant's father was a stag or boar or ram, perhaps wolf or fox or bear. There had been many masked men she'd lain with on the night of the Winter Feast, drunk on ecstasy and unwatered wine as she sought communion with the wine god. The child could even be half noble. The high priest had also mounted her as she worshipped. Despite wearing a bull's mask, his size had been disappointing. She'd expected more from the god's servant. She even enjoyed believing that her soul had merged with Fufluns, conceiving a son who would be half divine.

The baby kicked her again, reminding Semni that its holiness was a fantasy. She shifted her weight, trying to get comfortable upon her seat, her bulk hindering her posture.

Of course she had tried to purge it with the aid of laurel and lupin but, unlike other times, it did not slip early from her womb. And yet she did not try to scrape it away. Not when she'd watched one of her sisters die that way. Her lack of courage and the infant's stubbornness only made resentment grow.

Absorbed in her thoughts it took her some time to notice the other potters were standing. Lady Caecilia had arrived. A ripple of bows tracked the noblewoman's progress across the floor together with echoes of respectful greeting.

The Roman was accompanied by a small companion who gripped his mother's hand. The boy called Tas. The princip often brought one of her sons with her, always cautioning them that curious fingers could suffer burns. Aricia followed, grinning as she caught sight of Semni. The surly Arruns walked behind. Semni eyed him, pleased the Phoenician was once again detailed to look after his mistress.

Lady Caecilia was well liked by those in the workshop even if outsiders were wary of her. For she had freed all the potters and sculptors in her employ. Other owners were not so generous. Most of the artisans in the pottery quarter were enslaved. It was no wonder her staff was prepared to forget she was a Roman. They recognized her fairness, and admired her eagerness to inspect their work at the risk of dirtying her finery. They respected her, too, for knowing the names of their families and visiting them to offer medicine and food.

There was another reason Semni was fond of her employer. Lady Caecilia had become her patron. The workshop was renowned for its masterpieces. It was a world of treasure: fine terra-cotta, shiny bucchero. Most precious of all, though, were the vessels that boasted red figures within polished black. It was these vases that the noblewoman commissioned Semni to produce. A dream the girl had harbored since childhood. An opportunity to rival her father's fame.

Semni was only fifteen but all her life she'd been surrounded by ornament and beauty as well as noise and smoke and danger. Daughter of a sculptor famed throughout Etruria, she had spent her childhood mopping slurry and sweeping dust, collecting shards and fetching water. Yet the chance of learning how to throw and decorate pots was denied her. And before her father died he married her to Velthur, the workshop foreman, with an expectation she would produce grandsons, not artwork.

Her husband was easier to convince than her father. He was prepared to indulge his young wife in gratitude for her tricks in bed. It was a bonus when he discovered Semni was also skillful in another way. Her father may have bequeathed all he owned to her brothers but he'd left his daughter one thing—his talent.

A sudden thread of pain traveled from one buttock down her leg as Semni curtsied to Lady Caecilia. She lurched a little, then, arching, massaged the small of her back.

The mistress gestured to Semni to resume her seat at the flywheel. "Come and sit."

The girl hesitated before obeying, conscious that it was the noblewoman who should be seated. The little master lingered beside his mother, his amber eyes piercing. Semni found his stare unnerving, thinking it too solemn for one so young.

"Your aches will end after you have borne your baby," said the princip. "You must be due any day now."

"Yes, my lady."

"And then you will know a happiness you can't imagine."

Semni nodded politely. She doubted she would feel any elation. The burden of carrying the child would only give way to the load of rearing it. She glanced over to Aricia. Lady Caecilia had servants to care for her children. There would be no such luxury for Semni, just a cycle of suckling and dirty swaddling. She'd seen her mother worn out by the birthing of many children. Only four had survived. And the poor woman and her eighth had died together.

Lady Caecilia moved across to Semni's worktable. Tas trailed after her like a shadow. The potter stole a glance at the woman. The Roman was tall and slender. It was as though she had not borne three children. Semni doubted it would be the same for her. There would be sagging instead of firmness, padding instead of curves, slackening instead of tautness. Worst of all, Velthur had made it clear there would be no more flawless creations from pure clay. No loveliness from her labors. Semni's only job would be as a mother.

"This is very fine." The mistress examined a vase drying on the table.

Keen to show off her workmanship, Semni rose and stood beside her. A faint scent of lilies clung to the aristocrat, making Semni conscious that she must stink of sweat and clay.

Two lovers were etched onto the surface of the vessel. Fufluns and Areatha. The sheer robes swathing their nakedness seemed almost real as they embraced: faces close, lips almost touching, gazing rapt into each other's eyes. "See, my lady? I've incised the figures in readiness for painting."

Lady Caecilia examined the tracery with a bejeweled finger. "It's beautiful. Lord Mastarna is very fond of the wine god and his wife."

Semni was sure she caught sight of a fleeting frown at odds with the compliment.

Lady Caecilia carefully returned the vase to the artisan. "Such a pity it will be your last commission. I've come to tell all of you that the workshop must now only produce terra-cottas."

It took a moment for the girl to digest the news, her surprise momentarily overcoming deference. "But why?"

The princip raised her eyebrows. "Why? Because of the blockades, of course. The king has ordered that we must supply the army with essentials. It's no use creating goods that cannot be traded beyond our city."

Semni still struggled to understand. "Do you really think the Romans won't go home this winter?"

Lady Caecilia shook her head. "Rome means to besiege us until we starve, even if its soldiers must suffer hunger and sickness. Surely you must know that. Remember how they returned before the spring thaw this year? Now fall is upon us and they are still camped outside our walls."

Hearing the soft criticism in the princip's voice made Semni feel foolish. Then annoyed. She was not a child needing to be chided. Her memory of the enemy returning to dig new siege lines in the snow was vivid. Unease had filled her at how the Romans were breaking the rules, displaying gritty menace in the breach.

Then Lord Kurvenas had been elected as lucumo. Old Velthur worried taxes would increase and corruption spread as it had under King Tulumnes. To Semni, though, there seemed little dissimilarity between the reign of magistrate and monarch. War flourished under both.

Yet over the months, cocooned in the workshop, Semni could allow herself to forget the city was encircled. Her days were much the same as in other, more peaceful years, except for less food on the table. She let others worry. Even in a siege everyday life continued. Merchants still bartered, blacksmiths shod horses, and weavers cut cloth even as troops sallied forth from Veii's gates or showered arrows from its walls. Yet now Lady Caecilia was saying the workshop must become a factory manufacturing basics: bowls and beakers for the army, amphorae to store provisions, cauldrons for boiling oil or water. And, hearing this, Semni suddenly understood why others resented this woman.

Looking momentarily discomforted, the mistress drew her son to stand in front of her. "Believe me, Semni, I want peace as much as you do. Now, I must speak to the others. But perhaps Tas could stay and watch you."

Semni glanced at the boy. His small quietness throughout the conversation had made her forget him. She nodded, fond of children as long as they weren't hers.

Lady Caecilia patted the girl's hand. "Don't be too disappointed. I'm sure the time will come when you'll make beautiful things again. But for now simple terra-cottas must suffice."

Semni watched the princip greet the next artisan and break the news. It was kind of the mistress to take the time to speak to each one of them in turn.

Once his mother had gone, Tas ventured nearer to observe the potter prepare her brushes for painting. Aricia hastened to fetch a stool for the boy. "It's wonderful to see you again, Semni. I was so pleased when the mistress decided to bring the little master."

Semni nodded. She always enjoyed talking to the Greek girl when she visited the workshop. It bemused her, though, as to why the nursemaid was so effusive at such meetings.

"Sit here, my pet," said Aricia, hovering behind Tas.

Concentrating on stirring the paint, Semni said absently, "Where are his brothers?"

"With Perca, the junior nursemaid. I wanted to accompany the mistress so I could see you again."

Semni smiled but wondered whether Aricia had any friends. The girl seemed lonely.

Unused to the heat, Tas took off his woolen cap and laid it on his lap. Semni wondered if shyness hindered speech, yet he seemed confident enough as his strange golden eyes followed each of her movements.

Aricia peered over Semni's shoulder. Noticing the faint scent of violets, the potter envied the maid's good fortune to wear such perfume. There were benefits to being a princip's servant. She looked up from her task. "How is the Gorgon?"

The nursemaid glanced at Tas, reminding Semni that little children had big ears. She doubted, though, that he would understand that the Gorgon was Aricia's mother, Cytheris. Risking the chance the boy could report their gossip, she continued. "Is she still as mean as you say?"

Aricia nodded. "I'm sick of her slaps and pinches. She might be happy to remain in service but I'm a freedwoman and have other plans."

Semni frowned. "And what would you do?"

"Be a priestess."

The potter snorted. "Don't be silly. Only noblewomen can be ordained. Besides, you should be thankful for living in a mansion, plump with food and wearing Aegyptian linen and Milesian wool."

Arica flicked black curls away from her face. "You sound just like her. She doesn't understand me either. And now she wants me to marry Arruns."

Semni turned her attention to the Phoenician who stood guard at the doorway. Swarthy, shaven head, hooded eyes, hooked nose. All knew him for the blue tattooed snake slithering around his torso and neck, its fangs biting into his face. Arruns did not frighten her, though. Semni imagined him to be a potent lover.

She was sure she'd forget his grimness when squeezed beneath the expanse of his chest and between the strong thews of his thighs. "Why are you complaining? You have to marry sometime. You're already fifteen." She snuck a look at the guard again. "Don't you think Arruns is worth bedding?"

"It's not always about men!" Aricia snapped. "I don't want to be confined to the square of any man's home. I just told you. I want to be a priestess of the Calu Cult. I want to serve Aita."

Semni sighed. "You should forget about that dismal death cult. Revere Fufluns instead. Join the Pacha Cult. Enjoy his revels. Seek life. Hallow resurrection."

Aricia gestured toward Semni's belly. "I'm sure Velthur doesn't appreciate you worshipping the wine god."

Semni laughed at the unexpected quip. It suddenly made her warm to the nursemaid. She glanced at the guard again. She'd heard that Arruns had been the Phersu. Although she was not a follower of the death cult, it strangely excited her that he had performed holy deeds. "Arruns once acted as Aita's instrument. I would have thought that would appeal to you."

"He's no believer. He told me so. Just a killer Lord Mastarna has retained."

Semni frowned. Arruns was more than a bodyguard. He was a warrior who fought in the light infantry when his general rode to war. "Still, you could do worse."

To her surprise, Tas tapped her on the shoulder. "But Aricia would be very tired if she shared a bed with Arruns."

The potter blinked. Throughout their conversation the boy had been studying the vase. She'd thought him uncomprehending.

Aricia blushed. Semni giggled. "And why is that, young master?"

"Because Arruns never sleeps. He told me he must keep his eyes open."

Semni's laughter doubled. "Sleepless nights are exactly what your nurse needs!"

"Enough." Aricia scowled, then bent down to Tas, voice gentle. "Let's return to your mother, my pet."

"No! I don't want to!"

To Semni's disapproval, Aricia complied without question. Clearly the little master's petulance was often tolerated. Nevertheless, the nursemaid mouthed a warning behind the boy's head. "No more talk."

The potter smiled, returning to her work, deftly painting the background around the lovers, filling in the thin grooved outlines with precise strokes of a fine-bristled brush, the untouched clay giving form to the figures.

Unable to contain curiosity, Tas piped up again. "Why are you using red paint? It should be black."

"Because the slip is magic."

"Slip?"

"The clay and potash paint."

"It doesn't smell like magic."

Semni leaned toward him, tone conspiratorial. "Oh, that's because I like to mix a little piss with it."

He screwed up his nose, and when his expression remained skeptical, Semni pointed to the kiln. "See how the slave has placed a tile over the chimney so there is less air? It will make the furnace hotter. When the vase is placed inside, the slip melts and turns black, leaving the unpainted figures red as the fire cools. Is that not magic?"

Tas digested the information with a nod, then moved onto his next question. "Is she a goddess?"

"Who?"

He pointed to the woman on the vase. "Her."

"No, she is a mortal. That's her husband, Fufluns, the wine god. Her name is Areatha, but Greek people like Aricia call her Ariadne. Do you know her story?"

"Only that she helped These slay the Minotaur and then escaped with him."

"Ah, but on their way home they stopped at an island, and when she was sleeping These deserted her."

The boy frowned. "Areatha must have been very sad."

"Not for long because, you see, she fell in love with Fufluns. The god found her while she was sleeping and took her as his bride."

"And never left her?"

"Never. They live together even now. The most devoted of divine couples."

"But Aricia says that Lord Aita and Persiphnae love each other more than any others. They are rulers of the Beyond. I'll meet them after I die."

"Yes, my pet." His nursemaid tugged at the boy to stand, the gesture showing a nervousness the potter did not quite understand. "Now let's leave Semni to her work and find your mother." This time Tas allowed himself to be bustled away.

Shortly after, Semni noticed Tas's cap must have fallen from his lap. She retrieved it from the floor, brushing off the dust. Not inclined to heave her weight from the stool, Semni called to Arruns to fetch it. The Phoenician ignored her. He always snubbed her advances. To be perverse, she called even louder. He reluctantly approached.

"Master Tas dropped this." She handed him the hat. As he took it from her she ran her fingers along one vein of his corded arm. "You know," she said, voice husky, "I won't always be with child."

Arruns shook off her hand, hooded eyes cold. "You should look to your husband."

Semni laughed, studying the blue serpent on the Phoenician's torso. Her fingers drifted down his chest and stomach toward his groin. "Are you ever going to show me if it's a two-headed snake?"

His palm engulfed her hand, his touch light, but she knew he could hurt her with the merest pressure.

"I only lie with women, not spoiled children."

She pulled away, pouting and pointing to her belly. "Do you think I'd be like this if I wasn't a woman?"

"Semni, the babe inside you is probably wiser than you."

His barb stung. The baby edged its foot under her ribs. She poked it, cursing again.

The stoker called to her as he opened the furnace, querying whether she wished to check the pots before placing them into sand to cool. She gestured for him to continue, then picked up the vase, caressing it. Out of fire would come perfection. The child within her would never be as exquisite. What would it look like? Fawn or lamb, calf or cub? And what would her husband do if he found the child was not of his loins? Hopefully it would only bear a resemblance to her.

She thought of Lady Caecilia's announcement then realized that it didn't really matter that the workshop was to become a factory. With motherhood, any chance to gain fame would disappear.

Semni turned the vessel over and raised the scalpel, incising her name onto its base. Only the best artisans were entitled to do so. This would be the last time she would make such a mark. A spattering of tears darkened the clay.

THIRTEEN

The potters were standing again. Then kneeling. General Mastarna had arrived.

Semni curtsied as best she could, intrigued as to why Lady Caecilia's husband would visit the workshop. Here was another man whose unloveliness she could forgive. Out of habit she wetted her lips and primped her hair. Although she doubted he would be tempted even if she weren't pregnant. The lord only had eyes for his slender Roman.

The warrior was encased in armor, his round shield slung over his shoulder. He hastened to his wife, ignoring the potters who gave obeisance. Puffed up with importance, Velthur tried to greet him. The princip brushed past him. The old man's bony chest was already sunken; being rebuffed only made him looked more crestfallen.

Lady Caecilia stood, face ashen. "Vel, what is it? Is something wrong?"

He took both her hands, his deep voice buoyant. "Word has just reached us. The city of Falerii has declared war against Rome. They are in battle as we speak."

"The Faliscans? Why would they do that? Those people are not Rasennan."

"Because they see that they'll be next. They've been Veii's ally for too long and goaded Rome one too many times by providing us with their corn."

"But I thought the Romans had set up double siege lines. Isn't General Sergius ready to counter any northern attack from the rest of Etruria?"

Mastarna smiled. "The fool has been lax in leaving some of the northern forts unmanned. The Faliscans have taken his army by surprise. And while the Roman forces are preoccupied staving off the attack, I'll charge the trenches that face Veii. Then I plan to cross the northwest bridge and assault them from the rear. Our enemy will be squeezed between two battle lines."

The noblewoman's expression was as anxious as her husband's was eager. "But surely the main Roman camp in the south will come to Sergius's aid? And General Verginius's contingent is far greater in number."

"Kurvenas is already mustering his men to sortie against him should he make any attempt to relieve his colleague. Don't you see? This is the chance to flush out the Romans completely."

The lines creasing her brow deepened as she gripped his hands. "Do you have to lead the vanguard?"

Mastarna kissed her fingers. "I will be careful."

His wife gave him a small, unconvinced smile. "You are never careful."

"Don't worry, Ati. Apa will be victorious."

The parents looked down at their son, who had been standing silently beside them. Smiling, the father lifted Tas onto his hip. "You must look after your mother and brothers while I'm fighting." He lowered the child to the ground and swung his shield from his shoulder. "You must be ferocious." He pointed to the bull's head boss. "You must be the bull of the House of Mastarna."

The boy's golden eyes held his father's gaze, a note of bravery in his reedy voice. "Yes, Apa."

Semni saw how Tas trembled as he clasped his mother's hand. She felt sorry for him. Born into conflict, this boy had only known a world of armies and siege lines. At least she had memories of peace, even if they were clouded.

The piercing blast of a war trumpet sounded, one low, startling note held for moments, then lengthening and rising. Mastarna gestured to his bodyguard, then turned to his wife. "Two of my men will escort you home. Stay there with our family. Arruns will come with me."

Face upturned to his, Lady Caecilia put her arms around her husband. Watching them, Semni saw their embrace as an echo of the red-figured lovers on her vase. For a moment, the general's zeal dimmed. Husband and wife held each other's gaze as though no one else existed. He pressed his lips to her forehead, and then her mouth, the kiss lingering and tender.

Envy stirred within Semni. She'd never thought of being faithful. Wanted only desire. Brief and uncomplicated. Now, seeing the couple's reluctance to part, Semni wondered what it would be like to love a man. To have intimacy instead of lust. To welcome familiar caresses.

She'd never imagined, either, bidding farewell to a fighter. Even though she'd lain with soldiers, it was different than being their woman. And she knew little about the warrior class. Her brothers were merchants. Velthur and her workmates, craftsmen. Only noblemen and their vassals could afford to go to war. Their rank defined by how much coin they could spend on armor. There was a price for luxury and comfort in peacetime—the duty to die when war was declared.

She glanced over to Arruns. His demeanor had changed from bodyguard to warrior. There was keenness in his gaze, his body tense, a predator ready to stalk its prey.

In that moment the girl also saw him as a loner. Had he any family other than the one he served? Would any woman grieve for him? Did anyone love him? She knew nothing about him other than his harshness and disdain.

She moved to stand beside him, her gaze traveling along his tattooed body. "Be careful, Arruns," she said, no teasing in her voice. "I don't want the reason I'll never see all of that serpent to be because some Roman slew you."

She waited for his rebuke. It did not come. Inscrutable, he turned his attention to her. "Don't worry, Semni, it will take at least three of them to kill me."

The eerie martial horn blared again. Drums accompanying it. General Mastarna did not tarry. Face tristful, Lady Caecilia stood back, still holding her son's hand.

Semni knew she should also be somber, but as she watched the men leave she found herself pleased. For even though it was fleeting, Arruns had hidden a broken-toothed smile behind a nod good-bye.

FOURTEEN

News of the battle echoed through the marketplaces. The enemy was struggling to survive the Veientane and Faliscan onslaughts. A crowd of townspeople raced to the Tinia Gates at the northwest quarter of the city to assemble along the wall. They could not spy the fighting in the distance but they heard the clamor of battle drifting across the valley.

There was a mystery, too. The Roman contingent from the main camp in the south did not rally to aid their comrades. General Verginius held his army within the stockades. Never stirring. Letting the slaughter of Sergius's force continue. Not daring King Kurvenas to attack.

At sundown a clarion call signaled victory. Word spread. The surviving Romans had retreated.

The Veientanes were once again free to leave the city and there was no need to wait until winter and Fufluns's feast to celebrate. Soon a crush of people bumped against one another in the lock of the double gates as they hastened to be the first to reach the plain. Despite her condition, Semni wanted to share the fervor. Lining up, she seized a brand and dipped it in a bubbling vat of pitch before setting it afire. Then, to the accompaniment of flute and aulos, she joined the throng descending from the walled plateau as they sang a hymn to the god of war. Their torches formed a cascade of light as they streamed into a landscape already burning with color, the sunset's hues matching the russet and copper of autumn. Wagons followed, laden with amphorae of wine and cauldrons of pitch, one to quench thirst, the other to ensure the flames would ignite and incinerate all vestiges of the Romans.

Semni lagged behind, her bulk hindering her. Catching her breath, she slackened her pace as she shuffled through drifts of purple and orange foliage.

A breeze was blowing, setting pockets of yellow leaves swirling before they settled on the ruffled surface of the river. In the light of the setting sun, the water seemed pink as Semni crossed the wooden bridge through the wide ravine. The triumphant beat of drums drew her onward.

Ahead of her the crowd raced to the level ground where the earthworks and forts lay. Soon, though, Semni found herself bumping into those before her as they slowed, their singing petering out, merriment trailing. Pushing her way to the front she saw why they had halted. Aghast, she stared at the battlefield before her in the sore, bleeding light of dusk.

She had expected the same scenes as had met her every other winter: a deserted camp, sterile except for stinking cesspits and middens of rubbish. A forlorn silence. No foe remaining to confront them. No dead either. The Romans always took the deceased with them. The ashes tamped into urns then crammed into kitbags together with pots and plates and spoons.

Instead Semni stood frozen, heart beating hard, gagging at the stench of blood and ordure hanging in the air. Corpses were sprawled on the ground, their hacked limbs scattered like joints of meat. Brains, bowels, and blood, viscous and plentiful, splattered the leafy carpet.

A few of the dead boasted crested bronze Veientane helmets, but the greatest number wore the round oxhide headwear of Rome.

Many had been trampled in the confusion of retreat. And those Romans who'd fled must have abandoned their arms. Neglected battle-axes and spears were strewn among comrades who still bore weapons they'd never again brandish.

Quaking, Semni realized that not all around her were lifeless. The maimed lay groaning, bleeding, forsaken. And the victors, bloodlust still raging within them, were dispatching the wounded to meet their gods. In the distance Semni heard weird death-dealing ululation. She shuddered, realizing the Faliscans were exacting the same retribution at the outer lines.

The urge to punish was infectious. At the sight of the weakened foe, townsfolk were spurred to their own vengeance. It was as though people had lost all sense that the wounded were humans as fists pounded Roman noses and jaws, and feet kicked backs and ribs. Seeing that the civilians would not stop, Semni prayed that quietus would soon end the agony. Unlike the assailants, she felt no hatred. She lacked courage, though, to intervene lest her mercy be mistaken for treason.

Like hunters skinning a beast felled in a hunt the soldiers were claiming the spoils. Some forced battle-axes from stiffened hands. For others the task was easier as they unfurled supple fingers from around hafts, armbands from still-warm flesh, and greaves from just-dead limbs. As greed emerged discipline was forgotten. Fistfights erupted as they squabbled over the plunder.

The commoners knew better than to gather loot earmarked for warriors. There would be pickings for them tomorrow: gold teeth, amulets, even rings if they were lucky. Instead, they sped to the barricades to splash pitch upon the timber and set their torches to it. Their exclamations at the sudden whoosh as the wind god fanned the flames were almost childlike. Amphorae were unplugged, wine goblets passed around, pipe and drums played again.

The sun was sinking, a half-orb shimmering in a resinous haze, sliding from the edge of the horizon, dragging the light with it. Coughing from the acrid smoke, eyes stinging, Semni discovered there was worse to witness. The Veientane soldiers were exacting their final reprisal for long-harbored hatreds by sawing through tendons and bone and scything limbs and heads from torsos. Overcome by horror, Semni vomited as they began disembowelling bellies and severing genitals from once proud and virile men.

Suffocating from fear she backed away, but the crowd jostled her, tipping her over so that she fell next to a corpse. She closed her eyes, knowing that she would have to open them again; to fumble and crawl away blindly would only lead to more ghastly encounters.

She peeked at the dead Roman. The soldier's eyes were vacant, staring at a dusk he would never see. Mouth slack, blood was congealing from a cut in his gullet, the soft vulnerable space above his breastplate. His slayer must have been experienced. He'd not wasted time slashing at bronze when flesh was ready to be sliced.

Finally the girl summoned the nerve to look up. The colors of the battlefield were muted by encroaching darkness. And yet nightfall did not bring respite. A luminous harvest moon was rising, providing more light for the conquerors to continue their desecration.

Exhausted, Semni edged away from the fallen warrior and huddled, knees drawn up, hugging her swollen belly, burying her head, hiding her eyes.

The sound of hoofbeats gained her attention. A group of horsemen galloped through the chaos, their animals rearing, skittish with excitement. It was a unit of the cavalry that had chased the last of Sergius's men back into Roman territory. Bellowing in fury, their leader leaned down from his mount to heave one of the Veientanes from his grisly task. The rider's cuirass was embossed with Trojan heroes, the tiny figures engrossed in their own combat.

Semni recognized the bull's head boss on his shield. It was General Mastarna. The girl scanned around for Arruns but there was no sign of him. Then she remembered the guard would have no horse to accompany his master. He would still be returning on foot from the pursuit.

The control over his great gray stallion absolute, the general wheeled around so he could be seen in all quarters. "Cease defiling the dead! Otherwise you will suffer the same fate by my hands!" His bass voice resounded across the plain as he held his curved sword aloft to smite those who might disobey him. "You have fought bravely here today. But what you do now is cowardly."

The Veientane hoplites faltered in their butchery, although some appeared reluctant, muttering to themselves and glancing to the far side of the battlefield where they could hear the Faliscans continuing unrestrained. Semni was not sure what riled them more—being denied the right to mutilate their foe or being prevented from claiming plunder. Yet these men were Mastarna's troops. They knew better than to defy their commander.

Once again a blast of the curved war horns jarred Semni's nerves. This time it was a fanfare. Another band of horsemen appeared, escorting a warrior in a bronze-sheathed chariot. The driver's balance was perfect despite the jolting caused by flattening corpses beneath bronze wheels and hooves.

Already on her knees, Semni bowed her head before the king while all around her knelt. She had only ever seen the lucumo wearing purple vestments, his face painted vermilion as he presided over holy rites. Now he wore armor. A winged lion was depicted on his muscle cuirass, his helmet adorned with gold-leaf decorations, its horsehair crest purple. Close to his regal presence, she was dazzled. In the moon and firelight it seemed as if Kurvenas was surrounded by an aura, a princip above all others—shining and majestic.

The lucumo drew the chariot beside the warrior. To her astonishment Lord Mastarna did not kneel in fealty after he dismounted but gave a cursory bow. Both men removed their bronze helmets. Sweat plastered the general's short hair to his skull, his jaw dark with grime and stubble. The king's face was clean-shaven, his long hair oiled.

The lucumo did not address the princip but turned to call to Mastarna's soldiers: "You have been courageous. Veii is grateful for your valor!" Despite owing loyalty to the general, the men straightened their shoulders at the monarch's praise.

Then King Kurvenas gestured toward Mastarna. "Why then does your leader deny you the chance to wreak vengeance? To right old scores?"

The girl lumbered to stand, wanting to see the general's reaction. Mastarna was staring at his ruler, clearly annoyed that Kurvenas was challenging him. "Why shame men who've already suffered humiliation in battle?" Mastarna countered.

The king's contempt matched his. "And yet the Romans have sent too many of our forebears to the Beyond with the same marks of disgrace. They would have shown no pity to our fallen. They deserve to have their souls relegated to eternal torment!"

Mastarna pointed to a slain soldier. "If we respect Rome's dead, then Rome may show mercy to our fallen if needed. These bodies should be sent back to their families so they can cremate them with due honors."

Stepping down from his chariot, the king walked over to a decapitated corpse, blood spreading in a halo where the head should have been. "You talk of honor? My great-uncle suffered the same fate as this man more than twenty years ago. Only his head was spiked on a lance and paraded for all to ridicule. My ancestor was denied solemn burial. His ghost wanders in ignominy. Why should we not act as ruthlessly to the descendants of his defilers?"

Semni glanced around her. Both commoners and warriors stood transfixed by the argument between monarch and princip. Lord Mastarna still showed no deference to the lucumo. "Because my father died at the hand of the same general who ordered that desecration," he countered. "Yet I do not see how mutilating a dead Roman can assuage my loss."

Throwing his purple cloak over his shoulder, Kurvenas returned to his chariot. "Then you are weak," he said as he stepped up onto the vehicle. "Or maybe you are squeamish at the thought of dishonoring your wife's people?"

Lord Mastarna strode over to the chariot. Semni thought him fearless. It looked as though he wanted to drag the monarch to the ground; instead he checked himself by seizing the bridle of one of the two horses. "Are you questioning my allegiance to Veii?"

To Semni's surprise the challenge seemed to calm the lucumo, not incite him to anger. Ignoring his rival, he opened his arms wide to the troops. "Soldiers of Veii, because of you Sergius and his army are running back to Rome bleeding from wounds upon their backs. And now Verginius has been recalled by his city for not sending reinforcements. So there will be no claiming of their dead. No sacrifices made to their memory. Instead Rome is prepared to let the carcasses of their warriors be picked clean by crows." He smoothed back his hair as he looked across to Mastarna. "And yet your general wants you to respect a foe that has deserted its fallen."

The faces of the assembled soldiers registered shock, the announcement answered by the shifting and snorting of horses and the crackle of the fire.

General Mastarna's disbelief was clear as his gaze traversed the battlefield and the slaughtered hoplites. Yet to Semni's surprise he reached down and seized a shield from a corpse, then lifted the dead man's spear and laid it over the weapon. "Then let us pay them more deference than their own," he called to his men. "Let us take their possessions but keep their souls intact!" He added the helmet to the other armor. "Now stack all booty into this pile!"

Confused, his men glanced at one another before sullen expressions settled on their faces. Semni was also confused as she watched the general mount the great gray, guiding the restless horse to pass by the nearest of his soldiers. "And tomorrow," his voice boomed, "after you have stoked the funeral pyres with the Roman dead you will be rewarded—for I will not claim my right as your lord to the greatest part of the spoils. Instead you will all share equally with me."

There was quiet as his army weighed the incentive to gain booty against the desire to avenge. Then murmuring spread: those who had already gathered a hoard, resentful, and those with slim pickings, grateful. One by one they began stacking the loot upon the pile. Soon enthusiasm mounted, the pace of collection faster, the heap growing higher.

Semni looked over to the lucumo. Seeing his influence over Mastarna's army had diminished, he flicked the reins to signal his horses to draw his chariot away. He did not speak but the hatred in his expression made words unnecessary. Lord Mastarna smiled and bowed low.

As the girl watched the royal entourage withdraw she remembered Lady Caecilia bidding her husband to be careful. Now she understood such a warning. For here was a Veientane general, married to a Roman, who had chosen to flout a king.

FIFTEEN

There was a savagery to the celebration. As full-moon madness waxed and battle fever waned, some women realized too late that coupling could go beyond the cusp of lust into rape. Others, though, were undaunted that the soldiers took them roughly.

Wine encouraged the tipping of emotions: from tuneless singing and laughter to quarrels and brawling. Children scooped armfuls of leaves to throw on the fire, laughing as they watched them curl and spark, drifting in hot updrafts. The sound of their delight was at odds with the debauchery around them.

Semni cowered away from the commotion, beside a timber-clad trench, the heat from its glow giving no respite from fearful shivering. She was desperate to return to the city but was too scared of getting lost in the dark. Nor did she want to cross a river flowing with blood. She prayed, too, that no one would seize her, perversely wishing for the first time that no man would find her tempting.

A warmth flowed down her legs. For a moment she was ashamed that she had wet herself, but as she checked between her thighs her fingers came away slick with womb water. Panicked, she realized that if she could not reach safety there would be new life born amid the dead, a fresh soul to compete with phantoms.

She managed to stand and stagger a few steps before a pang overwhelmed her. Panting, she sank to her knees, hoping there was a midwife among the drunken women. She prayed to Uni, the goddess of children, to give her succor, but all she really wanted was her mother to be there to hold her.

Above the noise, she heard a footfall crunching through the leaves. A fiend from the Afterworld loomed from the smoke: face half blue, half red, half lit, half shadow. Two lances in its hands, a shield slung over its shoulder. It reeked of sweat and death.

Semni sobbed more than screamed. "Get away! Get away!"

The demon crouched beside her, placing a hand upon her arm. She thought her skin would burn, but its touch did not harm her.

"Semni, stop crying. It's me, Arruns."

Gulping, she stared at the dried blood upon the Phoenician's face, his reddened tunic, gore spattering his chest. Finding the vision was human made her no less terrified. She shied away.

"You should not be here," he said. "You should go home."

She shook her head, hiccuping. "I can't. The baby is coming."

In the moonlight, she could see his confusion; how he was confident with taking life but not so certain of delivering it. He stood and scouted around him. "I'll find a woman to help you."

Pain squeezed through her womb again. She clutched his leg, no longer fearing him. "Please don't leave me!"

Again Arruns hesitated. She raised her arms to him. "Help me," she gasped. "I need you to hold me up."

He grimaced at her moans, stabbing his spears into the ground and propping his shield against them. Then, behind the lee of this meager shelter, he pulled her to stand, placing her arms around his neck. When another spasm wracked her, she groaned and sagged against him, not caring that he stank. The pain momentarily eased as he bore her weight.

After a time she rested her forehead against him, the coarse cloth of his tunic scratchy against her brow. Another surge came, the intervals between the pains growing shorter, her breathing labored. "I'm scared," she whispered, her throat hoarse from crying, laying her cheek upon his shoulder.

"So am I," he said, resting his hands on her hips in a strange and tentative embrace.

Her labor was short, her son born at moonset just before the dawn.

As she squatted the babe slid from her, slippery with blood and birth fluid. Yet there was no first wail, only a choking sound.

She shrieked when she saw him, realizing she had convinced the gods to curse him. For the child was a demon, his face and body dark green. Semni rocked, filled with anguish. "No, no, no."

Arruns held the infant, smuts of ash floating around them. Taking care, he hooked one blunt finger to scoop green muck, sticky as tar, from the tiny mouth and nostrils. Gasping in air, the babe let out a frail cry that grew louder as though furious he'd been forced from his warm underwater world.

And then a sound that Semni had never heard before. Arruns was laughing as he wiped the child's body clean with his dirty cloak, revealing plump flesh, pink and healthy.

Semni stared at the man and baby covered in black smudges and blood and reached out to them. She was surprised at how powerful her happiness was, relieved that after her labor and fright her son was whole.

"Give him to me." She tugged at Arruns's tunic.

The Phoenician cradled the boy as though reluctant to surrender him.

"Please."

The infant flung his arms out in fright as the guard lowered him into Semni's hold. At first she thought she would drop him as his slippery limbs squirmed against her, but then she grew confident as she cuddled him. Opening her tunic, she pressed him to her. His nose and lips nuzzled her breast, searching for her nipple. She smiled at Arruns, proud now. "Thank you."

To her surprise he crouched beside her and stroked her sodden hair. "You were brave. Braver than I expected."

She nodded, pleased with the praise, wanting him to put his arm around her and build upon the bond they'd shared during the birthing. The three of them together. "You would make a fine father, Arruns," she said softly.

He grew serious again, his hooded eyes veiled, saying nothing, the serpent tattoo not the only thing masking his expression. Then, pulling his dagger from its wooden scabbard, he grasped the blue sinuous cord and severed it from the birth sac with one sure stroke, freeing Semni's son into war.

SIXTEEN

Rome, Autumn, 398 BC

Pinna bent to scratch the tiny bites upon her legs where the fleas had feasted. Her head was itchy too, the henna irritating her scalp. Her hair was no longer coated with ash; instead heavy red dye saturated the light-brown hair that hung to her waist. Instead of grave soil staining a heart-shaped face, albumen whitened her skin, carmine her lips. Her pallid face made her long-lashed eyes, rimmed with kohl, seem like dark holes within paleness, her fine arched eyebrows exaggerating her features as though she wore a mime actor's mask.

In the dimness of the brothel's corridor she sat on a stool outside her cell, naked, the nipples of her round full breasts painted. Merchandise on display. The leno liked his girls to smile, although such effort was not enough to hide wretchedness or boredom. He liked them to be sober, too, unless the clients required otherwise. Drunken whores were hard to rouse when their shifts started at the ninth hour of the day.

Inside the lupanaria Pinna easily forgot that the afternoon sun shone outside, except for the shaft of light slicing through the dark entry hall. It was always dismal here. The air was stifling, the dirty oil of the lamps causing acrid smoke to pool under the low ceiling, the vents choked, all surfaces covered with soot. At least the autumn chill did not trouble her. The braziers were always stoked, the heat preventing goose-pimpled flesh for both harlots and customers.

When she had first started there she would dread this time of day. She never knew who might stop at the large wooden phallus in front of the lupanaria to buy her services. Nor what vice they would prefer as they glanced at the price marked on the plaque above her doorway with "Lollia" inscribed upon it. Now she was resigned to whatever happened, and that until the goddess of the dawn appeared, there would be no respite.

Throughout the spring and summer, she had tried to sleep for only a few hours after finishing her shift. Ignoring exhaustion, she would take advantage of the shortened night watches to snatch some waking hours among day dwellers in the marketplace. As seasons cooled and working nights grew longer she was always weary, finding it hard to rise from her bed, downhearted upon waking. Denied the chance to drink wine or numbing elixirs, slumber became her only comfort. At least she was no longer skeletal. Her melancholy did not stop her eating. She remembered enough of hunger not to waste a meal. And her loosening teeth still had bite enough to devour what she was given. She had flesh enough also to add curves to hips and breasts that emphasized a waist that remained tiny. The other she wolves shunned her, scorning her for having been unregistered, although the leno forbade them to gossip about her. She noticed that clients preferred her, stoking further resentment in her sisters. Such favoritism gave her no pleasure. Her cheeks were hollow under high cheekbones, as were her eyes, her life reduced to a narrow bed in a little cell, grieving for Fusca.

— • —

When she and her mother moved to new lodgings, Pinna learned that her hopes of attracting men there would prove more difficult than expected. On that day in the Forum when she'd so admired Camillus, she had no idea that all-year campaigning would lead to a different kind of contest. There was fierce competition among whores for customers: artisans and merchants, tradesmen or landless farmers. Those men who sheltered behind the ramparts of the city wall and weren't qualified to defend it. Even the serving girls in the bakeries provided extra service in the back rooms to challenge Pinna's prices.

At first the lack of business did not worry her. It gave her more time to care for Fusca. Besides, she believed that Drusus's bronze would tide them over for a long, long time. She soon discovered, though, how costly renting accommodations could be. The medicine she bought for her mother proved both expensive and useless.

Yet for the last few weeks of her mother's life, Pinna wanted her mother to know there was food to fill her belly, clothes to warm her, and sturdy walls surrounding her. It disappointed her, though, that Fusca never knew her daughter's pride at being able to pay for her corpse to be burned upon a pyre rather than left to rot outside the wall of the Esquiline Hill.

Before the funeral Pinna washed the pathetic, blighted body, anointing her mother's hair and wrapping her in a clean mantle, before calling out Fusca's name three times and keening without sound. She could not bring herself to put on sackcloth. Not after she had finally felt clean wool against her skin. She did not sprinkle ashes upon her hair, could not bring herself to tread once again in the footsteps of a hired mourner.

On returning from the funeral, Pinna found her rooms ransacked and what remained of the bronze stolen. In that moment, staring at the broken firepot, smashed bowls, and strewn clothing, she fully comprehended just how alone she was.

The next day the leno came to her doorway. In one of his hands, blotched with liver spots, he jiggled the weights, declaring his role in the thievery with silent arrogance.

The bawd claimed to be generous. Rumor was that Pinna was no better than a night moth. He would pay her registration when it was next due. She need not fear being whipped or fined by order of the cross-eyed city magistrate, a black mark placed against her name. The leno would pay for her food and clothing. He would offer her shelter in his whorehouse. But such things were expensive. He too had rent to pay. And so in return she would give him her earnings.

Pinna thought of what it would be like to return to being a tomb whore. Remembered, too, how she had once been a warrior's child. Realized that she would now share the same fate as her father—a life of bondage. Thought how foolish she'd been to ever wish to be a brothel whore.

— • —

"Where is my Lollia?"

At the sound of Genucius's voice, Pinna managed a smile, relieved that he would be her first client. He was her favorite, if she could be bothered to claim such preference. His needs were unusual but harmless.

Calling to the slave boy to fetch a pitcher of warm water, Pinna turned over the wooden plaque to indicate she would be occupied and ushered the customer into her cell.

She drew the curtain closed. In the constricted confines between bed and wall the light from the phallus-shaped lamp barely illuminated the space between them. She ignored the thick pelt of black hair that covered Genucius's body as he peeled off his tunic.

"Ah, what a day it has been." He lowered his bulk onto the packed earthen platform of her bed, the thin mattress no relief from hardness.

Their routine began. Pouring the water into an ewer, she washed her feet, splashing her calves and thighs, taking her time. Genucius watched her with his one good eye. Unlike other men he did not brag how he'd lost the other. Handing him a cloth she placed one foot, dripping, upon the erection poking from his bush and dwarfed by his paunch.

Genucius dried each of Pinna's feet in turn, stroking them, sliding his palm along the soles, then leaned with difficulty to lick and suck her toes. "Delicious."

A politician and soldier of Rome ministering to a whore had at first shocked her. Now it merely amused her. As did his ridiculous hankerings. She kept such knowledge private—a secret and a trust that gave her power. In truth she almost felt affection for the plebeian as she let herself enjoy the luxury of his attention. His clumsy caressing of her feet always helped her overcome the oddness of what he would expect her to do next.

When he was satisfied, he lay with his head upon the wooden tablet that served for a pillow and adjusted his eye patch. Pinna reached for a flask of sweet-smelling balsam oil, and then, sitting at the end of the bed, drew one of his legs onto her thigh. Her back to him, she massaged the raised blue veins that riddled his ankles and snaked up his limbs. How they must pain him. Hands firm, she smoothed his calves before kneading arch, ball, and heel. And as she worked, Genucius talked.

According to the plebeian, his wife inhaled words and exhaled sentences with little interval, giving him no peace. So he paid extra for Pinna to provide a different service. To listen. And this was why he was her favorite—because, if she was lucky, his complaints would extend beyond domestic worries into worldly concerns.

For Genucius was a people's tribune. His right of veto over patrician law gave him both power and headaches. The cause of his latest anxiety could be heard outside the brothel. Men were running along the street shouting abuse and demanding justice, their noise permeating the walls of the dingy, windowless chamber. The unrest had been simmering for days now, erupting into scuffles and fistfights that would be quelled and then flare again in spasms of insurrection. Both the people and soldiers were roiling about the actions of the two consular generals who had caused so many warriors to die, and so many to be shamed.

All Rome gossiped. How the feud between Sergius and Verginius had led to a Roman army being routed. When under attack Sergius was too proud to call for help from his rival; and Verginius, just as obstinate, refused to provide assistance unless requested.

"Listen to that mob," sighed Genucius. "There'll be bloodshed soon. The pigheadedness of those two fools caused all this trouble. They blame each other for the debacle. And now they stubbornly refuse to resign even though the Senate and other consular generals agree that early elections should be held."

Pinna said nothing. She was not expected to offer an opinion.

Genucius closed his eyes. His silence lasted only moments. "Even if they do resign, the unrest won't settle until they are put on trial. Everyone is baying for their blood." He put his hand to his brow. "It wearies me. People come to me all day complaining that I should do something about it! Rome faces more enemies than ever so extra troops need to be levied. There is talk of recruiting old veterans to serve as home defense. They in turn are demanding a salary. And how do you think all these soldiers are to be paid?" As always, Genucius answered his own question. "By passing a law to double the war tax! The army has threatened to mutiny!"

He shifted his other leg onto Pinna's lap. "It's no wonder I'm aching. I've been standing in the Comitium all day trying to find a way through this mess."

"It must be so hard for you, sir," she murmured, stroking his ego as well as his ankles. "It is fortunate that you are so wise."

"You have no idea what I have to put up with!"

Pinna smiled, thinking how much more talkative he was than usual.

"Everyone expects me to use my power of veto to stop the bill," he whined. "They say the nobility should be taxed more heavily than others. But it's not so straightforward. Even if that happened we still could not raise enough funds to fight our foes. With the Faliscans, there are now four of them. The cost of war has to be borne by all Romans. The other people's tribunes don't agree with me."

Pinna frowned as she continued massaging him. She was not so sure about his sympathy for the wealthy. She quashed an urge to mention her father. How the war tax was one of the causes for his downfall. How it had led her to being a whore.

"And now there is a proposal to declare Camillus dictator to resolve the problem. More arguments. More debate!"

At hearing Camillus's name, Pinna paused in her task. She'd often thought of the patrician, and was a little disconcerted at how often she did so. She imagined what it would be like if he walked through her doorway one day. Would lying with him be any different? "Sir, what is a dictator?"

Genucius opened his eye at her query. Pinna could see he was deciding whether to pander to her curiosity. She bent and gently kissed his leg, brushing her breast against it. He moaned softly and gestured her to continue her ministrations.

"In times of crisis," he said, relenting, "the Senate can authorize one of the consular generals to appoint a leader to resolve an emergency."

"That is a lot of power for one man."

"That's why his rule is limited to six months so he entertains no ideas of becoming a king."

Pinna smoothed more oil over Genucius's scaly skin. "And why Furius Camillus?"

"He's a war hero. A brilliant strategist. Some think that, if he was given the chance, he might even succeed against Veii."

"And what feat did he perform to become a hero?"

Genucius chuckled. "When just a young officer he continued riding into battle with a Volscian spear lodged in his thigh. There is a touch of madness in such an action as well as courage."

"Then declaring him dictator might be the right thing to do?"

Genucius sat up, swinging his legs to the floor. "It's not like you to ask so many questions. It does not suit you."

"No, sir." Pinna was sorry that, in trying to converse, she had caused their time to end.

"Hear that? It's started to rain." He reached for his tunic. "I'll have to get that pimp to call for my carriage."

Pinna listened to the drumming upon the roof. The angry shouting outside had stopped, doused by weather and darkness. The protesters were no doubt going home or seeking shelter at inns to nurse their rancor over goblets of wine.

The politician patted her head as he stood. "Don't worry yourself about politics, Lollia. Leave that to us men."

SEVENTEEN

Genucius made his way to the vestibule, pausing to use the urinal at the entrance after paying. The smell of piss filled the air despite regular sluicing by the slave boy.

Pinna took up her place outside her cell, noticing that one of her sisters was also available. Two men entered, hair sodden, wearing heavy army capes, water streaming off the leather folds. Even without their armor Pinna knew they were officers. There was an arrogance about them, a sureness in their gait.

With the city teeming with disgraced soldiers, Pinna was getting used to a different clientele. Soft city bodies had been exchanged for hard ones; unmarred flesh for scarred. Some were rough, venting their frustration on whores instead of wives. The needs of most were simple, and usually brief. Seeing their calloused hands made her remember her father's. At least the early return from battle would mean these men could once again heft a plow. It reminded her that years ago her palms had also been coarse from farmwork, her body aching from wielding scythe and hoe. And yet even though such memories were tinged with the scent of fresh eggs and honest sunshine, she knew she did not wish for that life either, that she was making desirable what had been grueling. Yet the soft skin and clean fingers of a city prostitute brought her no happiness either.

Genucius glanced up from his task at the new arrivals. "Is that you, young Marcus Aemilius?"

Hearing the name, Pinna peered down the passageway. Heart pounding, she shrank back, realizing that the other soldier was Drusus. Even with the rain darkening his hair, she could see its russet color. He was even leaner and taller than she remembered.

She had never expected to see him again. The odds were long that they might meet again in this city of thousands. It was unusual for patricians to seek out a brothel. They had servants to meet their needs. Yet the stigma of being branded one of Sergius's cowards must have led these men to find a whorehouse that met their mood. Pulse racing, she was tempted to step back into her cubicle, but the leno had already seen her. He would only call her out if she disappeared.

Marcus nodded to Genucius. His manner was abrupt as though reluctant to rub shoulders with a commoner, even one as wealthy as this people's tribune.

Genucius did not seem to notice. "You are a rare man, Marcus Aemilius, to gain fame despite being one of a retreating army."

Marcus glanced at his friend before responding. "I did what any man would have done given the chance." Again he glanced at Drusus. "Others were not in such a position that day."

The politician stepped away from the urinal. "Come, don't be so modest. You made a stand although surrounded by the enemy." He clamped his hand on the younger man's shoulder while turning his back to Drusus. "You saved the lives of your men while others were fleeing. Yours was an honorable retreat."

The rebuff was brutal. In the eyes of Rome Drusus was a coward, even though he was led into and out of battle by a fool. His face colored.

"The gods blessed me that day, that's all." Marcus seemed embarrassed, even a little irritated, at such praise. Pinna felt respect for him. A warrior who had gained distinction and yet did not bask in glory.

"I imagine they were impressed by your valor."

Drusus pushed past Genucius, his own form of slight. "Come on, Marcus. Are you going to stand here talking or are you going to pick a whore?"

Pinna murmured a prayer that Marcus would choose her and leave Drusus to take her sister. The harlot was one of the oldest, at least thirty, well past her prime. The leno would have got rid of her but for the need to cater to the influx of soldiers. Pinna felt sorry for her. The woman's hair was falling out and there were lesions on her body. The leno allowed her to wear clothes to hide them. The memory of Fusca lingered. Pinna worried she had not escaped disease either. Her womb hurt when she lay with a man. It was the whore's curse—or blessing. She knew she was barren.

Marcus ruined Pinna's hopes. "I've changed my mind." The distaste on his face as he examined both of the she wolves was obvious. "Look at them. I don't want the pox."

Drusus frowned, grabbing the other's cloak. "You always make excuses. When did you last have a woman? It's been almost a year since we took that camp slut. You need to get your cock wet."

Marcus shrugged. "I'd rather wake up tomorrow with a sore head from wine than being bitten by fleas and infected by sickness."

"Try Lollia then," said Genucius, "she's clean." Then seeing his carriage had arrived, he slapped Marcus on the back. "Give my regards to your father."

When the older man had gone, Drusus further encouraged his friend to remain, but Marcus refused, making his escape despite the downpour outside. "I'll wait for you in the tavern."

Drusus signaled the leno that he wanted Pinna. Her stomach lurched, knowing that with each step the soldier took toward her he edged closer to discovering who she was. She moistened her finger with saliva and passed it behind her ear to avert evil, whispering a prayer to Mater Matuta, ever hopeful that the goddess of dawn would protect her. Hunched over, she entered the room before Drusus could draw near enough to see her. The lamp was guttering, the light on the point of being extinguished. For a moment she thought there was a chance that he would be content to continue in near darkness. The servant boy knew his duties, though, bustling in to refill the lantern and bringing more water.

The refreshed lamp did not add much brightness to the room, but as it flared it was enough for her face to be seen. She froze, expecting Drusus to show surprise, an intake of breath, but he said nothing. She relaxed, straightening her shoulders as she realized she bore little resemblance to the dirt-stained night moth he'd briefly met on that winter's night a little more than nine months ago.

The reprieve was brief. Her newest little Lacerta darted from its hiding place behind the flask of scented oil where it had been tied. Seeing the lizard, Drusus seized Pinna, raising the lamp so he might see her clearly. "You!"

His hand gripped her upper arm. She tried to ease herself from his grasp, perspiring, skin prickling. "Please, my lord, you're hurting me."

"I did not recognize you without the ash and grime. And yet you still ply a grubby trade. What happened to the bronze I gave you?"

"Stolen."

"Squandered, more likely." His long bony fingers pressed into her flesh. "Don't think you will get any more."

"Of course not, my lord." She'd not thought of finding him to milk him further. "Please let go."

He released her only to take her face between thumb and fore-finger, squeezing her cheeks. "Who'd have thought there could be comeliness beneath such filth?"

Knowing her past, Pinna hoped he would not want to take her. She was disappointed. He pulled the army cape over his head, letting it fall to the floor, and as he stripped she saw that he was hard.

She wiped herself with vinegar and oil, hoping it would be enough to moisten her dryness as much as protect her. Then she lay passive, outwardly calm, inwardly churning. Standing at the end of the bed Drusus dragged her by her thighs toward him. As he thrust inside her, he leaned forward, one arm straight, his hand flat upon the bed to balance him, and then deliberately covered her face with his other hand.

Struggling, she kicked out, thrashing her head from side to side. Her cries were muffled. Still covering her face, he slapped her hard upon one thigh to force her silence.

She heard the leno at the doorway but the bawd did not enter. Instead he inquired politely if all was well. He did not like his girls being beaten unless he administered the punishment himself. Yet he could not prevent the unexpected blow being struck before an alarm was raised.

"Tell him to go away." Drusus lifted his hand enough for Pinna to utter assurance to the brothel keeper to leave.

Chest heaving, Pinna tried to calm her breath, believing he would smother her if she resisted. When she was still, Drusus lessened the pressure so that she could breathe a little easier. "That's better." His voice was composed but she could sense his eagerness.

She flinched as pain shot through her womb. Quiet and unmoving, she prayed that his excitement would make him finish swiftly. Instead, he took his time.

His palm smelled of rain and grime as it pressed against her nose and mouth. He had been drinking, wine thick upon his breath as he leaned over her. And yet he did not seem drunk. Seemed to know exactly what he was doing. What he wanted. She could feel the touch of every finger pressed against her forehead and cheeks. It was a large hand. Broad and bony. Warm and clammy. She closed her eyes and counted to five, her knowledge of numbers ending at that figure. She counted again and again until panic rose that there would be no end.

He labored, his breathing strained, sweat, not rain, dripping from his hair and beard.

Thoughts edged into her terror. Was it the image of Aemilia Caeciliana he sought to obliterate? Or was it a punishment for the traitoress deserting him? Did he do this to all women that he took? This spite, this cruelty. Or was it reserved only for whores?

He shuddered, groaning. She gasped and coughed as he removed his hand. He continued to lean over her, his face looming above hers in the gloom. "Don't forget our bargain. Do you understand?"

Pinna nodded. He released her. Numbed, she lay watching him as he dressed. Her thigh hurt from where he slapped her. She was exhausted, empty. It was then she felt eyes upon her. Turning to the doorway she saw Marcus staring at his friend. How long had he been there? How much had he seen? It was not like the bawd to let another man into the chamber before a customer had finished. And she had never known soldiers to want to share a woman at the same time, not when it meant one must wait his turn. Warriors did not like to defer to the other when it came to claiming a woman.

Drusus noticed him also. "Ah, good," he said, smiling, "you've changed your mind."

Frowning, Marcus's gaze swiveled to Pinna. "Did you have to treat her like that?"

His friend glanced at her, his look showing a confidence that he no longer needed to fear her. He shrugged then collected his cloak from the floor. "What are you worried about? I was just taming a she wolf."

Marcus stepped inside. The room was so narrow Drusus had to edge past him to reach the corridor. He punched him lightly on the arm. "I'll meet you outside when you've finished."

After Drusus had left, his friend seemed unsure what to do. "Are you harmed?"

Pinna's cheeks were burning. Drusus had not left marks on her skin but she was wounded inside. What use was there in telling this man how she thought she would die? How she'd been made to feel like nothing. What use was there in complaining? No whore had the right to sue for rape.

When she didn't reply, he leaned closer. "Perhaps I should go."

She shook her head, resigned to continuing her work. Even if he left, others would take his place. There was no time to cry. She would have to wait for daybreak for that.

She studied him for a moment. A scar puckered the corner of one eye, the other blackened. A patch of blood was seeping through a bandage on his neck. The skin on his cheeks was faintly pockmarked above the line of beard. His bottom lip split. And yet there was pleasantness to his features, the cowlick in his hair appealing. And he had soft dark eyes that made a woman take notice. His kindness was unexpected.

She pointed to his cape. "Aren't you going to get undressed?"

He looked over to the door as though checking Drusus wasn't listening. "I'm sure he didn't mean to hurt you."

She flushed with anger. "Is that right? So just because I'm a whore you think he can abuse me?"

Marcus shifted away. Surprise upon his face. A sense of his discomfort filled the tiny room. It was clear he'd not expected her to lash back. She would not forgive Drusus. Nor forget what he had done.

"Don't use that tone with me." His tone hardened, sympathy ended. "I owe you no explanations."

She edged off the bed to stand beside the small table, impatient to be finished. "Do you want to do this or not?"

At the sharpness in her voice, his mood changed again. He was impatient now, but when he pulled his cape over his head his movements were stiff. After he'd unfastened his belt buckle, he was slow to remove his tunic as well. While his arms and legs were darkened from the sun, his torso was pale. There were shadows upon him, too, not caused by the play of lamplight.

The injury to his body made her wince. She remembered Genucius praising him for standing fast while others followed Sergius's orders to retreat. Bruising spread across his chest and forearms where his armor had not fully protected him from enemy blows, a gruesome rainbow of colors. Black and purple, green and yellow, the contusions melding into the dimness of the room.

"Come on," he said, confusing her with his haste after all the hesitancy and conversation. She was not about to be hurried, though. His early appearance at her door had prevented her usual routine. She poured some vinegar and oil into the ewer, but when she picked up the small cloth he grabbed her arm. "What are you doing?"

Pinna frowned, noticing how his cock was stiffening as he stared at the trickle of Drusus's semen running down her thigh. "Washing him off me."

"No." He strengthened his grip. She yanked herself away but not before spotting a row of neat cuts scoring the inside of his wrist. His rough treatment, though, quelled any sympathy she once felt for his injuries.

Marcus gestured to the bed. "Turn around and bend over. I can't wait much longer." Then he blew out the lamp so they were plunged into darkness.

There was no sound other than that of their rutting. No groans of pleasure or satisfaction. Just a quiet concentration, his fingers gripping her hips. Luckily he was the briefest that she'd had in a long time. It was a blessing after the effort of his friend. She barely felt his breath upon her back until he expelled it noisily, spending himself in what seemed an explosion of relief.

Then she heard him scrabbling for his clothes in the dark. Again, no words spoken as he left the cell.

Pinna lay on her back upon her bed. She stared at nothing in the blackness, trying to empty her mind of what had happened, thinking she couldn't bear to let another man touch her, and despairing that she had no other choice.

— • —

After the slave boy lit the lamp again and she had finally washed herself free of their seed, Pinna noticed a glint of metal on the floor.

It was the Aemilian's belt buckle. Iron. Heavy. A horse embossed upon it. She turned it over and over, instinctively turning her back to the door to shield her actions. She felt no urge to run after Marcus to return it. No obligation to give it to the leno.

Hearing the pimp calling, she looked around for a place to hide it. She was naked, her tunic and toga hanging on a hook upon the wall. The room was sparsely furnished. Only the little table for flasks, ewer, and pitcher. She hastily wrapped the buckle in the washcloth. Then, sliding it into the toe of one of her sandals, she tied Lacerta to the laces, knowing the slave boy did not like to touch the lizard. It scampered to and fro, waiting for Pinna to let it climb across the bedding to feast on fleas while its mistress slept. It would be hours before that would happen.

The leno poked his head through the doorway, his oiled hair combed over his bald patch. "Why are you dawdling, Lollia? Come back to work. There are men waiting. It seems a brothel is a good place to shelter from bad weather." He laughed at his own wit. He was not above giving her some praise, though. "What a night so far. We don't often see two officers and a people's tribune. You were popular with them, too. Other girls were available for young Marcus Aemilius to choose. He was most insistent that he wanted only you. Impatient, too. Demanding to visit you before his friend had even finished."

Aware that the leno would drag her out if she disobeyed, Pinna steeled herself to once again take her place upon her stool. She glanced at the sandals and the treasure hidden under Lacerta's guard. As far as she was concerned, the belt buckle was compensation for what she'd suffered. Drawing aside the curtain to the cubicle, she spat on the floor, cursing the two patricians who'd made her feel more soiled than any scum who'd claimed her beside a tomb.

EIGHTEEN

The odor rising from the Tiber was overpowering. The river had flooded, swilling out sewage and rubbish from the Great Drain, leaving tracts of stinking mud on the plain of the Campus Martius as the tide receded. To Pinna, the stink of the ooze was Rome. It had been one of the distinctive smells that assaulted her when she had first arrived in the great city, gripping her mother's hand, feet dragging from exhaustion.

The tombs in the Field of Mars were once her workplace, but beyond them there was open space nestled within the bulge in the river: a grassy stretch with copses of trees losing the vividness of the turning season, drifts of brown and blackened leaves rotting beneath them. Cows and sheep could graze there until room was needed for holding elections and mustering armies. Ignoring the stench, and glad to have found somewhere quiet to think, Pinna stood gazing at the brown churning water, pretending she was once again in the country.

Palm sweaty, she clenched Marcus's large iron belt buckle, too afraid to slip it into the sinus of her toga lest it fall out or prying fingers steal it. Weeks had passed since he had fled the brothel. Weeks had passed since his friend had raped her.

She'd slept little in that time. When she did, nightmares assailed her. Smothering again under Drusus's hand, his mouth whispering to her through his fingers, commanding stillness, demanding silence. And when she was awake she felt dirtied.

When she did push aside thoughts of her assailant they were replaced with suspicions about his friend. The image of the cuts on Marcus's wrist would not leave her.

She pondered the Aemilian's need to joylessly follow where Drusus had been, not even letting her wipe off her rapist's residue. How she'd overheard that the last woman with whom he'd lain had also been shared with his friend. And the leno had said Marcus refused the chance to take one of her sisters, preferring to wait for her. She could not forget his expression when she'd caught him watching—as if he saw no one else but Drusus. His concern for her had only emerged after the degradation had ended. And then there were the strange nicks carved into his flesh, resembling self-inflicted marks rather than battle wounds. Had he cut himself? Why? As punishment for being unable to take a woman unless he'd watched his friend have her first? Or was it worse? Did he hurt himself because he desired Drusus?

Her conclusions had led her to overcome despondency. For Mater Matuta had given her a second chance at coercion. Today she had summoned courage. Today she would pay a call on Marcus Aemilius Mamercus Junior.

The bawd was surprised when she'd asked permission to visit the Forum. She'd not ventured outside for many months. He had no reason to suspect she had no intention of returning. No inkling that, if she did not succeed with her scheme, she planned to let the current of the Tiber drag her into the passageway to the dead.

She'd left wearing her toga and sandals as required by her profession. The leno made no comment at her lack of cosmetics or the fact that the henna in her hair had faded. There was no expectation of her flaunting herself in the day, not when business was so brisk at night. Her face was still white, though, wan from tiredness instead of paste.

At the lupanaria's doorway she froze, breath shortening, pulse quick at the base of her throat at taking a first step from her dim cocoon into a world busy with daylight.

The Comitium was empty as she walked through it to reach the Campus. The early election for the six consular generals had finally been held. The results were astounding. Five plebeians had been elected. The threat of riot had been removed. There was carousing in the streets instead of violence. Her customers were drunk with triumph instead of discontent. The wound of a shameful retreat had been cured now that the soldiers were present in the city and once again able to vote.

Genucius's name had been scratched into the wax of many of the ballots. She was surprised at how pleased she felt at his being chosen. So far she'd only known him in his role of politician. Yet competing with the veins on his legs were scars, proof of past fighting under patrician leaders. No doubt the one-eyed soldier would wear the red cloak with pride.

Only one aristocrat had been chosen. Camillus had at last been returned to office. And it also made her strangely satisfied to think this man would again lead an army.

Hiding behind some trees Pinna checked that no one was observing her. She quickly coiled her hair into a demure knot and unwound her toga. Using a knife she had pilfered from the brothel's kitchen, she cut a length from the abundant material to serve as a shawl, then stashed the bundle of remaining cloth behind a tree. She would never wear the symbol of a harlot again. She drew the cloak over her head. The sensation of the cloth against her hair seemed odd after so many years of being uncovered.

She could do nothing about her sandals. Their leather was sodden from walking through the slush of the Campus. She could not exchange them for shoes because she had none. As a whore's life was led indoors, there was no need for her to wear them. She wished she had a mirror to check her appearance to see if she'd managed to feign decorum. One thing was certain: she did not need to check her reflection to know her face was hard and eyes bitter.

Returning inside the city, she paused at the cattle market to say a prayer outside the shell of the Temple of Mater Matuta. The Romans had become neglectful of the dawn goddess. The building's stucco facade was crumbling and weeds poked through gaps in the flooring. Even though the sacred precinct was deserted, she did not venture onto the portico with its cracked columns; the prohibition against a prostitute entering a place of worship was now engrained in her.

Untying the string around her neck she released Lacerta, bidding the lizard a farewell. Her companion did not hesitate to scurry between a crack in the steps, loyalty forgotten with freedom.

Pinna wiped her sandals clean as best she could, then, picking up her skirts to avoid the manure littering the road, she began to climb the Palatine Hill to the richest quarter of Rome.

— • —

The majordomo of the House of Aemilius was just as she expected, sniffing at the sight of a poor woman knocking at a nobleman's door.

At her request to speak to the young master of the house, he barred her entrance. "Get away with you!"

She scrambled for an excuse to be granted entry. "I have a message for him from Appius Claudius Drusus."

His eyes narrowed, disbelieving that an aristocrat would entrust an errand to one such as she. "Then tell it to me," he demanded. "I will make sure the master hears it."

"No," she said, growing in boldness. "I was bidden to tell no one other than Marcus Aemilius Mamercus Junior."

His doubtful expression remained, but nevertheless he led her through the vestibule. Wary that she might offend the household spirits she was careful to cross the threshold with her right foot.

"Wait here," he barked. "Don't touch anything."

Pinna surveyed the atrium around her. It was the largest room she'd ever seen, in the grandest house in which she'd ever set foot. She swallowed hard, overcome with apprehension that she may have embarked on too great a mission, feeling like a pig among princes.

A shaft of sunshine from the roof opening speared the otherwise muted light within the chamber. Wood smoke wafted through the ceiling hole from an enormous hearth fire, and a reservoir with a terra-cotta head beneath it boasted a private water supply. A fine loom stood to one side, indicating that Marcus had a mother or sisters who observed womanly duties. The painted timber walls were clean except for the soot that stained the rafters around the vent. Bunches of rosemary and chamomile hung drying, their scent perfuming the air. Pinna glanced at her feet, hoping she'd not brought too much of the stink of the river with her.

Near the hearth stood a tall cabinet, its doors closed. Her father had once spoken of such cupboards, how they housed the death masks of great and powerful family members within them. How many waxen faces of Aemilian ancestors were hidden in that space? No such storage had been needed in a farmer's hut.

Beyond a metal chest safe with a sturdy lock lay another room, its drapes drawn back to reveal shelves crammed with scrolls. A servant boy was busy mopping a large puddle on the floor, buckets around him full of water. It would seem being rich had not prevented the roof leaking during the downpour earlier that morning.

Marcus's disdain was equal to his manservant's at finding Pinna gawking at the splendor around her. His eye and lip had healed but he walked stiffly, the hidden bruising to his body still paining him. She noticed he was wearing wristbands today, lessening the chance of others spying the evidence of self-mutilation. There was curiosity in his expression. Clearly he did not recognize her. Why would he? The last time he'd seen her she'd been naked and painted.

"I'm told you want to speak to me."

She drew her shawl from her head. "Yes, my lord."

Hearing her response, Pinna saw him trying to recall her voice even if her face was not remembered. She stretched out her hand to reveal the horse crest buckle.

His eyes widened, then sharpened as he took in her garb. Then, noticing the servant boy was watching, he drew her by the elbow into one of the side rooms, drawing the curtain closed behind them. Startled by the intruders, cockroaches darted across the floor. It was dim and stuffy in the cell, the smell of damp seeping from the walls. There was a narrow bed also, making her feel as though they stood once again within the brothel, although the cubicle was far more spacious than hers. His shock had changed to suspicion. "What do you want from me?"

Pinna handed him the buckle. "A reward."

Relief apparent, Marcus reached for his money pouch. "Of course. You've been more honest than I thought. I'd not expected it to be returned after"—he paused—"after what happened."

She placed her hand on his. "My lord, I don't want your bronze."

"What then?"

Pinna lifted the hem of her tunic to reveal her sandals. "The chance to wear shoes."

He frowned.

"The chance to cover my head in modesty."

At these words, his confusion ended. "How dare you seek to parade as a respectable woman! You insult all those who are decent with your act. Why do you think I can help you? Your name is and always will be on the prostitutes' roll."

She bristled. "I am a soldier's daughter! Once a citizen. I am what I am because of patrician greed. My father died a bondsman and my mother a whore because he could not pay debts accrued while fighting for Rome! And now the leno holds me in bondage, too."

He stared at her, disbelief upon his face. His voice softened. "Then your family has suffered."

"Yes, we have suffered! I've been a harlot since eleven and no longer want to lie with men."

"But what do you expect me to do about that?"

"Become my patron. Take me to war with you as your concubine."

This time he laughed. "You must be simple."

"Why? There are always women who follow the army. I will wash and cook for you. I will mend your clothes and shine your armor." She pointed to the bandage on his neck. "I will tend to your injuries."

"Stop this nonsense." He opened the pouch. "Here, take this for your honesty and go away."

She took a deep breath, shaking her head. "I told you, I don't want your money."

Marcus shrugged and turned to leave. "Then you shall have nothing."

"Wait!" Her voice became a whisper. "How long have you loved him?"

The patrician swiveled around. "What did you say?"

Pinna took a deep breath. "Tell me, does your cock only harden if you are taking Drusus's leavings?"

He took a step toward her. "You little bitch, get out!"

To her relief he did not strike her. She stood her ground. "You want him. I can tell. Boys aren't enough for you, are they? Or freedmen? You want an equal as your lover." She pointed to the buckle in his hand. "You wear the loose tunic of a civilian today but when you wear your leather belt it marks you as a soldier. How would you feel if you couldn't wear it?" She gestured toward his wristbands. "I've seen how you've sliced your skin. Your own punishment for loving him."

His staring silence only fueled her. "Or perhaps you've already had courage enough to risk execution by using some other soldier who wants you."

He seized her. "Shut up before I make you!"

For a moment she thought she'd misjudged his reluctance to hit her but desperation drove her on. "How? By suffocating me, like your friend?"

He flinched. "You tell only lies."

"Not so. Your eyes and those wounds tell me I speak the truth. Besides, gossip can do much damage. I have many prestigious clients. Genucius, for example. I don't think he'd be slapping you on the back for valor if he knew you were lusting after a soldier."

Seeing his stricken expression gave her pause, then she remembered how he'd done nothing as his friend assaulted her, her violation taking second place to his lust. "My freedom for my silence," she hissed.

Marcus's fingers dug into her flesh but still she continued. "If you take me with you people will accept me as your concubine. No need to pretend you like women by going whoring with Drusus, unless, of course, you can't give up following where he's been."

He thrust her away and dragged his fingers through his hair. Then, as they glared at each other, there was a knocking at the entrance doors.

This time the majordomo was as unctuous to the caller as he had been condescending to her; she overheard the servant greeting the visitor in the vestibule. "Good morning, my lord. Master Aemilius was not expecting you but you are most welcome. He did not take audience today because he's ill, but I will let him know you are here."

"No matter. It is his son I came to see. Tell him I'm here."

Marcus peeked through the slit in the curtain then drew back quickly. He stared at Pinna, anxiety obvious. "Stay here, be quiet." He slipped through to the atrium.

Pinna moved one pace behind him so she could peer through the gap. The guest's voice was familiar although last time its level had been loud enough to hear across the expanse of the Forum. Her pulse quickened. No more than ten feet from her stood Marcus Furius Camillus.

NINETEEN

If the newly elected consular general thought it strange that Marcus appeared so abruptly from a side room he made no comment. He smiled as he clasped the younger man's forearm in greeting. "Ah, Marcus, I'm glad you're home. I hear your father is sick."

"A slight fever. And a fierce headache. I'm sure he'll be fit to see you."

The general laughed. "No doubt the election results only worsened his condition. And your good mother?"

"Visiting friends."

Marcus ushered him to the hearth. "Sir, come sit by the fire. I'm afraid the roof in the study has sprung a leak."

Pinna watched as the servant boy fetched indoor sandals for the guest then nervously helped him to remove his toga. It always interested her how a simple length of cloth could look so different on each man who wore it, their character defined by its folds, the way it was hefted upon the shoulders and draped across the body. Some men looked as though they had wrestled with it and been defeated. Camillus wore the unwieldy cloak with ease, no need for the purple-bordered hem to be weighted for elegance. The assured posture she'd admired from a distance was even more marked now that she was near him. The certainty of his movements, the confidence of his bearing, made the room seem small. His limp was barely noticeable but, knowing how he had gained the injury, she wondered what the scar upon his thigh would look like. And what others might be hidden beneath his handsome robes.

Marcus drew up a chair. "Congratulations, sir, on your being elected."

Camillus smiled and relaxed into the backless chair. "Perhaps that has also caused your father's head to ache." As he accepted a goblet of wine Pinna saw that his hands were broad, the fingers long and strong. They were calloused but she imagined their touch might be gentle. He wore a ring. Unlike most it was not of iron but of gold. A hint of wealth as well as vanity.

Marcus hesitated at the jest. "I'm sure he welcomes your appointment as much as I do," he finally said.

"Oh, I doubt that," said Camillus. "Poor Aemilius. He must be reeling. Five plebeian generals. Unprecedented. It must be quite a shock to a descendant of Romulus." Cup filled, he turned his attention to Marcus. "But that is not what I want to discuss. It's you that I really came to see."

It was a day of surprises. Pinna saw the younger man straighten his shoulders, his smile that of a pupil gaining unexpected praise from his teacher. Any revelation as to Camillus's purpose was interrupted, though, by the arrival of Aemilius. The senator's fat gray eyebrows and hair were awry and his cloak slipping from his shoulders. An annoyed look crossed Marcus's face at the conversation being disturbed.

The head of the house hailed his visitor with a voice that was hoarse and nasal. "Furius Camillus. I was not expecting you."

"Ah, Aemilius," said the general, standing to greet him. "You should not have got up from your sickbed."

"Nonsense." Aemilius sank into the armchair reserved for him, gesturing both guest and son to resume their seats. "I'm interested to hear what you have to say about this crisis."

"Crisis? I thought the danger of insurrection has been averted."

"By electing five commoners to govern us? To lead us into battle? To defend our city? What do they know of command? We need experienced men to lead us."

Camillus laughed. "Like Sergius and Verginius?"

Marcus glanced away to hide a smile.

Aemilius glared at his caller. "That plebeian dolt, Calvus, was just as incompetent as those two. Anxur is no longer in our hands, remember? The city you fought so hard to reclaim last year. He let it be retaken by allowing Volscians posing as traders into the stockades. And the Aequians are still causing trouble. And let's not mention the Faliscans." He paused to sneeze, and then continued. "Don't you think disaster will come from this election? There is a reason why patricians have always governed. We are the descendants of the founding fathers. Divine blood flows in us. Only we can hold the purification ceremonies to call an assembly. Next the people will claim we should be restricted to merely doing this just so plebeians can hold office."

The guest took his time to respond, sipping his wine, then placing the cup on the repository table. Pinna found it hard to take her eyes from him. She liked the way his beard was clipped. How it defined the strength of his jaw. Liked too how his hair was combed back from a deep brow, his nose that of a Roman, straight and aquiline. Masculinity emanated from him, no effeteness hinted in his grooming. His face was unscathed, a rarity among warriors, his cheeks grooved and the skin around his eyes creased. Good humor seemed to have formed such lines, because they remained intact even when he was not smiling.

"I'm as pious as you, Aemilius. After all, I spent my childhood as an attendant to the high priest of Rome. But you're exaggerating.

I don't see why the gods would be angry for avoiding internal bloodshed. Besides, consular generals don't hold supreme power like consuls. While martial law prevails, the compromise of granting limited power is worth it."

Aemilius gestured to the majordomo and boy to leave. Pinna guessed she would not be the only one eavesdropping; the pompous manservant was sure to remain in earshot.

"You and your brother, Medullinus, have always been sympathetic to the popular party, proposing that soldiers be paid this wretched salary in the first place. And now these plebeian generals will gain an honorary seat in the Senate! It's the beginning of the end!"

Unperturbed, Camillus smoothed his hand across his chest. "Be realistic. The latest unrest has now been solved by electing them. Although there is still resentment that Sergius and Verginius weren't fined enough when they were tried. Those two fools should have been ordered to pay an enormous figure toward the war tax." He gripped the armrests of his chair, voice clipped and deliberate. "This class war has to end. We can only conquer our enemies if there are no enemies within." He turned to the son. "What do you think, Marcus?"

Throughout the conversation, Pinna observed how Marcus listened enthralled. At being included, he grinned and sat forward in his chair. "As the majority of tribes voted for the plebeians, others among our ranks must agree with you, sir."

Aemilius's snort of disgust caused the younger man to stiffen. Pinna smiled to herself. The senator had failed to be elected by those same tribes.

Camillus smiled at the interplay between father and son. "You are worrying unnecessarily, Aemilius. The commoners won't find it so easy to carp and complain now that they hold office. Look at Calvus. He learned that the hard way, at Anxur."

"And you think incompetence should be rewarded by greater power?"

"With responsibility they'll realize the war tax has to be levied. How else are they going to pay the troops in the field? They won't want to deal with a mutiny. And perhaps soldiers will accept an impost approved by their own leaders."

Aemilius sneezed so loudly Pinna jumped. "But five of them," he moaned, adding a cough to his misery. "Five!"

Camillus slammed his hand upon the armrest. "Enough! Most of those elected are able men. Genucius is one of them. He has fought with me many times and is a cunning tactician. And he served me in good stead last year while he was a people's tribune. It's a pity I don't have as good a friend in that position this year."

The senator grimaced. "Another tribune in your pocket? Really, Camillus, it must cost you dearly in bribes. No wonder you were the only one of us elected."

The general's smugness was a goad. Aemilius continued his quarrel. "I suppose you also promised Genucius public land and private plunder this time in return for his loyalty?"

Camillus relaxed back and took another sip of wine. "I don't see why not. If Rome conquers enemy territory it would be politic to let both veterans and friends like Genucius gain a reward for their service."

Pinna gasped. Did Camillus truly believe patrician control should be loosened over state land? If only her father had been given the chance to take his own share of the spoils instead of giving all to the treasury, debts could have been paid. Her life might have been different.

At her noise, Marcus frowned and glanced toward the side room. She stepped back from the curtain, but when the other men remained absorbed in conversation, she resumed her place. The news that Genucius was Camillus's man was also surprising. No wonder the tribune had blocked his colleagues' proposal that the patricians should pay extra tax.

Blowing into his kerchief, Aemilius paused to rub his forehead. "Now you really go too far."

Camillus sighed. "I don't propose we hand over great tracts of land. And promises cost us nothing. Now that Calvus has lost face it will be difficult for him to be re-elected. As his platform is always about land, levies, and loot, let's deny him venom for his sting."

Pinna frowned to hear the general was not as liberal as she thought. What were his motives? Where did his sympathies truly lie?

Marcus turned in his chair to smile at Camillus. "We are fortunate that you are to lead an army, sir."

The head of the house bristled, his expression resembling that of Drusus when he'd heard Marcus praised by Genucius. Regaining composure, Aemilius leaned forward, one hand resting on his knee. "Oh, but it's not quite as grand as being a dictator, is it?"

Pinna focused on the senator. Although his appearance was disheveled, his mind was sharp. Such a man could not be dismissed merely because of a head cold. He had twice commanded an army of Rome. He had not succeeded in taking Veii, though. Perhaps he did not want anyone else to either.

This time it was Camillus who was irritated. "Perhaps a dictator is what we need. After all, your own uncle, Mamercus Aemilius, was able to defeat the Veientanes when he was given ultimate command."

For the first time, Pinna heard the older man laugh. "And you think you could do the same? Or better? Do you think you can take Veii when all others have failed?"

The general tapped his gold ring before he spoke. Pinna wondered if he did so to ward off the evil eye or merely the scorn of his host. "Don't worry, Aemilius, I won't get that chance. I'm to take my army to Falerii to rout our new foe. Genucius has drawn the lot to lead at Veii."

Aemilius's gloating annoyed Pinna. Now she understood why Camillus was frustrated. How childish it was for politicians to bicker among themselves.

The guest rose as though to leave but, instead of calling for his toga and shoes, he moved behind Marcus. "But my intention in coming here was not really to talk about the elections." He rested his hands on the younger man's shoulders. The gesture was harmless and yet laden with provocation. "I came to seek permission for your son to be one of the decurions in my cavalry."

The senator's glow of satisfaction disappeared.

"You see, I thought," continued Camillus, "that you would prefer him to fight with one of our own, not under a plebeian commander. And as I am the only patrician . . ."

At the request Marcus swung around in surprise. Unable to hide his eagerness, he turned to his father for consent.

Aemilius scowled and blew his nose again, maintaining silence.

"Father?"

Pinna felt a touch of pity for the older man. He must have realized that, no matter his decision, he'd already lost his son to Camillus.

Aemilius scanned Marcus's face. "Is this truly what you want?"

The soldier glanced at the general and then back. "Yes, it would be an honor." Then, in appeasement, he added, "Especially as I cannot fight under your command."

After long moments, the senator grunted and rose from his chair. "Very well. Marcus may join you for this campaign. Now if you will excuse me, I'll return to bed."

Camillus bowed. "Thank you, Aemilius, for giving me your son."

The older man halted, brow furrowed. "Make no mistake. The oath of allegiance he swears to you will end when you step down from office. My son knows where his loyalties lie."

"Of course, of course," said Camillus, still standing behind Marcus. "Know also, I will fully support him when he stands for his first magistracy. That must be very soon, mustn't it? He's nearing thirty. It helps to have as many friends as possible when you begin your journey along the Honored Way."

The contempt in the father's voice was unveiled. "So we are friends now, are we?"

The consular general smiled. "Of course, my good Aemilius. When has it ever not been so?"

TWENTY

As soon as the head of the house had retired, looking wearier than when he'd first entered the room, Pinna saw that any reservations Marcus may have had about offending his father had disappeared. He was grinning. "Thank you, sir, for asking me to join your staff."

Camillus thumped the young man's back. "I'm sure you will be most valiant. I heard what happened at Veii. How you stood your ground when surrounded by the Faliscans."

"Yes, sir." The young officer's smile faded. "But I was still part of a retreating army."

Camillus pointed to the bandage on the soldier's neck. "Your wound is on the front of your body, not on your back." He placed his arm around Marcus's shoulder. "Let me give you some advice. Modesty is a Roman virtue but it does have its limitations. Remember, Mars guards us in combat but expects us to be skillful before he grants us protection. By no means crow about your achievements but acknowledge praise when you have succeeded. Your deeds will tarnish if you don't remind your rivals about them." He tightened his grip. "And make no mistake, Marcus Aemilius, you are someone who should not be forgotten. Not with your battle skills."

For a moment the younger man stared, mouth ajar, at such flattery. "Thank you, sir. I will remember."

Camillus released him and turned to warm himself before the fire. Pinna followed his every movement, the feeling of attraction strong within her.

"So do you agree with your father about the current situation?"

Marcus glanced over to the inner passageway as though concerned Aemilius may be listening. Pinna smiled, thinking there could be more people eavesdropping in this house than conversing.

"Yes, it concerns me that plebeians are in power. But I can see merit in your viewpoint."

Camillus laughed. "Such diplomacy!" He turned from the hearth, serious now. "But what I really want from my officers is conviction."

Marcus stood at attention. "Yes, sir."

Camillus lowered his voice as though talking one conspirator to another. Marcus shifted his body toward him like a flower turning its face to the sun, or the tide turning with the pull of the moon.

"Can you cast off your prejudices, Marcus? Think of Rome not as a city divided but united. How mighty it would be. How our enemies would quake!" He held out his forearm for the other to grasp. "Join me. Help me make this happen!"

The vision was potent. And, hearing him, Pinna knew, more than ever, that she needed Marcus to take her with him. So that she could be near enough to hear Camillus quietly stirring loyalty instead of straining to hear him above the hubbub of a crowd. She could see that Marcus, too, was struck by the force of his words. He seized his commander's proffered arm.

Camillus nodded. "Excellent." Then, bond sealed, he broke away, ready to move on to other business. "Now I must go."

Marcus called the slave boy to fetch the guest's toga and shoes. "Sir, may I ask a favor?"

"And what would that be?"

"Let Claudius Drusus serve with you. He has long admired you. And he is an able decurion."

Suddenly the stuffy cell seemed airless, the smoky odor of the curtain stifling. Focused on coercing Marcus, she hadn't thought past convincing him to help her escape the lupanaria. Dreaming of becoming an officer's concubine had given her a reason to live. But the details of such a future had been sketchy. She'd not factored in his desperate need to always be with Drusus. Could she bear to travel in the company of her attacker? Perspiring beneath the weight of her shawl, she pulled it from around her and let it drop to the floor. She prayed Camillus would not agree to Marcus's request.

"Claudius Drusus?" The general frowned. "One of the men who fled on Sergius's orders? Wasn't he the lovesick soldier who made a fool of himself over your cousin?"

Marcus stood open-palmed. "It is unfair to judge a man whose leader failed him. And he no longer feels that way about Caecilia. That was eight years ago."

"I see. Instead he is bitter that she chose Vel Mastarna instead of him."

Marcus shook his head. "No. The only vengeance he seeks now is for our city."

Pinna raised her eyebrows. His love for Drusus was indeed deep if it drove him to deceive his general. The ease with which he lied was also surprising.

The slave hurried back. Camillus sat down to allow him to fit his shoes. "I'm glad to hear it, Marcus, because excessive emotions like infatuation and bitterness only weaken you. Love also." He lifted one foot and then the other for the boy. "Of course, have affection for your wife, and by all means satisfy your lust, but a Roman man should never let a woman possess his soul."

The cold way in which Camillus spoke gave Pinna pause. The swift change of his moods was disconcerting. She thought about loving a man. Would she recognize that emotion? Was there was anything left of her soul to lose?

The Aemilian cast a quick look toward Pinna's hiding place, making her smile. Camillus was right. Love did weaken a man. Here was Marcus, a decorated warrior, pining for another who would never return his affection. The power she'd felt when she'd first threatened Drusus returned. She stifled the urge coursing through her to shout that the Claudian still loved the traitoress. That he was no true Roman. That he was feeble with feeling. As was his friend.

When Marcus made no comment, Camillus looked up, eyes narrowing. "And you. How do you feel about your cousin?"

He hesitated. "Caecilia? Why, she has disgraced our family."

The general waved the slave boy away, concentrating wholly on the soldier. "Listen to me, one needs to be calculating when it comes to vengeance. Aemilia Caeciliana not only shamed your family but all Rome. When war was declared she had her chance to resume a virtuous life in Rome but she chose to warm the bed of an enemy general. So have no doubt. When Veii falls I will see that she is punished. If you have any qualms about that, you should tell me now and not waste my time."

This time Marcus met the general's gaze squarely. "I do not question what Rome expects of me, sir."

For a moment Camillus continued to scrutinize him, then nodded. "Good."

The majordomo appeared with the toga, officiously attending to the task of winding it around the guest. Marcus hovered nearby. "Sir? Will you consider Claudius Drusus? He would be more than loyal to you. He is brave also, already gaining three silver spears."

Camillus signaled the manservant to stop fussing about him. "Hundreds of men display bravery. I need soldiers who can gain fame. Men who, in a split second, decide to put their own lives in danger to either defend or lead their men to glory. If I recall, you earned an oak leaf crown in your first campaign by saving Drusus's life. And now you have gained renown for saving your fellow knights. So convince me there is an advantage in having him as a decurion."

To Pinna's surprise Marcus showed he was as shrewd as Aemilius—and just as determined. "Because he is very wealthy, and is head of his own House now that his father and grandfather have died. The Claudians have many friends. He would be a useful ally."

The general adjusted his toga, taking his time to smooth his hand along the edge before concentrating on the officer. "Leave it with me, I'll think on it."

Fingering her fascinum necklace, Pinna leaned against one side of the doorjamb and closed her eyes. She cursed Marcus for his perseverance, and prayed the general would not be convinced. Her prayer was cut short when she felt something scuttle across her foot. A cockroach. Instinctively she kicked it away, sending it skidding across the floor.

Her action knocked the curtain, attracting the men's attention. Holding her breath, she shrank back.

"Tell me," she heard Camillus say, "does Aemilius disapprove of you bedding the servants?"

"I don't know what you mean, sir," came an anxious reply.

"When I arrived, you scurried from that side room like a schoolboy caught filching sweets from the larder. Why bother hiding her? Or is it a boy you favor?" Then she heard footsteps. The hanging was thrown open.

Pinna took a tentative step into the room, heart thumping, apprehension and excitement merging. She avoided looking at

Marcus although she caught the astounded look of the majordomo. The slave boy, too, was staring at her as though she'd been
conjured. Marcus barked at the servants to leave. The surprise that
remained on the majordomo's face gave Pinna some satisfaction.

Curtsying to the general, she managed to summon enough
voice to be heard. "Good morning, my lord." Keeping her head
bowed, she tried in vain to pull her tunic down at the sides to cover
her feet, worrying that he might think it strange her indoor sandals were wet.

"So here is our eavesdropper. No wonder you hide her, Marcus,
she is fair."

The compliment was unexpected. Pinna thought he would
demand she be punished for listening to men's business or, at least,
that she be dismissed, but it seemed he could grant his attention to a
maid as much as to a noble. Or perhaps he liked flirting? But surely
this was a man who would not need to cajole a woman into bed,
nor use brothels to satisfy his cravings. Dozens of women would
gladly lie with him without expectation of praise or payment.

Pinna was used to men ogling her as she sat stripped of clothes
and dignity, so she expected the same from the general. Yet when
she raised her head she was surprised to find Camillus was not
appraising her form but her face. She blushed. Since Fusca had
gone mad, the girl had not been noticed for a long, long time.
Camillus's scrutiny leavened her spirit, reminding her of her happiness when Lollius returned from war and, for a brief moment,
would study her before swinging her into the air saying, "Well,
well, daughter, how tall you've grown!"

In the Forum, she'd been lulled, as all were, into believing
Camillus was addressing each of them individually. Now, with his
true attention, she felt uncertain what to do. It was difficult to meet
his eyes. What did he see? A girl aged beyond her years, features
honed by hardship, wretchedness etched onto her face?

As she finally met his gaze she saw his eyes were not special in shape or color, and yet they were compelling. He smiled briefly, then turned to Marcus. At the loss of his interest, Pinna experienced a disappointment she knew she was not entitled to feel. Not wanting him to ignore her, she plucked up the nerve to speak again, conscious of the crudeness of her vowels compared to his rich speech. "Thank you, my lord, for being a friend of the people."

Her words gained his attention. "Ah, so you have listened and not just heard. What is your name?"

"I am called Pinna, my lord."

This time his gaze traveled along her body. "Feather? I suppose that is apt. There is little enough of you."

Pinna reddened and realized she had lied when she'd professed to Marcus that she wanted no more of men.

"And are you concubine to Marcus Aemilius here or merely his fancy?"

Pinna glanced at Marcus, who glared at her.

"I am his woman." A tinge of defiance in her tone.

"I see." Camillus turned to his new officer. His good humor had disappeared. "A concubine is all very well but you should be married by now. It's every man's duty to wed and produce more citizens to fight for Rome."

"There has not been . . . time, sir," stammered Marcus.

"So you prefer to pay the bachelor tax I proposed?"

Now Pinna was amused. Another tax? And this one just to punish single men.

"No, sir." He shot another annoyed glance at Pinna.

"You Aemilians are too rich if you think you can bear the fine and continue to avoid marrying. There are too many good Roman widows because of this war. You should choose one," Camillus growled. "Or are you determined to have a virgin bride?"

"No, sir." Marcus was still struggling. "It's just that I have been campaigning."

"I've heard that excuse too often. Besides, you won't be taken seriously when you stand for office if you're not a family man. You should marry. It will assist your career." He nodded toward the girl. "Remember what I said about falling in love. I hope you're not smitten with Pinna here."

Marcus's look was anguished now. She felt a sudden pity for him after all. "No, my lord," she said, drawing his attention away from the soldier. "I share the master's bed only. He does not love me."

Camillus's eyes met hers again. "Good." Then he faced Marcus. "The legions are mustering in the Campus tomorrow. Report there at daybreak to swear an oath of allegiance to Rome. Also to pledge loyalty to me as your general for this campaign. I expect much of you. Do not fail me."

Marcus saluted, back straight, eyes steady. "I won't, sir."

As he turned to go, Camillus looked toward the buckets in the leaky study. Once again he bestowed a smile upon her. "Perhaps you should be more careful not to walk through puddles, Pinna. Your sandals are wet."

She curtsied, nonplussed to realize he must see her only as a woman. There was no indelible mark upon her, no brand upon her skin to declare to him that she was a whore.

— • —

Once the visitor left, the majordomo emerged like a cockroach from under a cupboard. For the second time that day Marcus ordered him to leave, causing the manservant's face to settle into disapproval, although there was a touch of comedy in the way he continued to observe Pinna as he left the atrium.

Marcus pushed her into the side room again. "How dare you say you are my concubine!"

Her confidence buoyed from surviving the encounter with Camillus, she stood her ground. "Why not? He will take more heed of me now if I tell him your secret."

He grabbed both her forearms and shook her. "The general wants me as a leader of one of his squadrons. This could have been the best day of my life except for you! I should beat you and send you away!"

Hearing the anger in his voice, panic rose that she had pressed him too hard. She sank to her knees. "Please, my lord. Take me with you. I have nowhere else to go. I will kill myself rather than return to the lupanaria."

He released her, standing over her as he raked his fingers through his cowlick. "Why do you think life with the army would be any easier? Military camps are dirty and dangerous."

"Because I'm not afraid of hard work or of living in wind and harsh weather. I was born on a farm and learned how to labor as soon as I was taught to walk."

"There is death and disease."

She sat back on her heels. "I already face them. After every man I worry that signs of the pox will appear. And then, in time . . ." The memory of Fusca's suffering returned. Suddenly the possibility that he might refuse overwhelmed her, her intention to suicide real. She could not go back to the brothel, could not continue living in that bleak world. She covered her face with her hands and wept.

Marcus paced the room, watching her weep before standing over her again. "You do understand, don't you," he finally said, "that when an enemy overruns the camp they don't spare the women. After they finish with them, their death is brutal."

Sensing he was relenting, Pinna wiped her eyes with the back of her hand. "But we will not be defeated, my lord. Not with Furius Camillus in command."

He frowned, rubbing the scar at the corner of his eye.

"You see, like you, I want to follow him."

"Why, so you can expose me?"

"No. Because he is like a flame."

Marcus sat down on the bed, legs apart, a hand on each knee, and examined her. And in that moment she knew he had finally noticed her just as his general had before him.

"Is it really true that you were once a daughter of a soldier, a citizen of Rome?"

"Yes, my lord, I am freeborn. A warrior's child. And I want all to see me as such again."

"A concubine still bears a stain on her reputation."

"Ah, but it is faint compared to that of a whore's, my lord. I might not be able to wear the stola of a matron, or woolen fillets in my hair, but no one will disrespect me for being a de facto wife."

Again he raked his fingers through his hair. He sighed. "If I take you there must be no tears or complaining."

Relief coursed through her. "Thank you, my lord, thank you." She kissed his feet, her lips brushing the soft fine leather of his sandals. "You will hear no complaints from me—ever!"

"And you will keep your side of the bargain?"

"Always."

"Very well." He rose, clasping her hands and drawing her to stand. "I will send a messenger to your pimp that he is to release you. How much must I pay him to cover your debt?"

Pinna had not thought that far. How much was her life worth? Less than the cost of an iron buckle. Less than two weights of Claudian bronze. "I am sure he will not haggle with you, my lord. He would not dare."

He was still holding her hands. She tried to slip away but Marcus held them tight. "And if the general agrees to Drusus joining his cavalry, what then? Would you still want to be my army wife?"

Her eagerness dimmed. Slowly easing her fingers from his, she met his eyes, her voice soft. "There is no going back for me now, my lord."

Once again he studied her. She bowed her head. The words were true. She could find strength to face his friend. She had none left, though, to remain a whore.

The sliver of silence passed. Marcus drew a small bronze weight from his purse and handed it to her. "Buy yourself a clean tunic and shawl. I can't have my concubine looking bedraggled." Then he walked to the doorway. "And you can sleep in the stables tonight so my parents don't find you. Tomorrow you can join the caravan that follows Camillus's army."

"I will be there before dawn!"

He drew the curtain aside, but before he moved through to the atrium he turned and shook his head, as though disbelieving he'd been persuaded to her scheme. "Oh, and Pinna," he said, glancing at her feet, "throw out those wet sandals. You'd better buy yourself some shoes."

THE WAR SEASON

TWENTY-ONE

Veii, Spring, 397 BC

His palm was warm. Caecilia placed her hand over his. "Be patient."

The babe stirred. She guided his calloused fingers to feel it.

Mastarna laughed. "He is determined to gain our attention."

"I keep telling you, he might be a girl."

Lying behind her on their bed, his arms around her, Vel kept his hand steady, waiting for another movement.

Caecilia shifted to face him. "You would not be disappointed if I bore a daughter?"

"No, provided she doesn't have her mother's temperament."

"Or her father's temper."

He ran his fingers along her arm. "I would welcome a little girl, and would be heartbroken if I was to lose her." Then kissed her forehead. "Or you."

Caecilia caressed his battered face, the scar that ran from nose to mouth and the curve of his lips. He kissed her fingers as she did so. There had been another wife before her. Another son and a daughter. All lost to him. A burden she could never share other than to offer comfort. They had lost a child also. In the time after Tas and before Larce. One terrible winter there had been no infant for Vel to claim. She'd been left to sorrow alone until he returned. The loss was as tangible as if she'd labored and held her baby. She always wondered if it were a son or daughter she might have suckled, for it had been too soon to tell. Experiencing this grief, she finally glimpsed the torment of Vel's first wife. She prayed she would never suffer the curse of watching children die before her eyes as had Seianta.

"Here." She directed him once again to the baby moving within her. His delight filled her with happiness. She had borne three sons to him, but her husband had never had the chance to see her with her belly like a gourd nor feel the first wondrous awakenings as their babe made its presence known within the womb.

Mastarna nuzzled the birthmark upon Caecilia's throat. As a young girl the blemish had worried her but now it went unnoticed when she gazed into the hand mirror. Her father said the stain meant her life would not be smooth. Mastarna claimed it meant their marriage would be blessed. So far both had been correct.

"Your skin is so soft." His fingers traced the faint natal line from her navel to the shadow of her mound.

"Again?" She laughed and held his wrist. "We've been in bed all afternoon. No wonder I'm buffeted black and blue by this baby. She is complaining that she must share her space so often with her father."

"Then she must understand that I am entitled to stake my claim before her."

Caecilia hesitated, wanting to have him but resisting. She had promised the boys she would play with them, and Mastarna had business to which he needed to attend. He had been home for over a year. At the beginning it was strange to have him as a constant within the family. Soon their sons grew used to having their father around them, squealing at his horseplay or standing with quivering lower lips when his deep voice chastised them. The novelty of him sharing her bed had faded but his presence was now an expectation. There was disappointment when he did not arrive from his post at the north of the city to hug his sons, share her dining couch, and make love. His attendance at the king's war councils had become a boon.

When she had fallen with child she'd worried that his desire for her would fade as her slender waist thickened. Yet as she grew large and her breasts heavy, his need did not diminish. Vel even soothed her doubts that he would no longer want her in the last months before the birth: "It will give me more of you to hold."

She stroked his hair. "You'll be late for your meeting with Vipinas."

Mastarna sighed. "I suppose you're right. He has become more irritable since stepping down as zilath." He kissed her, then rose, breaking the fit of their bodies.

Caecilia stepped down from the bed onto the footstool and called to the slave girl outside the chamber. Both Arruns and Cytheris had been granted the afternoon to attend to their own devices. She guessed that they also welcomed their master and mistress spending so much time together.

The heavy red curtain between the garden and chamber had been drawn back, letting light and warmth fill the room. Caecilia could see the ancient grapevine, fresh with spring greenery, entwining the columns of the arcade, and hear the water splashing in the fountain. Slaves were trimming the laurel hedges and cleaning the large banqueting hall, their industry emphasizing the luxury of lying abed in daylight. Caecilia had heard their hushed giggling at spying their owners in lovemaking but had not cared. Her Roman modesty had long ago been cast aside.

Caecilia held up her arms as the servant helped her don her chiton. The sheer linen slid like liquid over her skin. "What do you want to speak to Vipinas about?"

"His grandson. I've offered to take Caile on as my squire." Mastarna pulled on his tunic before sitting down to lace up his boots.

Surprised, Caecilia paused in choosing a string of pearls from her jewelry casket. "But you already have one, a boy from your clan."

"He is ready to ride his own horse into battle."

"Then why not another from your tribe?"

Mastarna gestured the handmaid to leave. Caecilia frowned, wondering what it was that he did not want to be overheard.

She grew nervous, too, when he became attentive, standing behind her to try and fasten the necklace with his soldier's fingers. "You know I've always fostered an alliance with the House of Vipinas. He has helped us in the past."

She swung around to face him. "And yet the old man was prepared to see Kurvenas step into royal shoes."

Irritated with fiddling with the clasp, Vel dumped the pearls into her palm. "I'm not denying he's a canny politician, but it doesn't hurt to have old Vipinas as my friend. That's why I am happy to help him with his predicament."

"Predicament?"

He grimaced. "You know very well what I'm talking about— Ramutha."

Caecilia sighed, not wanting to revisit the well-worn argument over her friend's infidelity with Vipinas's grandson Caile. The scandal had not been as great as she'd expected. Another example of the liberal mindedness of her adopted people. Ramutha Tetnies gave birth to her daughter, Metli, and called on neither her husband nor her young lover to claim her. Thefarie Ulthes was not pleased, though. The living proof of his wife's indiscretion challenged his manhood. Bruised pride and hurt marred his features every time Caecilia saw him. At least the child was a girl. It would have been unbearable for him if Ramutha bore a son only to find it was not of his blood. The nobleman longed for an heir, a young warrior to inherit both his name and armor. He still wanted his wife for that purpose but there was no doubt a rift had formed between them.

Vel had not been as accepting. His astonishment had quickly turned to disgust when Caecilia had told him. He and Thefarie were of a similar age. Staunch friends bound in common bond. In the year the war began, Thefarie had returned from the sea to find both a brother poisoned and a truce ended. Found also that Tulumnes, the murderer, had fled. Yet there was no time to pursue him. Rome needed to be defeated. And so a vow had been sworn to assume the role of avengers when the conflict was over. But it was not over. And there was no knowing when it would end.

"She's still meeting Caile in secret," growled Vel. "Such trysts are not as clandestine as she thinks."

Caecilia nodded. She would never understand why her friend sought such greenness. "I know she is being foolish. But she won't listen."

Vel took his tebenna from the hook on the wall. "Vipinas is livid. And it's wounded Thefarie, too. He's told me he dreads the thought of finding yet another bastard in his house."

"So you are helping both men by making Caile your squire."

"Yes, the youth is old enough to ride into battle with me."

A tiny pulse beat in her temple. "You mean to help you defend the Tinia Gates, don't you?"

His silence shocked her. She dropped the necklace, the pearls shooting and scattering across the tiles. "Oh, Vel, don't tell me you are leaving?"

Dropping his cloak to the floor, he crossed to her, his embrace giving her his answer.

Needing some air, she broke from him and ran into the garden arcade. At the sight of their mistress barefoot and with loosened hair, the garden slaves disappeared.

Mastarna followed and tried to hold her but she pushed him away. "Why must you go? You are needed here! Kurvenas has commanded you to defend the gates and hold fast the northwest bridge. Isn't the danger of leading skirmishes to harry Roman troops enough?"

"Please, Bellatrix, you must understand. While Genucius has yet to reestablish the forts and stockades, there's an opportunity for me to take reinforcements to the Faliscans. Thefarie is to do the same for Capena."

"Capena? When did that city need such assistance?"

"Because it fears Rome just as much as Falerii."

Caecilia felt faint. She sat down on the arcade seat. When was her world ever going to remain solid beneath her feet? "Then why not send Vipinas north? He can take his grandson with him."

"You know I'm familiar with the terrain. And Vipinas is seventy and too old to hold command." Mastarna sat down next to her on the stone bench. "Please listen, Bellatrix. The Romans fight through all seasons now. And when we thought we had driven them home by defeating Sergius, they returned just as fierce and persistent as ever by the end of that autumn. We gained the chance to gather fuel and restock our granaries in the lull, but you know this past winter was the harshest we've ever seen. No cargo boats could bear goods along frozen rivers. And the main roads to the west and south have been blockaded. The Romans are relentless."

Caecilia remained silent, clenching a thick branch of the grapevine entwined around the arcade column. She remembered the sick feeling in her stomach when she'd seen Sergius and Verginius return in winter. And now new leaders had been elected. The choice of five commoners amazed her, stirring memories of her father's ambitions. His chance to govern Rome as a commoner had always been denied him. How proud he would have been to finally see men such as Genucius lead an army. As always such thoughts were bittersweet, though. She was glad her father was not alive to see that the chief goal of the plebeian generals was to destroy his daughter.

And yet, in a way, shouldn't she thank the Romans? The constancy of their hatred had led to Vel remaining in the city. And though he could be harmed just as easily mere yards from the gates as he could miles away, it comforted her to know she could tend to him if he were wounded. And that if he died she would be able to anoint and wrap his body, kiss his lips, and hold him even if he were stiff and cold.

She let go of the vine and put her arms around him, laying her head on his shoulder. "I wanted you to see our child born. I wanted you to cut the cord."

"I will try. If I succeed at the League, I should be able to return by the time the babe is due."

Yet again, he had stunned her. "You are going to the League! What purpose will that serve? The other Rasennan cities have made it clear they have no interest in Veii's war."

Mastarna took both her hands. "I told you the Romans are like soldier ants, Bellatrix. It will take many to destroy them."

She stood up, staring at him, finally realizing what he was saying. There was a pain beneath her breastbone. "You promised you would not seek to conquer Rome!"

He did not try to touch her. "Furius Camillus's appointment has made me change my mind. He is ruthlessly occupying Faliscan farmland and has almost succeeded in cutting the main road to that city. There is iron within him. A resolve that does not falter. And he is gaining influence with the plebeians. He stirs them to continue fighting by promising them land. And with the harsh winter, Rome is suffering food shortages. Desperation alone will drive it to take Falerii, Capena, and Veii. And then who will stop them? The Twelve must recognize that."

Camillus. How she loathed him. The man who offered her consolation when she was first married to an enemy to seal a truce but then betrayed her. His drive to destroy Veii had once inspired her but then she saw him for the wolf he was. War was always his intention even if it meant she died a hostage at Tulumnes's hand. Her falling in love with Mastarna and choosing Veii merely gave him the excuse he needed to forsake her. "Why didn't you tell me sooner, Vel?"

"Please don't be angry. You know I don't want to leave you."

She shook her head. "That's only half the truth, isn't it? I know you too well. You love us but it is not enough for you. You hate being hemmed in by domestic dramas. There is always a restlessness within you. As if only by defying death you truly feel alive."

His face settled into harsh lines, heralding the familiar closing of emotions. "What more do you want from me? I've remained here all year because I wanted to protect you from Kurvenas. I angered him after the battle with Sergius, but my feud with him is over. I love you. I love our sons. I've not failed you. But launching raids on Genucius's army is not enough; I want a chance to ensure that our family and all Veientanes can finally live in peace."

"So suddenly you trust Kurvenas! Suddenly he wishes you to be his advocate. You who are his rival? Why doesn't he go to Velzna? It's more fitting that a lucumo represents Veii at the congress."

Mastarna sighed. "You know why. The stigma of Tulumnes hangs over him. Kurvenas understands this. He believes I would have a greater chance of persuading the Twelve to attack Rome."

"Or maybe he just wants to get rid of you by stroking your vanity. Lusinies could go just as easily. He is well respected. His battered and scarred countenance speaks of his valor."

"Lusinies has no influence with Aule Porsenna. That zilath leads the council this year. My ties with him might add weight to our submission."

At the mention of the Tarchnan magistrate, Caecilia felt a flare of resentment. He was Seianta's father. It reminded her that Mastarna had always been present when his first wife bore their children. And held them when they died. With Vel's news, her dream of handing their baby to him from the birthing chair had vanished. Then, as quickly as her jealousy spiked, she felt ashamed that his heartache over his lost family could cause envy. "And you really believe that Kurvenas will not harm our family while you are absent?"

"He has given me his assurance."

Caecilia walked into the garden courtyard to gaze at the sky-line of blueness and distant mountains where her husband would soon journey. Her bare feet felt the heat retained by the sun-warmed paving.

Was she wrong to beg for his sole attention when so many needed it? To expect him to put duty to family over his city? She believed he was faithful to her but this was different. Infidelity with an enemy was infinitely more consuming—and more deadly.

Mastarna stood beside her. She let him put his arm around her.

"I'm scared, Vel. What about the Veientanes? Many here believe I'm the one who caused the war. Animosity might grow against me."

"The people know you did not cause this. Rome had already decided to declare war whether you returned to me or not."

"But who will remember that if Kurvenas breaks his word and stirs up rancor? If he, like Tulumnes, wants to kill me? What happens if you don't return? If our sons are seen as Roman and not Veientane?"

"Hush. You worry too much. Nothing has happened to you all the other times I've left the city. You are granted more respect than you credit."

"But that was before the Romans campaigned all year round! You can't truly promise that I will be safe, can you?"

His pause made her heartbeat quicken. She clung to him, wanting words of reassurance even if they were baseless.

He kissed the top of her head. She could feel his breath on her hair. "Vipinas owes me a debt for removing his grandson from trouble. He will protect our family."

She turned to face him. "As long as he no longer resents the fact a Roman killed his son and left Caile without a father."

Grasping her forearms, he shook her gently. "You know he does not blame you for that. He has no score to settle with you. Please, Bellatrix, don't torment yourself."

She scanned his face, doubts churning. Yet she did not want him to leave with only memories of sharp words and anger that might never be recanted. She'd done that once before and nearly lost him forever. "I just want this war to end! I just want the Romans to go away!"

Vel pointed to the arcade. "We will be together in summer. There will be grapes on the vine when I return. I will hold our baby." He cupped her chin in his palm. "And remember, Nortia brought you back to me for a reason. She means for us to be together."

Caecilia tensed, the memory of the golden tesserae pricking her conscience. And as she kissed him all she could think was whether she should finally tell him her secret. But how could she? After all these years? Admit now that she had flouted, not followed, fate. For the dice throw had pointed to Rome, not Veii. It was her choice alone to betray her people and pledge allegiance to his. And retribution may well follow for defying the goddess. Rome might claim Aemilia Caeciliana after all.

TWENTY-TWO

She found Cytheris in the kitchen.

Caecilia liked visiting there. Its coziness soothed the vestiges of homesickness that sometimes filled her. The room was most like the atrium in her father's house where the hearth served as the heart of the home. A humble domain where spelt cakes were offered to the household spirits in the same place where meals were cooked or she sat reading.

Cytheris was gossiping with Cook. A favorite pastime. There was more than one tooth missing now in the handmaid's grin, her ankle-length plait coiled upon the tiles. The two women were laughing as they plucked ducks for dinner, a pile of feathers and down heaped on the floor around them. A sauce bubbled in a pot above the fire, the aroma of coriander, fish sauce, and honey marinating the air.

A boy was playing a flute as they worked, their task eased by his trilling. He sat, relaxed, feet propped against a chair, cheeks ruddy from the heat within the chamber. Caecilia usually enjoyed the Rasennans's delight in music, glad they used it for the everyday instead of saving it only for hymn or dirge. Today she barely noticed it.

All three servants stood and bowed when she appeared at the doorway, their amusement dwindling, surprise upon their faces. The mistress had already settled the menu for the day; there was no reason for her to attend there.

Cytheris hastened to Caecilia's side. "My lady, is there anything the matter?"

Needing the consolation of the Greek woman, and realizing she did not want to be overheard, Caecilia fumbled with the set of keys upon her girdle. "No, I've just come to choose a special wine for dinner. Fetch a jar and come and help me."

After lighting a torch, they entered the large storeroom, the piquant scents of cooking giving way to fustiness and a dry earthen smell. Clay amphorae, some tall as men, stood like shadowy figures in the dimness, crammed with figs and olives and oil. The siege had not yet threatened this household with starvation.

Cytheris placed the torch in the bracket and closed the door. Barely had she turned around when Caecilia threw her arms about her, laying her head upon an expanse of bosom.

The constraints of rank between mistress and servant often loosened. In that first bewildering year in Veii the handmaid had become a young girl's guide to the ways of men and marriage. The role had not yet ended. Hadn't Cytheris rubbed her back during birth pangs and helped deliver all her babies? And soothed her worries over raising those same sons? She was always relieved that the slave chose to remain in service to her as a freedwoman after she had granted both Cytheris and her daughter, Aricia, their freedom. Maid and mistress owed an allegiance to the other. The servant could not stand beside her as an equal but there was love there. There was friendship.

Cytheris held her quietly, the embrace of an older sister Caecilia had never known. The Roman had lacked maternal solace also. The icy bitterness of her patrician mother for her half-caste baby had never thawed. It was a comfort to feel the padding of hips and ample breasts, the soft frizz of the handmaid's hair, the aniseed scent of her hushed soothing.

"He is going then, mistress?"

No longer amazed that the maid could read her mind, Caecilia nodded, unable to form words as she sobbed.

She always resented the fickleness of her emotions when she was pregnant. It irritated her that she could be sensitive to the slightest upset. The virtue of fortitude had been beaten into her by Rome, and she prided herself on having endured bearing children when her husband was absent so many times. The years had matured her as well as her Roman resolve.

She did not cry in front of Mastarna on parting. She'd learned that from the very beginning. Their reunion after she'd chosen Veii over Rome had been brief. A few days together and then he was gone. Since then her tears of farewell remained invisible. Not because his sympathy was lacking but because she sensed his discomfort, his helplessness as to how to console her or cope with the anguish of his leaving their family. Now he was to travel to Velzna. It would be dangerous to move through enemy territory. No quick journey.

Today with Cytheris she was free to weep. Frustration had breached a reservoir of tears. She hoped the brick walls and stalwart wood of the storeroom door would muffle her weeping from the other servants.

The handmaid stroked her hair, crooning, her pockmarked face concerned. Then she drew away, holding Caecilia at arm's length so she could study her. "But it's not like you to cry over the master leaving. There must be more."

"He goes to seek the aid of the Twelve. Veii means to march on Rome and destroy it."

The Greek woman pushed the hair from her mistress's face, then, lifting the hem of her tunic, wiped Caecilia's eyes as if she was one of the children. "But, my lady, why should that matter? Rome is no longer your home."

Hiccuping, throat sore, Caecilia finally ceased her weeping, then, overcome with weariness, she leaned against one of the tall amphora, touching the Aemilian wristlet, remembering Marcus. "I don't want to see my Roman family die even though they may revile me. And that city is where memories of my childhood and the spirits of my parents reside." She placed her hand upon her chest. "Sometimes I think the legacy of my birthplace is like a canker within me. As malignant as the one that lay inside my mother's breast and killed her. Rome is part of me—as indivisible as flesh and blood. No matter how hard I try, the lessons of my childhood haunt me, the customs of my people echo within me. And even after all this time I can't help comparing the vices of the Rasenna with the virtues of Rome. One day I wish I could wake and be truly Veientane. To have no need to make a choice. To not judge if I should deplore or ignore those things that are still alien to me."

Cytheris touched the iron amulet on her mistress's wrist. "You gave me that on the night you went back to Rome so that I could remember you. And I returned it to you when you chose Veii because it had been a gift from your cousin. But, mistress, remember why you did not want to stay in Marcus's world. You did not want to live as a Roman."

Caecilia fingered the horsehead crest on the charm. Did Marcus miss her as she did him? She remembered the moment when he'd slipped the wristband on her arm. It had been on her wedding day as she trembled in her white bridal tunic and orange veil. Even then his earnest assurances that Camillus would save her were unconvincing. Rome needed the corn her marriage secured and was prepared to sacrifice a half-caste bride. There was never any intention of rescuing her. Yet Marcus did not know that when he comforted her. The kindhearted boy ached for her in her plight. When she'd been orphaned, he'd protected her against his mother's spite and consoled her. Later, though, when she'd naively returned to Rome, he'd not understood her need for Mastarna. To him there was no option other than a life limited to spindle and loom—and submission to Drusus, a man she did not love.

"You are right, I would hate that. Returning to them was as though walls were closing around me, as though I had been shackled. But even so, remnants of my belief in their laws still lurk within me. And I will never forget Marcus."

Cytheris sighed. "My lady, you know I come from Magna Graecia in the south where women don't have the freedom that we find in Veii. I would never wish to return there. Why would I hanker for Greek rules? I know there would be nothing there for me. Certainly not my family. And even what I remember fondly would not be the same. Time changes all. The Romans themselves may have altered the customs that you remember. And should Rome fall, your sweetest memories won't be lost or your ancestors forgotten. The rest is only timber and stone." The Greek woman stroked Caecilia's cheek with the back of her hand. "And as for your cousin, he is your enemy now, whether you like it or not. Your problem is that you think too much. The question comes down to this— which would you rather see destroyed? Veii or Rome?"

Caecilia blinked, then wiped her eyes with the heel of her palm. Such an absolute made the decision clear but did not remove the agony of choice. "You know my answer."

Cytheris squeezed the princip's hand. "Then stop fretting. It has always been the same, city against city, men against men, and the women crushed between. Let's worry about Rome falling when it happens." She smoothed the fabric over Caecilia's belly. "What's more important now is for you to bear another healthy baby, and to hug your sons whenever you can."

With a small smile, Caecilia brushed off the dust that had transferred from the amphorae to her skirts. As always, sharing her fears had lightened her spirit. "We'd better remember the wine or the cook will grow suspicious."

At the end of the storeroom lay the wine cellar, its door locked. Only she, Mastarna, and Tarchon possessed the key, the cache of fine wine kept safe from tippling servants. Every time she imbibed, she thought how her father and uncle would be shocked. In Veii, though, she did not fear being killed in punishment for what in Rome was a crime.

As she neared the door, she was surprised to hear male voices and laughter coming from behind it. Then a click of a key in the lock. The door swung open and Tarchon entered, leading someone by the hand. When he lifted the lamp to see who awaited him, his surprise seemed to match her own.

"Caecilia, you scared me! What are you doing here?"

"Choosing wine, of course." She peered over his shoulder to see who was with him, wondering why he would bring a slave boy to this cellar when a comfortable bed awaited them. When she spied his companion, though, she understood. For it was no servant but the son of a king. "By the gods, what is he doing here?"

Tarchon put his arm around the youth's waist, the gesture affectionate and proprietary.

The last time she'd seen Sethre Kurvenas, he was emerging from the murkiness of a prostitutes' den. How ardent these two must have been to risk being discovered rutting beneath the stand. Today, though, their furtive coupling was well hidden. "You must be mad!"

Discovered in the assignation, Sethre showed none of the arrogance he'd displayed toward her before. He blushed scarlet, instinctively turning to escape, but Tarchon restrained him.

"You don't understand, Caecilia. Sethre is my beloved. I am his mentor."

"You, his lover? What nonsense! You're not qualified. Nor have terms been struck with Sethre's father."

Behind them, Cytheris tutted. Tarchon bristled. "Get out!"

The maid stood firm.

"It's all right, Cytheris, you can go now," Caecilia bade.

The servant left, mouth pursed, shutting the storeroom door behind her, the light from the wall torch wavering in the draft.

Tarchon was holding Sethre's hand. "Rules again, Caecilia? Don't tell me you now condone a Veientane custom you detest."

"No, I still don't believe an aristocrat should take a noble boy in any circumstance. Freeborn with freeborn, it's immoral. But at least I've learned to respect the code that needs to be followed if he does. You broke that before and you are breaking it again. Only this time you are acting like Artile—corrupting a boy, disgracing our family!"

"This is different. I love Sethre."

"Oh? And are you saying you weren't besotted with the haruspex? If I recall, you saw no wrong in that liaison either before you saw him for what he truly was."

Tarchon glanced nervously at Sethre. The youth was listening with a confused expression.

"Enough talk of Artile. He manipulated me, manipulated you—and Seianta."

Now it was Caecilia who was uncomfortable. The conversation was shifting into territory she never wanted to traverse again.

"I am not a boy, I'm a man!" Sethre had finally found his voice, with a tone that reminded Caecilia of Tas when he protested his childhood.

She glared at him. "Truly? I don't see a full beard yet upon your chin, although it will be soon enough. And then what is happening between you and Tarchon would be even worse. Two freeborn men together."

Again Sethre reddened, making her soften. "Listen to me. I'm guessing you are not stupid, and I've seen you have the makings of a warrior. So don't let Tarchon spoil it for you. Go home and forget this foolishness!"

She was not sure if it was her condescension or her command that offended him, but the disdain the youth had once shown her reappeared. "Do not presume to give me an order, Roman. This is none of your business!"

Caecilia put her hands on her hips. "How dare you! You scuttle around in my wine cellar then question my authority? I'm your elder, wife of a general—and Tarchon's stepmother. I have a right to speak my mind. Your actions threaten to stir up the feud between our Houses. Think on that, and if you still wish to disrespect me, know also that you dishonor your father more."

Not expecting fierceness, Sethre's haughtiness vanished. Tarchon pulled the youth close. "Perhaps you should go, little chick," he murmured, brushing the other's lips. "I will deal with this."

Caecilia glanced away, embarrassed to intrude on their intimacy no matter how wrong they were to share it. Then it struck her that Tarchon must have led Sethre through the kitchen to reach the wine cellar for their tryst. She could scarce believe he could be so rash. "By the gods, Tarchon, have you already turned gossip into fact by letting the servants see Sethre?"

Tarchon pointed to the back of the wine cellar. "Of course not! I thought you knew there was a tunnel. It leads into the main drainage system. Just like the one we used under the Great Temple when I helped you escape to Rome. Here, I'll show you."

Caecilia followed him past the stacked rows of amphorae with their winemakers' seals. In that tiny room were vintages from distant places, their rich aromas mingling with dust and cobwebs, the wealth of the House of Mastarna patent in the trove of Carthaginian and Sardinian wine. Tarchon led her to the last rack. In all her visits she'd never noticed the slim opening in the shadows.

Managing to ease her bulk into the concealed passageway, she was overwhelmed by the dry, fusty smell of stone. A memory of the narrow vertical shaft gouged into the rock of the high citadel returned. An escape route hidden beneath the terra-cotta skirts of the mighty goddess Uni herself. Seeking what she believed was freedom, Caecilia had climbed down wooden rungs through clinging darkness to find herself in a shallow rock gallery at the foot of the cliff.

Why then should she be surprised that such a passageway existed within her own house? And she knew there were other tunnels, too. The earth beneath the wide avenues and bustling streets of Veii was riddled with them. A network that was a testament to city engineers. Stone-covered drains ran from each house into the street. Cisterns were filled with water. Wells were full. And hadn't Tarchon once shown her the marvel of a vast river cave, and also revealed irrigation channels under the very fields themselves? Feeding thirsty crops and creating a fertile landscape that would otherwise lie fallow with swamp and mosquitoes. Rome always envied Veii its corn, little understanding how the Rasenna diverted nature. Melted snow and rain were not wasted. The Veientanes were never going to die from thirst even in a siege.

Sethre hovered by his lover's side, face stricken. "I will see you again, won't I?"

Stroking his beloved's downy check, Tarchon kissed him again. "All will be well, little chick. Trust me. Now go."

Once the youth had slid into the gloom, Caecilia tugged Tarchon back into the cellar, disbelief and fury coursing through her. Then, uncertain if one closed door would be enough to shield them from eavesdroppers, she shut the cellar door, leaving only feeble lamplight to illuminate their dispute.

Tarchon raised the lantern. "Why, your eyes are swollen. Have you been crying?"

"It's nothing," she said, taken aback that he had noticed. "It's you who I'm worried about. How could you! Have you forgotten what happened with Artile? The principes had begun to shun you. Mastarna was about to disown you for continuing to lie with his brother after you had become a man."

"Again, that was different. The haruspex should never have become my mentor. He was one of our family. It was not fitting for him to be my lover."

"You're not eligible either. You're only thirty. You've not held high office nor gained battle honors. Sethre's reputation will suffer more than yours."

"I would never harm him. I love him."

Another memory filled her. The sick transcendent stare of Artile for his beloved. A jealous vigilance and longing that she could still glimpse in the priest's gaze whenever he was near Tarchon. He had feasted on a little boy's loneliness and hopes to lure him to his bed. And yet Tarchon had stayed with the haruspex even though it meant ruin. She doubted his passion then was any less than the one he declared for Sethre now. "You loved Artile too, remember?"

Tarchon scowled. "Yes, as much as I hate him now." He turned away, leaving her in blackness.

She grabbed his shoulder. "Don't walk away. Promise me this will stop!"

"I won't give Sethre up."

"That sounds familiar also. Your stubbornness will be his undoing."

As his hand shook, the oil in the lamp sloshed out of the vessel, the light flaring. "And if I don't give him up? What then? Are you going to tattle to your husband?"

Caecilia's breathing quickened, feeling a little nauseous from the oily smoke accumulating in the confines of the cellar. "No, you are going to tell him yourself. If you think you're so justified to take on this role then that should be no problem. But the very fact you're skulking around tells me you know you're trespassing on an unwritten law."

Tarchon raked his fingers through his curls, the shadows and light emphasizing his clean-skinned, sculpted features. "I've tried so hard to please Mastarna, but he will never see me as other than pathetic. But this is a chance for me to be counted. This liaison could heal the rift between the House of Kurvenas and ours. You know such relationships are often used to build alliances."

Caecilia laughed, her incredulity making him flinch. "You don't really think that is going to happen, do you? There will only ever be a brittle truce between Mastarna and the king. This would only break it asunder." She placed her hand upon his arm. "For goodness' sake, Tarchon, you can have as many slave boys as you like. Why complicate your life?"

He shrugged her off. "Do you think that is an answer? I could lie with a thousand slaves and it would not be enough. And I'm sick of disguising myself so I can visit molles in that quarter of the city."

Caecilia cocked her head to one side, raising her eyebrows. She'd seen such men in the marketplace. Soft creatures. Males who only lay with males. Their robes colorful, their eyebrows plucked, their lashes colored with antimony and cheeks with rouge. It was said they pampered their skin with bread poultices. If Mastarna knew his son kept them company, he would be furious. Not as livid, though, as when he heard what else Tarchon was doing.

"Sethre is clever and amusing," he continued. "We do not just pleasure each other. There is poetry and philosophy and politics between us. We have both read the sacred texts of our people. We are both principes. I could be his mentor if only Veii would let us. I want an aristocratic lover."

"Well, Veii won't, and you can't," she hissed. "How on earth did this begin between you? Our Houses are estranged."

"At the gymnasium."

Caecilia had visited one. Veientane women were also allowed to exercise there. Even after all this time, it shocked her. Ramutha often urged her to join in but she refrained. No doubt her friend's passion for Caile began in such surroundings, too. The thought of stripping to run and jump seemed ludicrous. There was laziness within her, too; she was glad she could remain thin without such exertion. She had to admit, though, that the honed figures of Rasennan women were to be admired.

In the precincts of a palaestra, Caecilia could imagine one such as Tarchon would attract a boy like Sethre. The darkness of his oval eyes, the curved bow of his lips, and his comeliness caused all around him to study him, even if, like Mastarna, it was merely to dismiss him for his beauty. With age, Tarchon had only grown more handsome, with his wide, strong shoulders and chest; narrow waist; flat stomach; and lean, muscled limbs.

Sethre must have enjoyed gaining his attention as he watched Tarchon's sweat-slickened nudity. She imagined the man would make the youth laugh, too, with his good nature, sharp intelligence, and quick humor. And how easy it must have been for the soldier to be drawn to the ebullient, graceful, and fearless boy when comparing him to the other awkward youths of the Troy Game.

Caecilia thought of Marcus returning from training covered in cuts and bruises. No poultices of milk and bread were used to soften his skin. She'd brewed nettles and stinking elder bark to heal his sprains and contusions. No elegant athletics were needed to harden a Roman soldier. They swam in the freezing Tiber and practiced with weighted spears and swords on the wide expanse of the Campus Martius. And yet Caecilia had to admit, both types of training produced potent warriors. Mastarna was proof of this.

"I thought the boys trained separately from men your age," she paused, "so they cannot be—"

"Seduced?" Even Tarchon laughed, although he sounded bitter. "True, but the boys are encouraged to watch and learn from their elders. Sethre was like no other of his age. I wanted him as soon as I saw him."

When she frowned, he once again turned to go. "You know," he said, unlatching the door and wrenching it open, "I think I liked you better when you were prickly and ignorant of our ways. Now, with a little bit of knowledge, your self-righteousness sickens me. After all, with what I know of your past indiscretions, you should not be the first to point a finger! Reformed sinners are always the first to decry the faults of others."

Caecilia flushed, knowing there was truth in what he said. He'd seen her stripped bare of clothes and dignity as he helped her to expel her addiction from Artile's Zeri potion, an elixir the priest tricked her into craving in her quest for Aita's salvation.

The baby moved within her. She touched the spot, gaining comfort from the infant's presence. Legs and back aching from standing for so long, she leaned against the doorjamb as he strode into the storeroom, the torch fire bright after only lamplight.

She wanted all to be well between them. As once it had. They had been strange confidants when she first came to Veii. He'd helped her when all others wouldn't. He'd championed her. He'd risked his life to save her. "What has happened to us, Tarchon? When did we grow so far apart?"

Perhaps sensing her sadness, he stopped and turned. His expression revealed a glimpse of the Tarchon of old. "You no longer need me to interpret words and customs and family secrets, Caecilia. You're no longer the lonely girl in a strange world. You've found your way, I can tell. You have become more Rasennan than I expected."

"I still need your friendship. You've been in the city for over a year now and yet we never talk. You used to share your own worries with me."

"I know." He sighed and nodded toward her belly. "But not just war, time, and distance have come between us. I'm an outsider. You must tend to your children and husband, not spend time with me."

"I will make time."

"There is no need. I have Sethre."

She searched for his hand. "Oh, Tarchon, please heed me. I listened to you when you told me I was mistaken about Mastarna all those years ago. Let me repay that favor by opening your eyes. What you are doing with Sethre is folly."

Tarchon covered her hand with his. "I'd rather you repay me with your silence. I kept your secrets once, remember?"

Unease stirred. "Yes. Shameful ones. But that is in the past. I do not keep things from my husband anymore."

He dropped her hand, tone hardening again. "Well, that's a lie. And we both know it."

Caecilia suddenly felt faint, yet she knew she could not blame the stuffiness of the chamber or the child within her for this dizziness. His words scared her. "It's for Vel's protection. He would kill Artile if he knew he tried to prevent me conceiving by slipping silphion into the Zeri potion. I do not want him punished for murdering his brother. You must not tell him! You promised."

He offered his arm to balance her as she swayed, but he remained unforgiving. "Don't worry, our little conspiracy will remain just that. I don't want Artile's blood on my hands either, no matter how much I despise him for what he did to you and Seianta."

A silence followed, broken only when the storeroom door creaked open. Cytheris called out tentatively, "Mistress, the master is asking for you. He's back from his meeting with Lord Vipinas."

Pulse quickening, Caecilia strived to remain calm. "Very well, let him know I'll be with him shortly." She looked at Tarchon.

Anxiety wreathed his features. "Are you going to tell him?"

Conflicting loyalties assailed her. Then she realized there was an answer. "I might not have to now that you are marching north. Mastarna has agreed to take Caile Vipinas as his squire to remove him from Ramutha's arms. Perhaps your absence from your beloved will also make you see sense."

This time it was Tarchon who seemed unsteady on his feet. "Mastarna is leaving the city?"

"Yes. That's why I was crying—he goes to seek support from the Twelve to attack Rome. He's taking as many troops as he can to reinforce the Faliscan army. As his son, you will be expected to ride with him."

Mouth set into a grim line, brow furrowed, Tarchon pushed past both Caecilia and her handmaid, storming into the kitchen. As Caecilia hurried after him, she heard him bellowing Mastarna's name as he ran toward the atrium.

TWENTY-THREE

A soft shower of rain was drifting from the atrium roof opening into the shallow impluvium pool, sending ripples across the water. The chamber was darkening, too, with the encroaching evening, the sacred fire wavering in spasms of breeze.

Mastarna was standing by the hearth holding Arnth upside down. Face suffused red, the tot squealed, his tunic dangling over his head, his chubby buttocks exposed. Caecilia was not surprised to see her youngest son there. His quest was to explore and conquer all territory around him. His father admired his daring. Favored him, too.

In front of them, Larce was jumping up and down in one spot waiting his turn. The nursemaid, Perca, stood shyly to the side. The laughter of the father and sons dwindled as Tarchon strode toward them calling to Mastarna.

Vel gently flipped Arnth upright and propped him against his hip. The boy clasped the man's neck and levered himself upward, glaring at his big brother for spoiling his fun. Larce tugged at his father's hand. "Apa, why is Tarchon so cross?"

"I don't know." He frowned and swung Arnth to the floor.

Tarchon ignored his little brothers. "Why didn't you tell me about Velzna?"

Mastarna cast a glance toward Caecilia, who expected him to bark a response. Instead he calmly patted both younger boys on their backs. "Go to Ati."

She held out her hand. The almost four-year-old ran to her, staring with saucer eyes over his shoulder at the men. Arnth stood his ground as though keeping guard. Mastarna crouched down to him and tousled his hair. "Enough, my young soldier. Now do as you're told."

The mother shepherded her sons toward their room, followed by the nursemaid. Behind them, the sound of Mastarna's booming voice signaled he was no longer composed. Arnth was still determined to be with his father, though, and Perca had to drag him. The twelve-year-old girl was timid at the best of times; now she almost tripped in her haste to put distance between her and the quarrel.

Anxious to return and calm the argument, Caecilia stopped in the garden arcade and drew both boys to her. "It's time for you to go to bed." She looked up at Perca. "Where are Tas and Aricia?"

"She was waiting for the little master to finish his lessons, my lady."

Caecilia heard another sharp spike in Tarchon's temper. Larce clung to her. "I want to stay with you. I don't like it when Apa is angry."

She gave him a squeeze. "It's nothing for you to worry about. Now go with Perca. I promise I'll come and kiss you good night."

Finally conceding defeat Arnth gave her a wet kiss and padded away, but Larce dallied, laying his head against his mother's stomach. "Is baby sleeping?"

She held his face in her hands and kissed his forehead. "Yes, and you should be, too."

Hurrying back to the atrium, Caecilia heard the hysteria in Tarchon's voice. "I refuse to go. I want to stay in the city."

"Of course you're going. You're one of my officers. We leave at nightfall tomorrow. I plan to move through enemy lines under cover of darkness."

"No, I'm staying to join Kurvenas's army."

Mastarna must have thought it a joke. He looked across to Caecilia as she approached. "Do you know what he is talking about?"

"I think Tarchon should tell you." She placed her arm around Vel's waist, making her allegiance clear.

The younger man swallowed hard as though needing to take a deep breath to survive the coming wave of his father's ire. "Because Sethre Kurvenas is now my pupil. I wish to ride into battle with him under the king's standard."

The force of Mastarna's bellow startled Caecilia even though she expected his fury. "By sacred Nortia, what idiot thing have you done now?"

"He is my beloved. I will not be parted from him."

Mastarna lurched toward him but his wife clutched the back of his robes. "Stop, Vel. Don't hurt him."

"Hurt him? I should thrash him."

Tarchon flinched but said nothing.

Mastarna also fell silent, but Caecilia could see the muscles in his neck cording. He walked to the winged terra-cotta demon on the atrium's wellhead, pushed with his arms against it as though summoning dark forces. Taking a deep breath, he turned back to face Tarchon. "You, a mentor? Do you really think Kurvenas would want a fickle weakling with a pretty face and too many emotions to tutor his son on citizenry and warfare? You leave a trail of debt roundels at every gaming table. You are always wide-eyed and jittery on some elixir. You have only survived this far in war because I surround you with the stronger and the braver."

Tarchon reddened. "You lie. I am no coward."

"Perhaps. But you have little skill at fighting. And you have not yet held high office. And I doubt very much if you ever will. You'll never be qualified to take on a pupil."

To Caecilia's surprise Tarchon stepped toward Mastarna, showing the courage he proclaimed. "Ah, but you have, haven't you, Father. Zilath before thirty and a great general for more than a decade. Is that why Vipinas is letting you take his son as a beloved?" He cocked his head toward Caecilia. "What does she say about that? She who still struggles with Arnth Ulthes being your lover when you were fifteen?"

Caecilia floundered for a moment, a gap between hearing and comprehending. It was a day to resurrect past hurts. And to revive lost loves: Artile for Tarchon. Mastarna for his dead family. Mastarna and a long-dead zilath. The image of Tarchon brushing Sethre's lips returned. Vel had kissed Ulthes that way to bid him a farewell to the Beyond. The memory was still painful. A hurt that never truly healed. The knowledge that her husband had been another man's beloved was hard to reconcile with the Roman in her. And yet, with Vel's reassurance that he loved only her, she had toiled to put such prejudices aside. Placing them like linen in a chest. Yet such a box could be reopened, the garments shook out, the weave reexamined and worn again. Was she now to envy a callow youth? Was what Tarchon said the truth?

Mastarna crossed to her, lowering himself on one knee beside her, taking her hand. "Take no heed of him, he's just making trouble."

Tarchon laughed. "Don't believe him. The arrangement Vipinas makes with your husband to mentor Caile is no different than that Mastarna's own father made with Ulthes. The politics behind any such liaison is the same. To seal alliances. Mastarna should be honest with you."

Vel gripped her hand. "The bond with the House of Vipinas was forged long ago without the need for me to become his grandson's lover. Besides, he will soon sport a full beard. He is my squire only. Just as all the others before him. He will lead my second horse into battle. I don't plan to bed him. You believe that, don't you?"

Her gaze traveled between her husband and her stepson. She'd never known Vel to lie to her. Never known him to be unfaithful. She slid her hand into his. "Yes."

Tarchon snorted. "Then you're a fool."

Wounded by his cruelty, Caecilia fought back tears. And in that moment she knew the companion she once needed no longer existed. Cytheris had warned Rome's present world would be unlike what was remembered. The same could be said of Tarchon's friendship. There was no going back to that time. "Why do you try to torment me?"

The chill of his answer confirmed he was prepared to cut deeper. "Because you are as bad as him. You both seek to deprive me! But I won't let you. I will go to Kurvenas tonight. I will pay homage to him. Perhaps he will see the benefit of our Houses forming a union through my mentoring his son."

Before Caecilia could stop him, Mastarna stood and took one long stride and seized Tarchon's tunic in both hands, dragging the man to him with an ease that was frightening. "Don't you understand? When Kurvenas hears that you're bedding his son he is going to kill you. And then he is going to want revenge. Against our House. Against my children. Against my wife!"

Tarchon fought him off. "I don't believe that. All the principes would rise against him just as they did with Tulumnes."

Mastarna clouted him across the head. The younger man reeled back, clutching his face, bent double with pain.

Caecilia cried out. She'd never seen her husband strike a man in anger even when goaded by conspirators. Fearing he would strike again, she pushed herself between them. "Stop this, Vel. Stop."

Tarchon straightened, the welt upon his cheek marring his honey-hued skin. And yet his defiance was astounding, proving the depth of his passion for Sethre. "You can beat me as much as you want, I won't give him up."

Mastarna broke from Caecilia and stood behind the large reception table, forcing space and marble to check his fury. The rain was harder now, small splashes exploding as the drops struck the surface of the atrium pool, the sound of drumming competing with that of confrontation. "How long has this been going on?"

"Since before the Troy Game."

Mastarna groaned. "That long? How have you kept it secret?"

"We've been using the tunnels beneath the city and bribed those slaves who saw us."

"Bribery? As if that has ever silenced rumor! Then I can take no further chances. You're forbidden to leave this house until we ride out. Arruns will guard you until then. I can't risk you putting all of us in any more danger."

Tarchon thumped the other side of the table. "You hypocrite, as if you haven't imperiled the lives of all around you when it suited. Dice are not the only things with which you gamble. You've shown no compunction in taunting Kurvenas and his clan members in the past. So why don't you stay here to watch over your wife and children if you fear I've unleashed disaster? Or is your desire for glory greater than your love for your family?"

Mastarna stiffened and cast an anguished look at Caecilia.

She hesitated, tempted to use Tarchon's accusation to try and bind her husband to stay. Instead, she joined Vel behind the table, saying nothing, her support evident.

Tarchon grimaced. "I see you have truly become his creature."

Mastarna placed his arms around her shoulders. "No. She is my wife and understands her duty."

With defeated shoulders, Tarchon turned his back to them and walked to where the rain streamed in a column from the roof opening. Puddles were forming on the floor where the wind was scattering the drips beyond the edges of the ornate bronze reservoir. He stretched out his hands to collect some water then splashed it on his face. When he turned, Caecilia saw he had not succeeded in hiding his tears.

"Please, at least let me see him one more time before I go."

She also found herself on the brink of crying, but Mastarna did not hesitate to show his disgust. As he strode from the room he gave his edict. "No farewells. Do you understand me? It's over."

Melancholic at the unwanted ending, Caecilia lingered. "I'm sorry, Tarchon."

His voice was hopeful. "Then at least send word to him for me."

She shook her head. "It is better this way. Trust me."

He turned back to watch the rain. "Know then that I will never forgive you."

Caecilia walked toward her children's bedroom. As she did so she noticed Arruns had arrived to stand in the shadows, silently keeping guard over his master's adopted son.

TWENTY-FOUR

This time Semni knew she was truly in trouble. More than when she discovered she was with child. More than when her husband divorced her.

There was a sick feeling within her. Her world had changed as surely as the seed within her had grown into a baby that could not be ignored.

It had been a week since her sister had ejected her from her cozy home, and Semni's stomach was hurting. She'd not known that hunger could cause pain. She was exhausted, too. Huddling under eaves or in the lee of buildings during chill spring nights made it difficult to sleep.

And Nerie gave her no respite. He was grizzling again, wriggling within his swaddling. It seemed he was always caked in ordure. Always needed changing. His fitful sleeping and demands to be fed frayed her nerves.

If not for him she would be a potter. If not for him she would be happy. Instead here she was trudging the steep hill to the windy heights of the citadel to beg mercy from the great protectress.

Catching her breath, she stood beside the stone altar within the sacred precincts and stared up at the facade of Uni's temple. Above her, antefixes with the face of the grim Medusa glared at her, and a parade of brightly painted gods adorned the roof ridge. She knew that some of these had been sculpted by her father. What would he think of her now? She cringed at the thought.

At first she believed all would be well with Nerie's arrival. Old Velthur had been delighted. Dewlap quivering, he bragged about his virility, the broadness of his grin prolonged and hearty. After a few months, though, his smile had vanished. To Semni's dismay the dark hair on Nerie's head fell out to reveal blondness. And so her curiosity was cured. Her son's father was the fair northern Rasennan who'd worn a ram's head mask at the Winter Feast.

Thrown out by Velthur, and with the whip marks of her beating needing salving, she knocked on her sister's door. It was winter. The coldest that Semni could remember, with snowdrifts choking the pavements and ice forming on the surface of cisterns and cracking drainpipes. Despite having three children of her own to feed, her sister convinced her husband to grant Semni and her baby refuge. In return for this kindness the girl was expected to help the fuller in his business of scouring and cleaning woolen clothes.

Semni sat down on a stone step of the vast temple portico. Nerie's whining had increased in volume. Sighing, she slid her chiton from her shoulder and pressed the six-month-old to the teat. Once he was settled, she stretched out one hand to examine her fingers. They were sore and red from working for the fuller. More so than when she'd used slurry and clay upon the flywheel. Wringing cloth saturated with a cleansing fluid of urine had caused the irritation. There were also tiny scratches from where she'd carded wool by skin of hedgehog. At least she was not expected, as were the slave boys, to tread and stamp the clothes free of dirt in vats full of the liquid. And yet coarsened hands and the lingering smell of piss were better than destitution.

It was the fuller's fault, too, that she was hungry and homeless.

No more than a month after Semni had moved into his house, she caught him eyeing her breasts as she suckled Nerie. She did not mind. He was broad-chested and pleasant-faced enough for her to consider him. Liking the attention, and out of habit, she gave him a coy smile and took her time to fasten her ties when the baby had finished. Soon he grew bolder. At dinner one evening he slid his hand along her thigh under the table while his wife ate her dinner. And needing a man after so many months without one, Semni guided his fingers higher.

After a while she merely tolerated him, bored with sneaking into the shop's storeroom to allow him grunting satisfaction amid wicker drying frames and casks of sulfur. She dared not spurn him. After all, she needed his protection. Her chance to earn money as a potter had vanished. The other craftsmen had shut their doors in allegiance to Velthur. And so her brother-in-law's groping was little enough price to pay for a thatched roof above her head and lentil soup in her bowl.

Every time the fuller took her, though, she thought of Arruns. Would he be skillful? Could he be tender? With her banishment from Lady Caecilia's workshop there was no reason for their paths to cross. It disappointed her that the Phoenician had made no attempt to seek her out. She thought a bond had been forged between them in the blood slick of birthing. And now that General Mastarna had ridden north with his army there was no chance she would meet him.

Nerie was fretful, pushing at her slackened breast, then biting her nipple. She yanked him away, which set him wailing. Her limits reached, she shook him. His cries rose in pitch.

Their prayers disrupted, the people in the sanctuary glanced at her in annoyance and a cepen priest bid her to quiet the child. Even the beggars who'd staked their territory on the temple steps raised their heads and frowned.

Emptiness squeezing her insides, Semni also began crying, aware at last that it was too late for remorse. There would be no reconciliation. Or assistance from her brothers after her disloyalty. She would have to sleep outside another night and every night thereafter. And if she did not gain food and shelter soon, Nerie and she would die.

She looked down at her bawling baby and took a deep breath. Shaking him would only make him scream louder. Regret overcame her. He was all she had now. Rocking him, she kissed his fine fair hair, whispering she was sorry. She did not always resent him. The first time he'd smiled she'd been joyous, and the first time he'd reached up to touch her face she'd kissed his fingers a dozen times.

After a time her lullaby soothed him. Thumb in his mouth, he fell to sleep. Weary, Semni closed her eyes and leaned against a tall red-and-black column, vulnerable, tired, and tiny against its breadth.

TWENTY-FIVE

She'd only meant to doze but when she opened her eyes it was late, the stone altar table and podium in the courtyard black solids. And the cippus stones scattered around the sanctuary were dark phallic shapes silhouetted against the deep-blue sky of evening.

Aware she'd not yet made her offering to Uni, Semni carried the slumbering Nerie into the goddess' sanctum.

The deity was immense, towering above her. The jeweled diadem crowning her head almost touched the terra-cotta-clad rafters of the lofty chamber, a goatskin cloak adorning her shoulders. The goddess held a lightning bolt in one hand, a spear of light to send her portents. Her posture was regal befitting her status. She was a queen, wife of Tinia, king of the gods.

The statue was ancient, created centuries past. For a moment Semni forgot her awe of the goddess to marvel at the artistry of the mortal who'd sculpted the masterpiece. It was beyond her ken, beyond her imagination.

Other supplicants were present, the susurration of prayers the only sound to break the hush. A novice cepen was lighting fresh bowls of myrrh, scent trails drifting in the air. Semni knelt and laid Nerie beside her. Little votives cluttered the space around the statue's feet, representing pleas and prayers. Among them were many small images of Uni, appealing to the vanity of the divinity as much as her mercy.

Semni's votive was a tiny lamb she'd fashioned from clay. Only the rich could afford to sacrifice a real one. As she offered the gift to Uni, she beseeched the goddess to give them succor, and grant long life to Nerie, son of a ram.

By the time she'd finished, she was alone. No doubt the other worshippers had homes to go to and an evening meal waiting. Even the young priest had disappeared.

As Semni considered whether to hide for the night in one corner of the heated chamber, she heard the faint sound of warbling and, above that, the reedy voice of a boy.

She glanced at Nerie. The babe was still sleeping. It was the first long rest he'd had for days. Semni covered him with her shawl and placed him near the warmth of a brazier.

Curious as to why a child would be present in the temple at night, she padded toward the sounds. The massive wooden doors at the back of the sanctum were ajar. She peeked through the opening into a long narrow cell that served as a workplace for the priests. Tall three-tiered candelabras lit the room brightly. The perfume of myrrh was stronger here, a fortune in resin heaped in deep salvers, the air stiff with headiness from it.

The cooing she'd heard was coming from cages on the wall. Semni eyed the plump pigeons shuffling on their roosts. For a moment she pondered offending the gods by stealing one of their messengers, before noticing the young novice was busy mopping the floor clean of white droppings.

In the middle of the room was a large oaken armchair and table, their legs carved into the shape of sphinxes. A small stone altar stood behind them. She scanned its surface, noticing golden patera dishes and a large knife with a handle studded with turquoise.

Tools for sacrificial rituals. Costly and sacred. There was a pile of linen books also, folded neatly.

To her surprise the child she'd heard was the young master Tas. He was standing on tiptoe trying to reach a bronze object with strange markings on it. Instead of his usual reserve, he was chattering to his nursemaid, who sat on a stool holding a bound rabbit by the ears. Semni eyed the animal, imagining tasting the victim after it had been sacrificed and cooked. There was little chance, though, that the priest who performed the ceremony would share his dinner with a beggar. "Aricia, is that you?"

Startled, the maid swiveled around. "Semni!"

The cepen looked up and frowned. Aricia hastily gestured him to leave. The youth heeded the girl, intriguing Semni as to why he would obey her. Tas fell silent, studying the intruder. Once again, Semni noted his unusual eyes, thinking his eyelashes darker and longer than she'd remembered.

Handing the rabbit to the boy, Aricia hurried across to her friend, drawing her by the hands into the chamber then throwing her arms around her. "Oh, Semni, I'm so pleased to see you."

As usual, the maid smelled of freshness and sweet orris, her linen robes clean. For a moment envy surged at the good fortune of her friend to live in a princip's house when she and her child had no home at all.

"I've missed you," continued Aricia. "I've not seen you since you went to live with your sister."

Tears welled in Semni's eyes.

The Greek girl raised her eyebrows. "My goodness. What's the matter?"

"She threw me into the streets."

"Threw you out? Whatever for?"

"Because of her husband. It was all his fault."

The nursemaid gasped. "Oh, Semni, you didn't? Not with your brother-in-law!"

The judgment irked her. "I said I was sorry but she wouldn't listen. Then she threw us out. Me! And my baby!"

Aricia looked past her. "Where is Nerie?"

Semni gestured toward the sanctum then restrained Aricia from going to the infant. "Please don't wake him." Then she put her hands over her face and wept. "I'm so tired."

Embracing her again, Aricia stroked her friend's hair, brushing away her tears. Her fingers were soft. Those of a pampered servant. Semni laid her head upon the girl's shoulder. The maid hesitated before kissing the top of her head. "Hush, all will be well. I will help you."

Semni drew away, wiping her nose with the back of her hand. "You will?"

"I will speak to Mother. I am sure there is work for you."

Semni thought of the ghastly faces of the Medusa antefixes and then of the pockmarked and stony-eyed Cytheris. "The Gorgon? Help me? I don't think so."

"Mother is not so bad. And even if she doesn't approve of you she wouldn't see a baby suffer. And besides, Lady Caecilia was your patron when you were at the workshop. I'm sure she'd agree to you being in her service."

Semni hugged, then kissed her, once, twice, three times upon both cheeks.

Aricia smiled, keeping her arm around her friend, one hand gently resting on Semni's waist. "And if you live in our house I won't be lonely anymore."

"Did you hurt your knees when your sister threw you away?" Tas had ceased his inspection of the table and was standing quietly beside them.

Semni had forgotten how disconcerting his questions could be. Always slightly askew in his understanding. "Not in body, master, but in spirit."

Distracted by the rabbit struggling feebly against its bindings, Tas stroked the animal's soft fur, calming it. Semni thought it strange the child was not in bed. Even stranger that he was here at all. "It's very late to be making sacrifice to Uni," she said to Aricia. "Are you waiting for Lady Caecilia?"

The maid avoided her gaze, instead busied herself retying her girdle.

"We've come to give sacrifice to Aita only," said Tas.

Semni remembered how the child had mentioned the god of the Beyond on the day he'd visited the pottery workshop. Aricia had been nervous then, too. Suddenly Semni felt uncomfortable, sensing something was amiss. Why was Lady Caecilia entrusting a nurse with the duty of attending to her son's salvation? Surely it was a mother's duty to seek immortality for her child.

Before she could question Aricia further, Semni noticed Tas looking toward the door, his mouth curved in a broad smile. "Uncle, Uncle!"

Semni turned, blinking when she saw who Tas was greeting.

The high priest of the Temple of Uni, the chief haruspex of Veii, the chief fulgurator, stood in the doorway, imposing in his long sheepskin coat and high pointed hat, his fingers clenched around his staff.

Semni cast a shocked look at her friend as both girls bowed. All Veii knew of the enmity between Lord Mastarna and his brother. None understood what caused it, but guessing why was a constant source of rumor. Had the rift been mended?

Tas ran to the priest and lifted the rabbit to show him. "Uncle, see what we brought this time."

Smiling, Lord Artile crouched beside the boy, resting his beringed hand upon his head and smoothing his hair in a tender motion. "Very good, little seer. Aita will be pleased to receive blood sacrifice."

The affectionate gaze bestowed upon his nephew changed from warm to cold in a matter of seconds as the priest stood and faced the two girls, his eyes accentuated with antimony. "Aricia, who is this stranger?"

The Greek girl stammered, bowing. "My lord, forgive me. I did not bring her here. She was making devotions to Uni and found us."

Semni barely heard her. She'd never been close to the gifted soothsayer whom king, zilath, and princip heeded. Last time she'd caught a glimpse of him she'd been packed tight with other people into the forecourt of this very temple as he presided over a sacrifice. A white bull for Uni. Even before the hammer stunned the beast it had been docile, ready for the knife, a good portent. And the haruspex, blessed with the sight, revealed the meaning of the divine sign hidden in the veins and membrane of its liver. A terrible omen that had come true—that Veii must endure a long and bitter war. Now she was in the same room as the prophet. His presence seemed to fill the chamber as much as the enormous statue of Uni standing imposing in her sanctum.

He glowered at Aricia. "I am displeased. Leave now—and take her with you. I will send word to you when it is time."

"But, your grace," the girl continued to stammer, "I should stay with master Tas. And I must give libation to Aita."

"No, you have broken my rules."

His deep voice was alarming. Aricia quaked. Again, unease spread through Semni, who realized she'd chanced upon a conspiracy in which she wanted no part.

Tas tugged at his uncle's sleeve, his tawny eyes anxious. "Please, Uncle, she must stay. She always stays. I need her with me." He pointed to the potter. "And she won't tell, will you, Semni?"

The girl nodded without knowing the full extent of the secret she must keep. She was certain, though, that she did not want to incur the priest's displeasure.

Artile stroked the boy's hair again. "Little seer, you do not need a servant to help you take the sacraments."

The child straightened, hands on his hips, stubbornness emerging. "I don't want Aricia to go!" He stamped his foot. "I won't perform the rites if she is not with me!"

To Semni's surprise, the priest did not chastise him. Chuckling, he placed his pointed hat onto the boy's head where it sat lopsided and low upon the brow. "Such a temper, little seer! But you must understand that Aricia has to be punished. I will not grant her the sacraments tonight." He held out his curved staff. "Nor can she remain in the sacred space that I create with my lituus. But I will let her watch over you from the doorway of Uni's cell. Will that please you?"

Cheeks high with color, Tas looked over at Aricia. The maid smiled, mouthing reassurance.

"Yes, thank you, Uncle."

The priest smiled at his nephew, but when he gazed at Aricia over the boy's head, his eyes were like flint. Semni shivered, disturbed by the effortlessness with which this man glided between emotions. To her dismay, he turned his attention upon her. "Come here, girl."

As she approached he recoiled slightly, making Semni realize that it was not only Nerie who was noisome. She thought he would shout but instead his voice was low, his menace laced with the scent of bay leaves on his breath. "Tell no one of this or I will call down disaster upon you."

Dumbstruck, Semni nodded then backed out of the chamber. Aricia followed.

Safe in the sanctum, Semni glared at her friend. "By the gods, Aricia, what are you doing? Lady Caecilia knows nothing about this, does she?"

Aricia gripped Semni hard enough to hurt. "You must tell no one. Not the mistress. Not my mother. Promise me. Otherwise, if you do, I will be thrashed and then dismissed."

Semni broke from her grasp, rubbing the sore spot on her arm. "How long have you been bringing him here in secret?"

"A year."

The girl's jaw dropped. "But why? Why would you do this?"

The nursemaid's expression hardened. "Because Lady Caecilia clings to her Roman religion and the general believes Fufluns will be his guide in the Beyond. But the Afterlife, where demons lurk, is perilous and fearful. Piety must be observed and eternal life sought through prayers and appeasement. I don't want to see Tas and his brothers damned—I want them to become lesser gods after they die and become one of the Blessed." She paused. "And I want to gain salvation, too."

Semni grimaced. She preferred Pacha Cult's blissful worship. The strictures required to satisfy the Calu Cult were rigorous and unforgiving. Blood sacrifice needed to be made often to gain Aita's favor. Providing a supply of victims was expensive. She doubted anyone other than the wealthy could afford to maintain such devotions. The common people were too busy struggling for staples. No wonder Aricia saw benefits in helping the young master. She was able to steal victims from the pantry for him and then offer them together—and all through the ministry of a priest whom Lord Mastarna despised.

What was she to do? The prospect of a bed, clean clothes, and food for both her and Nerie beckoned. Yet to accept them she must start her new life deceiving her mistress. She peered through the doorway at Lord Artile. His threat frightened her. Here was a man who communed with the gods. The punishment he could call down upon her was unimaginable. The very thought of his retribution made her shudder.

Behind them, Nerie stirred, whimpering in his sleep. Semni tensed, unable to bear the thought of having to cope with his misery.

Frowning at the mother's hesitation to comfort her infant, Aricia hurried to him, bending down to rub his back, soothing him until he settled into sweeter dreams. "He is beautiful."

Semni stared at her friend and baby, then made her decision. After all, it was really none of her business. She was not responsible for Tas. It was enough that she had to care for Nerie's welfare. "I promise I won't tell."

"Thank you." Aricia squeezed Semni's hand but her face was still lined with worry. She leaned against the wooden jamb, studying Tas and his uncle. Yearning was etched into her expression. Semni understood then that this girl was hurting. No doubt she would have to spend much time in expiation, begging forgiveness for her lapse in worship—a lapse caused by Lord Artile's cruelty. The haruspex knew that the servant was not at fault. And yet he was punishing her, making her suffer.

Sorry that she had unwittingly caused the problem, the potter placed her hand on the maid's shoulder. "He is spiteful to blame you."

Aricia swung around, shrugging her off. "Don't say that! He was right to punish me. I should have sent you away as soon as I saw you."

Semni frowned at the defense of the unjust priest.

The Greek girl returned to studying the haruspex and his nephew, nodding encouragement to Tas when he glanced over for reassurance. She slid her hand into Semni's. "Lord Artile is most wondrous. Just watch and listen."

TWENTY-SIX

The novice bustled past the girls, bringing warm water for the haruspex and flour to sprinkle on the sacrificial blade.

As Tas waited for the priest to wash his hands, he pointed to the strange bronze object again. "What's that, Uncle?"

"That is a model of a lamb's liver I use to teach pupils how to read divine signs."

The boy's eyes widened. "Truly? Will you teach me, too?"

"Why, of course, little seer."

"Now?"

The haruspex studied him for a moment, then wiped his hands. Sitting in the armchair, he drew his nephew onto his lap and handed him the replica.

Tas turned it over and over, examining the web of lines carved upon it. "What are these?"

"They represent the quadrants of the heaven. See how there are sixteen of them? In each segment a different god resides. And so, if I see a blood clot or other blemish in those sections I know which deity has sent the message." Lord Artile eased the model from the child's fingers. "Look. On this side the sun and moon is written. And on the other, the dwelling places of the gods. Those in the northeast where Tinia and Uni lie bring the greatest good fortune. Those in the northwest are to be dreaded."

Tas traced the grooves. "But how do you know what the god is telling you?"

Artile removed the hat from Tas's head and once again smoothed the young master's hair. His fingernails were painted purple, his hands white and soft, those of a man unused to labor. When Semni first noticed his caresses she had thought him merely kind, but with repetition, goose bumps pimpled her flesh. The soothsayer's fingers seemed to linger a little too long before he ran his hand down the boy's arm then rested it on the child's thigh.

Semni glanced at Aricia, wondering if the maid was also troubled about the uncle petting his nephew, but the maid stood rapt, admiring both priest and pupil.

The haruspex drew the linen books upon the table toward him. "Through the sacred texts, of course. The Great Discipline. They contain the wisdom given to us by Tages as to how to interpret prodigies and portents."

"Who is Tages?"

"Has your father not told you?"

Tas shook his head. "Apa talks about being a warrior but treats me like a baby."

Artile patted the boy on the back, a hint of disgust in his sigh. "Then listen and I will tell you. Once a man called Tarchon was plowing a field—"

"Tarchon? Like my big brother?"

Semni saw what seemed like sadness shadow the haruspex's face, and yet when he spoke his tone was harsh. "Are you going to listen to me or not?"

It was the first time the man had been stern with the child. Tas shrank back. "Sorry, Uncle."

"You must listen, little seer." Artile patted the child's knee, benign again. "Now, to Tarchon's surprise, a boy, innocent as a newborn, rose from the furrowed earth."

"A boy?" A frown creased Tas's forehead. "How could he live beneath the ground? He would not be able to breathe."

This time the priest did not chide him for the interruption. "Because he was Tages, the grandson of Tinia. More amazing was that he spoke with wisdom beyond his years. He was a child sage, ancient yet young, who bade Tarchon write down his words. The plowman thought this so astonishing he called all the priest kings of the twelve cities to attend there. And then they recorded all that Tages told them about prophecy." The haruspex pointed to the pigeons and the model. "Secrets about how to interpret portents from the flight of birds or from the liver of a beast. Or, most amazing of all"—he paused, watching Tas's anticipation—"from lightning!"

"Lightning!"

Lord Artile flipped open a fold of linen. "Here is the Book of Thunderbolts that Tages gave us."

Semni leaned forward as much as she dared through the doorway to view the sacred text. She was disappointed. There were only neat columns of black and red writing, the script no more special than that used by scribes to note down inventories and contracts. She'd expected the words of the gods to be written in ink of gold.

Engrossed in the scene, Aricia also craned her neck to see. Semni remembered how her friend desired to become a priestess. Today Aricia had a chance to overhear the lessons granted to her charge. "You wish Lord Artile would teach you, too, don't you?"

"Ssh," hissed the girl, keeping her eyes on Tas.

Their whispers must have been too loud. "Be quiet there," the soothsayer growled.

Aricia gave Semni an annoyed glance. Lord Artile concentrated on his nephew again, who was tracing the columns with his finger. "The words are too big for me."

The uncle leaned over him, his arms flanking the boy, their faces level and close as they scanned the book together. "Study as hard as you can and then you will become a great haruspex, my boy."

"Like you, Uncle?"

"Greater than me. And you will be a famous fulgurator, too, able to interpret what thunderbolts mean."

Tas turned and beamed at Aricia. The maid's smile matched his.

"Tell me what it says," he cried. "Please!"

The child's hand was still on the linen page. Lord Artile placed his over it. "No. Enough for today. It's getting late. We must give sacrifice to Aita so we might become one of the Blessed. We must appease and placate him. We must give thanks and expiate our sins."

Semni watched Tas's expression fall at the news the lesson was over. Sliding off the man's lap, he reached down to pick up the rabbit, which lay twitching on its side. The child was pensive, his confident manner dwindling. "Uncle, will Aita strike me with a thunderbolt if he is unhappy with me?"

"Aita? No, his realm is the underworld, not the heavens. He possesses no lightning. Why do you ask?"

His voice was small and lost. "Because he sends demons to scare me when I sleep. I thought, perhaps, that he was telling me that I was bad."

Crouching down, the man stroked Tas's face with one purple-tipped finger. "We must always be fearful of demons, little seer, but the gods do not speak to us through dreams. I am going to help you gain salvation so that no monsters will ever harm you."

The relief in the little boy was patent, shoulders relaxing, a smile returning. This time the priest's tenderness in comforting the child touched Semni.

Lord Artile clasped both of Tas's hands. "You remember your promise, little seer?"

The child nodded, golden eyes as liquid and gleaming as the man's. "Yes, Uncle. I must not tell Apa or Ati that I meet with you."

The haruspex smiled. "That is right. Because if you do they will not let you visit me ever again. And then how will you become a great soothsayer, the most powerful prophet Veii has ever known?"

Semni frowned, uncomfortable with what she had witnessed. Uncertain whether this priest's intention was not only to save this boy's soul but also to steal it.

TWENTY-SEVEN

The cries were faint through the brick walls, but even in her drunkenness Semni recognized her son, insistent and distressed.

She was supposed to be scaling fish in the washroom but had strayed next door to the stables. With the master and his son away at war the grooms had fewer horses to exercise and curry. Often these tasks were finished by midafternoon, leaving time for drinking a rough brew concocted on the sly.

Sitting up, Semni placed her hand over the groom's mouth to prevent another kiss and reached for her chiton, which had fallen to the floor. Tipsy, the youth clumsily sought to hold her, but she shoved him away, knocking over her half-finished cup. Wine trickled through the straw to the bank of pebbles that served as his bed.

Stumbling into the kitchen, she saw strips of swaddling trailing across the floor, the bands broken. Arruns was holding Nerie on his lap, murmuring stilted words of comfort as he rubbed the baby's back. The boy's mouth was wide, his scream earsplitting, eyes slits, face red.

Semni snatched him from the guard. "What did you do to him?"

The Phoenician's eyes narrowed. "I could hear his cries from the atrium. He has burned his hand."

Semni gasped, examining her son's reddened and puckered fingers. She kissed his head, rocking him, but the infant was inconsolable, gulping in air as he continued crying.

She thought she'd swaddled him tightly. And yet it had not been the first time he'd broken free. Her milk was plentiful and he was thriving. Strong-limbed and starting to crawl, he was always restless, eager to explore. And yet when she'd last seen him he was nestled safely asleep in the corner of the warm pantry.

Semni glanced across to the andiron, horrified she might have lost him in the flames. It was no wonder his exploration had led to the hearth. The bronze cookware was decorated with a menagerie of mystical and mortal beings: the huge cauldron on its tripod was decorated with the leering lips and mischievous eyes of a satyr, and dolphins adorned the sides of the saucepans. Even the brazier's handles were shaped as serpents. There were other attractions for a nine-month-old, too: necklaces of garlic dangled and sheaths of herbs hung drying, their aromas mingling with the ripe, gamey smell of partridges hanging on hooks from the ceiling.

A lion-handled poker lay strewn across the hearth. When Semni picked it up it was still warm. The stand with the tong and shovel had been knocked on its side.

This time Arruns did not hide his anger behind a cold and dreadful stare, but raised his voice in fury. "What kind of mother are you, leaving a child alone?"

Semni shrank back, thinking he might strike her. The right of a husband or father, when this man was neither. How dare he act as if he was entitled to berate her! "I am a good mother! It's not my fault he broke his swaddling bands." Rattled, she scanned the room. "I thought Cook and the kitchen slave were here."

"It's always someone else who is to blame."

Semni ignored him, kissing Nerie's face. Soon the guard calmed down as he watched her consoling the child. There was no doubt he was fond of the boy. Semni had often caught him in awkward play with the child, wary of his muscled touch when handling one so tiny. Hesitant, Arruns reached out to pat Nerie with clumsy gesture. Still aggrieved at his censure, Semni turned her back, denying him further contact.

When she'd entered Lady Caecilia's service she'd been surprised to find the general had not taken Arruns with him. And finding the Phoenician living under the same roof raised her hopes that he might want her. As soon as she could, she cornered him, believing that, with her figure returned to normal, he would desire her full breasts and soft curves. His rebuff had stung.

"Why not? I thought, perhaps, you'd think differently about me after what we shared at Nerie's birth."

"You've not grown any wiser from what I've heard."

"My brother-in-law took advantage."

He had shaken his head. "Semni, I would never take the chance that you could be the mother of my child."

"What's going on here?" bellowed Cytheris, who stood with her hands on her hips in the doorway, a slave girl behind her. There was a look of surprise on her face at seeing Arruns, then a scowl as she glared at Semni.

The man surveyed the three women and strode from the room without another word.

"Nerie's burned himself," said Semni.

Cytheris frowned, crossing the room to check the baby's fingers before ordering the slave to fetch some mint from the vegetable plot.

Semni shifted Nerie to her shoulder, jiggling him while kissing his head. "Hush," she cooed, putting the infant out of reach of the Gorgon. "Mama's here."

Cytheris pursed her lips. "And how did the boy end up near the fire?"

Semni gestured toward the slave girl in the garden. "Where was she? And Cook? They should have been keeping an eye on him."

"Cook is sorting out the day's menu with the mistress. And the girl was doing what she was told—picking herbs. So exactly what, pray tell, were you doing not to notice your child missing?"

"I was in the washroom. Nerie was asleep and swaddled in the larder."

The kitchen slave returned and began chopping the mint leaves before mixing them with some honey. She handed the lotion to the Greek woman, who smoothed the sweet stuff onto the baby's fingers. After a few minutes, Nerie's cries lessened, but Cytheris remained persistent. "Don't think I'm not aware of what you were doing."

Semni busied herself again with her son. "I don't know what you mean."

"Of course you do. You stink of musk and seed. And wine. Who was it? The gardener? The driver? Or one of those lazy grooms?"

Semni's head was aching, the effects from the drink souring. And she found it difficult to speak without slurring. "No one," she mumbled, thinking that if the Gorgon unplaited her ankle-length hair, snakes would slither from it. For certain the woman would turn her to stone if she were able.

"Listen to me, you little slut. If I catch you with another man I'll make sure the mistress dismisses you, and has you whipped for drinking. I only helped you because of Aricia's pleading. You've been here all spring and you've already stirred up trouble. Those stupid grooms are fighting over you." She paused. "And don't think I can't see you've been sniffing around Arruns."

Nerie had quieted. Semni laid him on the kitchen table and carefully wrapped him in the swaddling again. She was nervous, knowing Cytheris's threat was not an empty one. Lady Caecilia was fond of her handmaid. The Gorgon held much sway in the household. Semni knew, too, that the woman wanted Arruns for her daughter. "Yes, Cytheris." Her voice was meek, hiding her resentment.

"Good." The maid peered at Nerie, neatening one of the bands. "Poor babe."

Semni was relieved to see the fondness in Cytheris's gaze. Arruns was not the only one enamored of her child. When she'd first arrived, it was the sight of Nerie—dirty, hungry, and shivering—that had softened the Gorgon's stance. Hopefully the maid's affection for Nerie would continue to save them from being cast out into the streets.

Returning to the washroom to resume her work, Semni settled Nerie on a bundle of sheets. The thin membrane of gut and slats on the window did little to muffle the sound of traffic outside. Worn out with crying, the baby soon fell asleep despite the noise.

As the girl scaled the fish, she wished she didn't have to wait for darkness to visit Aricia. She needed to complain about Cytheris's latest injustice.

United in mutual resentment of the Gorgon, the two sixteen-year-olds' friendship had deepened. Their differences attracted rather than divided them: frivolous versus pious, wanton versus chaste. They often sought each other out. Aricia would bring the little masters to the kitchen, where Cook would spoil them with honey cakes sprinkled with a little pepper, and Semni would steal through the house at night to meet the nursemaid and gossip.

Her status as chief nursemaid entitled Aricia to sleep in a small antechamber next to Master Tas's room while Perca made do with a pallet in the nursery. And so, as soon as the other kitchen slaves fell asleep, Semni would creep along corridors tiled with mosaics and decorated with frescoes to reach her friend.

The House of Mastarna was full of servants all ranked according to the nature of their service. After her initial gratitude, Semni
soon made comparisons that fostered discontentment. How could
Lady Caecilia make her a kitchen hand destined to live out her
days washing crockery, plucking fowls, and gutting fish? After all,
she was a freedwoman and an artisan. Surely she should have been
appointed a housemaid at the very least. She'd half hoped, too, that
the mistress would take steps to restore her to a position in the
workshop, but it was not to be. The princip was not prepared to
upset Velthur. The Roman had been stern, rigid with disapproval.
"I would have expected fidelity to your husband and your sister. I
am prepared to give you a chance because of Nerie, but you are to
behave yourself here, do you understand?"

Semni bowed, irritated at being chastised. And, remembering
her own ungainliness, swollen ankles, and plodding gait when she
was pregnant, she could not help being jealous of the noblewoman.
The tall princip was seven months with child and yet remained elegant, carrying her baby well. Semni wished she could have worn
a chiton cinched under the breasts by a crisscross of beads, and
flowing golden pleats to hide a gravid belly.

Semni thought the aristocrat no beauty. The purple birthmark
on Lady Caecilia's throat was ugly despite layers of albumen and
powder. And her mouth was too wide and her nose too narrow in
her oval face. The girl had to admit, though, that the good humor
in the Roman's round hazel eyes and the charm in her smile drew
attention away from such defects.

She envied the princip's jewelry, too. She had never thieved,
but Semni could not stop herself imagining what it would be like
to fasten a necklace with tiny pendant bird charms around her
neck or wear teardrop earrings studded with granules of gold.

A different source of curiosity burned in Semni also. Any
mention of Lord Artile's name was forbidden in the house. The
haruspex was reviled. What had caused the rift?

Aricia could not say. "It happened when I was a little girl. Mother won't tell me. But it was one of the reasons Lady Caecilia ran away to Rome before the war began." The nursemaid raised an arm, twisting it so that four silver bracelets clicked and jingled. "The mistress gave me these on the night she left. She gave Mother enough coin, too, to buy our freedom. You see, I was to be sold to another House when I was eight years old and she could not bear to see Mother lose me."

Semni studied the bangles. Lady Caecilia had freed Aricia and her mother from slavery, and provided her with employment as a freedwoman ever since. Surely the nursemaid should be rewarding the Roman with gratitude instead of betrayal for such kindness.

Over the three months Semni had sheltered in this house, she'd often felt twinges of guilt at her own part in the nursemaid's plot. Yet the longer she remained quiet about Aricia's perfidy, the more her silence cemented her own. Resentment at the princip's refusal to be her patron again also made her continue to turn a blind eye.

Although the girl told herself it was better if she knew as little as possible, she found herself asking how Aricia managed to take the boy to the soothsayer without being caught. The nursemaid's explanation had amazed her. "A network of tunnels lies under the arx. Some are disused drainage channels but others have been hewn from rock as escape routes for the rich. There is a passageway from the wine cellar that branches into them. The high priest showed me the one to the Great Temple." The girl lowered her voice. "And there is gossip that Lord Tarchon uses one to visit Sethre Kurvenas in the palace. It is said that they are lovers."

Semni raised her eyebrows, thinking that both the people and the walls of this house concealed too many secrets and schemes. "Truly?"

"Truly."

"And what about Cook and the other servants? Don't they question you when they see you with the little master?"

"They are used to me bringing him down to the kitchen for a drink of warm milk at night to soothe his nightmares."

"But the wine cellar? No servant can unlock it without permission. Not even the majordomo."

Aricia had smiled smugly. "Ah, but Lord Artile used to live here. And he has given me the key."

Nerie whimpered in his sleep. Semni wiped her hands free of fish guts and patted him. Her son was the greatest reason for not exposing the cunning of the nursemaid and uncle. She knew what awaited should she and Nerie be cast out into the streets. Why then should she care about the conspiracies that lay beneath the same cobbled roads of river stone?

TWENTY-EIGHT

Aricia's cot boasted a feather mattress, a plaid woolen coverlet, and linen sheets. And her room was redolent with the smell of sweet violets. Semni had been mistaken about the scent of orris lingering in the nursemaid's hair and clothes. It was not perfume but the incense the girl burned to speed her prayers to Aita.

Semni sat on the bed and fed Nerie. The boy was fretful with pain. Loosening his swaddling, she smoothed more of the honey lotion on his hand before laying him down and stroking him until he fell asleep.

Aricia loosened Semni's topknot and combed her hair. Such ministrations reminded the girl of nights with her sisters. They would often gossip or squabble as they tended to each other's grooming, heaping bone pins into piles and combing out each other's tresses. Now she had lost both of them—one to death and the other to treachery.

Aricia had no such memories. She had no siblings. And the other servants kept her at a distance, conscious of her sanctimony. Her mother did not approve of her fervor for the death cult either. Semni knew, though, that Cytheris was proud that Aricia had been entrusted with the care of the heirs of the House of Mastarna. She'd overheard the Greek woman boasting of it to Cook. Yet the mother never wasted an opportunity to criticize her daughter to her face.

"She's dried up and old," complained Semni. "Why should I go without a man to warm me in my bed just because she's jealous?"

Between strokes, Aricia smoothed her hand along her friend's thick waist-length hair, saying nothing.

"Who would want her? She's over thirty summers old, ugly, fat, and toothless! And her breath stinks of aniseed. No wonder you have no brothers or sisters."

Aricia stopped combing. "Only a few of her teeth are missing. And I had a half-sister who died when she was a babe."

Semni swung around. "Truly?"

"Truly. And then there were my twin half-brothers, who were taken from her when she was a slave."

"By the general?"

"No. By my father."

"But if he was the boys' father he had that right."

"But he wasn't. Mother bore them to a different man."

"I'm confused."

Aricia sighed. "Mother has had many lovers but no husband."

Semni was stunned. That dour woman having many men? "So why don't you live with your father?"

"I've never met him. He is from Latium. When his wife discovered the Gorgon sleeping with her husband she took my brothers from her. Then Mother was sold to a Rasennan trader. She was pregnant with me."

Sympathy welled in Semni before she realized that Cytheris was demanding chastity when she'd been an adulterer just like her. "So she caused trouble in her time."

"You should not cross her, Semni."

"So you think she is right to deny me the chance for some pleasure?"

The nursemaid was quick to placate her. "No, it's just . . . I don't understand why you want so many men."

Semni's cheeks flushed with temper. She was fed up with Aricia's disapproval. There was no reason why the nursemaid needed to remain pure. She may have been plump and plain, but at least she had all her teeth. And instead of Cytheris's frizz, her pretty black ringlets were sinuous and shiny. Her smile could be appealing, too, when she chose to be amused. And her youth alone would encourage men to couple with her. "And I'd like to know why you want none!"

"Because I plan to be a priestess."

Semni snorted. "There's no rule that holy women have to be virgins."

"I don't want a husband," Aricia pouted. "He would not let me be a cepen."

"Who says he has to be a husband?"

Aricia clenched the comb, voice hard with spite. "Unlike you, I'm not prepared to bear a bastard."

Semni bridled at the mouse being prepared to bite. How dare Aricia judge her when the nursemaid was playing the traitor? She snatched the comb from the girl and brushed her own hair with sharp, hard strokes. "You might think me a slattern but I think you're a fool. The haruspex is not going to help a freedwoman become a priestess."

Aricia balled her hands, holding them tight in her lap. "You're wrong! He said if I learned to read he'll show me Aita's sacred text, the Book of Acheron."

"He only says that because he wants you to bring Master Tas to him."

At the sound of their anger, Nerie started grizzling. Annoyed that he'd been woken, Semni threw the comb onto the bed and picked him up, turning her back on Aricia as she rocked him.

The nursemaid pulled her around to face her. "You're a liar!"

"And as I said, you're a fool." Semni pushed the girl on the chest. "He'll never teach you!"

"And you'll never have Arruns until you stop opening your legs to every man!"

Semni stood up, propping her son against her shoulder, patting his back to stop him crying. "I don't have to listen to this. I'm going."

Aricia's expression changed from defiant to stricken in an instant. "No, stop, don't go. I'm sorry. Please don't be angry. I didn't mean it!" She clutched Semni's chiton. "Why don't you and Nerie sleep here tonight? It must be cold where you sleep."

Semni hesitated, hearing the neediness in her friend's voice. She thought of her bedroll on the hard floor of the kitchen, and the snores of the other servants who shared her space. It would be no hardship to swap that discomfort for sleeping head-to-toe with Aricia. The warm softness of the nursemaid's bed would more than compensate for cramped bodies. Hadn't she spent her childhood lying next to her sisters in this way? And after Nerie's accident it would be good for the babe to sleep in a room heated by a brazier.

"Very well." Her tone was haughty, making it clear she was doing the maid a favor. She sat down again, kissing Nerie's fair hair and crooning to him. When he was finally quiet, Aricia sidled up beside her and began plaiting Semni's hair into a loose braid. After a while the nursemaid laid her head on her friend's shoulder. "Mother can't force me to marry him, you know. But I don't know why you want him. Arruns is not a man to love, Semni. There's something missing in him, something chilling. He was the Phersu, after all."

Uncomfortable with the girl's nearness, Semni shifted away from her and pulled back the bedcovers. "I'm tired. Let's go to sleep." Cradling her son, she slid between the sheets, enjoying the first-time feel of linen against her skin. Aricia doused the lamp and climbed into the bed at the other end.

Semni lay on her side in the dark, taking in the smell of honey and mint as Nerie lay against her, and conscious of the nursemaid's back touching hers.

A tear trickled from the corner of her eye into her hair. Aricia was wrong. Arruns may have worn the scarlet mask once and now guarded his emotions behind hooded eyes and tattoo, but she'd seen through his guise. She knew he had feelings. And if he wanted her, she believed he might just make her desire no other man.

TWENTY-NINE

Falerii, Summer, 397 BC

Pinna was happy. Her arms and legs were brown. She liked the feel of the sun on her face, the slight tightening of the skin after she'd spent long hours in light. Although the ruddiness marked her as a peasant and in time would age her, the more she tanned the further away her life in the dim interior of the brothel became.

Under the hot noonday sun, perspiration soaked the back of her tunic, sweat trickling between her breasts and coating her arms as she carried a basket of provisions to her tent. She'd had to haggle with the trader outside the camp to get a decent price for olives and cheese. And the piquant fish sauce Marcus enjoyed was far too expensive for her liking. According to the sutler it was harder to secure supply lines from Rome when so far advanced into Faliscan territory.

Pinna looked eastward. Mount Soracte rose in the distance, its snowcapped peaks at odds with the shimmering haze. She had never known a summer like it. The earth retained its heat until evening and not even darkness brought cool. And yet it was preferable to the past winter when the wind scissored her skin and ice coated the ground. In that season the campfires were doused too often by falling snow, and the thin walls of Marcus's tent did little to ward off cold. The chilblains and shivers reminded her of her experience as a night moth, and made her wonder if she had made a mistake in becoming an army wife. After a time, though, camp life became bearable. It was not nearly as onerous as days spent beside her mother scything with sore back and blistered hands. And freedom, too, gave her cause to thank Mater Matuta every day.

Around her, soldiers, squires, and manservants were busy pitching tents on the gentle sloping field. General Camillus liked to change locations regularly to make it more difficult for the enemy to plan attacks. The march had commenced at dawn. Now ditchers were swinging shovels and filling wicker baskets with soil in the midday sun. Soon the wide trench dug around the perimeter would be finished. And the woodcutters felling timber in the nearby woods would then splinter the pine into pickets that would rise two yards high.

With no expectations of what a camp would be like, Pinna was amazed to find it was a small town on the move. Farriers and cobblers, leather workers and blacksmiths, all went about their business for the purposes of war. And she had grown used to the smell of dung and the odor of donkeys and milking goats corralled in the animal enclosure, their braying and bleating a constant.

As she walked through the encampment she was conscious of men's stares. Such attention always confused her. She thought herself unremarkable. At the lupanaria, customers had often chosen her over her sisters, but she thought the reason no more than the effect of cosmetics and lust. Now she found men still scrutinized her even though her face was devoid of carmine and kohl. And although she no longer sat naked outside a cell, it seemed her shawl and tunic failed to hide a narrow waist and full breasts. Marcus had remarked one time that it was lucky he was unlikely to be jealous. She had smiled at his jest, confident that men might ogle her but would never try to touch her. No soldier would attempt to steal an officer's concubine.

By the time she reached the tent, Marcus was already checking his armor, making sure sufficient beeswax had been used to polish the leather and metal of his corselet, and that his round bronze shield was burnished as befitting a knight.

She placed her purchases in one corner next to the lard and flour before arranging the clay jars of wine and water beside them. "I want to get everything in order by dinnertime," she said, finding a position for the cook pot, plates, and spoons.

Marcus smiled. "Disciplined as always. You would make a good soldier, Pinna."

"I have to be tidy since you insist on such modest quarters. I'll never understand why you don't have a bigger tent like the other officers."

Marcus checked the blade of his spear. "All I need is somewhere to sleep and some storage. I think myself lucky. The common soldiers must crowd together in their tents."

The last items unpacked were their mats. There was no need for sheepskin and blankets in this heatwave. Reluctant to lie under the stuffy tent of leather yet again, Pinna made a suggestion. "We've had such restless nights of late. Perhaps we could sleep in the open this evening. There might be a breeze."

Marcus stopped his inspection. "I don't think that's wise. It's more difficult to pretend that we are . . . well . . . together."

Headstrong, Pinna stood waiting with the mats at the tent opening. "Marcus, you know Roman soldiers don't show affection in public. No one will think it odd that we don't share a bed when lying under the stars."

He chuckled. "True enough. Set up outside then. But remember, you're to address me as 'my lord' in front of the others."

Pinna liked to hear his laughter. Proximity over the months had led to a friendship of sorts. The pretense of convincing others

she was his concubine had been a strain at first. He was irritated
that he had conceded to her coercion. Over time, though, his awkward greetings and stilted commands had relaxed into conversation as he realized she could survive without complaining. To her
surprise, she found he liked women even though he did not desire
them. And although there was no chatter or gossip between them,
knowing his secret led to understanding his fears and failings,
dreams and ambitions.

As she bustled about, one of the general's servants appeared.
"General Camillus is calling for you, sir."

Marcus nodded and immediately straightened his belt and
tunic. The commander expected his officers to be well groomed.

"The general is asking for Pinna, too, sir."

Her heartbeat quickened.

Marcus frowned. "Does he have one of his headaches again?"

"Yes, sir."

Pinna collected some puls bread and stashed it into her basket
together with various flasks. "Is his headache very bad?"

The man grimaced. "Bad enough to need you. Bad enough to
be ill-tempered, too."

The white flag marking the command tent's position hung
limp in the hot, windless day. Pinna and the manservant struggled to keep up with Marcus as he strode through the main avenue
toward it.

Camillus sat outside on his curved chair. Orderlies dithered
around him as he barked directions. The grooves on either side of
his mouth were deep, his forehead furrowed.

Drusus sat on a stool beside him, tall even when seated, his
corselet with the boar's-head crest emblazoned on its bronze pectorals emphasizing his frame. Disgust registered on his face when
he saw her. Pinna's sense of excitement and importance at being
summoned drained away. She braced herself for the familiar wave
of dread and revulsion that always swept through her at the sight

of him. Terror that he might harm her again. Self-loathing for how he'd made her feel unclean. And fear that he could reveal she'd been a night moth.

Then the surge subsided. She reminded herself he had reason to be afraid of her. She had power, too. They had reached an impasse, and she could tell that it infuriated him that he was frustrated by her ability to threaten him in turn.

Pinna steadied herself and met his gaze. He looked away.

"Ah, good," said Camillus, noticing her. "I need you to rid me of this pain."

"I will try, my lord."

Her skill with curing aches and injuries was well known. Marcus always boasted how he recovered faster than others. Word spread. Soon she was tending to his fellow soldiers, and then the general. Over the past three seasons she'd done this many times.

Her care was rudimentary, her supplies simple: bandages, bone needles, and the three cure-alls of mustard seed, castor leaves, and knitbone. Her mortar and pestle had become her dearest possessions. The rhythm of pounding and grinding such plants granted her satisfaction that she could do good, that she was no longer needed for her body. The poultices she brewed calmed contusions and drew pus from boils. Congestion was cleared, coughs soothed, and inflammations lessened.

Yet she was renowned for more than just her remedies. Her greatest talent was to heal by touch. Despite her slightness, her arms and hands were strong. She had been a farmer's daughter who'd labored at ten years of age, and with hard work her strength had returned. She used her hands to rub away pain and tension, and to help men exercise, which hastened the mending of muscle and bone.

"Shall I prepare a poultice for you?"

Camillus motioned to Marcus to sit down beside Drusus. "No. Just massage my neck while I talk."

Rubbing some oil onto her hands, Pinna stood behind him. She brushed his hair away before encircling his neck with her fingers and pressing her thumbs into the base of his skull. He gave a small moan then bent his head forward, exposing more of his neck.

The first time Marcus had recommended her, she was amazed to find Camillus remembered her name. She had flushed with pleasure, then shook with nerves at the prospect of touching him, aware that her hands were red and roughened from washing and other chores.

Soon he was asking for her whenever he suffered headaches. While it distressed her to see him grappling with pain so severe his vision sometimes blurred, it also pleased her that she was the only one who could provide him with relief.

He was a man of moods. His smile was warm, his laughter infectious, but she saw the dark side of him also. The frustration of his ambitions enraged him even as it spurred him to strive harder.

As the two soldiers waited for Camillus to speak, Pinna massaged the general in silence. Drusus scrutinized her every movement. She avoided looking over to him, but even so she could feel his contempt.

Marcus observed her without expression, but she sensed his unease at the familiarity between his commander and his concubine. Neither he nor Drusus could afford for her to whisper secrets into their leader's ear.

Camillus kept his head bowed, taking a deep breath whenever she probed any sore spots. Pinna concentrated on loosening the knots of muscle. She liked the way the sinews were strong, leading into the ridge of his shoulders. She spread her fingers along them, then across the base of his throat. There was a lump in his clavicle where the bone had not knitted properly after being broken in some past conflict.

Marcus ventured a question as the general relaxed under Pinna's touch. "Do you have orders for us, sir?"

Camillus lifted his head. His eyes were bloodshot. "Yes, I need both of you to escort the plunder back to Rome. And take the badly wounded with you so they may be tended in their homes."

Disappointment crossed both men's faces. Marcus's look was fleeting, wary of offending his commander. Drusus was less able to hide his emotions.

"Do you have some complaint, Claudius Drusus?"

Drusus was quick to shake his head, but the tense way he held his body signaled he was far from happy. "No, sir, it's just I think I might be better able to serve by fighting a battle than guarding a wagon train."

"Is that so?" Camillus lowered his head again to give Pinna greater purchase. "Well, there'll be no battles while you're absent. Only more raiding parties."

The two officers glanced at each other. The news was far from heartening. There was no need for valor nor any great danger posed from sacking villages. No chance for glory either.

Pinna had often wondered why the general didn't attempt to storm Falerii's citadel. Three seasons had passed with no siege lines dug or war engines constructed. Didn't he think the Faliscans should be punished for helping the Veientanes trounce Sergius? Marcus often complained in private about the lack of action. He longed to ride into battle with spear leveled while the heavy infantry clashed phalanx against phalanx. Instead forts were manned on crossroads to blockade trade, and Roman supply bases were established. There had been constant skirmishes, though. So far the enemy had failed to defeat Camillus when his troops remained mobile: attacking, pillaging, and retreating with lightning speed.

Every time Pinna served fruit, eggs, and vegetables or cooked fresh meat she tried to forget that they were seized from poor farmers. She could imagine only too well the desperation left in the wake of the attacks. It was harder to ignore her knowledge of the killings, rapes, and torture. She told herself they were the enemy. That if General Camillus did not act it would be Roman farmers and their families who would suffer such treatment.

When the decurions said nothing, the commander raised his head and growled, "I gather you expected me to have taken Falerii by now. But how exactly do you propose that be done? It is surrounded by ravines. Access to it is only from one side and that is protected by high walls, mound, and ditch. And it is no use meeting in battle outside the city. A phalanx formation collapses over broken terrain."

A slight stammer crept into Drusus's speech. "But Veii's defenses are the same, sir. Are you telling us we won't be able to take that city, too?"

Camillus straightened his shoulders, causing Pinna to stop her treatment. His movement was minor but ominous. "No, but I think Rome needs other tactics. Squeeze our enemies of supplies. Truly starve them. Neither Veii nor Falerii can afford to lose fertile farmlands. I intend to burn Faliscan crops and raze their towns instead of stealing grain. With their harvest destroyed their worst fears will come true. And then, instead of breaching Falerii's gates, we will force its people to open them from hunger and disease. We will finally make them pass beneath the yoke."

Marcus stared at him. "Burn their crops, sir? Surely we should send the produce back to Rome? What of the drought in our city? And the famine?"

"Do you question my strategy?"

Marcus swallowed. "No, sir. I just don't fully understand it."

The general rubbed his brow and sighed, but when he spoke his usual determination overcame weariness. "Rome has endured hardship before and will survive it now. As I've said before, sometimes there has to be suffering to gain benefit. We must stand strong in adversity. In time, rain will come."

Pinna was glad she was no longer massaging him. She was sure her dismay would be conveyed through her touch. This man was harsh. Was he right to let Rome starve while trying to inflict the same fate upon its foe?

Marcus nodded. "It will take bravery, then. From all citizens."

Camillus tapped his gold ring. "Yes, one that Calvus must understand." He gestured for Pinna to resume. She pressed her fingers into muscles that had once again tightened.

The general focused on the Aemilian. "Marcus, you must also persuade your father of the value of my plan. No doubt the commoners and nobles continue to bicker, thinking not of strategies but plots, not of tactics but conspiracies. That is another reason why I wish you to return. I need to know the politics in my absence. Speak to Aemilius and convince him of my reasons for not besieging Falerii. He most of all understands the difficulties of direct assault on such a city. He has been the only general so far who has come close to touching Veii's walls. I want him to direct his energies to supporting, not undermining, me."

The soldier saluted. "I will talk to him, sir. I will make him understand." His demeanor had changed from frustration to fervor. And Pinna knew that, despite his love and respect for his father, it was Camillus alone whom he would follow to the brink.

Drusus stood also. "And my orders, sir? Would you like me to canvass support as well?"

Camillus waved his hand dismissively. "Of course, of course. Do what you can with those of your friends who might listen."

Drusus's face fell. He and Marcus were already the commander's acolytes. At every opportunity they vied with other officers for the general's attention. Both lived to be praised; were despondent if ignored or criticized. Yet Pinna felt no sympathy that Drusus had been reduced to merely being an escort for a caravan.

The general had not finished with his decurions. "As for armed conflict, neither of you must despair. Vel Mastarna has not been successful at the Etruscan League, but his troops are shoring up the Faliscan army. I can't afford for him to thwart our blockades or come to the aid of townships we've already taken. We may yet have to engage him in pitched battle on the plain."

The red-haired officer clenched his fists by his sides. His stutter had disappeared. "I would do more than make Mastarna submit to our control, sir."

Camillus leaned his weight onto the armrest. "Oh, and what would that be, soldier?"

"Exact vengeance for Rome—torture the smooth-skinned bastard before he is slain. Then raze Veii to the ground."

Goose bumps rose on Pinna's arms, remembering the words carved into the lead defixio. Drusus now had a better chance to make real his curse.

"And Aemilia Caeciliana? What revenge would you mete upon her?"

Drusus was careful to avoid Pinna's gaze. "Execute her."

Pinna gasped. Given the love spell on the other defixio, it surprised her that Drusus would voice such false hatred. Her noise caused the general to glance around at her. She bowed her head and concentrated on her task.

Camillus knew the Claudian's history, though. "Such hatred coming from a man who shouted to the delegations of both cities that you wished to marry her. You smeared the blood from your wounded calf onto the spear used to declare war. Are you telling me you are no longer infatuated with Caecilia?"

Drusus stood to attention and rattled out his answer. "I was only twenty, sir. I now see her for what she is. I vow to do all I can to see her punished."

The general studied the tall, lean soldier for long moments. Pinna thought Drusus would buckle under such scrutiny, but he managed to remain straight-backed and unflinching. Finally,

Camillus turned to Marcus. "And you? Would you swear such an oath?"

Pinna wondered why the general was so persistent in testing Marcus's loyalty to Rome. The Aemilian had already declared that he put the state's purpose above all else, but pledging to see his cousin executed required ultimate allegiance. Marcus also stood to attention. "Yes, sir. She has dishonored my family. I swear to seek retribution."

His lack of hesitation was impressive, yet Pinna knew Marcus to be adept at lying. Hadn't he shown similar certitude before when assuring the general that Drusus didn't seek personal revenge? And his ability to repress his true feelings for his friend showed him to be a master at deception.

Camillus also examined Marcus as though weighing whether his sentences were a bluff. "Strong words," he finally said when the officer did not waver from meeting his gaze. Then he put his hand to his neck, stretching it from side to side, bored with continuing his inquisition. "Keep rubbing," he said to Pinna. "My headache has not shifted."

Marcus stood to attention. "Will that be all, sir?"

"Yes, you're both dismissed."

The officers saluted, but as they turned to leave, Camillus summoned Marcus once again. "I hope you would have no objection to Pinna visiting me while you're absent."

Surprised, the girl stopped her task, her hands remaining on the general as she waited for the answer. Yet what could Marcus do other than agree? He was hardly going to deny his commander relief from pain. He saluted again. "Of course not, sir. No objection at all."

Camillus bent his elbow and patted Pinna's hand as it lay on his shoulder. His action was so unexpected it startled her. The contact was brief, though. She longed for a repetition.

"Because, you know she's the only one who is able to ease my pain."

Pinna nodded to Marcus in gratitude for consenting. He ignored her. Then she caught sight of Drusus. The grim line of his mouth and the harshness in his eyes proclaimed that it was not just Vel Mastarna whom he wanted dead.

THIRTY

His decurions gone, Camillus groaned and pressed his fingers against his temples.

"A poultice will help you, my lord," Pinna said. "The heat loosens the muscles. Go inside and lie down while I prepare one."

"I don't have time to rest."

"It is because you sleep so little that you suffer. Come, none of your men would begrudge you some respite. And no man would ever accuse you of weakness."

Camillus rose and entered the tent. Pinna liked the subtle power she exerted over him. It reminded her of how Fusca could coax her father.

Breaking the hard puls bread into pieces, Pinna placed it in a cook pot and moistened it with water. When it had turned to porridge she ladled some of the mixture into a bowl, adding mustard and vinegar. The afternoon was hot and the fire only added to the temperature. Sunset would not be for hours.

Carrying her basket and the bowl inside, she found Camillus lying on his cot, eyes closed.

The interior was roomy enough for his officers to gather and consult with him. It was furnished austerely with only a pallet, chair, and wooden table. An unfurled map was held down at the corners with paperweights, and scrolls and correspondence were stacked in a pile together with his stylus. His panoply was positioned against one wall, the boss on his shield and the bronze pectorals on his corselet molded with a wolf's head, teeth bared, threatening and terrifying. A wolf's pelt, not a sheepskin, covered his bed.

When she knelt beside him, he opened one eye to view the bowl and bandages, then closed it again. "I suppose you're going to slap mustard on me."

She stirred the porridge. "You know the vinegar lessens the burn. Besides, a general should hardly fear a little heat."

He smiled and shifted his shoulders to make himself more comfortable on the bed.

Pinna was no longer worried about being bold. The first time she'd teased him she expected him to bark at her. Instead he indulged her joking. In fact she thought he rather liked it, when everyone else about him was careful of what they said. She also suspected he liked flirting, although there was a boundary set between them. He never made advances nor did she encourage them.

Sometimes he would talk to her. Like Genucius, he would tell her his worries in the quiet times when the pain eased. Their conversations were different from the plebeian's, though. Whereas Genucius expected her to keep her opinions to herself, Camillus let her speak. She knew she was not the only one to whom he listened. He made it his business to know all that happened in his camp. He visited the sick and injured, and inspected the healthy, too. Here was no patrician officer aloof from his soldiers. He recalled the names of all he commanded. He knew the veterans' histories, too: how they had gained their wounds, how often they had volunteered to fight for Rome. She saw how they would grin when he hailed them, appreciating being the center of his attention, even if just for one brief moment.

She was no different. He flattered her when he sought to learn her story. She only told him part of it: that she was a daughter of a soldier, that her father had been forced into bondage, that she was orphaned. He thought she was an impoverished citizen. The other part was fanciful. She was a little ashamed she found it so easy to lie, telling him that she'd found work in the House of Aemilius and then caught the eye of its young master.

She dreaded he would discover her secret. For there was another type of woman in the camp besides army wives. Whores escaping from Faliscan townships. Pinna kept clear of them, fearing that they would sense her old profession. Considering them disruptive, Camillus did not approve of their presence, but tolerated them for his men's sake.

"Please sit up for a moment, my lord. I need to apply the poultice."

Camillus complied without comment, resting his elbows on his knees as he leaned forward, his hands cradling his head.

His decision to raze Faliscan crops weighed on Pinna's mind. Rome needed that corn. And the camp would suffer also when supplies were low. Camillus was both courageous and cruel to allow Rome to suffer so that he could defeat a foe.

She pushed down the edge of his tunic at the neckline so she could smear the moist mixture onto his skin. "My lord, won't you find it hard to let our people suffer when they cry out for succor?"

He turned his head and frowned. "Do you think me heartless, Pinna?"

"Of course not, my lord." Her heartbeat doubled, worried she was displeasing him, and yet the memory of experiencing drought and famine drove her to continue. "It's just that I know what it's like to be desperate for food. To scrounge in the dirt for husks to eat. To watch the misery of withered cattle dying in dried-up river courses, their carcasses picked clean by crows."

He straightened his back and studied her. To avoid his gaze she began bandaging his neck so that the mess was held in place against his skin. He placed his hand on hers to hinder her. Her heartbeat trebled at his touch.

"What a hard life you've had, Pinna. I feel for the plight of your family. I am sorry your father was enslaved due to Rome's failure to reward him with booty and land. And yet you should remember that before his bondage he answered the call for the levy every year. He wanted to fight. He understood that failing to do so only threatened our city's safety. Don't you think he would be prepared to experience short-term privation for long-term gain?"

Pinna sat back on her heels and reluctantly withdrew her hand from under his. He talked of his sympathy for the common soldier and yet wagonloads of loot were stored in the enclosure ready for Marcus and Drusus to transport to the treasury. The sight of Faliscan armor, coins, and jewelry piled high next to water, food, and forage rankled. Camillus had the chance to lessen his men's debts and yet he never granted them part of the spoils. If not for their loyalty to the general, discontent could easily descend into mutiny. "What gains would that be, my lord? When all the plunder is sent back to Rome."

She waited for him to order her to leave. To her surprise, he sighed. "Little citizen, you must understand that the more booty paid into state coffers the less war tax need be levied. If I rewarded my own troops with some, less would be available to benefit all." Once again he pressed his fingers against his temples. "Rain must come soon, Pinna. And then Rome will be able to reap its own crops. And if I am successful, Romans will plant seeds on the land of our enemies as well. Warriors like your father will finally receive their share."

Seeing the yellow of the mustard was bleeding through the bandage, Pinna busied herself wrapping another layer of cloth around his throat. His words reminded her of his conversation in Marcus's house last autumn. She took a deep breath before she spoke. "Even though you said to Senator Aemilius that promises cost nothing when it comes to giving land to the plebeians?"

She was confused when he smiled, the creases around his eyes deepening. "Ah, I forgot that you listen, not only hear. But the matter is complicated." He lay down upon the bed and closed his eyes. "And until Rome unifies, then conquers, its enemies, all of this is merely talk."

Sensing he wished to be alone, Pinna rose, knocking over the oil flask. Thinking it a bad omen because she had challenged a general, she scanned the tent for the amphora of wine and then ladled some onto the floor without permission. When she looked up Camillus was watching her.

"What are you doing?"

"To spill oil is ill luck, my lord. Pouring a little wine afterward is a protection."

"That's just superstition."

She pointed to his golden ring. "And yet you tap that often enough. Is that not a way to ward off the evil eye?"

He swiveled the ring around his finger. "I took this from the Volscian who speared me in the thigh. I did not realize I tap it."

"Maybe you are more superstitious than you think, my lord."

His voice hardened. "No, I just like to remind myself what can be taken from you in defeat. Only women or weaklings who believe in dark forces need superstitions to protect them."

She bowed her head. "I am sorry, my lord. My mother taught me to believe in magic. I did not mean to offend you."

He settled his head on the pillow again, his tone less sharp. "Do not mind me. I am quick to temper today."

The afternoon sun was still strong as it beat upon the leather walls of the tent. It had grown stuffy, the lack of air causing Pinna to perspire. She saw that he was sweating, too. She checked the poultice. "It's not burning, is it?"

He rolled his neck from side to side. "No, but the warmth is spreading."

"Then rest, my lord, rest."

"You treat me like a child."

She smiled, packing away the bowl and flasks in her basket.

"But I do not want you to be my nursemaid."

Blushing, she swung around, not sure what to say. Was he merely flirting? He turned on his side to study her. "It's such a pity you belong to another."

Her heart raced again. She wanted to blurt out the truth that she was Marcus's concubine but he was not her man. Or was she just imagining that Camillus desired her? Her hands trembled as she gripped the handle. "Marcus Aemilius is a good man, my lord."

He lay back on the cot and closed his eyes. "Yes, and honorable. As am I."

She lifted the tent flap and murmured, "My lord, I do not want to be your nursemaid either." She did not know if he heard her. His eyes remained closed. He did not move.

THIRTY-ONE

Preoccupied with her conversation with Camillus, Pinna's footsteps were slow but her spirits light as she walked through the encampment.

Men were training. Some boxed, hands bound with leather straps. Others circled each other before lunging to wrestle. The hoplites were practicing in two formations, shields overlapping, charging each other. More often than not the sprains and breaks she mended were suffered in practice, not fighting.

Lost in thought, she did not notice Drusus until he stepped out in front of her. At every chance he would menace her. It was always unnerving. Her skin crawled whenever he was near. Pulse sharp and rapid, she tried to pass but he barred her way, his sinewy animal frame looming over her.

"The general likes you."

Goose bumps prickled her arms. "I soothe his headaches. I believe him grateful."

"You want more, though."

She tried to move on. "There is nothing between us."

Again he hindered her. "Make sure it stays that way."

Gaining courage that in truth she was growing closer to Camillus, she became defiant when he continued to block her. If Drusus exposed her secret, then it would be his downfall also. "It made me laugh to hear you bragging about killing Aemilia Caeciliana. Did you know the general despises those who believe in superstition? How I long to tell him you invoked magic to defeat an enemy, then inscribed an enchantment as you blubbered like a child, lovesick for the traitoress."

He gripped her wrist with his bony fingers. Panicked, Pinna dropped the basket and tried to wrench away, her heart thumping. In desperation she nodded toward the men training nearby. "Do you want them to see you mistreating your friend's woman? Let me go."

Turning his body to shield her from view, he held her firm. "You little whore. I should let all know your skin was once ingrained with dirt from fucking men in a graveyard."

Once again she tried to squirm from his grasp, determined to fight back so she could gain the attention of the other soldiers. "And I'll make sure Furius Camillus knows you're the type of man who needs to rape a prostitute."

Drusus pulled her closer, bending her wrist back. She gasped in pain. She could feel his breath upon her hair. His smell and nearness triggered memories. Just as on that night, she froze, reliving how he held her down. How he made her feel like nothing. "Please, you're hurting me."

His lips pressed against her ear, the bristle of his beard grazing her skin. Venom oiled his voice. No stammer. "I should slit your throat after dark." Then he shoved her so that she stumbled.

Regaining her balance, Pinna kept distance between them, a knot in her belly. As she nursed her wrist, she thought how this man was a brute when he'd raped her and would be a coward if he slew her.

Drusus attempted to seize her elbow. She shied away. "Please let me pass."

He glanced over to the training soldiers, who had not noticed anything amiss. "I don't understand why Marcus keeps you."

"I've already told you. As a reward for my honesty. And he took pity on me for what you did."

He spat in the dust. "I don't believe you."

She stood her ground although her heartbeat still raced and she felt as if she could vomit. "So what are you going to do? Reveal that I was a tomb whore? Marcus Aemilius would not thank you for letting me share his bed for months without such a warning." Her eyes narrowed. "Or would shaming him give you satisfaction?"

Confusion replaced his scowl. "What are you talking about?"

"Because whenever Furius Camillus praises him envy crosses your face as transparent as pain."

He flushed, stutter returning. "I—I don't know what you mean."

"Are you going to let me pass?"

Drusus stepped aside, no longer looming above her.

Relieved, Pinna picked up her basket and walked on.

— • —

Marcus was organizing his kit when she entered their tent. Pinna hastened to help him, her hands quaking after the effort of being brave.

He put down his shield. "What's the matter? Your face is so pale. And you're trembling."

Pinna struggled to calm her voice as she massaged her chafed wrist. "Claudius Drusus. He loathes me."

Marcus lifted her hand to examine the redness. "But he has hurt you. I will speak to him."

"No! Please don't. It's nothing. It looks worse than it is." She dared not tell him how sick his friend's hatred had become. That now he spoke of murder.

Marcus's expression remained troubled. She knew Drusus had expressed his disgust and puzzlement to him that he had taken her as his army wife, and that he doubted his explanation.

"Why did he accost you?"

"He still remains unconvinced as to why I'm your concubine. He wants to expose me as a whore but knows that would harm your reputation."

Marcus frowned and Pinna sensed his concern for her had changed to disquiet for himself.

"Do you think he suspects the real reason?" His anxiety deepened. "You aren't thinking of telling him the truth, are you?"

Pinna sighed, tired of being the key to these men's secrets, the cipher to their fears. "No, Marcus. I'll never tell him of your feelings for him." She moved across to his kit. "I don't want to talk about it anymore. Let me help you with your armor."

As she assisted Marcus to don corselet and greaves, she thought how fond of him she had grown. He emulated Camillus. Like the general he was popular with his men: fair when disciplining them, brave when leading them, and asking no more of them than what he asked of himself.

Yet he remained reserved, wanting only the camaraderie, not friendship, of the other soldiers to ensure there was no temptation to seek out those who shared a similar secret. For holding their gaze for long seconds could lead to doing what he dreamed of with Drusus. And the consequences of succumbing and being caught would mean humiliation, then execution.

In keeping with their sham, she always arranged their pallets close to each other. It was strange to sleep beside a man all night instead of briefly sharing a bed for coupling. Yet after a while what was odd became normal. It was pleasant to have someone next to her upon waking. She'd not had such company since Fusca. And she was grateful to him. She no longer had to service men every night. No longer risked catching the pox. And her womb pain had abated.

He lay with no one. Not even servant boys. The irony amused her. Both of them feigned sharing their bed and bodies but in truth were celibate and chaste. At dawn, though, he would satisfy himself by hand when he thought she was sleeping: working himself in small furtive movements, holding his breath, stifling sound. She thought the guilt trapped inside him was a sickness. She wished she could offer comfort but he asked for none. She guessed he would not welcome it either. The self-loathing with which he was consumed was distressing. He resorted to purgatives and mutilation, inwardly and outwardly punishing his body for the betrayal of his soul. She would often clean and bandage the small cuts he inflicted upon his wrists. He would pretend they were scrapes from skirmishes or training. She would not challenge this other than to comment that he was lucky his blood had not been poisoned.

Now, tightening a buckle on his corselet, she felt a twinge of pain. Seeing her wince, Marcus took her hand. "I'll strap this for you before I go. Mind you, I don't have your magic touch."

A surge of tenderness welled in her at a warrior being prepared to act as nurse to a woman. And suddenly she needed to understand his desire for his brutal friend. "Tell me, why do you love him?"

He let go of her hand.

"It's just that I don't understand how one who is kind could want another who is cruel."

When he said nothing, she grew nervous that he was so angry he'd lost the power of speech. Then, to her surprise, he collected their two stools and arranged them side by side. "Bring me a bandage and I'll see to that wrist."

He began wrapping the strip of cloth around her hand. His touch was gentle, his fingers nimble. "Drusus was wrong to treat you the way he did. But on that night he was upset at being unfairly branded a coward."

She controlled her irritation at his defense of his friend, not wanting to discourage his continuing. She kept her voice even. "Are you telling me I am the only whore he has ever mistreated?"

At her question, he became clumsy. Unwrapping the bandage, he bent over the task as though avoiding eye contact would make it easier to talk. "I know you think Drusus harsh. But he was not always so. He has grown bitter because of my cousin. He loved her, you see. He wanted to marry her but his father would not allow him. Cilla's mother was an Aemilian but her father was a wealthy plebeian. Claudius Drusus Senior did not want his son to marry a half-caste." He paused, shaking his head. "Poor Cilla, if only she'd been allowed to wed Drusus."

The register in his voice when he spoke of his "Cilla" hinted at melancholy. It gave her pause after the oath he'd sworn that day to see her die. And to learn Drusus had considered a commoner for a wife intrigued her. His patrician arrogance was another reason she despised him. "But did she love him?"

"I think, in the beginning, she did. And so Drusus thought she wanted to come back to him when she ran away from her husband. He was prepared to marry her despite the blood taint she bore for being an Etruscan wife."

Pinna remembered hearing how Drusus had shouted his intention to wed the traitoress to the world. Pity for the Claudian edged into her thoughts. Drusus had been twenty at that time. Her age now. She doubted she could ever feel such passion. "But she didn't love him after all."

Marcus shook his head. "Something broke inside him when she decided to go back to Mastarna. He could not understand why, when she'd only just returned to Rome. For a long time it was easier for him to claim that the Veientane had abducted her." He split the end of the strip of cloth and tied it off before finally looking at her. "But as time wore on he could no longer deny that she'd chosen Mastarna over him. I worry that his heart is scarred and will never mend."

Pinna didn't comment. She also doubted Drusus's soul could be repaired. "And you? Did you ever think her husband kidnapped her?"

"No. I knew the Etruscan did not take Cilla against her will. To say that is like believing a virgin with a swollen belly protesting she had never lifted her skirts. I saw my cousin's distress when she thought Mastarna was lost to her forever."

He raked his fingers through his hair. "Mastarna should have left her alone. He broke his word. He'd divorced her in front of ten witnesses. And Cilla promised me she would accept the life of a Roman woman again. She promised me, too, that she would never dishonor my father and our family."

He was agitated now, his voice ragged. Finally, given a chance to vent his frustration, he needed to purge himself. "My cousin gave these assurances and then she broke them. She should never have returned to Veii. She has disgraced the Aemilians and her father's clan, too. She has been a traitor to all Romans. For that I can never forgive her."

As he finished his tirade he pinched the bridge of his nose, squeezing his eyes with the fingers of one hand. Pinna rested her bandaged hand on his arm. "Do you really hate her? Want her executed?"

He stiffened, his face coloring. Pinna sensed she had pressed too hard. Yet after a pause, he lowered his defenses at last. "She should never have been married to Mastarna in the first place. I was angry at our politicians for treating her badly. Her father had died and she was vulnerable. And my own father took advantage of the fact she was half plebeian and patrician. He made her a symbol of unified Rome. A cynical move to try and end the class war so that poor soldiers would not balk at joining the levy. In truth, though, she was just a scared young girl sent to live with a foe." He squeezed his eyes again, removing any trace of sadness. "She was my friend. I confided in her things I could not tell others." He met her gaze. "As I do you."

Pinna smiled. It was the first time he'd acknowledged their friendship. It pleased her he was revealing memories he'd suppressed for years—of Drusus and the traitoress she'd been encouraged to revile. Was she wrong to condemn Aemilia Caeciliana? She touched his shoulder. "Yet you swore today to seek retribution."

He straightened his shoulders as though steeling himself. "I'm a Roman soldier, Pinna. My duty is to the state. There is no other choice. Her decision to return to Mastarna shamed my family. And I can't forget the torment she has caused Drusus."

Hearing his concern for his friend, Pinna wished she could tell him the Claudian still loved Caecilia even though he spouted words of vengeance. It also confused her that the man of whom he spoke was far removed from the vicious one who'd assaulted her. It made her even more curious as to why Marcus desired Drusus.

Marcus began to rise but she kept her hand on his arm to delay him. "You've told me Drusus loved Caecilia but you still haven't told me why you love him."

His brow creased. "Why is it so important to you?"

"Because I want to understand why he is worthy to be cherished." She ran her fingers over one of his metal wristbands. "I want to know why there are cuts in flesh that is protected by bronze."

He extended his arms, rotating them as he examined them. Then he eased back in his seat and sighed. "It goes back to our childhood. Drusus had little tenderness in his life. I fear the seed of violence was planted in him by a father who used his fists on his wife and daughters. And beat his only son when he tried to defend them. Drusus's body and face were always covered with both faded and fresh bruises." He rubbed the scar that puckered the corner of his eye. "And so when Claudius Senior died, I was glad to see the man who never spoke a sweet word smothered in honey and wine when they interred his ashes."

Pinna was stunned. She tried to reconcile the image of the battered boy with that of her assailant. Yet the legacy of hurt did not excuse Drusus's crime against her. "You say you met when you were young."

"Yes, at school. Drusus was long-limbed, awkward, and had faltering speech—a boy born to be mocked despite his height and weight and temper. And restlessness dogged him. He always fidgeted in his chair and called out constantly. Unfortunately, when he was teased he retaliated with such ferocity his bullies became victims, and punishment was exacted on him alone.

"I was the opposite. You might not believe it now but I was smaller than most. And the other boys disliked me for knowing answers that they struggled to remember. The stem of a stylus, not the haft of a spear, centered me then. Of course, that was not good enough for my father. I'll never forget the day I donned a man's toga at fourteen. He opened our ancestor cupboard to show me the death masks of Aemilian consuls, judges, magistrates, and generals. Then he declared his dream. He wanted me to be the youngest of our family to hold supreme office." He uttered a wry laugh. "After that I was glad such heroes were only displayed on special occasions. I was sure they had judged me and found me wanting."

Pinna frowned. She could not understand Marcus's apprehension. Over the past year she'd learned he was well qualified to meet Aemilius's expectations. After all, he had been a decorated war hero at twenty. And yet she knew he felt the pressure to drape a candidate's white toga around him and climb the Honored Way to a consulship. He'd often mentioned the need to capture fame when frustrated that Camillus would not engage the Faliscans. All Romans aspired to glory. It made a warrior manly. It added to family prestige. It gave an advantage in elections. The distinction of his great-uncle, Mamercus Aemilius, was a shadow as much as a beacon. "So how did you become friends when you were quiet and he was rowdy?"

For a moment Marcus's gaze grew distant as though not just recalling but reliving a memory. Pinna gently prompted him to continue. He focused on her again.

"Drusus was often bullied at school. I was, too, but for different reasons. And so we formed an alliance and then a friendship. One day after being taunted by another boy he stood up without permission and threw his writing tablet across the classroom. His tormentor went unseen by the teacher. Nor did he confess. Of course Drusus was ordered to be beaten. I could not bear the injustice so I championed him, challenging the pedagogue's judgment. As a result I was also birched."

Pinna thought of all the times she'd borne the brunt of her father's unfair beltings. Marcus's story of schoolboy punishment seemed scant reason for his lifelong devotion to his friend. "You stood up for Drusus. But what did he do for you that you so admire him?"

Marcus rubbed his scar again. "Because of what we shared that day. For I became the whipping tree over which Drusus was splayed to receive the caning. I was forced to bend my knees to brace his weight and pull his arms over my shoulders so he was stretched naked across my back. And then I had to listen to the sound of the switch as it rushed downward, the thwack as it split his skin, Drusus holding his breath, neither crying out nor weeping. He trembled, though. He could not hide that.

"I was not as brave. Drusus also acted as a tripod as I was thrashed. His blood was slick against my chest as I lay upon him. What agony he must have felt with my body upon his torn flesh. My tears must have been hot against his neck, my sobs loud in his ears. But after the punishment he whispered, 'One day we will be mighty generals, and this pedant will be nothing.'"

Imagining their pain and mortification, Pinna was confused to see Marcus smiling.

"Afterward, as we bathed each other's stripes, Drusus mimicked the teacher's reedy voice. He made me laugh despite my tears. From that day onward, we made a pact to always protect each other. And when we offered the clippings from our first beards to the gods and truly became men, we swore an oath always to guard each other in battle."

"One to which you have held true. Didn't you gain an oak leaf crown for saving his life at Anxur and holding ground until the conflict was over?"

His usual modesty emerged. "Not for any lack of courage on Drusus's part. His horse had been killed and his shoulder was dislocated in the fall so he could not raise his shield to defend himself. And his calf muscle was sliced to the bone, leaving him crippled, too."

Pinna had heard other soldiers professing that Drusus was brave. He had a reputation for never resiling from danger. Yet the risks he took were rash, giving equal balance to the chance of glory or disaster. He put the lives of his men in peril also, pushing them without praise. Pinna sensed they were wary of him. His zeal did not always impress Camillus either. He wanted his officers to be calculated in their war lust. It was clear he liked Marcus for his fearless but measured mien. "Even so, you showed the greater valor on that day."

Marcus shook his head. "It was more a case of nerves giving birth to courage. I managed to fend off three Volscians and drag Drusus to safety, then went back to continue fighting till the enemy was defeated. And all I could think as I rejoined my unit was that, despite our pact, one of us could die and one survive even as we fought shoulder to shoulder." He turned to her abruptly and held both her hands. "The thought he might be lost to me terrifies me more than the fear of dying. I would rather be dead than live without him."

This time it was the girl who looked down, unable to cope with his devotion. She suspected Drusus no longer felt bound by an oath made on the verge of manhood. "But, Marcus, I don't think he feels the same way. I think he now begrudges you delivering him from danger."

He stood up, knocking over his stool. "You know nothing."

"Don't I? Drusus owes his life to you. The burden of repaying such a debt can foster resentment as well as gratitude."

"That's not true. He knows I don't consider him obligated. And it would be the same if our positions were reversed."

Pinna stood as well. "Drusus is not like you."

"And you are colored in your judgment."

He stepped away and picked up his shield. Pinna felt helpless. "Please listen. You are blind to his failings and his envy! Even today he was aggrieved that the general did not recruit him to act as a diplomat. He knows Drusus would repel, not attract, possible supporters. Don't you see that your friend seethes with jealousy every time he is overlooked and you are chosen?"

"Enough!" His face was white, the pockmarks on his cheeks clear against his pallor, the scar on his neck livid.

Pinna obeyed, sensing that words of placation would only rile him.

Marcus adjusted his belt and balteus, ramming his sword into its scabbard and slinging his shield over his shoulder with a scrape of metal and squeak of leather. "Never speak to me of such things again. Drusus is loyal."

Anxious not to part on bad terms, Pinna hurried to fetch his helmet and pack some provisions before bidding him farewell. "Be careful, Marcus. The roads are dangerous. There may be raiding parties between here and Rome."

He remained gruff. "I will be back soon enough." Then, to her surprise, he held her upper arms. "Be warned, Pinna. I can see you are enamored of Furius Camillus. But to all in this camp you are my concubine. And remember you are indebted to me. I don't want to return to find you've been unfaithful—or that you have betrayed my secret."

Once again she claimed innocence but was nonplussed that her desire for Camillus was so obvious. "I only tend to his headaches. I would not do anything to dishonor you. Nor would the general."

As she helped him put on his cloak, she smoothed the material across his shoulders. "You saved my life, too. I pledge my fidelity to you."

He pulled away as though scalded by her touch. "Oh, but that allegiance comes at a price, remember?"

Pinna burned inside. His words were hurtful despite their truth. His earlier declaration of friendship had been retracted. She'd forgotten that the foundation upon which their confidences were shared was fragile and based on desperation: his to hide a vice, hers to escape degradation. "I swear I will never betray your secret."

Marcus paused. She could tell he was weighing her words and still found her lacking.

"I don't believe you."

She watched him throw back the tent flap and stride away, wanting to run after him and convince him that she was truly loyal. And to beg him to let her repair the flimsy bond she had broken between them.

PORTENTS

THIRTY-TWO

Veii, Late Summer, 397 BC

Semni found Arruns training at dawn in the brief coolness between stifling night and searing day. He was practicing with his spear on the small patch of lawn beside the stable. His lance thudded against the wooden wall. The tip embedded deeply, vibrating with the impact. The freshly splintered row of gouges in the timber was evidence he'd thrown it many times.

When he walked back to retrieve it, she expected the Phoenician to yank out the javelin, but instead he gripped the haft with one hand then laid his forearm against the wall, resting his brow against it.

His despondency was disconcerting. Here was a man who prided himself on repressing emotion. He did not seek companionship, either, encouraging people to be wary.

Conscious that she was as much an intruder upon his mood as on his exercise, the girl hesitated to disturb him. She heaved Nerie higher on her hip. The one-year-old had laid his head on her shoulder, sucking his thumb. When he saw Arruns, though, he raised his head and pointed. "Roons! Roons!"

The guard spun around then turned back to the wall to pull out the spear. "What are you doing here, Semni?"

She lowered her son to the ground. He tottered like a little drunkard toward the man, who crouched, then swung the infant onto his bare shoulders. Nerie squealed and tapped Arruns's shaven head as if it was a drum, unperturbed that his fingers were also touching the head of a serpent.

"Cook is punishing me. Setting me to work on the hand mill. I bet it was Cytheris's idea."

"What did you do this time?"

She stuck out her chin. "I haven't got into trouble for ages!"

Arruns said nothing as he lifted Nerie over his head and set him down. The boy sat with a bump onto his bottom and promptly raised his arms.

Ignoring him, the guard lay on his stomach on the grass and began doing push-ups. Thinking it a game, Nerie climbed onto his back. Arruns bore his weight as if the tot was a fly. The child giggled each time the man raised and lowered himself, slipping off and then climbing on again.

Semni ladled some grain from an amphora into the stone hopper of the quern. She was not looking forward to the monotony of turning the handle round and round for the next few hours. And so she dallied, pretending to ready herself but instead studying the Phoenician with surreptitious glances. She had not chosen daybreak to work just for its coolness. She knew Arruns always trained at that time. His master might have been absent but the guard needed to remain fit to protect Mastarna's family.

Most women recoiled from him, seeing him only as a hired killer. Yet it was this sense of danger that attracted Semni. His latent power. The broad fingers that carefully held her son's frail body could also pummel someone when curled into fists. She imagined them upon her, perhaps gentle, perhaps rough. Either way she grew excited.

Aricia thought the guard grotesque because of his tattoo. To Semni the markings were art wrought in flesh instead of clay. The snake's scales rippled under the flex and tightening of the musculature of Arruns's massive neck and back, the sloping shoulders and the curve of pectorals and ridges of abdomen. She wondered how many needle pricks he must have endured as the ink was hammered, inch by inch, into his swarthy flesh. She also imagined smoothing her hand along the coils that slithered around him. Wanting to satisfy her curiosity whether the serpent writhed beneath the guard's short kilt.

There was no intricate patterning upon his arms and legs but there were scars. Cuts scored his forearms and marks marred his thighs. The Phoenician was not entitled to wear cuirass, helmet, or greaves in battle. He may have been a rich man's protector but his only armor was shield, dagger, and spear.

Compact and proportioned, Arruns's physique was made for brawling, not the structured exercise of a gymnasium. His calves and thighs were sturdy, defined above the knee; his biceps brawny. Semni thought he was like a panther. A heavyset body endowed with explosive speed.

Semni did not fully understand why she wanted a man whose hooked nose had been broken and crookedly mended, and whose front and bottom teeth were chipped. She'd had so many lovers who were taller or more handsome. And yet, obsessed with him, she now found other men lacking.

The Phoenician had not yet shaven, his jaw heavy with stubble. Her son's blond hair was stark against his darkness. Semni remembered Nerie's father. She had noticed the fair-haired trader before the Winter Feast, and had tried to tempt him without the help of unwatered wine and worship. He'd not lain with her, though, until his face was masked and their spirits merged with Fufluns's. Thinking of the northerner did not stir any desire or regret. She wanted Arruns to be her husband. She wanted him to claim her son.

The guard sat up and rested his back against the stable wall, letting Nerie climb onto his lap. He gestured toward the hopper. "Hadn't you better do some work?"

"Plenty of time for that." She poured some grain into a pail before walking over to him and dumping the contents of the bucket in front of Nerie. The boy grabbed a handful, laughing as the granules slid through his fingers.

Sitting cross-legged next to Arruns, Semni hitched her chiton so he could see her thighs. Most men would have welcomed such a sight but he remained impassive, although his gaze wandered over to her every now and then, giving her hope.

Over the months his lack of interest had made her doubt whether he liked women at all, until she heard gossip that he slept with one of the seamstresses. Learning this, resentment flared. She could not understand why he would choose a widow nearly as old as the Gorgon instead of her.

Arruns scooped some grain and poured it into little heaps in front of Nerie. "You still haven't said why you are being punished."

"One of Cytheris's spies told Cook I was in the atrium."

"You mean one of the housemaids."

"Yes. They are one and the same."

"And what were you doing there instead of the kitchen?"

She reached in front of the tot and leveled the piles of grain, then drew a figure of a rabbit with her finger. Nerie cooed and clapped.

"I was reminding myself of what I used to be. I went to look at one of my creations."

The guard stopped observing the boy's play and instead searched Semni's face. "So you are unhappy here?"

"Why wouldn't I be? To know that my red figure vases and bucchero are only a corridor away is unbearable. The housemaid thought I was there to steal them. At least Cytheris and Cook did not believe her."

To her surprise, his voice was sympathetic. "It must be hard for you, but at least you are fed and clothed and sheltered during this siege."

She placed her hand tentatively on his forearm. For once he did not rebuff her. Her pulse quickened at the touch of muscle beneath flesh. "And you? What about you? You were hurling that spear as though you wanted to destroy the stable."

He leaned his head back against the wall and sighed. "The master has been away many months now."

"And you are bored with women and children?"

He straightened again, brow creased. "I do not question my duty to my mistress."

"Even though she is a Roman?"

"The Romans are not the enemy of my people, Semni. Besides, Lady Caecilia is a brave woman. I respect her."

"Enough to die for her?"

"If necessary. It is my job to protect all of Lord Mastarna's family."

"But you are a freedman. You don't have to risk your life."

He didn't reply, moving his arm away from her hand. She silently admonished herself for voicing her doubts about the mistress to so loyal a servant.

Spying some pebbles, Nerie toddled over to them, then proceeded to carry them one by one to drop them in the pail. One hit the edge and fell onto the grass. The man handed it to him. The boy dropped it again. Realizing it was a game, Arruns smiled.

Wanting to gain the Phoenician's attention, Semni picked up the stone and closed her hand around it instead of giving it to her son. "I don't understand. Don't you fear dying for them?"

Nerie whined, trying to prize his mother's palm open. She kept her fist tight. Finally the Phoenician focused on her. "I owe my life to the master. I will not leave him. He saved me from being the Phersu."

Semni relinquished the pebble to the child, who promptly gave it to Arruns. It didn't worry her that the man had been the Masked One. She was intrigued that he had once acted as an instrument of the gods. Stirred her, too. "What was it like to be the Phersu?"

There was a hint of anger in his voice. "Like a coward. A man called upon to set vicious hounds upon half-dead men."

"But the blood you spilled revitalized the dead. You must have felt great power when you wore the scarlet mask."

"Power? No, I just felt grateful I didn't have a sack covering my head."

She blinked, slowly comprehending. "You were a criminal?"

The boy began transferring the stones from the pail into a heap in front of the man. Arruns helped him. "My crime was to be a prisoner of war. Because of my strength, though, I was given the choice of being either a victim or the Phersu."

"How did Lord Mastarna come to rescue you?"

"One of his lictors died when the master was zilath. He saw me in the arena and chose me as a replacement. And then he kept me on as his guard after he left high office."

Nerie had grown tired of his game. He clambered onto Semni's lap, tugging at the neck of her chiton and demanding to be fed. Semni unfastened one side of her robe. Holding her nipple between two fingers she took her time offering it to her son. She glanced up as she settled Nerie, pleased to see Arruns watching. When he noticed her scrutiny, though, he looked away. Semni smiled. "So you never felt the divine within you?"

His tone grew impatient. "Don't you understand? I was sanctioned to murder men in the name of a god that was not mine."

Her eyes widened. The idea that Arruns might not worship the gods of her people stunned her. She thought her deities lived everywhere. "Who, then, do you worship?"

"Lord Ba'al. Lady Astarte. Gods of the land of Canaan."

"Canaan? I thought you were Phoenician."

"That is what the Greeks call us. Sidon is my city."

Hearing that name reminded Semni how she had once dreamed of her fame extending far beyond the Great Sea. "Why, Sidon is where my pottery was sometimes sent!"

Arruns nodded. "That is not surprising. My people are great traders, great seafarers."

Too absorbed in lamenting how her life had been reduced to kitchen, washroom, and courtyard, Semni had never thought about Arruns's past. Having been granted a glimpse into his world now, she was suddenly keen to learn where he came from, who he had been, and how he had come to be here. "And you? Were you a sailor?"

At her question, his expression clouded. "My story is simple, Semni. I was free, then a slave, and now a freedman who owes his life to this House."

"But how long have you been in Veii?"

"I was twenty when I sailed from my home. I have not seen my family for fifteen years. There is nothing more to know."

She did not press him, seeing that he was retreating, no longer prepared to share his story.

A silence fell between them as she nursed Nerie. After a time, the boy relaxed, his suck lessening. Semni stroked his hair and reached down to kiss him. When she raised her head she found Arruns was watching her.

"The impatient mother has grown patient."

She found herself grinning, pleased with his compliment. "It helps that he is so placid."

Arruns touched the boy's cheek. Drowsy, Nerie held the man's finger. "No need to be modest, you care for him well."

Semni placed her hand over both of theirs. "The boy needs a father," she murmured. "You saved him, Arruns. He would have choked if not for you."

Surprise registered upon the guard's face. "I am not what he needs." He started to rise. "My life is not my own."

Not wanting him to go, she eased Nerie from her lap and laid him on the grass where he curled up, thumb in his mouth. Then, scrambling to her feet, she caught hold of Arruns's hand. "Please stay."

He hesitated, then faced her. The girl stepped closer, running her finger along a raised vein upon his chest. "I have been good. I have been with no man for months."

Arruns grasped her hips, keeping distance between them. Yet Semni sensed he was restraining himself more than holding her at bay.

She edged nearer, her naked breast grazing his tattooed skin. His fingers tightened on her. Dipping her head, she brushed her lips across his corded flesh, tasting the salt of his sweat.

Taking his time to inhale and exhale, Arruns closed his eyes for a moment before meeting her gaze. Under the hooded lids, his eyes were the color of resin with dark rings around the irises. They were eyes that might have been kind before slavery, war, and violence made them guarded.

She encircled his neck with her arms and laid her head against his shoulder. The embrace was an echo of the one on the night of Nerie's birth. She raised her face to his. The snake's fangs only an inch away. "It meant something, didn't it? When you held me while I labored?"

He wrapped his arms around her so fiercely it made her gasp, then kissed her with hard lips. Eager, she opened her mouth to coax him, but at her urgency, he released her as swiftly as he had hugged her. Confused, she clasped his neck again, but he gently unlaced her fingers. "Don't, Semni. There's no point."

"Is it the widow? Do you love her?"

He frowned. "The seamstress? We satisfy each other sometimes. She means nothing to me."

"Then why won't you have me? I want to be your woman."

He clasped her forearms. "You think you want me, Semni, but you would soon grow bored."

"No! I would be faithful."

Arruns sighed. "Don't you see? I can't be a husband. I have the master's family to protect. I must put them above all others. You would not deserve that. Nor would Nerie."

Semni stared at him, disappointment deep and painful within her. "We would take what you give us. It would be enough."

"After a time you would want more." He glanced at the napping boy. "And so would I. Then I'd find myself putting both your and Nerie's welfare above my master and his family. I would fail in my duty."

Behind them one of the grooms led a horse into the courtyard, calling out the Phoenician's name. When he saw Semni standing with one breast bare next to the bodyguard, he smirked. Arruns let go of her. Semni hastily retied her chiton.

Expression grim, Arruns feigned disapproval as he said loudly to the girl, "You better get to work."

The groom was not fooled. He ogled Semni and winked at Arruns before delivering his message. "Lady Caecilia is looking for you. She needs you to accompany her to the palace."

The guard nodded and waved the youth away. Yet Arruns didn't turn to leave immediately, instead leaned over and whispered, "That night meant much to me as well."

Semni watched him go, then walked to the hand mill, grasping the quern's handle. The pivot creaked, the stones grating as she tried to gain momentum. Everyone thought Arruns was inscrutable. That he lacked feelings. She had known for a long time now that this was wrong. She'd seen him laugh in the half-light of a battlefield at the birth of Nerie, and had borne the brunt of his anger when she had neglected her son. And there had been a half-smile once. A hint of flirting. Today he'd shown desire. Just like the dye of his tattoo, she had got under his skin after all.

Knowing this only heightened her frustration. She could not understand his sense of duty. Could not fathom why he would choose another family when he could have one of his own. The memory of his skin against hers was still raw. She wanted to run after him and beg him to lie with her even if he would not wed her.

Nerie woke and sat up, his face crumpling when his mother was not beside him. Semni stopped her task and opened her arms, calling to him. As her son lurched toward her, tears pricked her eyes. Arruns was right. That would no longer be enough.

THIRTY-THREE

Clustered around the vast cistern at the crossroads of the citadel, the women paused to stare, pitchers balanced on their heads.

Caecilia did not miss their hostility as the driver urged the asses drawing the two-wheeled cart toward them.

The morning was scorching, no breeze. Ramutha sat next to her, chattering. The Veientane was immaculate despite the heat, waving a round fan decorated with spirals to cool her face and neck. Both principes held fringed parasols of bright hues above their heads to prevent their pale complexions turning ruddy. To the peasants they must have seemed like strange birds of gaudy plumage.

The resentment Ramutha felt toward Mastarna for removing Caile from her embrace no longer caused tension between the friends. The noblewoman accepted that Caecilia played no part in that decision. Yet the Roman's admiration for a woman having power enough to claim an illegitimate child didn't allay qualms over her being an unfaithful wife. She thought her friend's life complicated: pining for a youthful lover, caring for a one-year-old daughter, and weathering gossip. Yet she could not disapprove of

Ramutha's love for her baby. Metli Tetnies helped soothe her mother's longing for the young father. Nevertheless, Caecilia secretly hoped the princip's desire for Caile would disappear now that he was no longer near enough to spark temptation.

The sun was hot but Caecilia's palms were sweaty from nerves more than the heat. She'd woken to a summons from the king. As she fastened her jewelry, her fingers had trembled. Was today the day she would learn Vel was dead?

Ramutha would not let her see Kurvenas alone. Even though there was not much distance to the palace, the princip was determined that they drive there in her carriage. She didn't believe in mingling with commoners or risking hems and shoes being dirtied. Arruns kept an easy pace walking ahead of the donkeys, keeping a wary eye on people they passed.

Caecilia had not argued. She was overdue by more than a week, and her girth was ponderous and her tread heavy. She could not remember being so tired when carrying her three sons, nor having felt her back ache so. She was exhausted, dark smudges beneath her eyes. Warm nights led to sleeplessness, the small cargo within her buffeting her insides. She found it hard to be comfortable despite being propped up with pillows. At twenty-seven she was beginning to wonder if she'd grown too old to bear children.

She was also worn out worrying about Mastarna. There had been no word from him since he'd left Velzna. His promise that he would return in summer was now likely to be broken. There were only a few weeks left until leaf fall. Once again he would not be there to cut the cord or hold a babe slippery from the womb.

One of the women at the well had swung her pitcher from her head to the ground after climbing the stairs that gave access to the depths of the reservoir. Caecilia's stomach knotted at her glare. Those in the forum had easily spied her even in a carriage without the Mastarna bull's crest.

It was not the first time she'd encountered hostility. Camillus's blockades and the tightening of siege lines had threatened grain supplies. And now a brutal season had depleted reserves of water. Suddenly, for the first time, Veii was facing the prospect of thirst.

Caecilia no longer visited the workshop. Traveling through the city had become unsafe. The first time she'd run the gauntlet of catcalls, her heart beat so fiercely she thought it would rupture. Denied the chance to descend from the citadel into the hubbub was frustrating. Before she'd married Mastarna her whole life had been restricted to Rome. Now her physical world had been reduced to the limits of her mansion. The Veientanes viewed her as an alien, her birthplace defining her once again.

"Roman bitch!" Lowering her pitcher, one woman ran toward them, yelling. Arruns halted her progress, seizing her, but the peasant's spittle sprayed far enough to spatter the sides of the carriage.

Caecilia instinctively put her hand to her belly, protecting her child.

Ramutha half rose in her seat. "How dare you!"

The commoner struggled against the Phoenician's grasp. And yet, seeing her defiance, Caecilia felt pity rather than anger. This woman and her family would have shivered through the harsh winter and now struggled in the drought. "Arruns, let her go."

The jug the woman carried was simple earthenware, its surface crazed. No doubt she would have lugged it to and from the public well each day to provide water to cook and clean. Caecilia felt guilty that Mastarna's house boasted a private water supply, its larder well stocked despite the shortages, and numerous slaves to tend to domestic tasks.

She ordered the driver to stop so that she could alight. "I need to talk to her. I want to tell all of them to come to my door if their children are hungry."

Ramutha restrained her with a white and dainty hand. "Mele, you'll end up trying to feed half of Veii if you do that. Besides, you can't gain their loyalty that way. And I doubt they would be grateful for very long."

The peasant turned back to her companions. Caecilia glanced over her shoulder to watch them as the driver urged the donkeys to a trot. She wanted to cry out that she was part common, part noble. That she understood their hardship. And yet to do so would be lying. She may have been raised a plebeian but her father had been wealthy, deprived of power, not riches.

"Forget her, Mele. She is ignorant." Ramutha put her arm around Caecilia's shoulder and pointed to the palace. "And remember, you have greater concerns."

THIRTY-FOUR

Long years of war had led temples, houses, and public buildings to be neglected. Not so Kurvenas's residence and government office. The palace facade was magnificent. No faded paint here. Upon the pediment frieze a procession of warriors drove two-horse chariots depicted in glossy white against red, details picked out in light blue, violet, and green. And the scarlet-and-black pilasters were not chipped, the sculpted acanthus leaves on their capitals intact. Nor were there cracks in the antefixes on the watchtowers that guarded the forum.

The courtyard was packed with people waiting for an audience with the king. Caecilia realized it was the time of the quarter moon, the only chance each month for commoners to plead their cases to the lucumo.

Ramutha was incensed when the chamberlain advised them that they would have to wait their turn. Only one petitioner could enter at a time into the antechamber to the throne room. Caecilia checked her own irritation also. It was clear that Kurvenas was playing a game. Yet Rome had taught her patience when it came to petty men.

Needing protection from the sun, she directed Arruns to find some chairs. Both aristocrats settled in the shade of the overhanging gallery. The warm breeze that had sprung up gave little relief. Sitting there brought back memories of waiting in this palace to hear Artile decipher an omen nearly ten years ago. A portent sheathed in a thunderbolt that had foretold the downfall of a powerful man. Caecilia glanced at her friend. That man had been Ramutha's brother-in-law, Arnth Ulthes. Poisoned at King Tulumnes's hand.

Ramutha sat impatient, fiddling with one of the ivory rosettes appliquéd onto her chiton. The Veientane never balked at flaunting her wealth or her flair for fashion. Caecilia marveled at her friend's clear complexion and the glass-beaded diadem threaded through the soft waves of hair. To see Ramutha so elegant made her feel ungainly. The skin on her face was always mottled when she was with child, her hair lank. She wanted to loosen the laces of her sandals to ease her swollen feet but doubted she could reach them. She felt the babe kick. She smoothed her hand over its movement, the linen of her shift soft and sinuous. The child pulled away and her belly returned to a taut globe.

Tired of Ramutha's fidgeting, she reached for the princip's hand. "Thank you for coming with me. It mustn't be easy to see Kurvenas sitting on the throne."

The woman smiled. "I do this for you, Mele. Let's hope I annoy him by my presence."

Finally the last supplicant was seen. Directing Arruns to remain behind, Caecilia followed the chamberlain, butterflies competing with the baby in her stomach. As she passed through the tall double bronze doors, she was struck by the beauty of the lofty checkered throne room. When Vipinas was zilath, the chamber had been austere. He was not one to flaunt luxury while his citizens struggled. Kurvenas had no such scruples. The opulence with which he surrounded himself returned Caecilia to a Veii that existed before the war. Garlands hung from hooks entwined with ribbons, and platters of summer fruit were heaped upon side tables, the promise of sweet juicy flesh making her mouth water. Musicians were performing, the castanet player perspiring from the heavy plaid jerkin he wore over a diaphanous skirt. The cithara player and flautist were stylish in vivid striped tebennas.

Kurvenas had wasted no time stamping his mark. Winged lions had been engraved or painted on furniture and walls. A symbol of royalty and his family's crest. The largest was embossed upon the massive bronze throne upon which the lucumo sat. The last two kings before him had been his grandfather and cousin. It was clear that the newly appointed ruler intended that the Tulumnes clan would long be remembered.

The man sat upon the throne as if born to do so, his arms relaxed along the rests, his weight leaning to one side, legs crossed. Before he'd been elected, his good-humored camaraderie had endeared him to all. Now that he'd reached the pinnacle, Caecilia suspected he'd dispensed with civility to those who could no longer profit him. The laws he proclaimed and the taxes he levied did not favor the people but instead bought the allegiance of those principes he needed.

Morale may have been low among his subjects but the king appeared buoyant. With his bulk, his jewelry and robes made him impressive. Caecilia had to admit he looked regal. His cloak was embroidered with figures of Heracles performing his labors, and a wreath wrought in gold secured oiled shoulder-length hair. A winged lion was emblazoned on the wide bronze belt around his waist.

There were four others seated in the room. Three men and a youth. Caecilia's eyes widened when she saw Sethre's face. Both eyes were blackened, mere slits against swollen cheeks, and he held his body as though it pained him. She wondered if he'd come off second in a fight. For certain his usual cockiness was subdued.

Vipinas was sitting rigid in his chair, his face cadaverous and his cough no better. She wondered if he always attended upon the king when there was a public audience. This man had promised Mastarna he would protect her. Had he instead become a confidant of her husband's rival? She smiled to the old man, who nodded. His greeting granted her some reassurance.

Bored, the warrior Lusinies scratched his mutilated nose as he observed the women. He was wearing a kirtle, his heavyset chest bare, and a gold torque around his neck studded with scarab-shaped garnets. Caecilia never knew where this man's loyalties lay. He was cagey in declaring either his preferences or prejudices.

She stiffened when she saw the fourth man. For Artile stood behind an enormous bronze table with an ornate inkstand and two candelabras on it. Caecilia recognized the linen book open in front of him as a holy text. As always she thought him an echo of his older brother. Mastarna, with his masculinity and passion, was the first clear call while Artile, with his flabby body and cosmetics, was the fainter, lesser man.

The priest studied her. The honeyed persuasion of his gaze and voice and promises had once entranced her, but now she was strong enough to resist him. Repugnance gave her courage, refusing to be cowed. To her satisfaction it was the haruspex who was the first to look away.

Kurvenas scowled when he saw Caecilia had brought an ally. "What are you doing here, Ramutha Tetnies?"

The aristocrat squared her shoulders. "I was not going to let my friend walk into a winged lion's den lest she be eaten."

"Careful how you address me or I'll have you removed."

"I never thought you'd be one to fear a woman."

Caecilia put her hand on Ramutha's arm. "Enough. Now that we are here, let him speak."

"Very well." Ramutha glared at the men. "At least bring Lady Caecilia a chair. Her baby is due any day now."

For a moment the Roman thought the lucumo would refuse, but when Lusinies cleared his throat loudly, Kurvenas signaled the slave to fetch a stool. Ramutha was left to stand.

Caecilia felt more vulnerable once seated. With his height, and enthroned upon a dais, Kurvenas towered above her. Suddenly the pleasant atmosphere of music and beauty palled, the staccato clicking of the castanets grating upon her nerves. "Why have you asked me here? Do you have news of my husband?"

"Yes, I have news. He has failed miserably at the congress of the Twelve and is doing little better in assisting the Faliscans to thwart Camillus's forces."

Caecilia tensed, surprised at the vehemence of the slur even as relief filled her that Vel was still alive. From the corner of her eye she noticed Vipinas's attention sharpen.

Bracelets sliding down her arm as she shook her fist, Ramutha stepped toward the ruler. "Don't speak of Mastarna in that way!"

Caecilia leaned forward to grasp her friend's skirt and pull her back. Unlike the Rasennan woman, she was not about to trade insults with the lucumo. Hand to the small of her back, she lumbered to standing. "Thank you for informing me that he survives. Now may I be permitted to take my leave?"

"Sit down!" The volume with which Kurvenas bellowed the command stunned all within the room. He shouted at the musicians to leave. Discordant clicking and pinging of castanet and lyre marked their hasty departure, plums and cherries spilling across the floor as they knocked a repository table over in their haste.

Lusinies's expression was no longer bored. He frowned as he watched Kurvenas descend from the dais and stand behind Sethre.

"I have not summoned you here to merely report on your husband." Kurvenas placed his hands on his son's shoulders. The youth bowed his head, face scarlet. "Tarchon Mastarna has tainted Sethre and shamed my family! He was not qualified to act as a mentor."

Perspiration pricked Caecilia's scalp. How livid Kurvenas must have been to beat his golden child. Tarchon would be distraught to see that he'd caused his beloved to be thrashed. Dreading having to answer for her stepson's stupidity, she tried to remain calm as she settled back onto the stool. "I acknowledge Tarchon has acted foolishly."

"Foolishly? He has ruined my son's reputation."

"He did not intend to do so. He mistakenly hoped to create an alliance between our families."

Kurvenas moved across to her. "Are you mocking me? An alliance with your House? Mastarna caused my kinsman to be disgraced and deposed! And your great-uncle ordered my grand-father to be beheaded!"

Caecilia slipped her hand into Ramutha's. The noblewom-an's expression had been one of bewilderment at the revelation of Tarchon's affair but, seeing her Roman friend's need for comfort, she smiled in encouragement.

Bolstered by Ramutha's reassurance, Caecilia challenged the king. "Whatever enmity there may be between our two families, my husband has acted honorably. When he learned of the liaison, he forbade it and led Tarchon to war."

Kurvenas hooked his thumbs into his ornamental belt, loom-ing over her. The nadir of his loathing had been revealed. The shaming of his son had added to his own humiliation at Mastarna challenging him on the battlefield.

"Removing that mollis was not enough!" He strode to Sethre and placed his hand on the youth's brow, forcing the youth's head backward to face the others. Caecilia felt sorry for him. He looked so young and frightened as he gulped back tears.

"I punished my son when I heard," the king continued, "and I will shun him if he ever goes near his lover again. If Mastarna had done the same when Tarchon flaunted convention years ago, this never would have happened."

Caecilia's attention swiveled to Artile. He sat inscrutable, seemingly untroubled by the mention of his past affair. He had corrupted a young boy also. Why did Kurvenas not despise him? Yet again the priest had managed to escape condemnation.

The father released Sethre and glared at Caecilia. "Don't look at the haruspex. It was he who informed me of this betrayal. I owe him a debt of gratitude. He saved me from being ridiculed for not knowing Tarchon was riding Sethre. If I get my hands on your stepson, I will kill him!"

"No, Father!" The youth stood up, high spots of color on his cheeks.

"Go and wait outside!" Kurvenas abruptly clipped him across his bruised cheeks. The boy doubled over in pain but did not cry as he ran from the throne room.

Caecilia looked at Artile. He'd not spoken throughout the drama. The soothsayer gave her his familiar complacent smile and adjusted the gold crescent brooch at his throat that fastened his cloak. How had he learned of the trysts? She doubted it was through his mantic powers. More likely his web of spies. She never thought his love for Tarchon would sour enough to hurt his old beloved, or that his jealousy would lead to betrayal.

At the assault on Sethre, Lusinies concentrated on wiping sweat from his pate as though embarrassed. Vipinas, brow furrowed, watched the youth leave. "Sire, you are wrong to claim Mastarna has acted ignobly. He erred in not advising you of the liaison, but what Caecilia says is correct. He sought to avert disgrace by taking Tarchon into battle." He started coughing as he turned to Ramutha. "Just as he offered to help me by extracting my grandson from that slattern's grasp."

Ramutha's disbelief at what she had witnessed between Sethre and his father had rendered her dumb. Now she changed from staring at Kurvenas to glaring at the old princip. "I am no slut.

And I ask nothing of your family to raise Caile's child. I alone have claimed your great-granddaughter as part of my bloodline."

"Enough!" Kurvenas roared. He moved to stand behind the table with Artile. "I have no interest in listening to you squabble over a bastard child. There is a matter of more importance. That is why I have summoned Aemilia Caeciliana."

Curious, Lusinies sat forward in his seat. "What have you to tell us, sire?"

Kurvenas gestured toward the haruspex. "Lord Artile will explain."

After his long silence, the priest's bass voice seemed to reverberate around the chamber. "Rome suffers from drought and famine. This in itself is a sign that that city has offended the gods. But there is a greater prodigy."

Caecilia touched her Atlenta pendant nervously. Unlike Mastarna, she didn't doubt the power of the seer to foresee the future. His prescience had been proven too many times. His prediction had come true about Arnth Ulthes's death, and that Veii would fight a long and dreadful war. There was no doubt the haruspex was the supreme authority on sacred matters.

Ramutha also respected the haruspex for his gift. Her voice lost its edge. "What is this great miracle?"

"My spies have brought news that, despite lack of heavy rain or snowfall, the waters of Lake Albanus have increased so they now lap at the peaks of the mountains around it."

All fell silent again at hearing the mystery. Caecilia thought how tantalizingly close the prospect of such an abundance of water must be to the Romans. Only leagues away from their city, the Latin tribes were experiencing the solution to ending thirst caused by the relentless summer. A thirst that Rome must continue to suffer with no rain to fill its wells. The gods were indeed cruel.

Vipinas shifted in his chair. "A most wondrous omen, indeed. What does it signify?"

Artile smiled and smoothed one eyebrow. "That Rome has done more than displease the deities—it has angered them. And until our enemy can determine what expiation rites need to be performed, it cannot conquer Veii."

Caecilia knew of the Romans' limited ability to interpret such a sign. In contrast to the knowledge of the Rasenna, their skills were as infants compared to the ancients. Yet the patricians could still consult the oracle on how to placate the gods. "But can't the senators consult the Sibylline Books for direction?"

Artile tutted. "Those texts do not contain the answer. But our sacred codex does. And I am the interpreter of such secrets."

Caecilia smiled. It was the first time Artile had brought her good tidings. "Then Veii is safe if there is no chance for them to determine the correct rituals."

Kurvenas stroked the scar that furrowed the hair of his beard, his temper sparking. "Being spared an assault doesn't help me realize my ambition to rule your people!"

The baby stirred within her together with a twinge of pain. Caecilia flinched, stroking the baby's contours, hoping it was not a birth pang.

Vipinas coughed. "As Mastarna has failed to rouse the Twelve to march on Rome, such an endeavor is dangerous. Perhaps we should be satisfied that Rome's gods are unhappy. Our foe will need to be brave to continue to press a siege until divine wrath has been assuaged."

Kurvenas placed both hands on the table, arms straight. "Rome needs to be destroyed. But lack of support from the other Rasenna is not the only reason why I'll be thwarted. Artile has foretold there is a traitor among us. Until the betrayer is punished and our gods appeased, Rome will remain secure, too. And I will never be its king."

A sharp pain squeezed Caecilia's womb. She bit her lip, not wanting to reveal her discomfort. The talk of sedition was as unnerving as her dismay that her labor had begun.

Ramutha walked over to survey the linen book on the table. "What is the portent that signified there is a traitor?"

The priest placed his hand on the open page. "Thunder was heard on the night of the new moon. The Book of Thunderbolts warns that treachery should be averted."

Caecilia remembered the storm. How the gods teased and taunted the Veientanes, sending rumbles and flashes but no rain.

Kurvenas pointed at her. "You are that traitor, Aemilia Caeciliana."

She steadied herself, gripping the stool. This time her apprehension was not for herself. It was for her children. Would Kurvenas also exact punishment on them for having a Roman for a mother? Another spasm wracked her. She could not stifle a groan. Ramutha hurried to crouch beside her. "Mele, is it the baby?"

Caecilia nodded, breathing through the contraction, pressing her hands to her womb. Three times in her life she had borne a child and yet the intensity of the first pain always took her by surprise. When the pain had passed she focused on the king. "I am faithful to Veii."

The lucumo's expression was as though he needed to scrape a lump of dung from his boot. "Remember your boast at the Winter Feast? How, if anyone doubted your loyalty, you would return to Rome to meet a traitor's death? Well, I test that fidelity today. Tell us, would you see your city destroyed?"

"Rome is no longer my city."

"So you would welcome its annihilation?"

Caecilia faltered, the same reluctance emerging as when Mastarna spoke of such a course. "I want peace. I do not see how that is treason."

His eyes narrowed. "Ah, but if you truly loved Veii you would not balk at seeking Rome's destruction."

Another pang. She breathed deeply. Was she ever to be free of the threat of execution? First Tulumnes and now his cousin. She thought, too, of the women at the well. Antagonism would swell to assault with a decree she was a betrayer.

"Then you plan to kill me?"

"No, returning you to Rome will suffice. And when your people slay you, our gods will be appeased."

She found herself laughing. "And what if my death placates the rage of the Roman gods also? Both cities would be thwarted."

Ramutha put her arm around Caecilia, her gaze swinging between Artile and Kurvenas. "This sounds like personal revenge as well as holy advice." The king stiffened and glanced at Artile. The priest smoothed his eyebrow. Caecilia knew then that Tarchon's actions had catapulted their family into peril just as Vel had predicted.

Ramutha glowered at the men. "Lady Caecilia's time has come. Let me take her home."

Kurvenas grimaced, showing no sympathy, while Artile observed his sister-in-law with dispassionate gaze. Lusinies avoided looking at the women, clearly uncomfortable at the prospect of being present at a birth.

Vipinas, though, hastened to Caecilia's side and offered one scarred, liver-spotted arm to help her stand. He wheezed with the effort of propping her up as he glared at the king. "I have heard enough. I do not believe Lady Caecilia is the traitor we seek. I will not let you send her back to Rome. She is faithful to Veii and has borne three warrior sons." Coughing, he strived to finish his piece. "I gave my word that I'd protect her. And you should remember your own pledge to Mastarna. You talk of dishonor today. How can you think of sending another man's wife to her doom while he is fighting a war in your name?"

Caecilia clung to the aged man's arm, thinking how frail he seemed despite his defiance.

Kurvenas bristled. "I don't need a lesson on principles from a toothless old man."

The aristocrat's near-translucent skin reddened to the roots of his thinning hair. "I have been zilath more than once. At least respect my service to this city even if you choose to insult an elder."

Caecilia sagged as another pang seized her. Ramutha staggered a little as she held her friend around the waist.

The lucumo ignored Caecilia's distress. "Respect you, Vipinas? You failed to avenge my grandfather's death. You ensconced yourself as zilath and thereafter claimed no more tyrants would rule Veii. And then you negotiated a truce with Rome for twenty years instead of waging war against it. And don't think I've forgotten you joined Mastarna in deposing my cousin."

Astonishment registered through Caecilia's distress.

Vipinas was shaking as the lucumo listed grievances extending back decades. "Take care. I am still head of my clan even if I no longer ride into battle. You menace this woman as your cousin Tulumnes did before you. You would do well to remember that his oppression was not tolerated. And that all the other principes followed Mastarna in dethroning him and his cronies."

Kurvenas swept the inkstand and candelabras from the table. They crashed to the floor. "What you say is treason."

Vipinas flinched. He could barely speak for wheezing. "Are you accusing me of being the traitor?"

Lusinies rose and stood in the space between the two men. His circumspection was a relief after the fury between the king and princip. "Sire, this is a weighty matter. I ask that you not act hastily. Consult with the High Council. Let's wait until Mastarna returns to determine who this betrayer is. Then there will be no question that the College of Principes will support your decision."

Another contraction. Caecilia clenched her jaw, determined not to moan. It was as though a great hand was wringing her insides. Ramutha held her close as she shouted, "You should heed Lusinies. Otherwise you will need courage to survive Mastarna's wrath."

The king hesitated before turning to Artile. The priest bowed. "Sire, as lucumo you are the high priest of Veii. I am merely the chief haruspex of Uni. It is in your hands to determine what must be done. I have merely interpreted the omen."

Kurvenas kicked the inkstand across the room. Sweeping his cloak behind him with a swirl of frustration, he once again mounted the dais. "Go then! I will give Mastarna until the end of summer to return. And then the matter will be decided once and for all."

Skirts soaked, Caecilia tried to summon dignity as Ramutha and Vipinas helped her from the chamber. Unable to concentrate on politics and portents, absorbed with the agony of her labor, aware there was no guarantee Vel would remain alive.

THIRTY-FIVE

Semni leaned her weight against the handle of the quern, arms straight and back horizontal. Her legs strained with the effort, her breathing labored. The upper stone grated against the millstone, the iron pivot creaking from lack of grease. Flour flowed into the trough below before spilling onto the paving.

She was weeping again. Thinking of Arruns. She had done so on and off for hours.

A breeze, hot and mischievous, swept through the courtyard. The flour rose in an eddy. Semni knelt and hastened to scoop it from the trough into a sack, but the gust blew the powder onto her face and hair and clothes.

Frustrated, she sat on her haunches. She should not have been grinding a hand mill like some lowly slave. She should have been setting a flywheel spinning instead of trudging in a circle. She should have been perspiring from the heat of a furnace instead of sweating in the hot sun.

"Are you still out here after all this time?" Aricia hovered in the archway of the courtyard.

Nose red and eyes puffy, Semni wiped her tears with the back of her hand.

Aricia hurried over to her. "What's the matter?"

"Arruns."

The nursemaid frowned. "Why, what did he do to you?"

Semni rose, sniffling. "He wants me, Aricia, but he puts his duty first."

The nursemaid hesitated but made no comment. Then she scanned the courtyard. "Where is Nerie?"

"With Cook. She was cross that I was lagging behind and could see he was hindering me in my work."

Aricia pushed Semni's hair from her brow. "Come, dry your eyes. I'll fetch a broom and help you sweep up this flour, and then we can go to my room to talk."

Semni was grateful for such help. Her head was aching from laboring in the midday sun. "Where are the little masters?"

"Tas is with his tutor, and Perca is tending to Larce and Arnth."

The familiar smell of incense lingered in Aricia's cell, but after the fierce heat it was a relief to rest in the cool interior. Semni sat down with a sigh on the soft mattress and tried to wipe her face clean.

Aricia smiled. "Your tears have turned the flour on your face to glue." Spitting onto her kerchief, she rubbed the paste away as would a mother wiping the cheeks of a grubby child. Forlorn, Semni closed her eyes, tolerating the attention.

There was a bronze cista next to the bed. Aricia delved inside the container and brought out a silver mirror. She lifted it so Semni could check her reflection, albeit distorted, in the polished metal. "See, all clean."

Semni examined the looking glass. Engraved on the back was an image of Turan, the goddess of love, being tended by a winged and naked angel. "Where did you get this? It's beautiful."

"Don't tell. I stole it from Lady Caecilia."

Semni was stunned. Even her own resentment toward the mistress would never tempt her to steal. "Why do you take her things? She gives you everything you need."

Aricia sat down on the bed. "She has so much. Lord Mastarna spoils her. You should see in her chamber—one cista for pearl and amber and lapis, and another for all her gold. And besides, she has many mirrors. She has not even missed this one yet. Mind you, I don't know why she would want to look at her reflection with that ugly birthmark."

Semni was silent, disapproving of the maid's venom. And she could understand why the princip would collect mirrors if they were decorated as splendidly as this. The artist had talent. Again she wished she could display her own. "You sound as if you hate her."

"I told you, Lady Caecilia clings to her beliefs even though she claims she is Rasennan. She doesn't believe she will once again feast with her ancestors after she dies."

The girl traced the outlines of the etched figures. Why should she be shocked at Aricia's pilfering trinkets? It was nothing compared to the theft of the Roman's son. It also reminded Semni again of her own tacit involvement. She handed the mirror to the Greek girl, who carefully placed it back in the cista. "Do you ever feel guilty, Aricia? Taking Tas to Artile in secret?"

"Why should I, when she denies her sons immortality through Aita?"

Semni shrugged her shoulders. "Not all of us believe in the Calu Cult."

Aricia was undaunted. "The Romans believe you descend into a milling crowd of bodiless souls after death. Would you want that for Nerie? Well, that's what Lady Caecilia condemns her sons to suffer by not making sacrifice."

The bangles on Aricia's wrists jingled as she brushed some flour off Semni's dress. "What is worse is that the mistress once was a follower."

Surprised, Semni turned to face her. "How do you know that?"

"Lord Artile told me. To hear that she once believed but now has shunned Aita makes it even worse!"

Semni listened with growing concern. She did not believe in the blood rites of the death cult but she still expected to live beyond the grave. "How could the mistress not believe in the Beyond?"

"I know. It's terrible." Aricia lowered her voice. "Lord Artile told me something else that is worse."

Her hushed tones made Semni also whisper. "What?"

"She followed the Fatales Rites. She tried to defer the birth of Tas."

"I don't believe you." Semni's voice returned to normal level. "The mistress loves her children."

"Now, perhaps, but when she first came to Veii she wanted to stop herself conceiving. She thought bearing a Rasennan baby would mean spawning a monster. She appealed to Nortia to delay such a fate."

Semni struggled with the revelation, trying to reconcile the contented mistress who was heavy with child with the coldhearted schemer of whom Aricia spoke. And yet her friend seemed so certain. And the chief priest of Uni was her source. "Truly?"

"Truly." Aricia's eyes were stony with condemnation. "She failed in her purpose, though. Lord Artile says that she was not devout enough to gain Nortia's favor. Can you see now that I am right in taking Tas to visit his uncle? Lady Caecilia does not deserve to have such a son."

The story seemed so outlandish. And yet to believe it helped Semni to assuage her own guilt at remaining silent. Maybe the Roman wasn't such a good mother after all.

Aricia slid her arm around Semni's waist. "Do you feel better now? About Arruns?"

She shook her head.

"I don't understand why you cry over him. He's ugly and cruel."

"He's not cruel."

"His job is to kill."

"He is kind to Nerie." Semni tapped her chest, tears welling. "And to me."

Aricia's tone hardened. "Yet he does not want you."

"You're wrong. He does. Only he chooses Lord Mastarna over me."

Aricia brushed more flour from Semni's chiton. It was as though she had not heard her. "This is so grimy. Why don't you take it off and I'll lend you one of mine."

Semni glanced at the pleated blue-and-white gown hanging from a hook on the wall, distracted by the thought of feeling fine linen for the first time. She had always been jealous of the maid's wardrobe. She nodded and dried her eyes.

Aricia stood beside her. "You don't need a man to make you happy," she said, helping her friend strip off her clothes. The skin of Semni's rounded body was creamy, her arms and legs tanned, coated with a fine layer of flour.

She was weary of the refrain. "I do! And I've had no one to hold me for so long. All because of the Gorgon."

Aricia sat down behind her friend and encircled her waist, laying her cheek against her shoulder and placing her hands on Semni's belly. "Then I will hold you."

The offer was not the embrace Semni was seeking. Nevertheless, the cushioning of padded breasts and arms, and the faint scent of violets, was a comfort.

She felt Aricia's breath against her skin as the nursemaid whispered, "I want to make you happy. Can't I be enough for you?"

Surprised, Semni turned to face the nursemaid, not quite sure of what she was hearing. Over the past months she'd often slept on her friend's feathered mattress, welcoming the chance to abandon her narrow pallet and escape Nerie's squirming. And the tot also gained rest, snuggling upon a pillow beside the cot. And so Semni was not fazed when Aricia encouraged her to nestle in front of her in bed. It was less awkward than lying head to toe. Now she remembered how the maid always pressed a little too close, and how she would often wake to find Aricia's arm across her. She'd thought nothing of it, believing it the tangle of slumber.

And she'd been with women before. Twice that she could remember, at the Winter Feast. Yet even in the divine madness this had only happened amid shadows and bracken far from the bonfires' glow. There was no exaltation of Fufluns's promise of regeneration when woman lay with woman, just a quenching of passion that was unnatural and forbidden. Such coupling could be overlooked amid drunkenness, but to always seek it was shocking. Yet Aricia was an innocent. Semni wondered if the maid really comprehended what being a lover meant. "Do you understand what you are saying?"

The nursemaid blushed and bowed her head. "I love you."

Semni studied the earnest girl who was opening her heart to her. So different from the brooding Phoenician who rammed his emotions down within him. Leaning over, she coiled one black ringlet of Aricia's hair around her finger. It was sinuous and shiny. "Have you ever lain with a girl?"

Her friend shook her head. "Neither man nor woman."

"Then how can you be so sure it is what you want?"

Aricia took Semni's hand, entwining her fingers through hers. "I just know that when I'm with you I feel safe and cherished."

It was Semni's turn to shake her head. She did not want to hurt her. "You are a true friend, Aricia, and I love you for being so." She stroked the girl's cheek, then brushed her lips against hers.

Aricia drew back, her expression one of disappointment, then her eyes widened as she looked over Semni's shoulder.

Arruns was standing in the doorway.

Semni did not know what was worse, the hurt in his eyes or the anger and disgust that followed.

She grabbed her crumpled chiton and clutched it in front of her as she stepped from the cot. "Please, Arruns. Let me explain! It's not what you think!"

The guard rattled out orders. "The mistress's baby is coming. She has called for you to help her." He cocked his head toward Aricia. "And *she* is to take the young masters to Lady Ramutha's."

Semni tried to take his hand but instead he grasped her wrist, his fingers iron. "Why? Why would you do this?"

Panicked, a sharp pain rose in her chest. "Please believe me, I did nothing."

"Nothing?" His eyes raked over her as she stood barely covered by the chiton scrunched against her. "You're naked! In her bedroom in the middle of the day just like you used to be with those grooms."

"My clothes were dirty. I was changing into some of hers!"

He tightened his grip. "You were kissing her."

She gasped at his strength. "It was of friendship only. Please listen to me."

"Let go!" Aricia rushed toward the Phoenician, trying to yank his hand from Semni's wrist. "Why do you care? You don't want her anyway."

A look of confusion passed across Arruns's tattooed face before it settled back into harsh lines. He released Semni, thrusting the girls from him, eyes narrowing. "You both sicken me."

Semni slid to the floor, leaning her back against the doorjamb and searching for his hand as he stood over her. "Please! She means nothing to me, Arruns," she sobbed. "I love you."

He moved out of her reach. "You're a liar. Now get ready, the mistress needs you."

He strode away. Semni slowly dragged herself to her feet and dressed. Absorbed in her own misery, it took her a moment to realize she was not the only one who was weeping. Aricia lay huddled on her bed, shoulders heaving, tears streaming down her cheeks.

Stricken with guilt, Semni crossed to her, crouching beside her. "I did not mean what I said, Aricia. I was upset."

The nursemaid glared at her with the same vehemence as Arruns. "Liar," she hissed, and rolled over to face the wall.

THIRTY-SIX

Three menservants were sweeping the threshold and striking it with axe and pestle when Caecilia arrived home from the palace, birth pangs worsening. She murmured a prayer that such precautions would ward off the evil presence of the forest god while she was in labor. It was Juno whom she needed near this day. The Great Mother Goddess had not failed to protect her in childbed before.

The midwife had prepared the room for the confinement, the scent of willow bark tea heavy in the air. The sight of sea sponges and olive oil reminded Caecilia of what lay ahead.

Seeing the oak birthing chair with its crescent hole and the embroidered pillow beside it made her nervous. For over a hundred years, Mastarna wives had gripped the padded armrests, their backs and buttocks jammed against the swells and hollows of its surface. And for over a hundred years, heirs had been placed upon the bull's crest cushion after their mothers had borne them.

Caecilia breathed through another contraction. She had been one of those women. She had survived three births. And yet this labor was not like the others. The welling and ebbing of pain seemed endless. Face upward and stuck in the birth passage, her baby struggled to the light.

Afternoon slipped into sunset, sunset to evening.

Through surges of anguish, Caecilia's confidence drained. A great fist gripped and released inside her, the periods of respite growing less. Engulfed in pain, she found the willow bark tea was a feeble shield against her suffering.

Evening merged into darkness, darkness to daybreak.

Cytheris had called the young maid Semni to help with the lying-in. Ramutha was there also. The three women had all borne children. A sisterhood of mothers. They spoke in low voices, encouraging and gentle. They sponged beads of perspiration from Caecilia's brow and lips, and lodged a goat's bladder of hot water against the small of her back. Such ministrations brought little comfort. Caecilia shoved her companions' hands away, wanting to escape her body.

Daybreak edged into midday. Midday to afternoon.

The midwife, a freedwoman with soft fingers and calloused character, bade the three helpers to heave Caecilia onto the birthing chair, telling her that she must push or die.

Caecilia smelled the aniseed upon Cytheris's breath as the handmaid stood behind her to prevent her from slumping. Ramutha and Semni stood on each side, pressing on her abdomen, urging for her to bear down. Caecilia wondered if her fingers could fasten any tighter on the padded armrests.

"Remember, push from here." The midwife gripped the princip's thighs. "Not from your neck or else blood might burst in your eyes." Then, with weight on her left knee, the freedwoman knelt and rubbed oil to stretch the skin of the canal around the crown before wrapping her hands with softened papyrus to ensure the blood-slickened heir did not slip from her grasp when the babe finally was coaxed from the womb.

The infant clung fast.

She was shifted back to the bed again.

Afternoon slowed into sunset, sunset to evening.

Caecilia prided herself on her fortitude in labor, how she had always displayed forbearance: no hysterics, moaning only. This time she could not stop screaming. Pleading for it to be over. Her voice grew hoarse from begging Juno not to forsake her. Then, thinking she needed the goddess to see her as a Veientane, she also called the deity Uni, her Rasennan name.

Shivering, she vomited the useless tea until bile was all that remained.

Evening dragged into the late hours. There was only energy to whimper.

She heard voices. Anxious and fretful. None male. None Mastarna's.

The susurration of worry continued. Caecilia turned onto her side and fixed her eyes upon the leopard painted on the wall. The great cat peered at her from his laurel bower. Vel believed it was Fufluns's guide to the Beyond. She pulled Cytheris close. "I'm going to die, aren't I?"

The handmaid brushed sodden, matted hair from her mistress's forehead. "No, my lady, you are too stubborn."

Caecilia trembled. Death was coming without her seeing her husband. She would never hold her sons again.

At midnight, Cytheris and Semni helped Caecilia onto her hands and knees. Then, slinging a shawl beneath her belly, they bore her weight between them. And the midwife, thrusting her left hand into Caecilia's womb as she would some farm animal, finally delivered the trapped child.

Caecilia welcomed the familiar burn and release. Rolling over, she saw the midwife, apron bloodied, slap the infant.

There was a cry, piercing and indignant. Battle-stained, Mastarna's daughter had finished her fight to break free.

THIRTY-SEVEN

Falerii, Late Summer, 397 BC

A messenger, face red, brushed past Pinna, scurrying away like a camp mongrel that had been kicked.

She lifted the flap to the command tent. The sun had set but the temperature was oppressive inside. Camillus, a sheen of sweat upon his face and arms, was leaning over his table, one hand pressed to his brow, the other stabbing a knife into the wood. Dozens of marks scored the surface.

She knew to keep her voice calm in such moments. "My lord, you called for me?"

His eyes were soft with pain. "Yes. Vulcan is using the inside of my head as a forge, and my neck is stiff again. Come and rub it."

Pinna put down her basket and stood behind him. His muscles were tight, the joints fused. It would take much effort to loosen them.

Camillus continued to stab at the table. Reaching over, she placed her hand over his to stop him. "This is not helping."

He hesitated, then laid the weapon down. "You are right."

Curious as to why he'd scared the envoy, she ventured to question him. "My lord, perhaps it would help if you told me what is troubling you. It is better than brooding."

When he did not respond she realized she had overstepped the boundary. She concentrated on massaging him, spreading a little more balsam oil over his shoulders. She always liked to use it. For a short time it softened hands that were chore-roughened.

Camillus finally broke his silence. "The drought continues and now a plague has broken out in Rome."

"Is that why the messenger was here? Did he bring word of Marcus Aemilius? Is the sickness why he has not returned?"

Camillus swung around. "Do not fret, Pinna. It was Marcus who sent the herald. He and Drusus have retreated to the country to escape the plague. The wealthy are staying in their villas. Politicians and senators are breathing in fresh, not fetid, air. Although, sadly, Marcus's mother, Aurelia, has not been spared."

Pinna felt a stab of pity for Marcus's loss. He sometimes would joke about the cloying bossiness of Aurelia but, at heart, she believed him to be a dutiful son. She hoped the patrician woman had not suffered too much, knowing only too well what horrors the pestilence brought. She had survived one outbreak when she was a night moth. The sight of dead paupers heaped on wagons as they were carted to the burial pits outside the Esquiline remained with her. The air had been thick with ash from the funeral pyres of the rich and the stink of decaying corpses waiting to be fed into the flames. With the fear of contagion no customers sought satisfaction amid the graves either. And, although desperate for money, she and Fusca dared not seek work as hired mourners. Even the families of the deceased did not visit the tombs. They were either too sick themselves or fearful of anointing bodies covered with pus-filled sores. Yet Fortuna had spared Pinna and her mother. As always the blindfolded goddess had played a game: those she touched succumbing, those who could sidestep her surviving.

Pinna had prayed to Mater Matuta for protection every day, adding a bell to both fascinum and shell to ward off evil. Thinking of
Marcus's grief, Pinna silently murmured a blessing for the dead
mother he must be mourning.

Camillus picked up his dagger again, twisting the handle,
his body still tense. Why had the news of plague made him irate
instead of sorrowing? She eased her fingers through his hair, massaging the scalp. He sighed at such comfort.

"Something else is worrying you, isn't it, my lord?"

He turned around. "Ah, little citizen, as always you sense more
than others. The envoy brought only tales of concern or woes.
There has been a prodigy. Lake Albanus has risen to the tops of the
peaks around it despite the drought and its crater only being fed by
springs. All who see it say it is a prodigy—but one that favors the
Latin nation yet bodes ill for Rome."

Pinna shivered and fingered her amulets. It was indeed a powerful omen. Her ancestors had once lived beside the lake's shores.
She imagined how the Latin people must be marveling at the
abundance of water while Romans must witness rivers trickling
in hollow channels. "Do you really think it is because the gods are
displeased with our people?"

"What it portends no augur can say. But Rome needs to be
cautious. The Sibylline Books are to be consulted as to how to placate the deities."

He picked up the dagger again. "Marcus Aemilius has also sent
word that my opponents are making use of both the miracle and
calamities. They say the gods have been offended and are meting
punishment upon us—sending us a harsh winter and now a fierce
summer, spreading famine and now smiting us with plague."

"Because there are five plebeian generals?"

Camillus stabbed the blade into the table. "The patricians
say that families of distinction have been ignored and high office
debased. They hate that common men lead Rome's legions as ably

as any noble." He worked the point so it splintered the wood. "Yet in truth we have made more gains this year than any other. And there has been no bickering among the generals as there was between Sergius and Verginius. We share our strategies instead of hoarding them." He yanked out the knife and stabbed the timber again. Pinna wasn't sure if he was speaking to her of such matters or merely trying to convince himself of his argument. "The present consular generals should be gaining credit for their efforts, not criticism. This so-called explanation for the current misfortune stinks of human jealousy as much as divine disapproval."

Pinna closed her palm around her luck charms again, disturbed by both his impiety and his frustration. "Don't you believe the gods speak to us through signs, my lord?"

He rammed the dagger into the surface, leaving it standing upright.

"Of course I do. I take the auspices before every battle. I pray to Mars to grant me courage and to Fortuna for her protection." To her surprise he leaned his elbows on the table, pressing his palms against his eyes, his fury ebbing. "It is my fault that Rome despairs. I should be punished, not the people. I brought this plague upon them. The blood of many is on my hands."

His anguish was unexpected. He was always so strong in mind, so certain. Pinna knelt at his feet, drawing his hands from his brow. "My lord, I do not know why the gods sent such portents, but our city's suffering is not your fault."

Shoulders hunched, Camillus scanned her face. "But it is. Can't you see? Because of my decision to burn the harvest the famine has not eased. Starving peasants are flocking to the city begging for food. With none to spare, they are dying in the streets, rats gnawing at their bodies. The heat of the summer sun soon makes their flesh putrid. The messenger said the stink of the plague lingers over the Forum and streets. That they are dying in the hundreds."

Straightening his back, he tapped his ring. Pinna doubted he even noticed his tell. She placed her hand over his, halting the movement. "My lord, you have told us many times to endure all the gods send us, whether it is prosperity or hardship. To believe that both make us stronger." She squeezed his hand. "You were right to raze Faliscan fields so our foe starves. Romans will survive the plague and famine. And hunger for our enemies' land will overcome that in our bellies."

The corner of his lips turned upward for a brief moment. "You have been listening again. I have to be more careful." He looked down to where her hand still held his. Embarrassed, she released him.

Camillus massaged his temples. "Rhetoric is useful to urge men into battle. But this time my words were hollow. I have put all Rome in danger, including my family. What if they should die? The loss of my sons would be unbearable. They are all to me."

His sons. Pinna had heard that they would soon be old enough to be warriors, reminding her that this man could be her father. And yet she did not think of him that way, so different was he from Lollius. Vital instead of defeated.

What would it be like to bear children? She was so young when she became a night moth she had not even had a flux. And then later she was too scrawny to have them often. Nevertheless, Fusca made her wear a pouch containing cock's blood and testes as a precaution. At sixteen the amulet's power had failed her twice, although wormwood and rue had not. She did not regret ridding herself of those babies. In the brothel, her womb pain told her she was barren. "And your wife, my lord? Would you grieve for her also?"

"I already mourn for her, Pinna. She died two years ago."

"And did you love her?" Pinna said the words without thinking.

Camillus rested his hands on the table and studied her without responding.

"I'm sorry, my lord, you need not answer."

He leaned back. "Did I love my wife? No, Pinna. I don't indulge in such an emotion. It is for women. But she was a fine citizen from a noble family. Our marriage brought me both prestige and political advantage. And I was proud of her when she gave me two healthy sons. I miss her."

Tongue-tied, Pinna stood up and turned to leave, until she heard him groan. "My lord, what is it?"

"My back."

She hastened to stand behind him. "I think that's why you have the headache. Your backbone is very stiff. The tension spreads upward. Take off your tunic and I'll rub it."

He paused, surprising her. She did not expect him to be modest. He flinched again at another spasm. Sighing, he pulled his clothes over his head.

As he stripped she saw the cause of his reluctance. He wore a broad, heavy leather belt around his waist above his loincloth to support his back. Outwardly this man's pose was martial, but now she saw that he must suffer pain each day and hide it.

She tried not to study him but she could not help it. In the Forum she'd wondered what his body would look like, what scars were hidden by his robes. She found his torso was compact and lean, the muscles of his belly defined. Under the thick thatch of hair his chest was impressive for someone his age. Here was no stripling but a man. She glanced at his thigh. The scar was deep, the gash puckered where the sinew had snapped and not fully mended. There was also a semicircular scar from his shoulder to under his left armpit as though someone had sliced a line along the edge of his corselet.

The temperature was falling with the approach of evening but it was still hot and stuffy within the tent. Pinna pulled the wolf skin off the bed so that it would be cooler. "Lie down on your stomach."

Wincing, the general obeyed her.

She knelt beside him. "I'll need to remove the belt."

He nodded and she unlaced it, letting it thud to the floor.

Smoothing the oil across his broad back and shoulders, she worried if she could make a difference to his pain. Taking a deep breath, she pushed the heels of her palms between his shoulder blades with all her weight, causing him to grunt as he expelled air. He lifted his head. "Careful."

"I'm too little to hurt you."

He lay facedown again. "Maybe, but you have hands like iron."

She worked in quiet, the only sound that of his exhalations as she pushed down on him with short, sharp jabs, slowly inching up his spine to the base of his skull, feeling his muscles relax beneath her fingers and his vertebrae loosen. Then, when she thought she could achieve no more with her pummeling, she smoothed her hands across his skin, spreading the oil, massaging him with easy stroking until she was finished.

He remained still for a time. When he turned over he was smiling.

"Is the pain less, my lord?"

"Yes. The aching has stopped."

"I am glad."

Night had fallen in the time it had taken to tend him. He lay watching her as she stood and lit a lamp, placing it on the floor beside the pallet. "Pinna. Such an odd name. But I don't see you as a chick's feather, soft and downy. You are a pinion, light but strong. I like that about you."

She blushed, pleased to be admired, not quite sure what to say.

He raised himself onto one elbow and looked up at her. "Come, sit by me."

Pinna hesitated. Since Marcus had departed to Rome, the general had sought her services often. Sometimes she even fancied his headaches were not as troublesome as he claimed. Yet he made no advances, not even flirting. Did he want her after all?

He offered her his hand. Pulse quickening, she held it and sat down, her longing for him overwhelming.

"You know, just because I do not believe a man should fall in love doesn't mean I don't feel desire." His fingers glided along her arm. She shivered, the tingling sensation foreign to her. "You told me once that Marcus Aemilius did not love you, but do you love him?"

She bowed her head, wanting to blurt out that she had no lover, only a patron. Yet she had declared her fealty. She'd promised to be faithful.

He ran his fingers along her shoulder to her throat. Pinna closed her eyes at his touch. There was no need to use oil to wet her as she had in the brothel. Breathing deeply, she pushed thoughts of Marcus away. And yet she knew she must be careful of seeming wanton. "He is a good man, my lord."

"That is not what I asked."

She met his gaze. "Then no, I do not love him."

Camillus stroked her cheek with the back of his hand. "I want you, Pinna. Lie with me."

Pinna had never kissed a man even though many had forced kisses on her. She bent and brushed his mouth with her lips. His were warm, his beard soft. No whiskery jowls or probing sour tongue. For a moment she was clumsy, then she became eager.

He lifted her so she sat astride him. Pinna drew back, surprised. She had let men groan and thrust within her, or turn her on her belly, or use her as if she were a boy. There were men, too, who liked her to straddle them, but she had never, ever, ridden a soldier. A warrior would never show such weakness. Now a general was letting her act the lover, not the bride. The thought took her breath away as much as the touch of his hands upon her. It took a man such as Camillus not to be ashamed.

He was impatient with her hesitation. With hurried fingers, he reached up to undo the ties of her tunic. She slipped it over her head while he unwound his loincloth. After raising herself slightly on her haunches, she settled, moaning as he entered her. Then, straight-armed and flat-palmed against his chest, she began to rock.

The tent was inky black except for the small circle of light that oil and flame provided. Darkness had always been a refuge, a wall protecting Pinna's soul from her body. It had protected her as well from seeing her clients, even though she still felt and heard and smelled them: their sweat and weight, the stink of their breath, their shoving pricks, their piggish grunts.

This time it was as though the darkness was painting her. His hands were gentle despite calloused pads and palms. They were firm, too, as he held her hips or cupped her breasts. She hoped his groans were of pleasure rather than pain. She closed her eyes and lifted her face upward, feeling his hardness, grinding, lost in sensation. The brothel whores claimed that sometimes a woman could reach as high as a man. Pinna doubted them. Now it was happening. She felt herself unfurling then bursting inside.

Panting, she slumped forward and rested her head against his shoulder, their bodies slick with sweat and balsam. Camillus rolled her over beside him and she realized that he had finished also. This, too, amazed her. She always knew the exact moment when a man had spent himself within her. This time he'd made her forget everything other than the freedom of surging, soaring.

Breath calming, heartbeat slowing, she lay with his arm around her. In the dim circle of light she saw that the deep grooves upon his bearded cheek and the furrow upon his brow had disappeared, and the creases around his eyes had relaxed into good humor.

The languor of the embrace was unsettling. What did he expect of her? She had never encouraged a client to stay in her bed after their business had been conducted. "Should I go, my lord?"

He laughed. "Why would you do that?"

"No reason." She smiled and stretched her body along the length of his side in the narrow bed. "And your back, does it hurt you?"

He laughed again. "Yes. But it was worth it."

Strands of her hair had loosened from its knot. He stroked them. "So soft. Sleek as fur."

She smoothed her hand across his chest, fingering the lump in his collarbone and tracing a line along the curved scar around his shoulder. "How did you get these?"

"Aequians. One tried to thrust his dagger into my gullet. Luckily he missed but his blow struck armor and the force broke bone. The other tried to ram his sword through my armpit to pierce my heart."

"Were you afraid?"

"You need a seed of fear within you to drive you to survive. It is only when the dread takes root and grows that you can be defeated."

Lying close, Pinna thought she would never again be afraid as long as she was with him. And it was not just his desire that made her feel that way. Tonight she had possessed a small piece of his power. She was no longer insignificant. No longer puny.

— • —

She woke. It was still dark. Night on the rim of early morn.

Heart thudding, she sat up, disoriented.

The bed was empty.

Again she was disconcerted. To fall asleep and then wake in a man's bed was strange.

Camillus was at his desk writing by the feeble light of the lamp. He was fully dressed, hair and beard combed. A general again. No sign of the lover.

The temperature within the tent was warm. Night had done little to dispel heat. Pinna dressed and padded toward him. "My lord, can you not sleep?"

He glanced up at her. "No, I start work each day at this time."

"Before cockcrow? You have only slept a few hours."

"Even so little a time is a waste."

She hesitated, unsure whether he wanted her to remain. Camillus laid down his stylus. "I need to tell you something."

The words were ominous. It reminded her of Fusca when she was about to scold her.

"Pinna, last night should not have happened."

The girl's spirits plummeted as fast as she had flown only hours before. Disappointed she'd merely warmed his bed for a time, she resorted to a lie. "But, my lord, I think that Marcus Aemilius is growing tired of me. I don't think he would be jealous. And I am only his concubine, not his lawful wife. He can't punish us for committing adultery."

A frown creased his brow. "That may be so, but I acted dishonorably. Marcus is your patron. I betrayed him and in doing so shamed myself. And you have been unfaithful, too. Do you understand?"

She stared at him, thinking that not even the leno's beatings hurt as much as this. He had made her feel wanted. He had been tender. All these years she had built up a shell around her feelings. To reveal them only to be spurned was humiliating, as deep as any disgrace he might feel. Like a night moth immolating itself in a flame, she'd been drawn to his power and burned.

Throat dry, she swallowed hard as she turned to put on her shoes. "Yes, my lord."

"Wait." He took her hand. "Believe me, Pinna, you pleased me. If you weren't another man's, I would tell you to go gather your things and return."

It took a moment to comprehend. He wanted her to be his woman. Suddenly she resented Marcus for binding her to him. Why couldn't he believe that she would never betray his secret? Why should he prevent her from being happy? "My lord, if Marcus Aemilius and I agree to part ways, will you make me yours?"

Camillus dropped her hand and picked up the stylus again. "Yes, but until you can resolve this with him, we must not repeat what happened last night."

She smiled and reached over to kiss him, but he was aloof, already disciplining himself not to further breach his officer's trust.

"Then I should go?"

"Yes, it's still dark. It's best no one sees you leaving."

Collecting her basket, Pinna walked to the tent opening. Camillus was once again preoccupied with his work. As she pushed back the leather flap, though, he called to her. "And, Pinna, you will say nothing about my belt?"

She nodded. "I promise I will not speak of it."

"Or how I let you . . ."

Pinna realized the general was embarrassed. She had discovered yet another man's weakness. "Don't worry, my lord. I am very good at keeping secrets."

— • —

A rooster was crowing, its clarion call loud and boastful as the sun rose. Pinna watched the dawn goddess sifting light from the darkness, touching the world with color. Soon the heat would build and the camp would wake from a restive sleep to another blue-skied day.

She hurried past the red flags marking the officers' section, shooing away the chickens blocking her path. The birds flapped away, indignant, squawking. She was determined to convince Marcus that he was safe to release her. For the great Camillus wanted her. Murmuring her thanks to Mater Matuta, she gave a little skip.

THIRTY-EIGHT

Veii, Late Summer, 397 BC

Listless, Caecilia lay with her hand shielding her eyes. Her cheeks were tear-streaked. She had dreamed that Vel was with her in the bed. On waking she wept with disappointment.

A week after the birthing she was still melancholy. It had been a long eight days. She could not understand the sadness. After the birth of each son she had been keen to hold them, smiling at the first tentative mouthing of her nipple, the pain forgotten.

This time there had been no raising of the babe to her breast that Caecilia could remember. No kiss upon a small head covered in birth muck. Instead, bleeding profusely, she had fainted. When she awoke, Ramutha hugged her and welcomed her back from death. Exhausted, she had closed her eyes again. They let her sleep.

Her daughter was brought to her every day. The sight of her brought no happiness. Instead Caecilia felt empty. As if feeling had left her and at the same time overwhelmed her.

Caecilia could offer only a dry teat. At each failure the infant howled, enraged at being wrenched from cushioned warmth into a world of noise and hunger.

"Mistress, it's time for your bath. No excuses." Cytheris bustled into the bedchamber, bringing fresh robes and ointments. One slave girl followed, carrying bedding to replace the blood-encrusted sheets. Two slave boys lugged a tub and set it up beside the bed.

Stripped of her soiled clothes, Caecilia lowered herself into the icy water. Wrenching the baby from her had rent her. She gritted her teeth, cursing that she must suffer more pain to ensure the tear was healed.

After the cold bath there was a warm one, this time in the airy, light-filled bath chamber. Cytheris washed Caecilia's tangled hair and massaged her limbs and body with unguents. Yet sitting for such a time was agonizing. By the time the servant had tied back her mistress's hair with a ribbon, and dabbed carmine on pallid lips, Caecilia was exhausted.

"There, my lady." Cytheris fastened the sleeves to the chiton with brooches. "That's better. Now let us go outside and allow some sun to shine upon you. Your sons are anxious to see you. They have only just returned from their stay at Lady Ramutha's."

Aided by the servant, Caecilia hobbled from the chamber into the garden arcade. After the dimness of the bedchamber she blinked in the afternoon sunshine, smiling at the sight of her sons in the garden.

Tas was sitting near the fountain reading a book instead of playing with his brothers. He'd grown even more solitary of late, making her worry that her oldest son had inherited her Roman reserve but none of her laughter.

Larce and Arnth were kicking a ball stuffed with feathers. The house dogs yapped and chased them. She smiled. Arnth was becoming a handful. Nearing two, he was always venturing into small spaces, or climbing the precipice of chairs or stairs. His limbs and forehead were bruised from countless tumbles. Not satisfied to traipse after his brothers, the toddler set out on his own adventures. And Larce, ignored by Tas, had started to follow Arnth instead.

Larce. Here was a mystery. There seemed no Roman in him although he'd once formed inside one. Instead he was wholly Rasennan, with the dark sloe eyes and straight brow of his grandmother, and the curls of his father. She often marveled that two unlovely people such as she and Mastarna could produce such a beauty. Her son's exuberance did not reside within the characters of his parents either. If Caecilia had not known Vel was the father, she'd have wondered where Larce had come from.

Faces flushed from the heat of the summer's day, the boys were tussling with one of the dogs. The hound had snatched the ball from them, growling whenever Arnth tried to wrest it from its jaws. Larce was giggling. "Ra at him, Arnth!"

Unexpectedly, the dog let go, causing the tot to tumble backward. The older boy pounced on the prize and kicked it. The ball rolled near the cradle. Running over to retrieve it, Larce peered over the edge at his sister.

Aricia slipped her arm around the boy's waist. "Not so close lest you wake her."

Larce wriggled against her. "But I want to kiss her."

Caecilia stepped from the arcade, opening her arms. "Come, kiss me instead."

The three boys rushed to her, bumping one another to be the first within the circle of her embrace. Pain prevented Caecilia from crouching to hold them. She bent, kissing six cheeks one after the other. Arnth jumped up and down demanding to be lifted. Larce hugged her legs, burying his face into the folds of her robe, causing her to wince. "I've missed you so much. Don't send me away again." Caecilia stroked his hair, murmuring reassurance.

Tas had been forced back, denied access by his brothers. Unruffled, he studied the baby. "What are you going to call her, Ati?"

Of course Caecilia had decided on a name. What mother did not daydream over such choices? Tas's question, though, made her realize that she had not yet thought of her daughter as a person. The little girl was to be given her grandmother's name. Not the cold distant woman of Caecilia's childhood but the mother-in-law she'd treasured.

Larthia Mastarna had no daughter of her own but she had loved Caecilia, and Caecilia had loved her. The matron had taught her that Rasennan wives possessed the same fidelity and patience as that expected of Roman women. In quiet moments the loss of her still caused tears to well. More than anything, Caecilia wanted Larthia to be with her now. To feel her arms around her. To be mothered herself.

She gazed at the infant lying snug in her swaddling, face pink from heat. The babe's eyes were swollen shut and her head elongated from too much time in the birth canal. Caecilia dared not touch her, not wanting to wake her. She couldn't cope with failing to nurse her again. And yet wasn't it wrong that she did not hasten to hold little Larthia? Memories of her own ill, bitter mother lurked inside her. The patrician had kept aloof. Could scarcely bear to touch her. Had the Aemilian sewn seeds of detachment within her? Was she destined not to love this baby because she was a girl child?

Lost in her thoughts, Caecilia had forgotten her sons were waiting for an announcement. "She is to be called Larthia after your grandmother."

The three boys examined the occupant of the crib. Arnth tried to climb in with his sister but Aricia prevented him.

"I want to play with Thia." The tot struggled to say the full name.

"Thia's ugly." Larce's declaration was said without malice.

Caecilia smiled. "Not for long. She will be pretty in no time."

"I don't want any more brothers or sisters." Tas was scowling at the baby.

Thinking her oldest son jealous, Caecilia indulged him. "Why ever not?"

"Because Aricia told me that she"—he jabbed his finger in Larthia's direction— "nearly killed you. She said I must pray for your soul."

Caecilia tried to control her temper, angered that Aricia should stoke, not douse, her son's fears. She had sent the boys to stay with Ramutha to avoid them hearing her in childbed. And had asked her friend to keep them longer rather than have them see her in a weakened state.

Cupping Tas's face in her hands, Caecilia kissed his forehead. "I am here now. You must not blame your sister for my pain."

Cytheris extracted her mistress from the jumble of boys, swinging Arnth onto her hip. "Come away now, let your mother lie down."

A canopy had been erected over a divan for shade against the sun, and a slave stood holding an enormous feathered fan to cool the mistress in the sluggish heat. Larce scrambled up to snuggle beside Caecilia on the deep, wide mattress. At Arnth's insistence, Cytheris let him sit beside his brother.

Caecilia patted the kline. "Tas, there is room for you, too." The boy climbed up and sat beside Arnth.

Caecilia looked across to her daughter, thinking Arnth's nickname of Thia would suit her well. "Thia sleeps soundly, Cytheris. What a pity it took hunger to tire her out."

The handmaid fussed with the divan's bolster, propping it behind her mistress. Her lack of response stirred her mistress's suspicions. "Cytheris? Is there something you're not telling me?"

The servant hesitated, then became matter-of-fact. "The truth is I had Semni feed her. The girl has not yet weaned her son and has milk enough. I could not bear to hear the babe crying."

Jealousy spiked. No wet nurse had ever suckled her babies.

"Just until your milk comes in, my lady," the maid hastened to add.

Caecilia closed her eyes, wondering why she should feel such resentment when she herself had been reluctant to even hold her daughter. It made sense that Thia be fed by Semni. Why should the child starve just because her mother's breasts were slack and empty?

"Ati, play knucklebones with me." Tas pulled out five tali from a pouch and handed them to her. Glad for the distraction, Caecilia deftly flipped and caught all of them on the back of her hand.

"You're too good," complained Larce.

"Then we shall take turns." She handed the tali to him. The boy laughed as he tried to copy her.

After a time, Caecilia's attention wandered from the game to admire the blue sky reflected in the pond, and the grapevine and the laurel hedges. She was content lounging amid such beauty. Although the summer had scorched the edges of the leaves there was greenery enough to be pleasing. In the lengthening shadows of the lazy afternoon the dogs lolled in the shade, occasionally snapping at flies. Even Arruns sat relaxed, idly throwing the ball up and down in one hand.

Caecilia studied Mastarna's shadow, the man who'd once been the Phersu. He had saved her life once when he slew a Gallic marauder who'd attacked their caravan on her journey from Rome. It was the first time she'd seen a man killed. The only time she'd washed the blood of an enemy from her face and clothes. The easy brutality of the guard had scared her then, but her wariness of him had waned. His fealty had been tested many times, and Arruns had never failed. The Phoenician was only a few years older than Tarchon and yet life had molded two very different men. She thought of her stepson. And then of Kurvenas's threat. Once again, she prayed that Vel would return soon.

The majordomo's face was unusually drawn and his tone tense as he approached his mistress. "Pardon me, my lady, but you have a visitor." Caecilia saw the reason for his unease. Artile Mastarna followed close behind the servant.

She sat up, the suddenness of the movement causing her to flinch. Swinging her legs over the side of the divan, she stepped from the footstool, pointing to the doorway. "Get out of my house!"

The priest merely smiled. "Now, Sister, that is not the way to greet one of the family. Especially since I have not seen the inside of my home for so many years."

Larce and Arnth were gawking at the stranger who so resembled their father and yet was no soldier. Tas was transfixed as he slid from the couch to the ground, his recognition of the priest apparent. Caecilia frowned. Until now all her children had been quarantined from their uncle.

Arruns stepped forward, waiting for a command. Conscious of her sons' presence, Caecilia hesitated to have the guard eject her brother-in-law in front of them. "Aricia, take the boys to their chamber."

The girl did not obey, instead bowed to the haruspex.

"Aricia! Do as I say."

From the corner of her eye, she saw Artile nod to the nursemaid. The girl curtsied, then lifted the younger boys from the kline, calling for Tas to follow. As Caecilia's oldest son was led away, he kept looking over his shoulder as though reluctant to lose sight of the caller, his tardy steps disturbing her.

Cytheris was gaping at the sudden appearance of the man who had been forbidden to cross the threshold. She stood beside her mistress while Arruns flanked Caecilia's other side.

The priest smoothed his eyebrow, seemingly unperturbed at a possible eviction. "Sister, I ask for only a moment of your time. My news will be to your advantage." He scanned Cytheris and Arruns each in turn. "Dismiss your lackeys so we might speak in private."

The Greek woman did not move, mouth set in a grim line. Caecilia was grateful for her loyalty, knowing how Artile had assaulted the handmaid in the past. She knew, too, that Arruns would relish the chance to manhandle the soothsayer into the street. And yet, as always, curiosity stirred. Her brother-in-law spoke of favorable news. Was the king no longer asserting her treachery? Was she no longer to be a scapegoat?

Hoping she was not being foolish, she bade both servants leave. Cytheris touched her sleeve. "Are you certain, my lady?"

"Yes, and take the baby."

The handmaid stood firm, standing in front of her mistress with her back to the priest. She lowered her voice. "I'm sure Lord Mastarna would not want you speaking to his brother alone."

Caecilia hesitated, knowing she spoke the truth. "Don't worry, Cytheris. I will merely listen to what he has to say and then send him away."

The maid retreated, carrying Thia in her arms. Her glare was baleful as she walked past the haruspex.

The Phoenician refused to go. "I do not think the master would want me to leave you, my lady. He gave me instructions that I was not to allow you to be harmed."

Artile was smiling at the interchange between mistress and guard. "I can assure you, Sister, I do not plan to assassinate you."

The tattooed man did not shift.

"It's all right, Arruns. Wait in the atrium. I will summon you if I need you."

The Phoenician bowed, then backed his way to the arcade, his eyes fixed on the seer. Arms crossed, he stood sentinel under the archway between the garden and the entrance hall. To see apprehension on his usually stony face caused Caecilia to doubt herself.

Taking a deep breath, she leaned against the divan and faced the seer, hoping she had not made a grave mistake.

THIRTY-NINE

Artile surveyed the garden, strolling to the pond, pausing to trail his fingers in the water. He had grown up in this ancestral house but had long been denied entry. He was never destined to possess it. Her three sons and Tarchon barred his way.

The arrogance of his inspection irked her. "What is it you want to tell me?"

The wrinkles around his dark eyes creased in amusement. "You look pale, Sister. I hear the birth was long and difficult. You still look in pain. If you would like I can give you some Zeri. I am sure it would give you relief as it did before."

She colored, remembering the slow seduction of the joyplant, how each vial she drank of the elixir shackled her to him, granting her bliss when he provided it and misery when he'd deprived her. Remembered, too, how he had laced it with silphion to prevent her from conceiving or to guarantee any child she bore would be deformed. Yet she was no longer that frightened girl, her nails bitten, her mind bewildered by an alien world. "To taste Zeri again would be like drinking gall. Or do you want to poison me again? As you did Seianta. Her children died because of you."

Artile smirked. "If I recall, you drank the Zeri greedily, and were equally as eager to follow in your predecessor's other quest. To defer your fate." He adjusted the fibula on his cloak, his kohl-rimmed eyes hard. "To the detriment of your husband."

As always, the man's needling was unnerving. Suddenly she regretted dismissing her servants. "Vel and I have put that time behind us. I no longer seek to control my destiny."

"If you say so, Sister." Artile gestured to the empty cradle. "What have you called the child?"

"Her father will name her."

"But he defers to you. Surely you have already chosen one."

"Then it is Larthia. I wish to honor your mother."

She was surprised at the anger that crossed his face. "Then you sully her memory by making a half-caste her namesake. Or is your daughter a bastard like Lady Ramutha's child?"

"How dare you! Mastarna is her father."

He ran his finger along the edge of the crib. "Ah, but he is not here to claim her, is he?"

"Vel will do so when he returns. There has never been an issue before when he has been delayed."

Artile nudged the cradle. "But you have not borne a son this time."

Disquiet spread through her. "We are not in Rome. The Rasenna do not abandon girls."

He set the crib rocking. "Have you not noticed, Sister, that starvation will soon grip this city if your people are not vanquished? Feeding a future warrior is one thing. Giving succor to a worthless female is another. Your daughter will not be viewed favorably. Especially when she is half Roman."

So long abed, Caecilia's legs were unsteady from standing. She put her hands behind her, leaning her weight against the divan. "My husband welcomes the birth of a girl. He claimed his first daughter even though she was a cripple."

Artile prodded the crib again, maintaining its momentum. "Yes, my brother has a soft spot for children. But as I said before, he isn't here. Nor do I think he will return before the ninth allotted day elapses. It is only two days away. Who else, I wonder, could claim the child for the House of Mastarna?"

If he had struck her she would have felt no less shock. She sank her fingers into the couch, shoring up support. "So now I am to beg you to establish my daughter's legitimacy?"

The priest stopped the cradle and smiled. "You have no other choice, Sister. The day after tomorrow I will make the decision whether to let you keep her or expose her to die."

There was a clawing in her chest. "Then I will claim her myself. As did Ramutha Tetnies with Metli."

There was a chill in the deepness of his laughter. "You? Claim a child? Your friend is of noble heritage with wealth of her own and her family behind her. You, on the other hand, only have relatives who are among those beleaguering our city or assailing our allies."

She had been threatened so many times, in so many ways. Panic spiked but she tried to remain calm. "How you must detest me."

For a moment an emotion flickered across Artile's face other than smugness. Black and sour and seething. "I ache with hatred for you, Sister."

"Because of Tarchon?"

Spittle flew from his mouth. "You turned him against me. He was my all and you took him from me."

"Not so. The scales fell from his eyes when he saw your malice. Seianta's son was born horribly disfigured and weak because of you! And you held her captive with your Zeri. Just as you tried to do with me."

He pushed the cradle so hard it threatened to topple. "If not for you, Tarchon would have been Mastarna's heir. And as his lover I would have governed this House."

"You are blind. Your plan was flawed. Vel was going to shun Tarchon because you would not give him up. He would have known nothing other than shame as a mollis."

"I would not have let that happen."

Caecilia thought of Kurvenas and his fury over Sethre's corruption. "You declare you love Tarchon and yet you've informed on him to the king. Your jealousy has put his life at risk."

He crossed to her. She could smell his cleanness. "No, Sister. The seeds of his destruction lead back to you. If the lucumo kills him it will be your fault."

She flinched but was not prepared to cower. "How did you learn about Sethre?"

"Tarchon has always been careless. A bribed slave is always open to a higher offer."

"Get out of my house," she hissed.

The priest breathed deeply, slowly. She saw the veil descend over his feelings. The brief, sharp spurt of passion dissipating. "Do you want to prevent your daughter being exposed?"

The question caught her off guard. "Of course I do!"

He picked up the tali left on the mattress. "Then I have a suggestion that might appeal to you. Did you know your oldest son has the gift of sight?"

Goose bumps prickled her skin. "Tas? What do you know of Tas?"

"He is different, is he not, than your other boys?"

The hair rose on the back of her neck.

The haruspex scattered the knucklebones on the divan. "It would be a pity if his talents were not encouraged. For I believe he might become the greatest soothsayer Veii has ever known."

"Tas will be a soldier, like his father."

Artile remained poised, the slippery, conceited smile reappearing. "I think not, Sister. He has proven to be a keen pupil. I wish him to live with me so I can continue to train him in the art of prophecy."

It was as though her legs had been kicked from under her and she had fallen on her face with no chance to break her fall. This man was seeing her son in secret. Someone in her household had delivered Tas into his hands. "Who is it? Who has betrayed my trust?"

"Someone who despises you for your lack of piety. Your sons' nursemaid would see them gain salvation after their death. She has been my devoted servant even as she has been unfaithful to you."

Caecilia sagged against the divan. "Aricia?" She whispered the name, trying to convince herself that the little girl she'd freed had grown into a conspirator. Had she not treated her fairly? Kindly? Bestowed gifts upon her, clothed her, fed her? Skin crawling, she swallowed hard as she remembered Tarchon's story also. How this priest had beckoned an eleven-year-old to his bed and then corrupted him. He had promised the boy that he would teach him to be a cepen, cajoling him with flattery and gulling him with sick affection while beating him whenever envy and temper flared.

She launched herself at him. "If you have touched my son I will kill you."

Artile fended her off, grasping her wrists. For one used only to pampered living, his reflexes were deft and his grip surprisingly strong. "Calm yourself. I have not tainted him. He is my nephew. To do so would offend the gods."

"And Tarchon was your cousin and Mastarna's adopted son. That did not stop you."

He released her. Caecilia clenched her fists, restraining herself from trying to hit him.

Once again, the irritating smoothing of his eyebrow, the adjusting of his crescent brooch. "The role of haruspex is hereditary. As I am unlikely to have a son, given my abhorrence of your sex, I am prepared to make Tas my heir. This is the news I thought you would welcome." He stretched out his hands, palms open. "Would you deny your son the chance to read the future? He is hungry for knowledge. Thirsty for enlightenment. People will hold him in awe. He will be honored and revered. You could declare your pride at being a mother of such a seer, as did my own."

Dumbstruck, she stared at him. It was true. Larthia had been proud of her priestly son. She had sent Artile away when he was ten years of age to learn the holy discipline. She claimed it caused her heartache and yet it had not stopped her. Artile was delivered, alone and vulnerable, to the Sacred College. Much as Caecilia admired her mother-in-law in so many ways, she did not want to emulate her in this example. "I will not surrender Tas to you."

There was no mercy in Artile's eyes. He was no warrior and yet he was brutal. "Then you will lose your daughter. And when confirmation comes that your husband has died, I will control all three of your sons."

She hated that tears pricked her eyes. Hated to show him weakness. For a moment she considered begging. She doubted it would make a difference. "Mastarna may yet return."

"Within two days? Unlikely."

"And when he does? Do you think he will spare your life when he finds either his daughter dead or his oldest son in your thrall?"

The priest scooped up the tali again. "And yet he did not slay me for what I did to you and Seianta." He tutted. "Or have you kept that a secret from your husband?"

Caecilia reddened. Vel knew of her addiction to the Zeri but she feared telling him of the silphion's effects. Only Tarchon knew of the priest's perfidy in preventing her from conceiving and causing Seianta's children to be malformed.

"I only kept it from Vel to prevent him from being executed for killing you."

"So you no longer wish to shield him from suffering the same punishment?"

"This is different. Your murdering his daughter would give him a defense."

The priest leaned closer. "No one would condemn me. After all, I would be acting within my rights as the head of the House of Mastarna in my brother's absence."

Face inches from hers, his bay leaf breath struck her with each word he uttered. "Besides, a holy servant is protected by the principes as much as by the deities. And the lucumo relies upon me. My brother will sign his own death warrant if he harms me. And if he does, at least I will die knowing that I have caused his downfall."

He drew back and shook his head as though speaking to an imbecile. "Don't you understand, Sister? You have no power here. I plan to take everything from you just as you did to me. Your children, your husband, Tarchon."

Tas's tali were still in his hand. He opened his palm to show them to her. "You like games of chance, don't you, Sister? Mastarna often boasts of how Nortia brought you back to him with your throw of the dice." He jiggled and scattered the knucklebones across the kline. "Tell me, do you cheat at tali as you did with those tesserae?"

A shiver ran down her spine.

"You say you no longer seek to control your fate but that's not true. You are destined to return to Rome, Sister. I have read it in the liver of a beast. And you saw Nortia's decision that day, didn't you? You cannot avoid that destiny. The goddess may be blind but she is all-seeing. Your subterfuge has not gone unnoticed."

Gloating, he edged back from her. The space granted no relief. Caecilia felt as though she were suffocating. The seer might well have had his hands around her neck.

From a distant room in the house, a shrill wail drifted through the garden. Thia had woken.

Artile grimaced at the sound. "I will give you until midday on the day after tomorrow. And then that noise will be silenced forever if you do not give Tas to me."

Turning on his heel, he strode from the garden, an assassin after all.

— • —

Thia was shrieking. Desperate to hold her, Caecilia ran toward the kitchen.

Semni had been given the babe to feed.

"Give her to me!"

The girl shrank back, frightened at her mistress's shout.

Caecilia kissed Thia's swollen face and her downy head, nuzzling the folds of the baby's neck, sweet with rose water. Untying the bands, she pulled the swaddling away. She needed to feel the babe's skin against her own. The gentle nudging warmth. To be as close as possible to this little being. Thia's puny legs wriggled, her body long and skinny, the black stub of cord protruding from her navel. Caecilia quickly counted ten small fingers and toes.

Unfastening the fibula on her chiton, she pressed the baby to her breast, sensing the fluttery racing heartbeat beneath her fingertips, her own pulse frantic. And face upturned to Juno, Caecilia prayed the goddess would grant her enough milk to finally suckle Mastarna's daughter.

FORTY

Semni stepped back, shocked and uncertain what she had done wrong. She watched as Lady Caecilia tried in vain to nurse her daughter. She had never seen her so angry. There was a desperation about her as the noblewoman held the naked infant tight. Freed of her bands, Thia squirmed and squealed, the fierceness of her mother's actions distressing rather than soothing her.

Semni frowned, wondering what had happened to cause such frenzy. Earlier Cytheris had emerged from the garden and promptly handed the infant over without a word. The girl realized the Greek woman was perturbed but didn't ask what was wrong. The Gorgon was unlikely to share any of her burdens. And now the mistress had appeared and wrenched the baby away to feed her. And yet everyone knew that Lady Caecilia could not give suck.

A week had passed since the infant's birth. Semni wished the princip's milk would come in soon. She resented her new role. As wet nurse she should have gained status as a house servant; instead the babe was brought to her in the kitchen, not the nursery. And no sooner had Thia been fed and rested than she would wake and demand the teat again. It reminded Semni of the hard months after Nerie was born.

Her memories of Lady Caecilia's confinement were troubling. She could not forget how she had stood transfixed as the color leached from the mistress's face and blood gushed from her womb. She could not forget Lady Ramutha either. The princip's beaded dress was drenched in red as she had held a vinegar sponge to her friend's nose, urging her to open her eyes. Seeing this, Semni realized that bearing Nerie in the aftermath of battle had been nerve-wracking but uncomplicated.

While the midwife stanched the bleeding, Cytheris had barked at Semni to take the baby. Thia bawled, her battered face scrunched and little tongue ululating. The servant was nervous of dropping the small girl as she wiped her clean of blood and vernix with salted barley water.

Then the Gorgon had issued another order. "Feed her!"

She had obeyed, nursing the mite amid the rush and urgency, noticing the infant's feebleness after being used to the confidence of Nerie. Worrying also that the abundance of her milk might drown the babe.

The other servants in the kitchen were staring at the princip, too. Cook wiped her hands on her apron, wary of speaking, and the slave boys in front of the fire forgot to turn the spit. The aroma of roasting rabbits permeated the room.

Cytheris signaled for one of the naked boys to fetch a chair for Lady Caecilia, then she crouched beside her, face concerned. It was not the first time Semni had noticed the bond between maid and mistress. When they were together the Gorgon was not shrill or ill-tempered. Indeed, to Semni, it seemed the depth of Cytheris's affection for the Roman and her sons meant there was none left for her own daughter. "What is it, my lady?"

"Where's Aricia?"

"In the nursery with the boys."

Lady Caecilia shouted to one of the slaves. "Go and fetch her. Tell her to come alone."

Cytheris's brow furrowed. "What has she done?"

Thia's cries were piercing. Lady Caecilia rocked her, not answering. When the child would not be consoled, the Greek woman touched her mistress's shoulder. "Perhaps Semni should take her," she murmured, "until you are calmer."

The mother shook her head. The babe grew hysterical, her tiny fists balling against her mother's bosom. Thia's face was no longer swollen but all Semni could see was a wide howling mouth. Finally the mistress relented, kissing her daughter's head as she handed her to Semni, reluctance obvious in the transfer. Semni felt guilty at how quickly the infant settled once she'd wrapped her again and put her to the breast.

Semni could feel perspiration soaking her armpits and trickling down her back, guessing why Aricia was being summoned. The judgment day had arrived. She prayed her friend would not expose her as an accomplice. Since the day when Arruns had accused them, Aricia had kept distant, her silence laden with reproach and hurt and self-pity. Pleading forgiveness had proven futile. Semni's thoughtless denial hung between them.

Crestfallen after relinquishing her child, Lady Caecilia ordered Cook and the slave boys to leave. The freedwoman did so, protesting that the dinner could burn. As they left the kitchen, Arruns appeared and stood observing the fuss. As always, there was contempt in his gaze.

She'd tried more than once to convince him he'd been mistaken, but when she repeated her explanation he refused to talk to her. She thought of all the times she had shifted blame, cursing injustices that in truth were her own fault. Now faced with the reality of unfairness, she despaired. Time and time again, she relived the moment when the briefest brush of lips had turned two people whom she loved against her.

Cytheris hovered at her mistress's side. "I don't understand. What has she done?"

The princip nodded toward the doorway. "Let her tell you herself."

Aricia hovered there. "You called for me, my lady?" There was a tremor in her voice as she scanned the expressions of the three women before her, in turn angry, anxious, and confused.

Lady Caecilia gestured to the space in front of her. "Stand here."

The nursemaid curtsied, gulping, and duly obeyed.

"Tell your mother what you have done, Aricia. Tell her how you have betrayed the House of Mastarna."

The bracelets on the girl's wrist jangled as she stood speechless and trembling.

Cytheris stepped over and grabbed a handful of her daughter's hair. "Tell me what you did!"

Semni found it difficult to watch, a sick feeling in her belly. She wished she could hide and listen, instead of being an audience to the drama.

Aricia gasped at her mother's grip but the rough handling provoked rebellion. "The chief haruspex is my true master, just as Aita is my god. I sought salvation for her sons so they could be one of the Blessed. I performed the rites of the Calu Cult for them because the Roman wouldn't."

The Gorgon yanked at the roots of the girl's curls. "Are you telling me you took them to see Lord Artile?"

Aricia stood on tiptoe, leaning her head to the side to lessen the pain of her hair being pulled. "Only Tas."

There were two high spots of color on Cytheris's pockmarked cheek. She continued to hold the girl fast. "How did you manage to hide this?"

Aricia spoke through clenched teeth. "We went through the tunnel leading from the wine cellar. Lord Artile gave me the key."

"Cytheris, let her go."

The Greek woman hesitated at Lady Caecilia's command, then released her daughter.

Aricia held her hand to her head, rubbing the sore spot as she faced the mistress. "Did you know your son has the sight? Lord Artile recognized Tas's gift. But he said you would deny the boy the chance of greatness because of your hatred."

To Semni's surprise, Lady Caecilia did not shout. Instead, after a chilly silence, the noblewoman unclasped the necklace she always wore. Semni had often admired the craftsmanship of the pendant and the figure engraved upon it—Atlenta the huntress with her bow and sheath of arrows.

Prizing the locket apart, the princip laid it on her open palm. Within it were two locks of hair—a small black curl and a frizzy wisp. Intrigued, Semni glanced at Aricia and her mother, realizing she'd combed the coils of one and mocked the Gorgon tresses of the other.

Aricia stared at the amulet, clearly nonplussed.

Lady Caecilia pointed to the four silver bangles encircling the nursemaid's wrist. "Do you remember when I gave you those?"

Dragging her attention from the locket, the girl fingered the bracelets. "Yes. It was when you freed Mother and me. On the night you escaped to Rome."

Lady Caecilia closed her fingers around the pendant. "Why do you think I carry such keepsakes?"

The nursemaid shook her head.

"Because when I first came here I was scared and homesick and bewildered. Your mother was a comfort to me and still is. She cut off these tresses on that night and gave them to me as mementos. And so I keep them to remind me of such friendship and how, for the first time in my life, I had the power to save a little girl from being taken from her mother."

She extracted Aricia's curl from the necklace and tossed it into the fire. "But you repay my kindness by giving my son to the man I detest."

There was an acrid whiff as the hair incinerated. Aricia watched it flare then turned back to Lady Caecilia, no longer distracted by sentiment. "The chief haruspex has told me everything. Every bad thing there is to know about you. He has told me how you never wanted to bear the master's heir. You do not deserve to have such a son!"

Lady Caecilia grasped the armrests of her chair as though bracing herself. Semni thought how vulnerable she looked, how frail. The princip's normally coiffed hair was unloosed and held back by a simple ribbon. The brief flush of color that fury had engendered had vanished, carmine and antimony emphasizing her pallor. The servant sensed that only a brittle resilience prevented the Roman from weeping. When Lady Caecilia spoke, though, her voice was so loud Semni doubted there would be any need among the other servants in the house for speculation or rumor.

"Do you know what you have done? Lord Artile visited here today. He has given me an ultimatum. Tas or Thia. I must choose one or the other. If I do not surrender my son to him your high priest will expose my daughter!"

Aricia's insolence faltered. She gaped at the mistress, her aghast expression proof she had not been party to the priest's cruelty.

Cytheris had been rendered mute, but now she took up a switch from beside the fireplace and ripped Aricia's chiton from one shoulder. "My lady has given us everything! She does not deserve such treachery."

Back bared, Aricia cowered as she was beaten. Semni flinched with each hit, remembering what a hiding felt like. How the anticipation of each cut was nearly as awful as the smarting blow.

Lady Caecilia was known for her leniency. Few slaves were whipped at her orders other than those who had thieved or were caught fighting. Yet even though Aricia deserved a birching, the mistress bit her lip as she watched the mother thrash her daughter. After a few strokes, she bade her handmaid to halt.

Cytheris was deafened by fury. The switch split the skin on Aricia's shoulders over and over, the white skin webbed by livid stripes.

Above the sobbing came a high-pitched command. "Leave her alone!" Tas raced to his nursemaid at the risk of being hit. Chest heaving, Cytheris stopped, startled by the arrival of the eavesdropping boy.

Aricia embraced him as she sank to the floor.

Face ashen, Lady Caecilia held out her hand. "Come here, Tas."

The boy clung to the servant. "No! I hate you, Ati. I hate you. I want to go with Uncle!"

His mother stepped over to him, grasping him by his arm. "Be quiet. You do not know what you are saying."

Tas stamped his foot, golden eyes tear-filled. "I want to be the greatest haruspex Veii has ever known. I want to be a fulgurator and see the future in lightning and thunder."

Lady Caecilia tried to hold him but he wriggled free, running back to Aricia. Once again, Semni's guilt pricked her conscience.

The mistress sank into her chair. She was haggard, dark smudges beneath her eyes, lines harrowed between cheeks and mouth. "Arruns, take Master Tas to his room."

The Phoenician had been viewing the commotion with an impassive face. When the boy would not budge, he wrapped one arm around the child's waist and hefted him from the chamber. The guard ignored how he tried to kick and hit him. Tas's shrieks could be heard echoing along the hall.

The noise upset Thia. She stopped suckling, edgy and mewling. Semni placed her against her shoulder, amazed the baby settled when being patted by tense hands and rocked against a thudding heart.

Tas's declaration of loyalty had calmed Aricia. With painful motion she rose, swaying as she regained her balance. Then, one by one, she pulled the bangles over her hand and threw them at Lady Caecilia's feet. There was a rattle as they hit the tiles, one rolling until it wobbled onto its side. "Your choice is easy. Keep Thia. Give Tas to Lord Artile."

Cytheris raised her stout arm again, the birch ready. "How could you do this to the mistress? How could you do this to me?"

Aricia raised her elbow to ward off the blow. "I owe no thanks to the Roman for keeping me with you! All I have ever known is the blunt edge of your hand and the sharp edge of your tongue."

The Gorgon hit her.

Lady Caecilia stood. "Cytheris, stop."

The maid paused, rod in midair, then lowered it to her side. Obedience to her mistress had not halted her wrath, though. "You are no longer my daughter!"

Aricia glowered. "And I do not want you as my mother!"

Lady Caecilia covered one side of her face with her hand as she sank into her chair. "Be quiet, both of you."

The roasting rabbits were sizzling. Semni could smell them beginning to burn but she remained intent on the mistress as all waited for Aricia's sentence. She looked over to her friend, perspiration pricking her scalp when she saw Aricia was staring at her, face devoid of emotion. Semni froze. Did the girl expect her to confess? To show fidelity through sacrifice? "Please," she mouthed, seeking mercy.

Her blank expression unchanging, Aricia looked away. Semni relaxed her shoulders but her pulse did not quiet.

Raising her head, Lady Caecilia sighed. It was as though outrage had been drained from her and all that was left was heartache. "Aricia, I do not make this decision lightly. You are banished. Salve your wounds and then leave."

Semni's stomach lurched. She had not thought Lady Caecilia would go this far. The cosseted, spoiled housemaid would not survive when cast into a starving city.

The silver bangles were scattered across the floor. The princip pointed at them. "Take those. Sell them. They will buy you food and shelter."

Hunched over, Aricia did not beseech forgiveness. "Lord Artile will take me in. He will train me to be a priestess."

Lady Caecilia frowned. "Don't you understand? He is base. Now that you can no longer serve his purpose, he will shun you."

At the words, Aricia's posture became less defiant, her demeanor no longer triumphant. Doubt flickered. Fear, too.

The rabbits had caught ablaze, smoke billowing and pooling under the ceiling as the kitchen vents clogged.

Cytheris knelt before her mistress. Her eyes were watery. Semni thought it was from the stinging haze until she saw her anguish. "Please, mistress, don't throw her into the streets. I will beat her daily instead. I will keep an eye on her. Otherwise she will starve, my lady. She will die."

Distressed by the smoke, Thia gave a choking cry. Lady Caecilia stood and reclaimed her from Semni. Then, as she turned to leave, she paused and rested her fingers on Cytheris's forearm. "Forgive me. The priest has stolen both of our children." Her touch signaled sadness. There was regret, too, in her round hazel eyes. "I am sorry. I cannot risk having Aricia under my roof."

The servant nodded but tears were flowing now. "It must be, then. It must be."

As the princip left the kitchen, Semni stared at the Gorgon, touched by the grief shared by mistress and maid.

One of the slave boys appeared and scurried to the fireplace. There was a hiss as he threw a bucket of water over the burned dinner. As the flames were dampened, an odor of scorched herbs filled the air. Cook followed, flapping her apron to dispel the smoke.

Semni ran and threw her arms around Aricia. The nursemaid gasped, the cuts on her back paining her. Yet she did not shrink from the embrace, laying her head upon her friend's shoulder. She smelled of smoke and fear and violets.

Cytheris dropped the switch and wiped her tears with a corner of her chiton. Then she moved to examine the welts on Aricia's back, frowning at the damage her anger had wrought. There was concern in her tone. "I'll get some yarrow to lessen the bleeding."

Contemptuous, her daughter shied away, remaining huddled within Semni's arms. "You offer comfort now? And tenderness?"

Once again, Cytheris tried to reach out to touch her daughter. "You are the only child I have left."

Semni could feel Aricia quaking as she pushed the proffered hand away. "Then you have lost me just as you did my brothers and sister."

The sorrow on the Gorgon's face made Semni glance away.

Cytheris's long plait brushed the floor as she stooped and collected the bangles. "At least take these."

Aricia broke from Semni and snatched the bracelets, tossing them into the fireplace. "I will not need them. Lord Artile will help me."

Cytheris stared at the jewelry lying amid the smoldering ashes and charred carcasses. She was so still Semni thought the woman had turned to stone, as if petrified by Medusa's glare. Slowly the mother's plump face sagged, her double chins quivering. "Then I will mourn for you, Daughter. Today and on the day news is brought that you have died."

FORTY-ONE

Falerii, Late Summer, 397 BC

Half waking, half sleeping, Pinna was in the brothel again. She could hear Genucius.

His voice grew louder.

Opening her eyes she realized it was past daybreak, fresh sunlight spilling into the tent, the heat already beginning to permeate through its walls.

Her heart tottered and lurched. The plebeian general was not in her dream. He was standing no more than two yards away. His manservant was unfolding the cross struts of a chair for him so he could sit next to Camillus. Closing her eyes, she hoped the men had not noticed she was awake.

She concentrated on feigning sleep, hoping that by remaining still she could avoid recognition. She was naked beneath the thin sheet, her hair loosened, partially covering her face. No different in appearance than all the other times Genucius had seen her except for lack of paste and henna. She could hardly believe her misfortune. For nearly a year she'd coerced Drusus into silence and bargained with Marcus for protection. Now her chance for happiness would be destroyed by one random meeting.

Why had Camillus not woken her? She should have returned to her tent by now, creeping back in the hour before sunrise. Yet after their lovemaking, the night had been stifling, making sleep fitful. The cool of the early hours must have granted her deep slumber. Perhaps this had happened to him also.

His vow that they should not lie together had been broken the first time she'd soothed his headache again. The continual lapses made him guilty but did not hinder repetition. In a way she wished that Marcus would return. She needed the matter to be settled. Then Camillus's conscience could be salved. Hers as well. She was desperate for Marcus to trust her enough to release her despite her infidelity. And sometimes she resented the general's intention that he would not pressure his officer should he object.

She visited him when the sun had set and the moon risen, returning to her tent before he met with his officers at sunrise. The hours with him were similar to those she had kept in the lupanaria. At least there she could rest at dawn whereas now she was expected to work in daylight as well. She did not mind the lack of sleep. Not when it meant she could spend treasured time with him.

There was no declaration of love. Pinna told herself never to expect one, to be content with what she had. Yet she could not help wanting to possess his soul. For certain he'd stolen hers. She hoped to convince him there was no need to check emotion, no shame in letting her share a place in his heart. Wanted to believe that, because he'd not stopped lying with her, there might be a chance.

Although they strived to keep their affair secret, those in the camp were not foolish. Nor were his servants. There were whispers. Gossip was spreading that Pinna was not just skilled in rubbing the general's shoulders. It made her nervous, making urgent the need for Marcus to return.

"Was the whore any good?"

Pinna tensed. Genucius must have been looking at her. She kept her eyes shut.

"You know I don't use prostitutes. I leave that to city idlers and weak soldiers. I've tried to expel those poxy Faliscan whores but it is like trying to rid a scab-skinned cur of fleas."

Pinna felt a flush of heat. She'd not known the depth of his scorn. Suddenly she realized there would be no redemption if he discovered her past. He would think of her as vermin, feel stained by her touch. She prayed he would not flay her.

"Then you have taken a concubine. Something new for you since your wife died."

Camillus was curt. "You've arrived here earlier than expected. Why not make use of your time by talking of war instead of women."

"Certainly." The one-eyed officer sounded uncomfortable. "But I am parched and hungry. I have been traveling most of the night."

Hearing this, Pinna opened her eyes a slit, her muscles aching from the strain of stillness. Camillus must have been taken unawares by his colleague's premature arrival, giving him no time to rouse her.

The general gestured to his manservant. "Of course. I'll see to it that your aides are fed as well." Then he called to her, voice gruff. "Pinna, wake up. See to my guest. Bring us some water."

Her panic heightened, knowing she couldn't escape. She murmured a reply, realizing that even though she'd listened more than talked to the plebeian, he might well recognize her voice.

Tense with nerves, she sat up and turned her back to them as she drew on her clothes. Then, flipping out the hair trapped by the neckline of her tunic, she twisted it into a knot and pinned it tightly. Head bowed, she hurried to the clay water jar, lifting the dipper and pouring the liquid into the cups. Maybe if she served the men as fast as possible the chance of detection would be lessened.

Genucius was sitting on his armchair, one leg hooked at a right angle upon his other knee, rubbing his calf muscle. He had lost some of his size. No doubt campaigning had reduced his diet.

He was still hairy, though, beard wild and bushy, tufts poking out from the top of his tunic. Even with the reduction in weight his bulk was not made for summer. He was already sweating.

Pinna concentrated on quelling her jitters. Standing on his blind side, she offered him the cup together with a plate of figs and cheese. To her relief he didn't look up at her as he drained the goblet and asked for another.

Accepting the drink, Camillus nodded his thanks. "You must wash the general's feet, too, Pinna, after his long ride."

She froze, remembering how Genucius had once kissed and sucked her toes. She wondered if the plebeian had found another whore to tend to him as she had.

Camillus took a swig of water. "It is good that you have come in person. It's time to destroy Mastarna once and for all. He may have failed to raise all of Etruria against us but he is not a man to be underestimated. If he succeeds in opening the routes to the north, our plan to starve our enemies will flounder."

"So what do you propose?"

"My spies have confirmed he is making his way back to Veii. He is weak enough to want to be with his bitch when she whelps another pup. To return to her he will have to break through your defenses. Are the outer siege lines secured?"

"My men have replaced much of the timber cladding with stone on both inner and outer trenches, but the work is hot and exhausting. Quarrying the tufa from the ravines is a long process."

"But you have built more forts?"

"Yes, and replaced the hides on the siege engines with iron. All the roads to the north and east are now blockaded. The main camp is doing the same in the south and west."

Pinna listened with amazement as she fetched the pitcher and ewer. Genucius was no longer the world-weary politician complaining about the burdens of office. It was obvious he was clearheaded and resourceful. And a good ally to Camillus.

"And the bridge across the river leading to the northwest gates? Have you taken it yet?"

The plebeian paused. "We've launched assaults, but Kurvenas holds it fast. Skirmishes prevent us from constructing a siege tower at the most vulnerable entrance to the city. The king is also a leader not to be ignored."

"Then we must cut Mastarna off before his army reaches the bridge. Destroy his force and we may yet forge a corridor to the walls of Veii."

"I will order more troops to defend this section immediately."

Camillus stood and paced. Since the news of the plague, his enthusiasm for razing crops had faded. Over the past weeks he had left behind fields of blackened stubble and ruined villages to slowly edge into Veientane territory. His discontent at being denied the primary command was eating into him. He needed a victory.

Kneeling at Genucius's feet, Pinna unlaced his boots. The tortuous blue veins were raised and thick, the skin bruised with tiny blood vessels. Stomach churning, she guided his foot onto her lap. Then, after wringing the wetted cloth, she wiped the grime from his calves and ankles.

"Ah, that is good. My feet and legs ache in the heat, you know."

"Pinna is skilled in massage."

She smoothed her hands along heel and arch. As she did so she sensed Genucius's attention. He leaned down so he could see her with his good eye. "Why, Lollia, is that you?" A pain twisted in her gut. She cursed that it was her touch, not voice, figure, or face, that had revealed her.

Inhaling deeply, she raised her head. "I think you are mistaken, sir. My name is Pinna." She squeezed his ankle. "Your feet are so swollen; perhaps you would like me to do something 'special' for you?"

Even behind his beard she could see him redden. He wiped the sweat from his forehead and fiddled with his eye patch. She fixed her eyes on him, hoping that her candid stare would act as a warning—remain silent or risk revelation of his fetish.

Alert to their conversation, Camillus frowned. "Have you two met before?"

Genucius was quick to recover. "I'm mistaken. Pinna here looks like a servant girl I once knew."

"And no doubt bedded." He grew impatient. "Dry the general's feet and help him on with his boots, Pinna. And then you may go."

She hastened to finish the task, sloshing water from the ewer in her rush to leave.

A familiar voice halted her progress. Looking around she saw Drusus asking permission to report. He was travel-stained, dusty from his journey. She could scarce believe his arrival at this moment.

A tremor ran through her. For weeks she'd been spared Drusus's malice. She'd felt freedom, glad for the respite from the exhausting tug-of-war between them. Now, as the emotions that he always evoked swept through her, she realized she'd been lulled into a false contentment.

And yet Drusus's shock at seeing her barefoot in Camillus's tent was almost comical before he regained composure and saluted the commander. Denied the chance to sneer at her because of the general's presence, there was an edge to him. He was disconcerted. His worst fear had come true. Pinna now possessed the power to whisper secrets into Camillus's ear as she laid her head upon his pillow.

Marcus entered the tent, his brow creasing in puzzlement when he saw her. She was nonplussed to glimpse hurt in his eyes before they hardened. And suddenly she understood Camillus's sense of dishonor. This is not how either she or the general wanted Marcus to learn of their liaison.

The Aemilian's gaze traveled from her to Genucius, his confusion returning. The last time he'd met the plebeian was in the brothel, and yet it was evident Genucius had not spoken to Camillus about her. The half-blind man also looked perplexed to learn the two officers had not revealed her profession either.

She could no longer control her hands from shaking. She bent down to clean the spill from the ewer. All four men in this tent had taken her in different ways. All four had a secret that she alone preserved. Three of them could destroy her if they had courage to expose themselves. She prayed that none of them could summon it, that her schemes would not unravel.

To her surprise, Camillus showed no embarrassment that Pinna was present in his tent in the early morning, her shoes beside his pallet. Instead he seemed annoyed that his officers were distracted by her. "Don't just stand there. Tell me the news from Rome. Is the sickness still spreading?"

Marcus stood to attention. "The plague still rages, sir."

"And Aemilius and the other senators? Do they still claim divine anger is caused through the military consulate being debased?"

Marcus glanced at the plebeian before replying. "Yes, sir. The gossip is as virulent as the disease. I tried to make Father understand that the accusation serves no good purpose but he will not heed me. The Senate is agitating for only patricians to once again be elected. And there seems to be little opposition to the proposal. The commoners are preoccupied with the mystery at Lake Albanus. Even Calvus's complaints about the war tax are of less concern."

"Are you telling me no ceremonies have been conducted to placate the gods?"

"Only those in relation to the pestilence and extreme weather. The Sibylline Books don't contain the answer to the miracle. Rome remains ignorant as to which rites should be performed in response to the unnatural rising of the water."

Pinna murmured a prayer. If her city did not know how to appease the gods, what disaster would befall it?

Genucius shifted in his chair. "This is indeed ominous. What do you think, Camillus?"

The general tapped his gold ring as he contemplated the news, then he leaned forward and slammed his fist onto the table. "What do I think? I think the time has come to glorify the gods by dedicating a victory to them. Let's defeat Mastarna and then divine wrath may be assuaged. And it will provide proof that the current leaders of Rome's legions are not the reason why such prodigies have occurred."

He gestured to Marcus and Drusus to approach. "You are going to get your chance for battle after all. We may not be able to storm Veii but we can destroy its greatest warrior and its largest army."

Both officers grinned, joining the other commander at the table. Camillus unfurled a map. "Genucius, my friend, tell me what you think of this strategy. Mastarna's troops should reach Veii tomorrow. Return now and feign that you no longer guard the outer siege lines. And when the Etruscan arrives, lead your forces out to meet him on the plain while my troops—"

The plebeian smiled. "Circle behind and attack from the rear."

"Yes, let's crush him between us, just as he and the Faliscans did to that idiot Sergius."

Genucius grinned. "And in glory we'll show those bastards in Rome that they cannot pull us down."

Camillus stood and clapped his hand on Marcus's shoulder. "No doubt Aemilius worries that his ambitions for you are hindered by your association with me?"

Marcus showed no rancor at the two leaders' disdain of his father and friends. "I'm afraid so, sir. But I have sworn an oath to follow you on this campaign. I owe my allegiance to you."

"And you do not regret that?"

Marcus faced him squarely. "Never."

"Good. Then how would you like to be promoted to command a turma of knights? You have proved yourself an excellent decurion. It's time you led thirty men instead of ten."

The officer's mouth fell open. "Yes, sir! Thank you, sir!"

Unexpectedly, Marcus looked over at Pinna as though wanting to share his excitement. To be promoted to lead a turma was one of his dreams. Seeing her barefoot, though, must have reminded him of her betrayal. His expression clouded. He turned his back on her.

"And me, sir?" Drusus's zeal was childlike, his desire to also be promoted obvious. "What are my orders?"

"Ah, Claudius Drusus." Camillus placed his arm around the officer's shoulders. "You are to escort General Genucius back to Veii. You shall have your chance to meet Mastarna head-on rather than circle behind him. And if the gods are kind, the opportunity may come for vengeance as well as fame."

The Claudian saluted him, but Pinna glimpsed disappointment as he bent his head to adjust his belt. Marcus's career had been advanced. His friend, once again, had gained greater favor.

Camillus sat down at his table and focused on examining the chart with Genucius. The plebeian studied it intently. Pinna guessed he no longer noticed his aching feet.

The two knights stood waiting for orders.

Their general raised his head. "Go, Marcus Aemilius! Give the command to break camp. Then ride ahead and scout for a suitable site. We must march to the outskirts of Veii by the end of the day. Tell my other officers to report also. Advise them that tomorrow they will taste victory." He addressed the russet-haired soldier. "And you, Drusus, ready yourself to ride with General Genucius."

The Claudian saluted, then glared at her before he hastened away. Marcus also turned on his heel, but then paused and looked back at her, rubbing the scar near his eye. His silent reproach shamed her. And the way he held himself stiffly suggested he felt vulnerable that she was Camillus's mistress. She wanted to go to him, to say that she was sorry, to tell him he could trust her, but this was not the time.

Noticing the exchange between the concubine and her patron, Camillus kept his expression blank. "I will speak to you about Pinna later, Marcus."

Genucius glanced up and frowned, then returned to inspecting the chart.

Watching Marcus leave, Pinna suddenly wondered if there was more to his advancement. Was it a sop to ease the general's conscience? A bribe to ensure the young officer would not cause trouble?

Wanting reassurance she glanced across to her lover, but he'd already resumed conversing with his colleague.

Miserable, she sat down and put on her tunic and shoes.

FORTY-TWO

Camillus's Camp, Outside Veii, 397 BC

The new camp had been erected by the time Pinna arrived in the midafternoon. Each of the soldiers and workmen knew their role, their tasks completed with efficiency. Rows of tents were pitched, red-and-white pennants fluttering to mark the sections. The enclosure between tent line and palisade was ready to be crammed with horses, cattle, mules, supplies, and fodder. Ready also to be filled with booty and prisoners.

Pinna sought out Marcus amid the noise and heat haze. She was tired and grimy from the journey. There had been no time to speak between the breaking of camp and traveling to the new location. From the moment the two consular generals had formed their plan there had been no rest. In full armor the troops quick-marched in advance, leaving the women, noncombatants, and beasts straining to catch up.

Guilt consumed her, regretting that she had humiliated him. She should have heeded Camillus's counsel instead of stoking his passion every time he called her to him. Not truly being Marcus's lover had blinded her. Having gained credibility as his concubine she could not now shuck off the role like a snake shedding its skin.

Hurt, pride, and anger were not precluded merely because jealousy was lacking.

Marcus was in the enclosure checking his mount. Pinna observed how the stallion trusted him, responding to his touch and command alone.

After a time he noticed then ignored her. Determined to talk with him, she risked standing in front of horse and rider. Whinnying, the bay reared, hooves slicing the air. Pinna scrambled away. Sullen, Marcus calmed the steed and dismounted. He motioned the groom to hold its reins, barking at the servant to see that the horse was watered. The boy smirked as he led the animal away, leaving the officer and his woman to their recriminations.

Pinna touched Marcus's sleeve, but his disdain caused her to drop her hand. "I need to explain."

"I have nothing to say to you." He headed to the entrance to the main area of the camp.

Pinna scurried behind him. "Please, Marcus. I am sorry."

He halted, thrusting his face close to hers. "Don't ever call me by that name again! Don't forget your place."

She bowed her head. "I'm sorry, my lord."

Her humility only riled him. He dragged her by the arm to stand next to the high pickets, safe from the traffic. "What good are all your sorries? The reason why I agreed for you to become my concubine was to shield my reputation from gossip. Now you've caused me to be ridiculed."

She couldn't meet his eyes. "I did not mean to hurt you."

Marcus clasped both her upper arms. "Look at me! Are you saying that you never thought this would affect my honor? Everyone here sees you as my woman. Do you think being cuckolded by a general makes my embarrassment any less?"

Pinna raised her head, surprised at his anger toward Camillus. Even with the commander's part in the betrayal she never thought he would see his idol as flawed. "Don't judge him too harshly. He wanted to delay until I could speak to you and end our union. It was my fault. I tempted him. I could not wait."

His face was white and pinched under his helmet, the scar on his neck livid. "There you were barefoot in his quarters like the whore you are. The shoes I gave you did not change your ways. And it was obvious he was confident that a subordinate would not challenge him."

"It is not like that. He respects you."

He shook her hard enough to make her head fling back. "Tell me, did you tell him that you were a citizen? Wait till he learns your name is listed on the prostitutes' roll."

A sharp pain stabbed inside her chest. Marcus released her abruptly and tried to move away but had to wait for a wagon of grain to trundle past. Flustered, she tugged at his cloak, remembering the desperation that drove her to pressure him in the first place. Yet hadn't she sworn she would never reveal his love for Drusus? She couldn't let him spoil all that she'd achieved, though. And there was a lesser threat she was prepared to use. "And what will Camillus think of you? When he discovers you made a harlot your concubine? He despises men who go with whores."

Marcus gave a sour laugh. "Is that why Genucius did not speak up about you?"

"All men have their secrets," she murmured.

His look of surprise quickly changed to contempt. "And you gather them like a spider traps flies in a web, don't you?"

Another cart passed by, dust stirred up by wheels and hooves. He pulled his cloak from her grasp. "Believe me, Pinna. I can weather Camillus's disapproval. Better than allowing him to become a laughingstock for unwittingly taking a whore. I may be disappointed in him as a man but I have sworn an oath of loyalty to him as my general."

Pinna grabbed onto the edge of his corselet with its horsehead crest. "I beg you, please don't tell him. I love him."

Derisory, scoffing, he prized her fingers away. "And I suppose you think he loves you, too. Let me tell you something. Furius Camillus is just satisfying his lust. He is not a man to be manipulated by romance." He paused, his eyes narrowing as he glanced toward the command tent, then back to her. "Unless, of course, he has a secret, too."

She stiffened. "No," she lied, then quickly added, "even if he did I would not divulge it. Just as I would not betray you again."

His look was withering, as though she was some base creature that should be trod upon or kicked. "Do you take me for an ass?"

Fear made her forget her earlier restraint. She clutched his arm, the metal of his wristband hard beneath her fingers. "And what of the proof of self-loathing hidden beneath this bronze?"

Menacing him only provoked greater scorn. "So you would break that promise, too, Pinna? The one you swore when I left for Rome. How right I was to doubt you only weeks ago. You're a true she wolf after all. Conniving and venal." He wrenched away and walked away from her.

The ache in her chest tore at her. Shame and anxiety merging. Did she really hate him that much? Frantic, she ran around him and sank to her knees, prepared to abandon all chances of coercion, seeking mercy instead. "Forgive me, my lord. Take pity. I truly will never speak of your love for your friend."

He halted, head cocked to the side, examining her. "Is that true, Pinna? Are you saying that even if I tell Camillus you're a prostitute you won't try to take revenge on me?"

She bent and kissed his boots, tasting the grit, smelling the odor of leather. "That's right, my lord. I'll remain silent." She looked up at him. "But please, my lord, please, can't we just free ourselves from each other instead?"

Marcus crouched beside her. For a moment she thought all was well. Then she realized she had not calmed his fury but forged it like iron. The man who could be kind had vanished. She had managed to drive compassion from him.

"Then know that if I return alive I will tell him exactly what you are. And I will pray that respect for my valor in battle will soon override any contempt he has that I kept a whore in my bed. He will thank me, too, for sparing him ridicule."

The pain became a deep, sharp-bladed hurt. Disbelieving, she sat back on her haunches and watched him stride off. She felt numb, scarcely comprehending what had happened. She'd always thought it would be Drusus who would destroy her.

A muleteer shouted at her to move as he drove his animals into the compound. His curses did not penetrate her thoughts. It was only when the donkeys were almost upon her that she lurched to her feet, the herd passing only a foot away.

Dazed, she headed into the main camp, passing through the commotion of shouted orders and soldiers training. Hoplites were practicing their phalanx formation. When some pretended to fall, the next line stepped over them and re-formed. In battle tomorrow the knights would charge forward as the heavy infantry cut a swath. And for one brief, guilty, savage minute, Pinna wanted Marcus to be slain.

FORTY-THREE

Veii, Late Summer, 397 BC

The night demon sat upon her chest, snakes slithering around its arms, breath rank from its vulture's beak, flesh rotting, scaly wings arched.

Caecilia woke, heartbeat frenetic, gasping with fright at the vision of her old tormentor. To her relief light was filtering through the vents and slit in the curtains. Then she remembered Artile. She swallowed down a knot of panic, feeling as trapped as she'd been in her nightmare. Nausea returned. She'd vomited twice yesterday from constant nervous churning. The priest's threat was so huge it was inconceivable. Even now she could not reconcile the menace with reality, the terrifying choice of either delivering her son to evil or her daughter to death.

Her sons were lying asleep beside her. When night had fallen she wasn't prepared to let any of her children out of her sight. She'd brought them into her bed: Arnth and Larce on either side and Thia nestling in the crook of her arm. She found comfort in their body warmth and cuddles. Tas, though, remained sulky and silent, refusing to speak to her after witnessing Aricia's beating.

The younger boys had thought it a game but soon grew irritable with their sister's squirming. In the end, Caecilia relented and let the babe lie in the cradle next to the bed. Even so, the heat and cramped space still led to disturbed slumber. And sleep evaded her completely, although she must have finally dozed only to be visited by the monster.

Curled beside her, Larce stirred at Caecilia's abrupt wakening. Drowsy, he snuggled up to her. She stroked his cheek, resisting the urge to wipe sand from the corner of his eyes. "Hush, no need to wake."

She looked across to Arnth. He was lying on his back, confident as always. No nightmares for this child. He would be a demon slayer.

Caecilia checked on Tas, who had huddled on the edge beyond his brothers. He'd refused to lie beside her even though he was the one she needed to hold nearest. He was awake, his hands clasped on his chest, staring at the ceiling.

"Tas? Will you talk to me now?"

He didn't respond, instead turned to study the leopard on the wall.

Easing herself from between her two younger sons, she climbed from the bed and came around to face him. He rolled onto his other side.

She touched his shoulder. "Look at me. I'm sorry you saw Aricia whipped, but she should never have taken you to see Lord Artile. I can't trust her anymore. That is why she must leave."

Suddenly he sat up and rounded on her. "You let Cytheris hurt her! And now I won't see Uncle again! He told me this would happen. He said you would stop me if you found out."

Caecilia tried to remain calm, disgusted with the priest's manipulation. How much poison had he poured into her son's ear? "Apa and I don't want you to see him because he has been cruel to me in the past. You must believe me, Tas, it's for the best."

"How was he cruel? Did he hit you?"

Once again Caecilia restrained her temper, resentful that the soothsayer had placed her in such a position. She was not about to describe the history of the haruspex's sins to a child only nearing seven. "No, Tas, he did not strike me, but it's hard to explain what he did. You must believe me, though, that your uncle is not a good man. And Apa will be very angry when he hears what he has done."

The amber eyes brimmed with tears. "He was going to make me a seer. Now I will have to be a soldier. That frightens me. I don't want my chest cut open like Apa."

Her heart ached for her little boy. He'd known nothing but siege and combat since he was born. And she was as guilty as his father in impressing upon him the expectation he'd be a warrior. Roman or Rasennan—a man was taught to be proud of such a future. There were always doubts, of course. Hadn't she calmed those felt by Marcus? In the end, though, valor was required. Tas's inheritance was of brutality and glory, not prophecy and fame. Now she saw how he would be drawn to Artile. The prospect of being a sacred messenger was wondrous compared to the danger of gaining scars. She tried to hug him but he wanted no part of her. He climbed from the bed and ran into the arcade.

She let him be, knowing that Arruns was standing vigil.

The thought that she may have already lost her son to the priest infuriated her. Artile's hold over Tas had to be broken. She was not prepared to surrender the boy. She could no longer afford to sit brooding or rent her clothes and tear out her hair as though already in mourning.

Leaving her other children to sleep, Caecilia sat at her table and put stylus to paper. Then she summoned a slave girl and issued orders. "Fetch the steward. I wish him to deliver an invitation to Lady Ramutha."

— • —

Ramutha Tetnies, clever and charming, had been the first of the principes' wives to welcome Caecilia into her home. Other noblewomen in Veientane society had not been impressed. The princip's liking for the Roman was as blatant as their disapproval. At first Caecilia thought the aristocrat paid attention to her to annoy the snobbish clique, but it did not take her long to realize her new friend was sincere in her affection. And both women shared two things in common: their lives were grist for other people's gossip, and they adored their children.

At Caecilia's call, Ramutha attended upon her immediately, bringing her girls with her. Thefarie's two daughters were as comely as their mother and as richly dressed, ribbons and tassels trailing, their hair crimped into curls. And it was clear that they loved their little sister as they fussed over her. Metli had yet to walk or speak because her siblings would carry her everywhere and do the talking for her. The toddler only needed to point and her every whim was granted. Larce and Arnth had all three squealing as they chased them around the fountain. Their shrieks and laughter lent a strange counterpoint to the hushed and worried conversation of their mothers. Tas sat watching their play, refusing to join in.

Noticing the boy was listless, Ramutha frowned. "How you must hate Artile for filling your son's head with such ambitions."

The sick feeling in Caecilia's stomach deepened. "It torments me to think he might have touched Tas as he did Tarchon, although he claims he would never taint his nephew."

Ramutha studied the child, expression grave. "You would be justified in having your brother-in-law killed, Mele. Take matters into your own hands. Mastarna would not hesitate to slay his brother for such wickedness."

Caecilia shook her head. Arruns had offered to assassinate the priest. Until yesterday the thought she might commission a murder would have repulsed her. Now, in her desperation, it seemed a possibility. Yet even though Artile was prepared to spill her daughter's blood, she could not bring herself to have his on her hands. And she could not condemn the Phoenician to a death sentence for following her orders.

Instead she had come to a different solution. What if Thia was claimed by another princip? Then the priest would be thwarted. To forfeit her daughter to another House would be heartbreaking, but the price paid was small compared to the toll the seer sought to exact. "I have another idea. One over which I have thought long and hard. Lord Vipinas has vowed to protect us. Do you think he would adopt Thia?"

The Veientane raised her eyebrows before growing serious. "Ah, Mele, that is inspired, but I doubt he would intervene. His pledge was to ensure Kurvenas did not harm you, not to interfere in family matters. He would consider that the high priest is the head of the House of Mastarna in his brother's absence. I'm afraid he would respect Artile's wishes."

Caecilia covered her face with her palms. Her scheme had kindled hope, now Ramutha had doused it.

The noblewoman gently pulled Caecilia's hands away. "But, Mele, I will claim Thia myself."

The plan was bold. Wide-eyed at the simplicity of the suggestion, Caecilia felt her spirits lift. Once she had condemned the freedoms of Rasennan women as licentious. Now she was grateful for such independence. She thanked the gods she lived in Mastarna's world. Never would she have been allowed to claim a child in the name of the Caecilian clan in Rome.

Ramutha picked up Thia. Her daughters clustered around her, jostling to hold the baby. Metli shuffled over to them on her bottom and held up her arms, indignant she'd been deserted by her sisters. One of the older girls once again obliged her. Arnth and Larce scampered over, not prepared to be left out.

Ramutha laughed. "Don't look so astounded, Mele. I have already claimed Caile's child for the House of Tetnies. Of course I would do the same to save Thia's life."

"But what about Thefarie? Would he mind you claiming her?"

"He would do the same, Mele, if he were here. As your husband's friend he would not want to see your daughter harmed. And when Mastarna returns, I will relinquish her. In the meantime she will still be known as Larthia Mastarna. I would not seek to deprive her of her heritage."

Caecilia kissed her on both cheeks in gratitude and yet her mention of Vel stirred anxiety as well. "I wish he was here. I fear he will never come back."

The princip returned Thia to her. "Come, you must not think that. The great general is not going to let any Roman dog savage him."

Caecilia pressed her lips to her daughter's forehead, aware that her friend was trying to jockey her. She told herself she should concentrate on those things in her control, not what was in the lap of the gods. She must cast aside her worry over Vel. Rejoice instead that her quandary had been solved.

Metli had become fractious. Her older sister handed her to Ramutha, who sat the tot on her lap and began retying the child's hair ribbons. Watching her friend with Caile's child, Caecilia remembered how Ramutha thought Mastarna justified in removing Sethre from Tarchon's arms. And yet the princip had been furious with Vel for granting Vipinas the favor of keeping her young lover far from her. Did the noblewoman still pine for the youth every time she gazed upon his daughter? Or had absence and distance finally dampened her passion? And what about Thefarie? Did the wife even spare a thought for her husband?

"Do you miss Thefarie at all?"

Ramutha kept her head bowed, prinking her daughter. "Of course. He has long been at Capena."

Caecilia placed her hand over her friend's, trying to gain her attention.

"And Caile? Have you forgotten him?"

The Veientane stroked Metli's head before looking up at her. "No, Mele. He is in my thoughts always. My heart still aches."

STORM

FORTY-FOUR

Camillus's Camp, Outside Veii, 397 BC

If there had been no danger, Pinna would have thought the ravine beautiful. Red-and-yellow tufa walls rose beyond a stream dappled with sunlight while beech and oak provided welcome shade. Before she had become an army wife she would have found no menace in this landscape. She knew now that a camp set within a valley could be surrounded, that a forest could hide a lurking foe. Pinna prayed the palisade stakes were tall and sharp enough, the ditch deep and wide enough, to offer protection.

Camillus would not normally have chosen such a vulnerable site, but he needed to be close to Veii yet hidden from Mastarna. He did not plan to stay long. He sought victory by sunset.

Around her, the place was eerily quiet, devoid of almost all soldiers except those few left to act as defenders. Warriors resentful at being denied battle to protect women, workers, and sick and wounded soldiers.

At sunrise, after lustration had been made and the auspices taken, Camillus had moved into position to wait for the signal to ambush the foe. Companies of hoplites marched past with the clank of armor and thud of boots while cavalry reined in high-stepping horses. Leves followed, equipped with only shields and spears, then the low-classed axemen together with slingers. Last of all came the units of trumpeters. Their horns were silent but soon would add to the din of war cries and fighting.

An undercurrent of dread had been left in their wake, a tremor of fear at any motion or sound outside the picket. Hours had gone by, but the animals in the enclosure remained restive, shuffling and snorting at the sound of combat in the distance, the trumpet calls tinny, the shouting faint.

The only break in the tension was the sight of a cloudy sky, a gray expanse that promised rain. The chance the drought might be broken raised morale.

Pinna sat baking a fresh batch of bread with the other women, cook pots in the fire, lids covered with embers. When she'd first joined the camp she'd been reluctant to seek their company. She was not practiced in making friendships, having known only the disdain of the she wolves and the solitary life of a tomb whore. And her status as a knight's concubine also created a barrier until they saw she did not want to lord over them. In time, though, she enjoyed gossiping with them as they sat mending clothes or swapping recipes as to how to sweeten the bland porridge of puls with raisin and honey, or make it savory with vinegar, beans, and salt. There were no children to fuss over. The general would not let any woman remain who had borne an infant. He did not want his camp to become a nursery or schoolyard.

This morning the wives were subdued, their laughter false. All knew that at the end of the day a blood toll would be paid and some would mourn over their lost men. Conscious of Pinna, their chatter was nervous, too. Rumor had been made certain. Her argument with Marcus had been witnessed and reported. Now there were murmurs that both the commander and his aide should spurn the troublemaker.

The night before battle, unable to bear Marcus's hostility, she'd placed her mat outside his tent while he remained inside. He'd said nothing when he saw this. And he rested for only a few hours. On the eve of combat there were too many nerves and too much excitement. He was surly when he departed, ignoring her. She was weary from lack of sleep and worry, and felt powerless and humbled. And, despite her brief spurt of malice yesterday, she feared for his safety.

As a child, Pinna would gaze at the night sky and reach up to try and sweep stardust from the constellations, the sparkles so dense that such a theft would surely go unnoticed. Last night, during the long hours awake, she had stared at the dark universe, ruing that the little girl who played with twinkling patterns had become a schemer whom her father would despise.

Turning the dough over and over upon the board, Pinna strewed it with salt and added more water before she kneaded and flattened it with her palms. She had believed the rhythm of the task would empty her mind of cares; instead she found herself pounding and slapping with greater effort than was needed as her feelings revolved: fear to anger, anger to shame. She could not concentrate, going over and over Marcus's threat. She considered Drusus, too. Strangely, she'd not needed to contend with his bile. In his haste to leave with Genucius he had not approached her. Instead, with the bronze boar's head on his corselet and shield burnished to gleaming, he'd ridden out with a scowl upon his face. His reticence alarmed her as much as his spite. Yet what did it matter what the Claudian did or thought? It was his friend who had condemned her. Bitterness surged. She was being forced to grieve for Camillus whether or not he was slain.

Her lover's farewell had been rushed, curtailed by his desire to rally his troops while the dew was fresh upon the grass and the sky rosy with early sun. If not for Marcus, she would have been ecstatic that the general was prepared to break the rules, that with the risk of death he'd wanted to summon her to him.

When she'd entered his tent she'd found him keyed up with anticipation, his mind roiling with tactics, pushing through exhaustion. His squire was helping him don his armor, a routine established between them. She'd wished she could be tightening the buckles on his corselet and handing him his balteus and sword. Instead she'd stood watching, not warranting his attention until he was attired for the charge.

After dismissing his attendants so he could speak to her in private, he'd made it clear he didn't want to invest time in good-byes nor listen to whispered warnings of concern. He'd showed her that he cared, though.

The iron dagger had been heavy in her hand. Blade polished and honed, handle weighted, a wolf's head crest embossed upon it. He had presented it to her not as a gift but as a precaution.

"I don't plan to give the enemy the chance to raid the camp but, should it happen, you must use this."

Pinna had stared at the knife, afraid to touch it. "I don't think I could kill someone."

Pressing the weapon into her palm, he closed her fingers around it. "No, it is to kill yourself."

Taking two of her fingers he guided them to her throat. "You must cut here." He pressed against the pulse. "Make sure your stroke is firm enough to slice through muscle and artery, not just flesh."

The practicality of horror chilled her. "I don't think I could do it."

He gripped her hand. "There will be more than one of them, you know. Bloodlust is infectious. And they will not stop at rape."

It was as though she was standing on a precipice looking downward, her knees weak, her belly churning. And yet she knew he was right. She could expect no mercy. There had been more than soldiers and farmers slain in skirmishes. Wives and daughters had been defiled. The Veientanes would relish the opportunity to redress the balance for their Faliscan ally.

"Please, Pinna. Seize courage if it is needed. I don't want to return to find you mutilated and broken, a ghost tormented."

Before she could respond he kissed her, intense and swift. Then, slipping his arm through the leather strapping of his shield to grasp its handle, he left without a parting glance or reassuring smile.

Now the dagger was hidden in the basket beside her. And as she pressed her knuckles into the dough, she relived the brief glimpse of his emotion. She prayed that Marcus would somehow forgive her and change his mind. Wished also that he was wrong in claiming Camillus would never love her. Pondered whether she should use the knife anyway if the Aemilian did not grant her a pardon.

The sound of a camp mongrel's frenzied barking broke through her thoughts. The women stood frightened, clasping each other's hands, anxious as to what was causing the disturbance. Seeing the soldiers at the guard posts had not raised their weapons, Pinna ran to the gate. She was optimistic that it was the footsteps of a victorious army that the dog had sensed.

There were no warriors, only a messenger, flushed and filthy from his ride. Coming from a direction away from the battle. As he swung from his horse, he hailed the duty officer and asked to speak to the general. "I come from Rome. Lake Albanus has risen so high it has broken its banks. A deluge sweeps all in its path as it gouges a route to the sea. The plowed fields and plantations of the Latins have been inundated. It is a catastrophe of major import. The Senate thought General Camillus should know."

Pinna listened, disturbed by the news. The rising of the lake in drought had been a prodigy. Here was a greater omen.

The officer frowned. "But the Roman people have not yet appeased the gods. What are we expected to do?"

"The Senate counsels caution until they learn what rites must be performed."

The soldier groaned. "Your message comes too late. The general led his force into battle this morning."

Pinna gripped her fascinum and shell so tightly the cords bit into her neck. She ran to the altar in front of the command tent. Shortly after dawn Camillus had sought confirmation that he would succeed. The sacred chickens had pecked at the proffered puls, eager to eat it. The greedy sound of the grains dropping from beak to ground revealed divine favor, not malice. Was the result of the auspices faulty?

Until now Pinna had felt the peril Camillus was facing unreal. There was always an aura of invincibility around him. One he aroused within his soldiers, too. Hadn't he once defeated an enemy with a spear dragging in his thigh? The gods had spared his life on that occasion. It must have been for a reason. She could not imagine an Etruscan killing him just as she could not believe she could slit her own throat. The danger he faced now terrified her.

She knelt and prayed. Soon she was joined by all the women and camp workers. And as they made supplication, gray fists of cloud gathered, the air cooling. After so many months of arid summer it took Pinna a moment to realize it was showering. She closed her eyes and let the rain drift down upon her.

The pleasure of wet cheeks, lips, and brow soon faded. The darkening skies could bode ill. If the drops grew heavier, dust would turn to mud. The battlefield could become treacherous. Horses would stagger through mud, their speed slowed. And warriors would struggle in the downpour, their footholds and handgrips slippery as they fought their foe. Pinna cradled her head in her hands, no longer anxious about her own troubles. Once again the deities were bending nature to their will. Were they truly angry with Rome or could it be possible they wished Mastarna to fall? Fraught with worry, Pinna repeated one prayer to Mater Matuta: "Bring him back to me. Don't let him die."

FORTY-FIVE

Veii

The sound of the war horns was faint, drifting on breezes from the north.

Caecilia ignored it as Arruns drove her carriage along the main street of the citadel. The clarion call was common. There were often skirmishes launched from that part of the city to protect its most vulnerable side. She noticed, though, that there seemed to be more people about, and more carts heading down from the arx. The mood was buoyant. For the first time in months the sky was gray. The prospect of rain was welcome.

Caecilia was light of heart, too. The ninth day had passed. She wanted to confront Artile rather than wait for him to visit her. Whom did he think she would sacrifice? Son or daughter? The thought of depriving him of both filled her with satisfaction.

She held Ramutha's hand. Her friend had insisted on accompanying her. The thought of thwarting the priest pleased the noblewoman as well.

Since the war began, Caecilia had not set foot inside the Great Temple of Uni in case she met her brother-in-law, and so it concerned her that Juno might be offended. Yet it seemed the deity had forgiven her for such neglect. Hadn't she given her succor on many occasions? And now the goddess had saved the children against her chief priest's wishes.

Caecilia expected the haruspex to be presiding over the daily sacrifice. He was not there.

The women ventured inside, where the bejeweled statue of Uni stared down upon them from her chamber. Kneeling, Caecilia covered her head with her yellow shawl and laid a terra-cotta figurine of a baby at the feet of the statue. A thanksgiving for Thia being rescued and Tas saved.

Noticing a cepen was lighting bowls of incense, she called for him to advise his master that she and Lady Ramutha had arrived.

The novice shook his head. "But King Kurvenas summoned my lord this morning. Have you not heard? Your husband is fighting Genucius at the northwest bridge."

Caecilia ran, pain ripping through her at the sudden movement.

Calling to Ramutha to hurry, she cursed that she must rely on donkeys instead of horses to pull her the miles to the Tinia Gates.

Flicking the reins, Arruns urged the animals to a trot. They skidded on the cobblestones of the steep single road from the arx but regained their footing once driven onto the wide, straight avenue dissecting the city.

And then, as they neared the north of the city, they slowed.

Traffic was clogging the artery, crowds streaming along the pavements. The mood was cheerful. General Mastarna was always victorious. At last they would be able to escape the city. There would be revelry more joyous than when Sergius's army had been defeated. The siege lines would be destroyed. Trade would flow again. Hunger assuaged.

To Caecilia's relief there were no catcalls when people spied her, instead encouragement. Her husband was returning. And his wife, no longer seen only as Roman, was hastening to meet him.

Her own excitement was intertwined with apprehension, though. Vel was so near and yet in danger. The thought churned inside her that she could lose him while he was within reach.

The sea of carts and litters, wains and wagons, serried the vast boulevard, a spectacle of color and racket. The odor of animal dung was strong as oxen and asses left droppings where they stood. Soon drivers were shouting at each other in the crush, their progress delayed by having to take turns passing between stepping-stones laid at intervals along the street.

Aggravated by the slowness, Caecilia rose in her seat, ready to step down and push her way through, but Ramutha stopped her. "Don't be foolish, Mele. You could be trampled."

They waited.

It started to sprinkle, the temperature cooling. A thousand upturned faces gazed at the darkening sky, spirits lifted by the feel of the mist. A cheer rocked the air.

Finally they reached the northern forum only to find the carnival air dissipated, voices querulous, chatter anxious. Caecilia heard snatches of conversations.

"Camillus has joined Genucius."

"Mastarna's army is surrounded."

"The general has called for reinforcements."

"The king is refusing to open the Tinia Gates."

This time Caecilia almost tripped in her haste to leave the carriage. Arruns climbed down and stood in front of her. "It's too dangerous, mistress."

She was impatient. "Stand aside. I have to find out whether it's true. Whether Vel is trapped."

To her surprise he lifted her into his arms. She held on tightly to his neck, her cheek inches away from the snake, conscious of the hardness of his chest, the ease with which he held her as she bumped up and down with each step he took.

Barging through the masses, Arruns bellowed for the people to stand aside. The crowd parted. The bodyguard and his mistress made their way to the wall.

There were archers stationed along the rampart, and she could see others on the bastions projecting from the curtain wall. Kurvenas's men. There were more atop the two pylons that flanked the entrance, the stone lions decorating them keeping vigil. She frowned when she saw that the bowmen were passive. She was reassured, though, that there were rows of soldiers assembled behind the inner door of the double gates, carrying aloft the standard of Vipinas's clan.

Using his shoulder, the Phoenician shoved his way up the long rampart's slope to the bulwark where the lucumo and his advisers were gathered.

The king's lictors barred them. Arruns placed Caecilia on the ground.

"Let me through!"

The guards looked doubtful, rods and axes raised to defend their ruler. If she was not so distraught she would have thought such security laughable against a wan, frail woman. Her tone changed to entreaty. "Please, I merely wish to speak to the king about my husband."

More hesitation and then they relented. Caecilia was allowed to pass, Arruns restrained.

The war horns were louder here. Strident. Brassy. And she could hear the noise of battle rising from beyond the walls: men shouting, the clash of metal, and screaming. The breastwork was too high for her to see over it. A pulse beat at her temple as she realized Vel was on the other side.

In the lee of ashlar blocks, Kurvenas and Vipinas were arguing, beads of moisture coating their cloaks and hair, droplets of rain showering them with each gust of wind. The king's arms were crossed, chest pushed forward. Vipinas's shoulders were hunched, his wheezing voice loud. Caecilia had seen the lean old man offended and forceful before but now his fury was patent. She searched for Artile, frowning when she found him absent.

Sethre stood next to his father, the bruising on his face less noticeable but the skin around his eyes still puffy. He was trans-fixed on another warrior sitting on a stool, his armor grimy and bloodstained. A wound on his thigh was bleeding. He was also shouting. It was Tarchon.

Pushing through the bronze-clad officers surrounding the king, Caecilia knelt and threw her arms around her stepson. Startled, Tarchon reared back but then embraced her. There was an earthy smell of drain water about him.

"How did you get here?"

"Through one of the drainage tunnels. Mastarna sent me ahead to call for reinforcements."

She examined the gash. "You are hurt."

He grimaced. "I'll survive."

She hugged him again. "So Vel is alive?"

Tarchon drew her from him. "Kurvenas is ensuring that he dies. Mastarna's cavalry broke through Genucius's forces at the bridge and planned to charge the Roman phalanx from behind. But then Camillus launched a surprise assault, giving the oppor-tunity for some of Genucius's troops to turn and block our horse-men. Our infantry is now squeezed between both Roman armies on the plain. And Genucius has ordered all his cavalry and skir-mishers to attack Mastarna. Our knights are stranded between the river and the city, and are heavily outnumbered." He pointed to the lucumo. "If this coward does not send reinforcements or open the gates they will be slaughtered."

Bewildered at his news, Caecilia rose and faced the king. Her hand trembled as she rested it on Tarchon's shoulder. "Why won't you send assistance?"

Kurvenas ignored her. Talking strategy to a woman was beneath him. He yelled at his lictors, "Get her out of here!"

Vipinas moved to Caecilia's side and fronted the monarch as well. "Why not answer her? It is her husband's fate you determine today."

The ruler was disdainful. "Mastarna has failed. There are two enemy forces out there. Why should I risk Veii by opening the gates and letting her people swarm over this city?"

Before Caecilia could protest, Vipinas challenged him again. "I've already told you. The Roman hoplites are still engaged beyond the bridge. At this stage only their cavalry and leves have been sent to slay those who are caught beneath the city wall. My men are already marshaled. Let me march to help Mastarna, or at least allow his troops to retreat inside."

"And you think your men can defeat two armies?"

The nobleman drew himself erect. "At least we can show our foe we are not afraid."

Kurvenas flicked his head, smoothing his hand over his damp hair, vain even in crisis. "Veii is safe behind ditch, mound, and walls. It's no use adding to the casualties by ordering another of our armies to venture out."

Vipinas's hands were shaking, voice cracked. "At least let me die saving my grandson!"

Too consumed with her own concern over Vel, Caecilia had forgotten Caile. She understood how the grandfather was feeling—the shock that a loved one would die while they stood helpless behind masonry.

When Kurvenas failed to respond, the princip left Caecilia's side and strode over to him. "Then at least allow Mastarna's cavalry to retreat inside! The lock of the double gates will protect us from the Romans should they follow. Our archers can keep them at bay while our soldiers enter the space between inner and outer doors. Then we can let our men inside once the area is secured."

The king stood over him, snarling. "Can't you hear me, old man? I'll not risk Veii being overrun. I have given my command."

Vipinas's usually waxen skin suffused with color, but before he could respond, Tarchon staggered to his feet, blood flowing down his thigh. "You do this because you want Mastarna dead. You have never forgiven him for defying you." He leaned against Caecilia. She lurched. Sethre stepped forward, hooking Tarchon's arm over his shoulder. The lovers smiled at each other, a fleeting glance of affection passing between them.

At the sight, Kurvenas wrenched Sethre back toward him. "Get away from that mollis!"

Suddenly deprived of support, Tarchon toppled. He groaned as Caecilia helped him onto the stool. Swearing beneath his breath, he studied Sethre, realizing their liaison was no longer secret. Misery exuded from the youth, his shoulders slumping.

Kurvenas loomed over the injured man. "I'm going to throw you over the wall so a Roman can stick his sword into your gullet—if you survive the fall."

"No, Father!" As Sethre called out, Kurvenas cuffed him, sending him reeling.

Seeing his beloved struck, Tarchon made the effort to stand again, stooped over in pain. "Punish me but leave your son alone! I will gladly join Mastarna. At least it will be an honorable death."

Caecilia slid her hand into his. She felt a tremor run through him, his bravery forced. And yet she admired him. Tarchon always impressed her with unexpected displays of valor.

Anger surged, too. The pulse throbbing in her head matched the frantic beating of her heart. Out on the plain, and just beyond the walls, Mastarna and his clansmen were being slain to satisfy one man's revenge. "Why not cast me over the wall, too? Why not make it clear that your decision is based as much on vengeance as it is on caution?"

Kurvenas sneered. "Rash defiance as usual, Aemilia Caeciliana? The thought is tempting, but I'm not inclined to provoke outrage by throwing a woman onto a battlefield. Not even a traitoress. As I've said before, I prefer Rome to exact its own punishment on you. And make no mistake, by the end of today I will send you back to your city. And your husband will not be here to hinder me."

Caecilia sighed in disgust. The well-worn threat was irrelevant compared to her despair that Vel was going to die.

Vipinas grabbed Kurvenas's arm. "Are you confirming that this is personal retribution? Would you have Caile die, too, because you hate Mastarna?"

At the princip's action the lictors seized him, not prepared to allow him to touch their king. Vipinas collapsed into a coughing fit, striving to gain breath between his words. Phlegm rattled in his throat. Caecilia knew the sound. It was more than illness. It hinted of death. The death her father suffered.

Vainly struggling against his captors, the lord glared at the lucumo. "Is this revenge against me as well? For not supporting the Clan Tulumnes in the past? I should never have agreed for a monarch to be elected again."

She felt pity for him. This man's son had died fighting for Veii when only eighteen. Now his daughter's child would be slain also. A dynasty lost. Just as Caecilia had felt powerless when faced with Artile's ultimatum, she could see emotion working within the old warrior, how he was grinding his false teeth, eyes hard with hatred. No doubt he had braced himself many times to hear his grandson had fallen—but not in this way. Not when Caile could so easily be saved.

The king signaled the lictors to release the nobleman. Vipinas straightened and readjusted his robes, the cloth darkened with wetness under the steadily increasing rain.

"You are mistaken, Vipinas," said Kurvenas. "I make this decision for Veii. Your grandson will be remembered for dying with courage."

Sethre found his voice, still prepared to question his father. "Please, Father, at least command the archers to let loose volleys. It might drive the Romans away." The youth's determination made Caecilia realize that perhaps Tarchon had taught the boy to be a man. That perhaps her stepson had been a true mentor after all. The thought reminded her of Artile. Where was the haruspex?

Kurvenas was dismissive. "Don't be stupid. A barrage isn't going to repel the enemy for long. And our horsemen below could be pierced by our own arrows."

Tarchon snorted. "Yet you'd allow them to be killed by Roman spears."

The ruler flinched and squared his shoulders as he shouted to his bodyguards, "Pitch the mollis over the wall."

Caecilia felt Tarchon tense beside her. She squeezed his hand. She was not sure if his palm was moist from water or sweat. He glanced down at her, his expression grim, his beautiful face streaked with grime and rain. He was about to be murdered by a madman after surviving years of fighting. Before the lictors could seize him, though, Sethre stood in front of him. "Please, Father, I beseech you. Spare him . . . or . . . or . . . I will kill myself."

Caecilia felt sorry for the youth. His display of manliness had been brief. His earnest plea seemed childish. It had the same plaintive note that she'd heard from her own children. Behind him, Tarchon was wise enough to counsel his beloved to be silent.

Kurvenas shoved the youth aside with a clip to the head. "Be quiet! I'm ashamed of you." He gestured to one of his lictors. "Guard my son." The black-clad man seized the youth by the arms. Sethre tried to thrust him aside without success. "I will never forgive you, Father. I will hate you always." His voice rose in pitch. "And so will the people."

To her surprise, Kurvenas paused. And at his hesitation Vipinas pressed the point. "Your son is right. Your subjects might forgive you for sacrificing men for the sake of the city—but killing Mastarna's son at the same time as his father is dying for Veii? The people will see you as a tyrant as base as Tulumnes. And remember what happened to him."

The drizzle was heavier. The king's armor was glistening, his hair slick from both unguents and rain. Wiping his dripping face, he showed he was canny despite his quest for vengeance. "Very well, Vipinas. I will spare him such a death."

"Thank you, Father, thank you." The lictor allowed Sethre to kneel and pay homage.

Kurvenas raised the youth to his feet. "I have not finished with this dog, do you understand? I will deal with him later."

Sethre cast an agonized glance at his lover. Ashen, Tarchon nodded shaky reassurance. Seeing the exchange the lucumo roared, "Take the soft creature away."

Despite pain and loss of blood, Tarchon held himself with dignity as the lictors seized him. "Be brave, Caecilia," he called over his shoulder as, limping, they dragged him away. "Mastarna would expect it."

Kurvenas now concentrated on her. "Take the woman, too."

Caecilia shied away when a lictor tried to seize her with his calloused hand. "No! Let me stand upon the rampart. Let me see my husband one last time."

Bent over from wheezing, Vipinas moved to her. "I do not think that is wise. Do you really want to watch Mastarna die?"

Smug and implacable, the king smiled as he interrupted the princip. "On the contrary, Lord Vipinas," he said, rubbing the groove of scar on his bearded chin. "I think that it is an excellent idea."

FORTY-SIX

The lamp was enormous. A maenad's face adorned it. Two slave boys were needed to unhook it from the ceiling. It would take hours to burnish.

Semni used the tweezers to extract the spent wicks from the sixteen nozzles, then with olive oil and elbow grease she set about removing the soot. She always hated polishing the bronze. There was so much of it: candelabras and incense burners, wine jars and rhytons. Her delight in the artistry of their decoration had palled the first time she'd cleaned the crevices of their engraved or embossed surfaces.

Her brief spell as a wet nurse had ended. Her short-lived sense of importance also. She thought the mistress's decision premature. Thia was still hungry, her cries jarring everybody's nerves. Yet she understood the mistress's persistence to suckle her baby, and her resolve to keep all her children within sight, given Lord Artile's malice.

Arruns had said the Roman was brave. Semni knew this was true. And since the confinement she'd come to admire the princip more and more. Lady Caecilia had showed courage in her lengthy labor.

In the birth chamber, boundaries of class had been suspended. The lowly had rubbed shoulders with the highborn, and roughened hands had touched soft ones as she and Lady Ramutha held the mistress on the birthing chair. And for once there was no hostility from Cytheris as she issued instructions to fill the goat's bladder or brew the acrid tea.

At least the foreboding that had loomed over the household had lifted. Yesterday Lady Ramutha had visited, trailing her brood of prissy daughters behind her, and had left hours later, having found a way for the mistress to thwart Lord Artile's plot. Today, though, as Semni rubbed the grimy lamp, she could not help feeling a little resentful at the solution to Lady Caecilia's dilemma. With a fortune of her own, the haughty Veientane could weather scandal. Her husband had accepted her illegitimate child. Now Lord Thefarie would have to cope with his wife adopting another man's daughter. How different it had been for her. As soon as Velthur had spotted the blond patch on Nerie's head he'd cast her aside. Raising a bastard was not so simple without rank and riches. And yet Semni could not truly grumble—at the end of the day her son would be raised in a princip's house as well.

Nerie perched on the washroom bench beside her. His face, clothes, and hands were covered in oil. Having grown tired of copying her, he was now arranging the molded ladles and wine strainers in a row: griffins nudging centaurs, and docile lions next to deer.

Semni brushed her hair from her eyes with the back of her hand, glad for the day's coolness and hoping that, after the searing summer, autumn might not tarry after all. For she had woken to a dismal sky. The prospect of the drought ending caused those in the household to smile.

The horses in the stable were neighing with a fractious shifting of hooves at the distant notes of war horns. Above their sound Semni heard a herald calling for all to gather. She lifted Nerie and hurried into the kitchen.

The youth was breathless. "Lord Mastarna is attacking the Romans at the northwest bridge!"

Message delivered, he departed, repeating it to all he met.

Keen to plunge into the crowd that would be heading to the Tinia Gates, Semni started toward the courtyard. Although she never again wished to view the aftermath of battle she relished the chance to join in carousing when victory was announced. It had been such a long time since she'd reveled.

Cook paused in adding salt to the cauldron. "Where do you think you're going?"

"To see General Mastarna and his soldiers returning."

The woman pointed to the washroom. "You're not traipsing after any rabble. Get back in there. When the master returns home there will be chance enough to celebrate."

Pouting, the girl turned to resume her work. She ached for the freedom she'd once had to leave her potter's wheel and share the thrill and heartbeat of the city. Yet she'd only taken a few steps when she heard cries of delight outside.

Fine mist was drifting from the sky. Smiling, Semni stood with the others in the yard enjoying the feel of droplets upon hair and skin. Nerie laughed, squeezing his fingers open and shut, trying to catch the sprinkles.

After a time the novelty faded and the servants retreated inside. Semni trudged to the washroom. Settling Nerie at her feet she resumed polishing the lamp. Rain pattered on the roof. And the creak of wagons and clip-clop of donkeys outside was proof that wetness was no deterrent for the curious heading to the Tinia Gates.

"Hello, Semni."

She froze, recognizing the voice.

Head covered with a shawl, Aricia stepped inside the doorway, flattening herself against the wall so she could not be seen.

Nerie laughed, lurching toward the nursemaid. Semni picked him up and swung him onto her hip. Her whisper was panicked. "How did you get here?"

"The tunnel from Uni's temple, of course." The girl held up the wine cellar key. "Lord Artile had more than one of these." She tilted her chin. "I'm going to Velzna to the Sacred College just as he promised."

She was radiant, exuding sanctimony and smugness. Her blue-bordered chiton was not dirtied. It was clear she had not suffered from the expulsion. Instead she was triumphant that any doubts about the priest were unfounded.

Semni remained skeptical, though. "I don't believe you."

"It's true. The haruspex is leaving the city today and is taking me with him."

Astonishment was heaped upon disbelief. "But the mistress is on her way to tell him that Lady Ramutha is to claim Thia."

Aricia frowned, unsettled by this news. She soon recovered. "Then she will find my lord missing."

It was still difficult to believe the girl's story. "And how are you going to get to Velzna? The Romans surround us. And now a battle is raging."

"There's a tunnel to one of the sanctuaries outside the city. From there Lord Artile knows a way through the ravines. And he has coin enough to buy us passage through one of the remoter outposts. A priest and his family would pose no threat to the Romans."

A sense of disquiet stirred. "What do you mean, 'family'?"

Aricia peeked through the doorway and back to Semni. "Tas is to come with us."

"But you can't take him! He is the heir to this House."

Aricia placed one finger to her lips. "Shh! I am doing what is best for him."

"You're crazy. His father is fighting his way here at this very moment. You cannot deprive him and the mistress of their son."

The girl drew her shawl from her head. Her eyes were intense. "Have you ever wondered why I shielded you? For certain it was not for love. Not after you made it clear that I mean nothing to you. I protected you so you could help me now."

Semni swallowed, shifting Nerie farther up her hip. "I'm sorry I hurt you, but I thought you knew we are only friends. I love Arruns. That doesn't mean I don't care for you."

A glimpse of the old Aricia returned. "I would have done anything for you, Semni. Anything, if only you had chosen me."

Compassion filled her for her friend's unrequited love, but pity was not enough to convince her to abet Aricia in her plan. She was already remorseful that she'd aided the nursemaid in the first place. And she would never be able to bear Arruns's hatred once he learned she'd been complicit in the abduction of a beloved child. She avoided the reproach in Aricia's gaze by concentrating on Nerie. The boy put his arm around her neck and sucked his thumb.

"I can't. It would break Lady Caecilia's heart."

The girl's expression hardened. She gestured toward Nerie. "He is safe because of me. You owe me a debt." On hearing his name, the tot leaned forward and stretched out his arms for Aricia to take him. She ignored him. "I wish you to repay me now."

Heat prickled Semni's skin. She was being dragged into a conspiracy again. "I don't understand. What do you want from me?"

Aricia glanced yet again into the corridor. "I want you to bring Tas to me."

Semni stared at her, the request so astounding she struggled to understand.

"The Roman never wanted him in the first place," Aricia hissed.

Semni cuddled Nerie, thinking how she'd tried to rid him from her womb. Should she judge the mistress for not wanting to quicken? After all, people change. She thought of Arruns. If he was her husband, she would welcome, not dread, bearing his child. And everyone knew the story of how the Roman returned to marry the general for a second time. Would she have done so if she did not love him? If she did not want to bear his sons? And hadn't she kept vigil over Tas and Thia with obsessive determination when they'd been threatened?

She studied Aricia. A girl who had never borne a babe. And in that moment Semni knew she could not assist her. As a mother she could not let her take another mother's child.

Suddenly Nerie leaned so far forward she thought she would drop him. "Maa-sta." He pointed at the doorway. "Maa-sta!"

Semni could not believe her eyes. Tas was creeping along the hallway. How had he escaped from Perca's care?

Risking discovery, Aricia stepped into the corridor and called out softly.

Tas halted, the fear in his face dissolving when he realized he'd not walked into trouble. His former nursemaid drew him into the washroom and hugged him.

His voice was squeaky with excitement. "You've come, you've come! I knew you would. I tried to visit the storeroom yesterday but Ati would not leave me alone. I wanted to go through the tunnel again." He extracted himself from her embrace. "Can I visit Uncle now?"

Aricia nodded. "He has sent me to fetch you."

For a moment, the boy's anxiety returned. "He is not angry with me, is he? For not making sacrifice to Aita?"

"Of course not, my pet." She kissed his cheek. "He longs to see you."

Semni realized that Aricia was not going to reveal the priest's true intentions. Lowering Nerie to the floor, she crouched beside

Tas. "Little master, Lord Artile does not just want you to visit him. He wants to take you to the Sacred College in Velzna."

Tas knitted his brow. "Velzna? But that is far away, isn't it?"

Aricia pulled him closer, putting distance between him and Semni. The boy clutched the folds of the nursemaid's chiton, looking up at her. "I don't want the Roman soldiers to get me!"

She stroked his hair. "Hush, you need not worry. Your uncle knows a way to keep us safe. This is your chance to learn how to be a prophet."

Semni rose and reached down to touch the boy's shoulder. "Little master, you might never see your mother again. Nor Larce or Arnth or Thia."

In the dim light his pupils were dilated within amber irises, his expression wary. "Leave Ati?"

Semni nodded.

Aricia pressed him against her.

Conscious that the girl could still convince him, Semni persisted. "Do you hear those trumpets, Tas? That is your father's army trying to return to the city. Don't you want to see him?"

Aricia peeked around the corner, ready to scurry to the wine cellar. "We must hurry, my pet. Let's go to the tunnel while we have the chance."

Dazed, the boy would not budge. "Apa?"

Semni pitied him as his gaze swung between the two girls.

Aricia tugged at him, stepping into the hallway. "Come on."

Desperate, Semni grabbed Tas's other arm; then, with as much force as she could muster, she shoved Aricia's chest. The girl tumbled, landing hard on her bottom. As the nursemaid sat stunned, Semni yanked Tas and ran, voice hoarse from the force of her shrieks. The boy did not resist her although he looked back toward Aricia. Frightened, Nerie began crying, toddling after his mother.

Semni burst into the kitchen, pulling short when she found a roomful of servants startled by her entrance. Cytheris was one of them. The relief on the handmaid's face at finding the truant boy was followed by indignation that he was with Semni.

"What are you shouting about? And what are you doing with the young master? I've been looking for him everywhere. That witless Perca did not notice he was missing until now."

Semni glanced back over her shoulder, trying to catch her breath. "Aricia was trying to take him."

"Aricia?" Nonplussed, Cytheris peered down the corridor. "But I can't see her."

Semni relaxed and let go of Tas's hand so she could pick up her grizzling son. The young princip stood rigid beside her. "She was going to take Master Tas to Lord Artile. The haruspex planned to take him to the Sacred College."

The handmaid's confusion changed to shock. Semni had always thought her old but now she seemed ancient.

"Are you sure?"

Tas interrupted. "Yes, Cytheris. And Aricia scared me."

Sitting on a stool the woman covered her face with her hands. Semni sensed her helplessness to control her daughter. As though she herself had failed in raising such a deceiver.

Alarmed by the drama that had erupted in her kitchen, Cook put her arm around her friend. "She never did deserve a mother like you."

At her friend's words, Cytheris straightened, the Gorgon in her emerging. "We have greater concerns than my own."

Cradling her son's head against her breast to soothe him, Semni scanned the other servants gathered in the room. They looked gloomy. After her frantic dash from danger, she suddenly noticed it was quiet outside. No sound of traffic. As if the citadel was deserted. "What is it? What has happened?"

One of the grooms spoke up. "Camillus and Genucius are both attacking the general. The king refuses to open the Tinia Gates for those in retreat. The warriors of the Clan Mastarna are being massacred beneath the walls."

Shocked, Semni glanced down at Tas, dismayed that he was listening. The boy was no longer at her side.

Her search led her to the courtyard. The sky was filled with a translucent light that made the grass and leaves more vivid.

Drenched, Tas was a forlorn figure as he stood in the rain: thin-limbed, all knobbly knees and bony elbows.

On gusts of wind, Semni heard the intermittent sound of distant wailing. The hairs on her neck rose. It was no paean but a discordant din of despair.

She offered him her hand. "Come, little master."

He shook his head, covering his face. Semni bent down and gently prized his fingers apart. There was no gift of sight in his eyes, only the tearful gaze of a frightened boy. He let her lift him, legs straddling her waist, arms clinging around her neck. He laid his cheek against her shoulder. "I want Ati. I don't want Apa to die."

FORTY-SEVEN

The first thing Caecilia noticed was the wind. In the lee of the tufa blocks there had only been a breeze, but on the heights of the rampart currents tugged at her damp hair.

There was a green tinge to the sky, the light no longer dull but eerie. Spindrifts swirled across the landscape from sudden squalls. Droplets splattered her, smacking onto her face and hands. The wind was capricious, undecided from which direction to blow.

As she perched on the curtain wall, Arruns sat anxiously beside her. His headstrong mistress had ignored his pleading. Now he was resigned to her madness. Holding a shield in front of her, he tried to protect her from any Roman shot. Each time a stray stone thudded against the metal, Caecilia instinctively ducked.

Behind her, the crowd in the forum had already begun keening, weird mournful strains of resignation that their family and friends would lose their lives that day.

Bows at their sides, Kurvenas's archers were troubled, clearly disturbed at their king's order. They had become spectators instead of combatants. They were confused, too, to find Mastarna's wife beside them on the wall.

The rain was heavier. Visible lines of water. Caecilia hooked wet hair behind her ears to prevent the wind whipping it across her face. Water dripped down her neck. The linen of her yellow shawl and embroidered chiton was drenched. At the risk of being hit, she peered out from behind the shield. Looking over the edge, the sense of falling was strong within her, but the desire to find Vel overcame her fear.

Carnage lay before her. Dead men. Dead horses. Hacked limbs and severed heads. The maimed sprawled, bleeding. Too much gore. Too much bloodshed.

Caecilia shut her eyes and just as quickly opened them, forcing herself to search for Mastarna again.

Sounds that had been detached from action when hidden by masonry were now connected. She saw, not just heard, men yelling. Shields clashing against shields. The screaming of the wounded and the dying. Horses whinnying and squealing. There must have been two hundred Veientane cavalry trapped in the corridor below.

Some were crowded at the gates. The seasoned wooden barrier was only the thickness of one foot of timber between safety and annihilation. Some tried to climb it, their hands stretched upward, pleading for the gates' lock to be opened as the Romans slashed at them from below. Caecilia could not stop thinking they might yet be saved if Kurvenas found a conscience.

Others had been pushed off into the deep ditch next to the road, which was fast becoming a moat as the rain filled it. The earth that had been caked and dry was now thickening. The men floundered in the quagmire, their faces and padded linen corselets spattered, their limbs slick with mud as they tried to wade back onto higher ground.

Some of the townsfolk were lowering ropes and ladders, but the king's men forced them to drop them. They could not afford for the Romans to use them to scale the walls.

Vel was not among those at the gates.

Caecilia scanned the area where the remaining Rasennan horsemen were fighting, desperate in their last stand. Proud noble warriors of Clan Mastarna to the end.

Then she saw his gray steed. The bright-blue horsehair crest of his bronze helmet. The spiraling pattern on his cuirass. The bull's head upon his shield.

She froze with the shock of finally seeing him. Suddenly she was not thankful to the gods for granting her wish. For now she must truly watch him die.

Arruns must have seen him, too. She could feel him tense beside her. At the same time a slinger found his mark as a stone smashed into Vipinas's borrowed shield. Caecilia ignored the danger, beyond caring, blood coursing through her.

Mastarna's face was hidden by his helmet's cheek pieces. She longed to view his dark eyes, battered nose, and scar. Wanted to call out to him also, but she doubted he would hear her above the din. He was leaning down from his stallion, fending off an axeman who was trying to drag him from his mount. Caecilia watched, riveted, heart pounding.

The ground was becoming treacherous. Skidding on the slippery surface, Vel's horse lost its footing and fell on its side, unseating its rider. Mastarna lay stunned, his spear jerked from his hand by the impact and landing a yard away. Axe raised, the Roman skirmisher advanced on the fallen man.

Recovering, Vel drew his sword and staved off the attack while still lying on his back. Then, scrambling to his feet, he rammed the foe with his shield before using it as a club. His enemy felled, he stepped over him to meet another.

As Caecilia watched him she overcame horror, concentrating instead on his survival. She needed him to be brutal. Death-dealing. Smiting all who attacked him.

Roman knights were riding through the strife, horses' hooves spraying mud as they chased down Veientanes and trampled them. Others rode parallel to the fleeing soldiers before piercing them with spears.

Arruns touched her shoulder and pointed to the horizon through the rain. Her shoulders tightened and her neck muscles strained as she saw a Roman cavalryman riding at full pelt toward Vel, his horse churning through the boggy ground.

Mastarna had his back turned, dealing with two leves. Armed with only javelin and shield, the men were game to take on the hardened warrior. Vel booted one in the stomach, sending him sprawling. Then, shouldering the other aside, he dispatched him with his sword with one swift, lethal blow to the throat.

The knight was drawing closer. Caecilia screamed, trying to warn her husband, but her cries were lost in the rain and wind and clamor.

As Mastarna thrust his blade through the second levis's chest, he was unaware that the horseman was racing toward him, spear raised high to make the blow as powerful as possible on his unsuspecting prey.

She steeled herself to watch, determined to remember the coward who attacked her husband from behind. The Roman's face was exposed under his conical helmet, his mouth a bleak line. His corselet was emblazoned with the boar's head crest of the Claudian clan.

Caecilia gasped, disbelieving.

It was Appius Claudius Drusus. The man she'd once adored.

FORTY-EIGHT

Drusus's spear swung downward in a deadly arc.

Sensing danger, Mastarna swiveled around, elbow raised. Enough to avoid the lance piercing his neck. Too late, though, to prevent the iron tip slicing through his upper arm. He staggered a little with the impact but regained his footing, twisting around to face his foe.

The Roman readied his horse to make another pass.

Roaring in rage, Mastarna stepped in front of the stallion and raised his shield to startle it. Hooves flailing, the animal reared, unseating its rider.

Drusus crashed, his shield and spear sent flying. Yet he recovered quickly, scrambling to his feet, years of training ingrained in him. Mastarna was faster, though. As Drusus drew his sword, Vel barged him, using his colossal shield to drive the soldier backward. Then, chest heaving, and with his right arm bleeding, the general dropped his shield and gripped his sword in both hands to slam it down upon his foe. The force of the blow cleaved through the leather of the knight's corselet. The breastplate gaped open. Tunic and flesh was sliced from shoulder to groin. Drusus crumpled, his helmet knocked off as his head thudded against the ground.

Watching from the walls, Caecilia's breath exploded after being held throughout the attack. The assault seemed to last forever and yet was so speedy it stunned her.

Drusus lay unmoving. Dead by her husband's hand.

Emotions raced through her, as swift as Mastarna's attack. Relief for Vel's survival. Horror at his savagery. Concern for his wound. How was he to fight on with his arm injured? The vestiges of his energy had been expended by dealing the blow. His arm now dangled by his side as he sank to his knees. Blood dripped from the laceration to be soaked up by the mud. His instinct to survive was strong, though. A battle was still in progress. With his good arm, he dragged his shield to him and lodged it upright in the soft soil. Then, leaning his weight on it, he levered himself to stand over Drusus. Caecilia glanced at the corpse, feeling only disgust for the coward.

Arruns stiffened beside her, scanning the battleground, checking for other Romans who might harm his master.

A stone whistled past. The Phoenician once again protected Caecilia with his shield.

Another missile struck the metal. She frowned. It sounded smaller than a slingshot.

Then something hard hit her cheek, stinging her. Hail.

Tiny at first, the icicles grew larger. Harder. More frequent. Smashing against the stone wall, pinging against the metal of the shield. Hurting those parts of her that were exposed.

Caecilia cursed as she was again forced to shelter in the lee, unable to check how Vel was faring.

A command was shouted to Kurvenas's archers to fall back. She glanced around. The line of people stationed along the curtain had disappeared, bolting down the rampart to seek cover. They crowded into shops and houses and temples as they waited for the storm to pass.

Abandoning the protection of bronze, Caecilia ventured to peek over the wall, flinching as the ice hammered her.

Mastarna stood bearing the brunt of the hail pounding him. She was glad his armor offered him some protection as the sky rained down dozens of blows upon him and the Romans he'd slain.

Ice coated the ground. The balls, some the size of fists, rained down so violently they bounced as they hit the earth. All around, other combatants crouched under their shields, peering up at the heavens, wondering which city's gods were angry.

Trumpets blasted, their sound as eerie as the weird glowing green sky. Their notes competing with the noise of frozen rain against metal and stone and earth.

The horns continued. A call for retreat. The Romans responded, withdrawing at pace to avoid bombardment.

Her relief caused Caecilia to sway with dizziness. Arruns steadied her as he balanced the shield above them. Recovering, she laughed in astonishment, realizing that Vel was safe, that they would be reunited. To gain his attention she screamed so loudly her throat and lungs hurt. It was to no avail. The wind and hail deadened the sound. She waved frantically, still yelling. The bodyguard joined her, his voice loud and abrasive over her high-pitched cries.

The movement of the solitary figures on the rampart caught Mastarna's eye. He looked toward them and raised his hand despite the hail striking his helmet and armor. The thrill of gaining his attention was exquisite.

Her delight was short-lived. From the direction of the conflict on the plain, a lone Roman knight was braving the weather on his skittish steed. He plowed through the current of withdrawing troops, not heeding the call, instead searching among the corpses of his countrymen—until he spied Mastarna.

To her dismay he spurred his horse through the sheet of white toward her wounded husband.

She clutched Arruns's arm. "Help him!" Yet even as she uttered the command she knew she might be condemning him to death. The height of the wall was great. The jump could kill him.

Arruns nodded. He had been too long a nursemaid. He wanted to be a warrior again. Then she saw him hesitate. To leave meant denying her protection. The shield was too heavy for her to hold. "Go," she urged.

With the grace of a panther, he sprung from the rampart over the wall. The drop to the mud-filled ditch below was nearly thirty feet. To her horror, he hit the soggy ground hard and pitched forward. Caecilia's stomach lurched when he did not recover. She'd thought Arruns indestructible. Shock set in at the sight of his motionless body being struck by the ice.

She dragged her eyes back to the battlefield, panic rising. The Roman was drawing closer, spear held aloft.

Mastarna was now aware of his stalker. He hauled his shield from the wet earth with his good arm, and heaved it up to cover his body, staggering a step from the effort and weight. Caecilia's chest hurt, anxiety tearing her insides. With his right arm useless by his side, Vel had no way to wield a weapon against the horseman. Instead he would be vulnerable to a spear thrust from the knight as he made a pass on his stallion.

Caecilia uttered little cries of pain as the hailstones beat upon her head and shoulders, hands and back. But still she kept watching her husband. She could scarce believe she was going to see him die after all. She gripped the rough edges of the ashlar wall as the cavalryman advanced. There was something familiar about him. Poise in his stature and confidence in his riding.

For the second time that day Caecilia reeled with surprise. There was a horse emblem on the soldier's shield and corselet. The Aemilian crest. The knight was Marcus.

Two ghosts from her past had come to haunt her. Drusus and now her cousin. It was the first time she'd seen Marcus in nine years. Her tension eased, glimpsing hope. They had been so close. Surely he would not murder her husband?

Suddenly the hailstorm ceased as swiftly as it had started. The wind dropped, the rain eased to a drizzle. And in the lull came a strangled cry as Marcus spied Drusus.

Kicking his stallion's sides, he circled Mastarna. Yet Marcus did not take advantage of attacking from a height. Disbelieving, Caecilia saw him command his horse to halt, then, discarding his spear, he jumped down to stand in front of his enemy, slapping the horse's rump to order it away. Shield held close, he drew his sword, ready to strike. And in that moment she saw there would be no mercy. Fear rose in her. This man had won an oak leaf crown. He would be a master at killing.

Mastarna raised his shield to parry any blows, planting his feet firmly, knees flexed.

The attack never came. A lance struck Marcus's shield, the impact throwing him backward so that the warrior lay spread-eagle in the mud, the javelin piercing the metal and embedding in the bronze.

Stunned, Caecilia looked around to see who'd hurled the missile.

Arruns had only been winded. He was sprinting toward his master, coated in muck like some monster from the Beyond. Without even breaking stride, the Phoenician leaned down to collect another abandoned spear from a dead levis. Caecilia murmured a prayer of thanks to Juno for saving both her husband and his servant.

Reaching Mastarna, Arruns raised the lance to impale his foe, but his general dropped his shield and grabbed the guard's arm. Poised for the kill, the Phoenician was reluctant to respond, his need to strike signaled in the steep angle of the lance and the clench of his fist. Yet his master did not have to command him twice. Maintaining discipline, Arruns lowered his weapon.

Caecilia fought to understand Vel's clemency after he had faced death at her cousin's hand. Even so, she was relieved that he had chosen to spare Marcus's life. She did not want to see him executed. There had been too much blood already shed this day.

Mastarna confused her even more when he offered his hand to Marcus to assist him to stand. The Roman stubbornly refused. Weighed down by his armor, he struggled to sit up, then lumbered to his feet, his forearm bleeding. His face was exposed under the conical helmet but she could not see his expression. His body was tense, though, his hands balled into fists. She could hear his shouts but not his words as he argued with Mastarna.

Vel was also angry. He shoved Marcus on the shoulder, pointing up to her.

Caecilia froze. If only there was no war. If only there had been forgiveness. How gladly she would have welcomed a chance for a reunion. Instead, as Marcus raised his eyes to hers, loathing settled within her as she stared at a loved one who had become a stranger.

In the long moments while Marcus scrutinized her, Caecilia felt time slow. She heard the rise and fall of her breath, noticed the sprinkle of rain upon her cheeks, and her sodden clothes clinging to her. After the din and clamor of men and nature, the intensity of the encounter centered her.

The first to break the stare, Marcus turned to Drusus. Grunting with effort, he hefted his friend to standing, but he was unable to lift his deadweight onto the horse. Mastarna nodded to Arruns, who helped heave the corpse into place on the bay's back, where it sat slumped forward over the beast's neck. Marcus did not acknowledge the assistance. He quickly mounted and edged behind his fallen comrade, encircling Drusus's waist, the gesture almost tender.

The Roman steadied his horse, speaking to Mastarna before looking up to the wall to stare at Caecilia again. Then, holding fast to his dead friend, he twisted his stallion to face the bridge, galloping across the blood-soaked battlefield, hurdling any Veientane corpses in his path.

FORTY-NINE

Camillus's Camp

·

Leaves and twigs were strewn across the ground. The hail had left a swath of devastation. Swelled by the rain, the stream was running fast, and the ground was slushy from the melt. Many feared the ferocity of the tempest was because Camillus had provoked gods who had not yet been appeased.

The strains of distant fighting had been deadened by the storm. The silence was foreboding. Clothes soaked, hair plastered to their heads, the women clustered at the perimeter, waiting for their men to return.

A reverberation. Hoofbeats. Shouts drawing nearer.

Whooping. Cheering.

Excited, Pinna stretched on tiptoe to see Camillus as the cavalcade erupted through the gate.

Mud- and blood-drenched, the general rode into camp surrounded by horsemen and followed by his exultant troops. A wall of stench exuded from them, soil and ordure and death.

His cheek was bleeding, the pectorals on his corselet spattered and dented. Two hoplites took hold of him as he dismounted, carrying him aloft on their shoulders. Balancing himself between them, Camillus roared with laughter as he progressed through the ranks, calling out the names of men, extolling their deeds.

Pinna stood to the side, watching him. Around her the army wives looked for familiar faces. Smiles broke when they found them. Others looked bewildered as column after column marched by. Soon all that was left to search were the wagons bearing the maimed and the dead. Sobbing followed.

Finally carts of plunder and lines of prisoners were driven into the enclosure. The captives' hands were bound. Bent under the blows of staves, the Veientanes must have thought themselves cursed to have been captured, not slain. Instead of being proud warriors they'd been stripped of their armor, reduced to being part of the spoils. A Roman soldier might not be able to share in the booty but the bravest among them might be granted a slave.

Pinna was ready, her basket packed with medical supplies. Although the casualties did not seem numerous, she knew she'd be busy aiding the worst of the wounded. Those with heads cleaved by axe or stove in by slingshot, those with necks pierced or with broken limbs.

Camillus was surrounded by men wishing to congratulate him or hear words of praise. She wanted to push through the crowd to embrace him and tend to his cut. She dared not do so, though. And she was certain he would put the badly injured before a flesh wound.

She scanned the ranks of horsemen for Marcus. When she found him, he was not jubilant but drawn. Drusus sat slumped before him on the stallion, more blood than mud covering one side of his body. His breastplate hung loose by one strap. His head lolled. His helmet was missing.

Pinna called out and Marcus steered his horse through the host. Reaching her, he dismounted, then rolled Drusus onto his shoulder, taking all of his weight as he guided him down. "Help him, please."

Peeling off Drusus's damaged corselet like a shell, both of them ripped away his shredded tunic and heavy linen kilt. A laceration extended from collarbone down his chest to his groin, the muscle exposed, ribs broken, shoulder dislocated. He was lucky his lungs and other organs had not been punctured. This did not stop Pinna from panicking. She thought it a wonder that he was still alive.

She made an effort to calm herself. The thick flow of blood had to be stanched before the man's life drained away. Grabbing wads of bandages, she ordered Marcus to try and pack the huge slice along his friend's body. The task was near impossible given the length of the rip. The warrior did not balk at obeying her. Until Drusus was treated, she was in charge.

The stink of the two soldiers filled her nostrils: stale sweat, dirt, and dampness. For a moment Pinna stiffened, recalling the smell of grime and rain on Drusus's hand when he tried to smother her. If he died she'd be liberated from at least one threat. Yet she could not let him suffer. She would never wish this end on any man.

There were other odors that made her gag. She glanced at Marcus and saw his beard was speckled with the remnants of enemy brains and his armor was slick with blood. She tried to concentrate on torn flesh instead of gore. "I'll have to fix his shoulder first."

Pinna never thought she would feel sorry for the russet-haired patrician, yet she felt only pity when Marcus assisted her to shove the joint back into its socket. Drusus shrieked, his eyes focusing on her briefly, not with hatred but with anguish.

She directed Marcus to lay him down then fetch water so she could wash the hacked and bruised skin. The liquid in the bowl turned pink as she wrung out the bandage. "My lord, it might be kinder if you knocked him out."

Marcus looked aghast as he knelt beside his friend. The prospect of striking Drusus on the head clearly alarmed him. "He survived hitting his head on the battlefield; I won't risk killing him now with another blow."

A pain gripped Pinna's belly at his refusal. She hoped her nerves would hold when hooking thread through flesh while her patient was awake.

Face tinged green, lips white, Drusus moaned when she poured the strong-smelling castor oil on the slash to clean it. And when she began sewing the long seam with flax thread, his groans made her fingers tremble. She resisted the urge to hurry, anxious that the stitches hold firm as she felt the resistance of jagged skin beneath the needle. As she worked, tears pricked her eyes, aware she was adding to his agony.

Screaming, Drusus crushed his friend's hand, clenching it to try to ride the waves of pain. Tears ran down his cheeks, forging runnels through streaks of mud. Just before he fainted she heard him whisper in a croaky voice, "Tell Camillus . . . Mastarna . . . I smote him."

Pinna stopped stitching the wound, eyes widening. "Did he actually fight the Veientane?"

Marcus grimaced, sitting behind his friend and resting Drusus's head against his chest. "I did not see their combat. When the call for retreat sounded, I went to find him. There was no sign of his horse. As I was searching the battlefield I recognized Mastarna from his blue crest. Drusus was lying in the mud at his feet. I thought him dead but he was just unconscious." Marcus held Pinna's gaze. "Mastarna's arm was paralyzed. Drusus had crippled him yet somehow the Etruscan had managed to fell him."

"So did you attack the general also?"

He ignored the question as he pulled off his rounded helmet. The mud and grime on his face did not mask its harsh contours, his mouth set in a grim line. "The Etruscan dog believed he'd killed him. But that wasn't enough. He also sought to sully his name. He claimed Drusus attacked him from behind." Marcus bent his head over his friend's. "I know he is lying," he said, his hoarse murmur as soft as an endearment. "You are no coward."

Then, defiant, he raised his head, eyes intense. "Whether he lives or not, I will ensure he is lauded for his courage. Engaging an enemy general in combat and striking such a blow should be rewarded."

Pinna studied the two men as Marcus returned his gaze to his wounded friend. She was not so quick to believe the Claudian would not launch a sly attack. Had jealousy driven him to cowardice to ensure his curse came true? He had nearly been the instrument of the Etruscan's destruction. And yet Mastarna had wrought terrible damage. Drusus had been defeated. His foe had been the better man that day. "My lord, I don't think he will be triumphant that he failed."

Marcus looked at her sharply. "I suppose you would celebrate his death."

Pinna regretted her words. She had not meant to rile him. She bent her head to resume her neat stitching. There was a seed of truth in what he said, although it would be relief, not joy, she'd feel if her tormentor died. She tied off her needlework. "I'm helping him now, aren't I? Now hold him up. I need to bandage him."

Marcus winced and groaned as he lifted his friend. Absorbed in tending to Drusus, she'd not noticed the bruising that darkened the entire length of the officer's shield arm and that he'd lost his wristband. His already scarified forearm was bleeding from a gash. She wondered if those wounds he inflicted himself were any less painful than that received in battle. Pinna nodded toward the damaged flesh. "My lord, you're also hurt."

Marcus clenched his teeth as he concentrated on bearing his friend's weight. His face was gray with pain as well as fatigue. Sweat beaded his brow. "I suppose you wish I had not returned either."

Shame over her brief desire for his death returned. And yet hadn't she regretted such an idea as swiftly as she'd thought it? "No matter what you think of me, my lord, I do not want you dead."

Marcus grunted and scanned the crowd of soldiers around them until he found Camillus. "Even if I said I am still duty-bound to tell him?"

The tightness in her chest from yesterday recurred. Rather than replying, she concentrated on winding a bandage over and around Drusus's shoulder before commencing the immense task of strapping his body.

In the hours of nervous waiting, she'd rehearsed different ways of begging in the hope that Marcus might yet relent. Now it seemed he was determined to hurt her. It made her realize she could not surrender without a contest. "I gave my word I would not harm your reputation but I feel no such obligation to your friend. And so, if you speak out against me, I will tell the general what Drusus did to me."

"You're a prostitute," he growled. "It's no use crying rape."

Pinna flinched, not expecting such callousness. "Maybe, but I'm sure he'll think a man who abuses a woman is pathetic. Even if she is a she wolf. So excessive. So weak. Furius Camillus already doubts the Claudian can control his emotions. The revelation may well affect your friend's career."

Marcus's eyes narrowed. "You bitch. He showed audacity today. He can display these scars proudly."

"And he was lucky he didn't have ones on his back after he retreated under Sergius!"

The same flicker of hesitation passed across Marcus's features before he wiped the gray flecks from his beard. "I detest you."

His words were cruel but it hardened her resolve. She nodded toward the unconscious decurion. "Will you keep silent for his sake?"

Marcus arranged his cloak around his friend, chill hatred in his eyes. "For now. But know this, Pinna, should he die, I will speak out."

FIFTY

Veii

The hail stopped. The bank of clouds parted. Ice shards glinted in the sunlight.

The Veientanes ventured from their hiding places. The rush of bodies was strangely hushed as people hastened to discover if any of their loved ones lived.

The outer gates were opened.

Caecilia pushed into the anxious surge of people streaming into the lock. Then she paused, summoning courage to pick her way through the bodies heaped at the entrance of the outer doors. There lay soldiers who'd been deserted by a heartless king. Soldiers who might have been saved if Kurvenas had allowed their rescue.

There were few survivors on the battlefield. Weeping, mothers crouched over sons, wives over husbands, embracing corpses half buried in hailstones and slush.

A paean was being sung. The notes of grief clear and pure compared to the low lament and high-pitched keening.

The ground was white. Like snow in summer. Caecilia stumbled, her sodden skirts hampering her as she crunched over the frozen earth. With each step she sank through the crust of ice to the layer of mud. Pain shot through her but she didn't care as she lumbered closer and closer to Mastarna.

He wrenched off his helmet when she reached him. His face was bearded, his eyes fervid. She sensed the battle fever had not yet ebbed from him.

Throwing her arms around his neck, she hugged him. His breastplate was hard against her. She ignored his stink. Holding her with his good arm, he rested his injured one on her waist. She lifted her mouth to his. Their kiss was deep, making up for lost time.

They said nothing. Holding each other.

Finally he drew her away, touching the red marks upon her cheek and brow. His scurfed fingers scratched her skin. "You should have sheltered from the hail." His deep voice was achingly beautiful after not hearing it for so long.

"I could not leave off watching once I sighted you. I could not believe Marcus tried to kill you."

Mastarna frowned, searching her face. "Did you expect otherwise? He is our enemy. As was the Claudian."

"Yet you spared my cousin."

"I don't believe in killing a man after a battle has ended."

She cupped his face between her palms, his beard wiry beneath her fingers. "Marcus did not observe such a rule."

Vel's face was harrowed, his weathered skin pale beneath the tan. "That was different, Bellatrix. I had killed his friend. Rage blinded him."

Caecilia pressed against him, laying her cheek against the embossed Trojan figures on his cuirass. "At least he fought you fairly, unlike Drusus. He was a coward to attack you from behind."

"Still, he meant something to you once."

She shook her head. Her infatuation had been for an awkward youth, not a malicious warrior. "It was horrible to see him die, but I will not weep for him."

Vel kissed her and held her close again. She wished she could feel his body, not bronze.

"Master, mistress. The general is losing much blood. We need to stop the flow." Arruns stood impatient beside them. He had caught Mastarna's horse, which snorted and shook its head at finding its master after galloping off during the battle.

Caecilia plucked up courage to look closely at Vel's wound. Color drained from her face, queasy at the sight. The arm appeared broken as well as slashed. Tearing the patterned border from her chiton, she then handed it to the guard, who tied it tightly above the wound. Her rain-drenched shawl was then bound around the damaged flesh, blood staining the yellow fabric. Mastarna groaned, finally connecting injury with hurt.

The Phoenician assisted Mastarna to mount his horse then lifted Caecilia so she could sit sideways in front of her husband. Always nervous with horses, she clung to Vel, scared of falling as the steed shifted impatiently.

She could not contain her curiosity about her cousin. "What did you say to Marcus?"

"That his friend lacked valor in not facing his opponent. He did not believe me. It angered him. Also that it would sorrow you if either of us had been killed in front of you."

Caecilia hesitated, steeling herself to hear all Marcus had said. "And what did he say?"

She sensed Vel's reticence as he flicked the reins with one hand, urging the horse to move.

"Please, tell me."

"He said that you were dead to him."

A flush of heat spread through her from belly to scalp. She clung tighter to Vel, wishing he could hold her with both arms.

There were other warhorses amid the carnage. Some wandering lost and aimless, some nudging masters who were lifeless. Other animals lay dead or squealing in their death throes.

Mastarna carefully led the gray through the battlefield to avoid treading on corpses or the maimed. Caecilia could not bear to look at the torsos, limbs, and heads around them, how the white was sullied with crimson and dirtied with sludge as soldiers and townsfolk dragged the wounded onto litters or laid the deceased out for their relatives to collect. Gagging at the sight and stench of the butchery, she fought her nausea, hiding her face against Mastarna's neck. "Kurvenas wanted you dead, Vel. He refused to open the gates even though Lord Vipinas's clan was prepared to assist you."

She could feel the spurt of energy as the anger rose in him.

— • —

Caecilia thought the worst was behind them. And yet, as the stallion trotted along the road to the forum, she heard commotion, people yelling and the clash of weapons.

Mastarna urged his mount to a gallop. The crowd parted at the threat of being trampled.

Before them some of Vipinas's men were attacking the king's officers and lictors. One royal bodyguard clutched the old nobleman's arms behind his back while another beat him with his rod. The princip's nose was broken. His false teeth had been knocked from his mouth and lay smashed on the ground.

Caecilia noticed a man collapsed nearby, blood pooling in the grooves of the cobblestones. Kurvenas. His throat was cut, a fine spray of scarlet splattering his armor.

To her surprise, Tarchon was holding Sethre down. He winced as the youth thrashed against him, the bandage on the wounded soldier's thigh bright with fresh blood.

Ramutha knelt next to Caile, who was lying on his shield. It had been used as a bier for the young warrior. Rocking and wailing, she smothered his face with kisses. The youth's eyes were open but unseeing. His had not been a glorious death. His skull was fractured. Not pierced by a hoplite's spear but brought down by a lowly slinger. Caecilia remembered his lack of skill in the Troy Game. The soft bristles on his jaw reminded her how a beard could falsely proclaim a boy was a man. She glanced across to Sethre. Like Caile, this youth had been thrust into the world of men. One had fallen, the other was overwhelmed.

"Cease fighting!" At Mastarna's bellow, both groups separated, although some still stood close to their rivals, keeping fists and weapons poised to strike.

"Unhand Lord Vipinas!"

The lictor obeyed by shoving the princip to the ground. Coughing, the beaten man lurched to his feet, trying to regain his breath.

"Tarchon, let Sethre go."

On release the youth lunged at the aged princip, causing Tarchon to grab him again. The boy screeched. "He murdered my father. Let me kill him! I want retribution."

"And Kurvenas killed my grandson!" Vipinas pointed to Caile's crumpled body, over whom Ramutha remained prostrate, oblivious to all around her.

Astounded, Caecilia glanced at her husband. Shock registered as he took in the mayhem.

"All of you, quiet!"

Refusing Arruns's proffered assistance, he dismounted. Sweat beaded his forehead at the effort, but he drew himself erect, not prepared to show weakness even though his arm dangled by his side. The Phoenician helped Caecilia down so she could stand beside her husband.

The people who'd gathered in the forum craned their necks to see how the general would control the situation. Veii's lucumo had been murdered and its greatest general defeated. The fabric of the world was in tatters. The gods had visited both wrath and mercy upon the city in equal measure. The mood wavered between outrage and disbelief. Catcalls were heard—either howling disapproval at Kurvenas's tactics or demanding Vipinas be punished.

"Tarchon, explain all this."

The soldier held tight to Sethre, clearly disconcerted that his beloved had not calmed in his arms. "The lictors were holding me in the forum when Kurvenas and his retinue appeared. The villain was returning to the palace as the dead were being carried inside the walls. When Lord Vipinas saw Caile's body being borne into the city, he drew his sword and attacked the king so swiftly there was no time to stop him."

Sethre's voice cracked. "My father was no villain. And his murderer should be executed now!"

Wheezing, Vipinas hobbled to Mastarna. With his teeth missing, the nobleman's speech was muffled. Caecilia cringed at a proud man made pathetic. Her heart ached to see his grief.

"Kurvenas could have sent reinforcements. Your troops could have retreated inside. Instead he was prepared to sacrifice you and your army. All for personal satisfaction. It was he who committed murder today, Mastarna. And I who meted out justice."

The king's son bucked and wriggled, trying to break free. Caecilia could see Tarchon was suffering as he struggled to restrain him, distressed by both his beloved's resistance and the pain of his wound.

Sethre would not be silenced. "No, my father was protecting this city. The Romans would have overrun us."

Caecilia stared at him, stunned at how he'd forgotten his qualms about Kurvenas's decision. Vengeance for his brutal father now consumed him.

Suddenly the people scattered as Lusinies and his officers rode into the forum. The scarred veteran's expression was one of horror as he took stock of the scene: a slain king, a battered princip, and an injured general. He slipped from his mount, examining

Mastarna's wound. "By the gods, what's happened here? I heard Kurvenas would not open the gates."

Vel grimaced and held his bandaged arm against his side. The fervor of battle was ebbing. Fatigue and pain were now exacting a toll. "While your army was defending the south of the city, chaos ruled here. Kurvenas let my vanguard be slaughtered."

The bald officer frowned, grappling with the news as he crouched down beside the lucumo's corpse. "And who killed the king?"

Sethre called out, his chest heaving as he gulped back tears. "Vipinas. He needs to be punished. Mastarna won't execute him. You must do it, Lord Lusinies."

The crowd had swelled. Reports of the assassination must have trickled through the jam of bodies to race along avenues, streets, and lanes into every house and inn and brothel. More protests were heard. Caecilia feared a riot. The king's men pushed back those who threatened to break the cordon.

Mastarna put up his hand for quiet. "Silence! There has been enough blood spilled today."

To Caecilia's relief the mob settled. She was alarmed, though, to see Vel swaying on his feet. He gripped onto the side of his horse's mane for support rather than lean on her. The gray neighed and shook its head but held steady. "This is a matter for the High Council. They rule until it is decided who must govern this city."

Sethre spat toward Vipinas. "No. Justice must be served. He should be put to death this instant. His crime was witnessed. And I accuse him of being the traitor who Lord Artile predicted lives among us."

The former zilath tore his gaze from his dead grandson. "How dare you!"

Confused, Mastarna scanned the square. "What prediction is this? And just where is my brother?"

In the furor Caecilia had forgotten the priest. Now she remembered his earlier absence. It was not like him to defy his ruler. Nor miss the chance to gloat over Vel's impending death.

Tarchon's expression mirrored her own. "It's strange. I was present this morning when Kurvenas summoned Artile."

Mastarna snorted. "No doubt he shied away from the danger of an enemy at our gates."

Caecilia noticed Vel was finding it difficult to remain upright. He tightened his hold on the horse. The fine shawl was saturated, blood dripping from his fingers to spatter the ground. Caecilia could smell it, rich and sickening. She clutched his arm. "Please, Vel. We need to see to your wound."

He shook his head. "Not yet. Don't worry."

Wrinkles furrowed Lusinies's brow below his bald pate. He ordered an aide to fetch the haruspex. "The king's death may well be a portent. For certain this is a matter where the gods need to be consulted. The chief priest's counsel is needed."

Mastarna grunted. "I don't need a soothsayer to tell me Veii is in peril."

Sethre had calmed himself enough to encourage Tarchon to lessen his hold. The soldier still grasped the boy's forearm, though. Sethre held himself stiffly as he wiped his eyes and nose with the back of his hand. "So you are going to do nothing about this betrayer?"

Vipinas crossed to him, a blue vein visible beneath the pale skin at his temple. "Your father was that traitor. A traitor to his people. I was justified in putting him to death."

Sethre smirked at the princip's garbled speech. Vipinas flushed and raised his fist. Caecilia could hardly believe how grief had loosened all control in such a dignified man.

Lusinies stepped between the elder and the youth. "Stop it, both of you. I agree with Mastarna. This is a matter for the High Council until another lucumo is elected."

Bridling at being dismissed, Vipinas moved from Lusinies so he could view the general directly. "And that man must be you, Mastarna. You must be king."

Vel grimaced and pointed to Kurvenas. "I think we have had enough of monarchs."

A sheen of sweat coated Lusinies's skull, trickling down the sides of his face into his beard. The extraordinary circumstances were affecting him as well. "Perhaps I should keep Lord Vipinas under custody in my home until the High Council can convene."

Sethre jabbed his finger toward Mastarna. "Why? So you will have time to conspire with him to let an enemy of the state go free?"

Lusinies could no longer keep his temper. "You do well to remember to whom you speak, boy. I claim no alliance with either of your Houses. And Lord Mastarna and I are generals who have risked our lives for this city countless times. Do not question our loyalty to Veii."

Caecilia expected Vel to be scathing; instead he remained even, recognizing the youth could not rein in his emotions. "I assure you, Sethre, your tribe will be given time to elect a new leader. Until then the High Council will defer determining this matter." He gestured to Tarchon to release the aggrieved son. "Now it's time for you to tend to your father's body. Just as so many of us must wash and anoint our loved ones."

Lips and nose blotchy, eyes red-rimmed, Sethre crossed to his father and knelt beside him. The rawness of his hurt was painful to watch. Seeing his anguish, Tarchon limped over to him and placed his hand on his shoulder.

Sethre recoiled, elbowing him away. "Leave me be! I want no comfort from Mastarna's son. Our Houses have always been and will remain enemies."

Caught off guard, Tarchon tripped slightly then righted himself. He walked backward with slow steps to stand beside Mastarna, his gaze locked on the youth. Caecilia rested her fingers on his wrist in comfort. His hand was shaking.

Ramutha was still weeping, her head upon Caile's chest. Her sorrowing had lent a sad accompaniment to the shouts and accusations. Seeing the matron still lying across his grandson, Vipinas bent down and jerked her away. "Get away from him! He is not yours to mourn."

Defiant, Ramutha tried to resume her place at her lover's side.

Caecilia could understand the grandfather's disgust despite sympathy for her friend. It was somehow unseemly to see the depth of this married woman's passion on display. And so she moved to the grieving noblewoman and touched her shoulder. "Hush, let his grandfather hold him."

Ramutha was dazed. "He is gone, Mele."

Caecilia clasped her hand and helped her to her feet. "Yes, he is gone. Now come with me. There will be time for you to bid him farewell later."

Blood crusting around his broken nose and one cheek swollen, Vipinas signaled to four of his men to lift the shield upon which Caile lay. The grandfather brushed hair over the hole in the youth's head, and closed the staring eyes. He was as quiet in his torment as Ramutha had been noisy. His daughter had died giving birth to this boy, and his wife had passed away together with his son. All of his family but him was now in the Beyond. How terrible it was to have outlived them all.

As Caecilia led Ramutha by the hand, she heard the gray stallion whinny as Mastarna sagged to the ground. His face was ghost-white above his black beard, his eyes liquid with pain. Caecilia ran to him while shouting to Tarchon to help her. He tried to support his father around the waist but, weighed down by his armor, Vel was too heavy for either of them to hold.

Without asking permission, Arruns pushed both wife and son aside and heaved his master over one of his shoulders. Caecilia marveled at his strength, thankful for his devotion.

After Vel had been placed on a tray of a wagon, Caecilia stopped his son from climbing in beside her. "You must stay. Represent our House. Make sure Lord Vipinas is not treated harshly."

Tarchon nodded, pride apparent, then he squeezed her hand. "Don't despair, Caecilia. Mastarna has survived worse wounds than this. And he has you and your children to live for."

She ordered Arruns to urge the donkeys on. The Veientanes stood aside to allow the cart to pass, jostling to gain a view of the great general.

Terrified she had already lost Vel so soon after the gods had delivered him to her, Caecilia hunched over him and placed her mouth on his. She was relieved to feel the susurration of his breath. She cradled his head on her lap to prevent it from lolling as the wain jolted over the bumps and ruts of the road. She murmured to him not to die. She wept but chided herself as she did so. She needed to be dry-eyed. Vel did not like to see her cry.

FIFTY-ONE

Giggling, the boys had thought the hail a marvel.

It pelted down, causing dollops of water to rebound upon the pond's surface. And the foliage of the laurel hedges shook with the missiles so that leaves, made brittle from a summer's scorching, scattered and were buried beneath balls of white.

Cytheris struggled to keep Arnth from running into the open. Larce, more cautious, wriggled and hopped up and down in one spot as he held on to Perca's hand. Thia's crying was drowned out by the hammering on the roof as she lay in her crib.

Grave-eyed and pensive, Tas refused to leave Semni's side. No amount of coaxing could convince him to join his brothers. It had been the same for hours. She alone could provide solace to him, bereft of his mother and nursemaid.

There were no smiles as the servants watched the younger boys' antics. No delight to be had in childish pleasure with the deluge of ice. Cut off from the news of the carnage to the north of the city, they could only imagine the worst. Were the gods trying to stone the Veientanes? Semni hoped Arruns was safe. And despite

Aricia's sins, she prayed the girl had not been added to the death toll when she fled with the haruspex.

When the storm passed, Larce and Arnth slipped the restraining hand of their caretakers and raced to kick or throw fistfuls of hailstones at each other. Despite being taunted as scared, Tas remained glued to Semni's side.

Despondent after learning of Aricia's continuing treachery, Cytheris let them play, not scolding them for getting wet as they sloshed about in the melting slush. Perca jogged Thia in her arms, sniffling as she carried the sleeping baby to the nursery. The twelve-year-old was still upset at failing to keep her eye on Tas. Miserable also from being chastened by Cytheris's hand and tongue.

Outside they heard the timekeeper herald the hour as well as bring tidings.

The enemy had retreated.

Mastarna's army had been slaughtered.

King Kurvenas had been murdered.

The hail had indeed been an omen.

— • —

The steward was shouting orders to the porters to open the massive bronze doors to the street.

The general was carried into the arcade upon a litter, eyes closed, his arm bleeding and maimed. Yet Lady Caecilia's expression told Semni he was not dead. It was one of worry, not sorrow, as the princip hobbled beside her husband.

A mud-drenched Arruns followed. Semni's stomach lurched, thinking that the guard was also wounded, but she soon realized the blood saturating his tunic was not his own but his master's. Preoccupied with his lord, he did not acknowledge her.

The border of the mistress's chiton had been ripped away. The torn hem was coated with both wet and drying mud. Elsewhere blood spattered her fine robes. There was vigor in her despite her pallor. Her husband's need had given her purpose. She directed the bearers to take the master to the bedchamber while bidding a maid to fetch bandages and salves. Then she dispatched a slave boy to fetch the Greek physician before handing the cellar key to the steward. "Bring wine. The strong one from Sardinia. Do not mix it with water."

"Ati, Ati!" Tas raced to her and threw his arms around his mother's hips, the force of the embrace nearly unbalancing her. For certain it astounded her.

Larce and Arnth halted their play, appalled at the sight of their wounded father. Seeing Lady Caecilia, they clustered around her like puppies fighting for the dug. She winced in pain but smiled as she bent and hugged them.

"Is Apa dead?" Larce's eyes filled with tears.

"No, but we must pray for him." She kissed each one in turn. "He needs me now. So you must go to the nursery and listen to what Cytheris tells you. Kiss your sister good night for me."

With reluctance, the younger boys allowed the Greek maid to take their hands, but Tas clung to his mother. "I want to stay with you."

The mistress stroked his hair. "Hush now. You must show your brothers not to be frightened."

"But Aricia tried to take me away. Uncle Artile wanted me to go to the Sacred College."

Bewildered, the princip stared at him in disbelief. "Aricia?" Then she glared at her servants. "How did she get near him? Where was Perca?"

Cytheris bowed her head. "Do not blame the girl, my lady. It was my fault. I should have kept a closer eye on all of them. Aricia snuck through the tunnel again. It seems the priest gave her another key. We were lucky Semni found her before it was too late."

Tas tugged at his mother's skirts. "That's right, Ati. Semni stopped her this time."

The girl tensed at the telltale words, thinking that at last she would be questioned for being complicit. The noblewoman must have thought the statement unremarkable, though. No questions were asked.

"Then I owe you a debt of gratitude."

Semni bobbed, pleased to gain credit, relieved to put guilt behind her. As she raised her head, though, she noticed Arruns had emerged from the master's bedroom and was listening. She grinned, glad to have gained his attention, but his response was a frown before he bowed to the mistress.

"My lady, the general is awake and asking for you."

Caecilia's face brightened, but when she moved to go, Tas continued to hold fast to her. "Don't leave me!"

"It will be all right, Tas. Stay with Semni and Cytheris. Apa needs me."

Arruns cleared his throat. "Mistress, he wishes to see the young masters as well."

Lady Caecilia's brow furrowed as she surveyed her three sons. Then, taking a deep breath, she clasped Tas's hand and signaled Perca and Semni to follow with the younger boys. "Let us see your father. Let's show him how brave you are."

— • —

The odor of damp cloth and wet leather permeated the room. And more. Semni tried not to inhale the stench of battle gore.

Lord Mastarna lay propped up with cushions on the bed. Still in his armor, he was sunk deep into the mattress. The sight of the warrior lying on the fine linen was out of place. Blood seeped into the jaunty greens and blues of the plaid coverlet, war intruding into pampered living.

Arruns was untying a yellow shawl stained crimson, and a strip of embroidered cloth from around the general's bicep, a dainty pattern for a gruesome wound. The Phoenician smeared yarrow onto the cut before pressing clean bandages against it to stanch the flow.

Lord Mastarna's face was waxen. The heavy growth of his beard was stark against the whiteness, the scar from mouth to nose livid. There was no color in his lips; grooves of pain scored his flesh.

Head sagging against the pillow, he drank wine from a rhyton held to his lips by Arruns, downing it with grim concentration. After he'd drained the cup, his guard poured him another.

Lady Caecilia wiped the sheen of sweat from her husband's brow. "Our sons are here, Vel," she murmured, "but perhaps this can wait."

Semni was unsettled to hear the master's usually honeyed voice rasping, "No, Bellatrix. Let me see them."

Tas hovered next to the bed, his eyes transfixed upon his father. Arm shaking, he saluted. "Hail, General Mastarna."

The man touched the boy's cheek with calloused and stained fingers. "Hail, Vel Mastarna Junior."

Tas whispered. "Are you dying, Apa?"

"Not if I can help it."

The son frowned. "But I don't think you can be of any help with such a sore arm."

Lord Mastarna closed his eyes.

"That is enough, Tas." The mother ushered the boy away.

Larce and Arnth stood rigid beside Cytheris. The bed was too high for them to reach their father. Arruns lifted one and then the other by the waist so the general could kiss them. Larce burst out crying, unable to keep his gaze from the scarlet seeping through the bandages. When placed back on the floor, he hid his face in his mother's skirts. Arnth, though, wanted to see his apa again and began dragging the footstool toward him. As Lady Caecilia caught him, the general managed a smile. "Later, my young soldier."

Semni wondered if it would have been better to have spared the children such a viewing. It was an early start for witnessing such damage. And yet was this not their destiny? These little principes of warrior stock. The specter of the battlefield already pursued them. Like their father, they were fated to ride to war. Were born for that purpose. In time thin limbs would strengthen with muscle, tiny bodies would gain bulk to be encased in bronze. There was an expectation that they must seek scars of their own.

She studied Tas, the heir, who dreamed of separating heaven from earth with a lituus but instead must wield a sword. He would be more comfortable wearing a fringed sheepskin cloak than a military cape.

Lady Caecilia bade Cytheris take the boys to their chamber. Once again, Tas slipped his hand into Semni's.

Seeing this, the mistress left the bedside. "You are to take Aricia's place now, Semni. Perca is too young and silly. Go with Cytheris. Feed my daughter. She must be hungry."

The girl curtsied a thank-you, amazed that she would finally break free of the drudgery of washroom and kitchen.

Lady Caecilia smiled. "Oh, and Semni, thank you again for saving my son."

— • —

After lullabies and consolation the brothers fell asleep, the arc of eyelashes curving upon soft cheeks, their breathing shallow but steady. Semni prayed there would be no nightmares after such a day.

Replete, Thia dozed in her cradle while Cytheris sat in a chair keeping vigil. The woman's stare was vacant, thoughts far from that room. Semni recognized Aricia in her. The nursemaid may have been faithful to Lord Artile but there was steadfastness in Cytheris also. Her own sons and daughters lost, the Greek maid was devoted to the mistress and children of the House of Mastarna.

After a time she focused on Semni. "Do you think she is still alive?"

What could she say that would reassure her? The haruspex's influence with the gods needed to be great if the fugitives were to survive. She hoped Aricia was right in believing the Romans would take no interest in a priest and his servant. "All we can do is pray for her."

Cytheris sighed and nodded toward Aricia's cubicle. "That is your room now, Semni. Bring Nerie here and rest awhile."

FIFTY-TWO

Camillus's Camp

Marcus sat with his sleeping friend propped against his chest. The closest embrace he was likely to have with the man he dreamed of as his lover.

Pinna rose and left them alone after tending to Marcus's wound. She was downcast. For he had trapped her. The Claudian's wounds were near mortal. She would have to spend long hours feeding, bathing, and changing his dressings daily. Even with such care his wounds could turn septic. The beeswax she'd spread upon the wound was a scant barrier to infection. She would have to pray hard and often for the dawn goddess to save the man she loathed.

Hoping to see Camillus, she walked toward the command tent. She did not need to go far. He was visiting the hurt, praising them for bearing pain for the glory of Rome. She could see how his words rallied their spirits. Even the gravely wounded responded with feeble smiles.

When he saw her, he grinned and strode over to her. Lifting her by the waist he swung her into the air, kissing her as he set her down. She dropped her basket in surprise.

"We routed them, Pinna! We destroyed the army of the great Vel Mastarna! The river ran red with Veientane blood. We now hold the bridge!"

Giddy with elation, she hugged him, not caring that the odor of combat was heavy about him. Her euphoria was not for his victory but because he'd held her in front of others. And in that moment she dared hope that she may have stolen a small piece of his soul.

Laughing a little too loudly, she touched the gash upon his cheek. The blood had dried, the skin swollen. "You've been cut."

He laid his hand over hers. "Just a nick."

"I was so worried about you, especially when the messenger told us about Lake Albanus. I thought it might be an omen that you would die."

"Lake Albanus?"

When she explained he frowned. "And the Sibylline Books still provide no advice as to how to placate the gods?"

"No. The Senate is at a loss." She laid her head upon his shoulder. "I am fearful, my lord."

He kissed her again, stroking her hair. "The gods favored us today, Pinna. If anything, the lake's flooding is a portent that our city will finally triumph." He broke from her. "But now I must continue to inspect my men."

She didn't want him to go, longing to throw her arms around him and bid him take her to his tent. Wanting to delay him, she picked up her basket and searched for the dagger. "Here, take this. I did not need it."

Camillus slid the weapon into its scabbard. "Let's pray I never need to lend it to you again."

She smiled and shifted the basket into the crook of her arm, the movement catching his eye.

"Tell me. Who have you been treating?"

"Claudius Drusus."

His brow creased. "Then take me to him."

Marcus still held his friend. When he noticed the general, though, he eased the unconscious man from his lap and stood to salute.

The general clapped him on the back. "I hear you fought well today, soldier. Slaying many. You will be rewarded for your deeds."

"I do not deserve it, sir. Claudius Drusus showed greater valor."

Camillus crouched down beside the injured warrior. "How so?"

"He fought Vel Mastarna and wounded him badly, whereas I failed to kill the Etruscan when I had the chance."

The general looked up sharply. "Vel Mastarna? Then not only have we massacred his army but we also struck him a personal blow." He rose and pointed to Marcus's forearm. "No doubt there will be other opportunities to kill him. And you will bear a scar to remind you of your purpose."

Marcus's eyes narrowed. "Do not worry, sir. I will not rest until Veii, Mastarna, and my cousin are destroyed." He stared down at his friend. "Doubly so if he dies."

Camillus scrutinized Drusus's injuries again. "So he nearly got his wish."

"Yes, sir."

"Then rest assured, Appius Claudius Drusus will gain honors, too."

For the first time that day, Marcus smiled.

The general nodded, returning to the business of command. "Genucius's army will remain in place to tighten the siege, but this campsite is perilous. We need to move back to Faliscan territory. I don't want our victory today spoiled by King Kurvenas trapping us in this valley. And there is danger that the stream might rise and flood us if there is any more rain."

"What about the dead, sir?"

"There is no time to build funeral pyres. We'll take the fallen with us. Tomorrow night when we are on safe ground we shall give burned sacrifice for those who have joined the Shades. At least our losses have been few and we will not need to commit too many to the flames."

Marcus stood to attention. "So I am to tell my men we break camp at dawn?"

"Yes, and advise the centurions to give the order."

Command given and received, Marcus glanced across to Pinna.

An uncomfortable silence followed. Finally, Camillus placed his hand on the knight's shoulder. "I have acted badly, Marcus. Pinna is your woman, but I would like to make her mine. So speak if you don't wish her to leave you and I will respect your decision."

Pinna's jaw dropped. How could her lover be prepared to relinquish her after his public display of affection? Nervous, she waited for Marcus's answer. Once again she was in his hands. She stared at him, knowing that the problem of disclosing her past would be solved if he kept her, even if it meant maintaining a liaison based on mistrust and hatred.

He took his time to respond. To Pinna, the pause seemed endless.

"I no longer want her. Take her."

"You are generous, Marcus Aemilius. I am grateful."

Being treated as a chattel reminded Pinna of how money was exchanged for her services in the brothel. Any resentment was forgotten, though, when for the second time that day Camillus put his arm around her waist and drew her near.

The blatant gesture of possession fed her confidence as she realized that she had at last washed herself clean of the graveyard, escaped the oppression of the leno, and gained the affection of a general. She smiled at Marcus, relieved and thankful. He deliberately looked down again at Drusus then raised his eyes to her. A pulse beat in her temple, knowing her future was clouded. She needed the gods to help her heal the decurion.

Camillus broke from her embrace, preoccupied again with visiting the wounded.

Pinna turned to follow but Marcus restrained her, his words cutting short any delight she might feel to belong to Camillus.

"This changes nothing, Pinna," he said, his expression threatening, his disgust concrete. "You may no longer be under my patronage but our bargain remains. So don't overly rejoice that you've gained the general's protection. For if Drusus dies, I will ensure that you will suffer as well."

FIFTY-THREE

Veii

"You need to take this off." Caecilia unbuckled the straps of Vel's corselet.

His voice was raw, smile frail. "Don't worry, I plan to."

She leaned over and kissed his pallid lips. He groaned as Arruns helped her to remove his armor. It made her guilty that Vel must be caused anguish. She wondered whether it would have been better to leave him as he was until the doctor had seen him.

The muscle cuirass with its linen strips thudded to the floor, followed by high greaves, boots, and armbands, until Mastarna lay only in his damp tunic.

The Greek physician bustled into the chamber with a youth and confidence that declared his nerves were not yet frayed from listening to the screams of his patients. She thought how spruce he was with his short clipped nails, well-combed hair, and pleated chiton. When he donned the leather apron, though, it was clear he was prepared for his profession. Opening his square bag, he drew an array of instruments from its compartments, which he laid on the side table, taking care to place them in order. The iron forceps, needles, and scalpels looked as if their purpose was to inflict torture rather than repair.

Discarding the fouled bandages, the healer examined the misshapen bone and lacerated flesh, muttering to himself as he peered at the damage. As nausea rose within her, Caecilia chided herself for being squeamish. At least the yarrow leaves and pressure had helped. The blood flow was now sluggish. Yet the thought that Vel must suffer further when the physician set the bone sent a shiver, strong and visceral, through her.

Sweat beaded Mastarna's upper lip and brow, his face alarming in its grayness. Despite the wine being the strongest vintage, its effect had only taken the edge off the pain.

Mercifully, the Greek showed compassion. He poured some liquid from an alabastron into yet another goblet of wine. "Here, drink this, my lord. The mandragora will help you sleep."

Caecilia placed her hand over the rhyton. Arnth Ulthes had died from drinking such a potion. Witnessing his slow and ghastly death still haunted her. "No, it may be a slumber from which he never wakes."

The healer was terse. "I would be a poor doctor if I poisoned my patients." Then he nodded toward Arruns. "This man looks brawny enough, though, to hold down the general if he chooses not to use it."

His sanguine attitude chilled her.

"Of course, I doubt he will stay conscious once I start straightening the bone. Fixing broken elbows is excruciating."

Mastarna lowered the cup away from his wife's protective hand, then drained its contents. "I trust him, Bellatrix. Besides, I do not want our sons to hear me screaming."

Soon he grew drowsy, the muscles in his face relaxing as the elixir spread within him. Wincing, he shifted his weight toward her. "I have not asked about the baby."

Caecilia brushed his sodden hair from his forehead. For the first time she noticed silver strands. "A daughter—fine and fair and very noisy."

"A girl?" He smiled. "Then isn't it time I claimed her?"

It was the declaration for which she had yearned, yet now that Vel was home she could wait a little longer. "Then she will be your first visitor when you wake."

Just as with his desire to see his sons, Mastarna was pigheaded. "No, bring her to me. In case the Greek is not as clever in measuring mandragora as he boasts."

Anxiety stirred again. What if in the end the father was on his deathbed, unable to claim a daughter in her cradle only one room away?

Well fed, Thia was contented when Perca carried her into the chamber. Caecilia laid the baby in the crook of Mastarna's arm, the fresh swaddling bright against his soiled tunic.

He was awkward with the miniature girl. "She is smaller than the others."

"That is because you've never held a newborn." Caecilia uncurled Thia's small fist with one finger only to have the baby clench her palm around it. "This is only her tenth day of life."

Lethargic, Mastarna needed to concentrate to form words. "And what is she to be called?"

"Larthia, after your mother."

Caecilia realized she did not have an amulet to place around her daughter's neck. So she unfastened her Atlenta pendant. The silver locket was large upon the tiny breast. "This will serve until you bestow one of her own upon her."

"Then she is to be a warrioress also?"

"She is a child of war."

"Then may this bulla protect her from the evil eye."

He could not raise the baby aloft; instead he bent and kissed her head, speech slurred but his intention clear. "I claim Larthia of the House of Mastarna. She is the child of my loins and that of Aemilia Caeciliana's."

There was no welcoming crowd to hear his proclamation. Only three witnesses: a bodyguard, a healer, and a nursemaid. After threat and despair and terror this more than sufficed.

— • —

The physician was skilled. Caecilia saw how careful he was as he worked on her unconscious husband. He used both hands with equal ease and his fingers never trembled as he stitched the flesh and set the bone with a wooden splint.

Her spurt of vitality was flagging. Now that Vel had been tended, she noticed the aches within her own body: the rent to her womb, the welts upon her cheek where the hail had hit her. Her eyelids were heavy with both tiredness and the sharp beating pulse in her forehead. And the acrid smell of resin cerate smeared on the bandages made her feel faint. It was an odor to which she must grow accustomed. Such a plaster would ward off infection.

Evening had fallen. In the soft glow of the candelabras the leopard on the wall peered at her from its laurel bower. Vel believed it would keep them safe from the perils in the Beyond. As always its gaze was steady and calming as she whispered to it, "I pray he will not need you today."

Arruns stood to the side in the shadows observing the general. For the first time she noticed how weary the Phoenician was, the snake tattoo unable to mask exhaustion. There was an air of satisfaction about him, though; the subtle uncomplaining discontent she'd sensed within him over the past months had been dispelled. He was no longer a mere guardian of women and children. Today he'd been able to display valor. Once again, he'd risked his life for his master. "Thank you for protecting him, Arruns. Both of us now owe our lives to you. Go eat, rest. I will watch over him."

He hesitated, then checked Mastarna one more time before bowing and leaving the chamber.

Sinking into the armchair, Caecilia tried to clear her mind, but soon troubles disturbed her.

Tas.

The vehemence of his embrace after days of quiet resentment had stunned her. Yet on the heels of surprise came the news of his attempted abduction. The sense of danger having been evaded when she was not aware of its existence was unnerving. She'd thought she had outwitted the haruspex. If not for Semni, she could be bemoaning the loss of her son.

Thinking of Artile upset her. A nerve flickered in her cheek. She hoped the Romans would be ruthless. The priest's sins against her had been so many and so great. At least Mastarna would not risk punishment. With his brother fled there was no need for murder.

Lost in thought, Caecilia did not notice Tarchon enter.

Standing at the end of the bed he studied his father, crinkling his nose at the heady smell of pitch within the chamber. "At least he looks peaceful, but I would not want to be him when he wakes."

"The physician has done all he could. Now we must pray Vel's blood is not poisoned."

The soldier drew up the other chair in front of her. His thigh had been dressed with fresh bandages. "And what about you, Caecilia? You are so drawn you look as though death has hunted you. Was giving birth to my sister difficult?"

"I must admit that she was a little stubborn about leaving the womb."

"Then she takes after her mother." He smiled and patted her hand. "Let's hope she is as brave as her mother, too."

Caecilia did not feel courageous. Seeing Tarchon was a reminder that the world outside the sickroom was frantic with confusion and grief. He'd not even had time to wash the dirt from his face, his beauty marred by lines of weariness and worry. "What is happening in the city?"

"Lusinies is convening the High Council. Many are calling for Mastarna to be lucumo."

She rubbed her temples, the throbbing in her head worsening. "Vel would never agree. And the dead of our clan are still on the battlefield waiting to be buried. There are few left to vote for him."

Tarchon leaned forward. "Other tribes wish him to rule, Caecilia. Many believe he is the only one who can lead Veii to victory."

"Victory? How can you speak of victory after today?"

"Because of the alliance."

"Alliance?"

"The one Mastarna formed with Tarquinia."

Her eyes swam with fatigue as she struggled to understand. "But the League of the Twelve rejected Veii's petition."

"That's true, but Mastarna convinced the congress to allow those cities wishing to assist to join us. He has succeeded in persuading Aule Porsenna. That zilath is mustering a force as we speak. And there are others, too, that see Rome as a canker that must be excised before it can spread. Thefarie is riding from Capena to parley with them."

Caecilia glanced over at her sleeping husband. "Then we need not despair?"

Tarchon took both her hands in his. "The gods have not deserted us yet, Caecilia. The Romans may well be routed if enough of the Rasenna rise." He looked across to his father. "But we need him to lead us. We need him to be our ruler."

Caecilia shook her head, aware the pressures of command were already mounting even as Vel lay injured. "We need him to recover first."

"May he heal swiftly then. There is much to do. Many are now agreeing with Sethre that Vipinas is the traitor."

She remembered how the grieving princip wept over his dead grandson. Perhaps the old man would welcome death. "He is no traitor."

Tarchon grimaced. "He is a king killer, Caecilia. Few would agree with you."

"Kurvenas said I was the treacherous one."

"That is a chorus we have heard before."

The wry reply made her smile.

He patted her hand again and stood. "You must rest. All this can wait until tomorrow."

Raking her fingers through her hair, she massaged her scalp, trying to ease the ache, doubting she could sleep. "Has Artile truly gone?"

"He cannot be found. And although we may welcome his departure, the loss of the chief haruspex will be keenly felt."

"Then they should seek him in Velzna."

He raised an eyebrow. "How do you know that?"

"Because . . ." Suddenly she could no longer be brave, no longer calm. The horror of the day, and all the days before, welled in her. "Because . . ."

She halted, unable to make a sound as the sob rose within her. Her distress hung suspended until, surging, it was expelled in one long, loud lamentation.

Tarchon lifted her, then sat down with her on his lap, ignoring his wound. Crying, she put her arms around his neck. "So much has happened."

"Hush, all this can wait until tomorrow." Stroking her hair, he held her as she wept. A closeness between them. The foundation of their friendship solid, past arguments forgotten. With Tarchon she could be vulnerable. He had comforted her this way many times before. He was a confidant on whom she'd relied when first a bride and now a matron.

After a time she wiped her eyes, realizing she'd not consoled him about his own sadness. "I'm sorry about Sethre."

Tarchon eased her from his lap before standing. His small smile did not hide dejection as he kissed her cheek. "I will think about that—tomorrow."

FIFTY-FOUR

In the dimness outside the circle of the candle's light, Semni sensed Arruns before she saw him standing at the cell door.

She left Nerie sleeping on the bed and ran to him, slipping her arms around his waist. "I feared you would be kill—"

He did not wait for her to finish, instead lifted her by the waist and pressed her against the wall, his kiss urgent. Her astonishment lasted only a fraction, then she opened her mouth to his tongue as she hitched up her chiton. He no longer wore his battle-stained tunic. Bare-chested above his short kilt, the muscles of his chest and abdomen were defined beneath the coils of the snake. His skin was still wet from where he'd washed away the mud and his master's blood. He rammed into her as she stood on tiptoes, crushed against him. She'd not been taken so roughly for a long time and welcomed his power.

Grasping her wrists, he held her arms above her against the wall. She wanted to run her hands over the broad expanse of his shoulders and back yet the restraint heightened her excitement. She moaned at each thrust but, intent and hungry, he made little sound. His head was bent to hers, the tattoo flush against her skin. She drew back, licking the inked pattern before nipping his earlobe. He grunted and bit into her shoulder through the cloth. With the pain and surprise came her rush. Shuddering, she cried out, sensing him following, but then another surprise—groaning, he pulled out of her suddenly, his hot seed spurting over her belly.

Her disappointment was strong, her anger, too. She struggled to free herself from his grip. "Why didn't you finish inside me?"

Releasing her wrists, he wrapped his arms around her, his breath uneven. His hug was tender after the fierceness of their coupling. "Because I want no more of our children to be born into this war."

Semni wriggled from his embrace to look at him. "Our children?"

"I want to claim Nerie. I want you to be my wife."

"Truly?"

His face with its hooked nose and hooded lids was serious. "After facing battle today—after seeing the general injured—I was glad to be alive. I've wanted you for so long."

She laughed, happy, so happy, but as she raised her arms to encircle his neck, she winced, the bite on her shoulder hurting.

Arruns noticed her flinch. He slipped the chiton from her shoulder to reveal teeth marks in her flesh. He touched the spot gently with calloused fingers. "I'm sorry if I hurt you."

Semni thought of the aged Velthur, and how both needed to use a switch to stir them. "I don't mind a little pain," she teased. "At least you didn't draw blood like my old husband."

He raised his eyebrows, causing her to laugh.

The touch of Nerie's hand on her leg startled her. The toddler was grizzling, bleary-eyed from being woken from his slumber. "Hush," she said, picking him up.

Arruns smiled, scooping up both mother and child and carrying them to the bed, where he sat with them on his lap. Content between them, Nerie nestled close.

She laid her head on Arruns's shoulder. "So you believe me? Believe that I did not want Aricia?"

He nodded. "I believe you. I do not think you would have prevented her taking the young master if she was your lover."

Idly tracing the line of the serpent around his neck and across his torso, her hand drifted down to his kilt. She had yet to discover if it was a two-headed snake. "So you are proud of me?"

He covered her hand, his palm engulfing her fingers, preventing further exploration. "Yes, now tell me what happened."

Semni felt uneasy, regretting she'd drawn his attention to Aricia's plot. "The haruspex sent her to take Master Tas. The three of them were to travel to the Sacred College. I stopped her when I found her coming from the wine cellar after she'd been through the secret passageway."

His eyes narrowed. "And of all the slaves and servants in this house it was you who happened upon her?"

His suspicion nonplussed her. She concentrated on Nerie. The tot had fallen asleep again, sucking his thumb. She laid him down on the bed, tucking in the coverlet around him rather than look at the Phoenician.

Arruns shifted her off his lap when she didn't reply. "Quite a coincidence."

Again Semni was sorry she'd raised the subject. She'd expected praise matching the gratitude of the mistress; instead Arruns was asking the questions Lady Caecilia should have asked. "Yes, it was good luck, wasn't it?"

His frown showed he remained unconvinced. He crossed his arms. "There was something Master Tas said that was strange. What did he mean by 'Semni stopped her this time'?"

Nervous, she spoke rapidly as though rushing her words would convince him. "Nothing. Only that I thwarted her."

He seized her wrist. "Did you know Aricia had taken the boy to visit the haruspex before?"

Her heartbeat doubled, feeling trapped. "Of course not."

His fingers dug into her flesh. "You're lying, Semni. I can tell."

Now the pain of his grip scared her. Suddenly she could pretend no longer. She wanted all to be right between them. For him to hold her and love her again. Taking a deep breath, she prayed honesty would earn her a reprieve. "I did not help her but I did keep quiet."

His silence was worse than if he'd struck her.

He let her go, staring at her as though overwhelmed in understanding what was unforgivable. "Why? Why would you do nothing? You must have known Aricia was wrong."

She rubbed her wrist then knelt before him, grasping his knees. "Please, Arruns. Don't you see I have been good? What does it matter what happened before? I did not let her take the boy today."

His look was withering. "You are such a child, Semni. Selfish and unthinking. You're a coward, too. You should have confessed when the nursemaid was punished."

"And be thrown out too?" She pointed to Nerie. "He would have suffered."

Arruns glanced at the sleeping boy.

The desperation she'd felt when her sister shunned her returned. She had not been pardoned then and she sensed there would be no forgiveness now. "Are you going to tell on me?"

He stood up as though he could not bear being near her. "No, you are going to speak out when my lord has recovered and the mistress is stronger. And you must beg their indulgence and pray for their mercy. Lady Caecilia is kind and may well be lenient because of your actions today. But the master . . . well, he may not be so compassionate."

The general. Semni had never seen him angry, but she guessed he would be terrifying. Stomach knotted, she steepled her fingers in supplication. "Please, Arruns, please don't tell. Do you want to see me whipped? Do you want Nerie to die of hunger when we are thrown into the streets?"

Arruns reached down and lifted the boy into his arms. A killer cradling innocence. Groggy with sleep, Nerie woke again briefly, closing his eyes when he saw it was the guard who held him. The Phoenician placed his hand upon the child's head. "I said I'd claim him as my son. I will not see him come to harm."

Semni sat back on her heels, relieved. "Then you still want me as your wife? You will stay silent?"

In the flickering light from the candle, she saw him pause.

She stood and retrieved Nerie, holding him against her shoulder. The child whimpered at being woken. "Don't punish me now for my past sins. What if the master sends me away? What then? Will you tear my son from me? Deprive him of his mother? I never thought you could be so cruel."

The furrow creasing Arruns's brow deepened. "To protect you means I must deceive the master."

"You will not be deceiving him. The threat has passed. He need never know." She placed her hand on his chest. "And I have changed. You know I have."

Arruns stepped back from her, retreating inwardly, too, leaving passion and affection in his wake. "It is not so simple." He reached over and placed his hand on Nerie's back, scanning Semni's face, reproach in his resinous eyes. "Why do you have to make it so hard to love you?"

As Semni watched him leave, she sat on the pallet and cradled her son. The headiness of lovemaking had vanished, the creeping fear that she had lost Arruns making her despair. His fleeting look of hurt on parting made her ashamed that he must fail in his duty if he was to protect her.

Yet was hope truly splintered into shards so minute it could never be repaired? She rocked Nerie, this boy whom she'd not wanted. The son of a ram had at last been claimed. Now he was her savior. She kissed his fair hair, determined to prove to Arruns that she could be a worthy wife. Then, like a broken pot that could be mended if enough pieces were intact, she hoped their son might be the glue that would bind his new father to his mother.

FIFTY-FIVE

Camillus's Camp

The rain was teeming again, beating on the leather of the command tent. Inside, the air was steamy, the humidity heightened by high spirits and body heat, the sour sweat of battle augmented by fresh perspiration on flushed faces.

Pinna was the only woman present, having been called to tend to Camillus's wound. She may have finally moved her possessions into his quarters but this was a time for men. Marcus was absent, though, keeping vigil over his damaged friend.

The general squeezed her hand. "I'm ready for you to do your patchwork."

"Patchwork? Why, it will be embroidery."

He laughed. "Just remember, it is flesh you sew, not fabric."

She teased him when he flinched at the sting of the castor oil but grew serious as she stitched the gash. He made no sound as she worked. The wine dulled the prick of the needle and tug of the thread. Nevertheless, she noticed how he gripped the armrests with whitened knuckles until she'd tied and broken off the last knot.

The rain had not doused the fervor of the men's drinking party. The mood was rowdy, exhilaration matched by inebriation. BAmid boasting of brave deeds, their heroics were soon inflated. And the stack of empty wine jars confirmed that the journey northward tomorrow would be with sore heads as well as aching bodies and injured limbs. Camillus had given the order, though, that no man would be punished for drinking unwatered wine that night provided he was sober enough to march at sunrise.

Camillus was animated. As with everything, he led his officers, refilling his cup as soon as he'd drained it. And as usual he outdid them. While others flagged he continued imbibing. He grew cheerful but not drunk. She knew, too, that in the morning he would suffer no headache and would also expect a clear mind and sober stride from those around him.

Some of his staff were not merry. The thrill of battle had disappeared. Exhausted, some drank solemnly while others grew maudlin over fallen comrades. Some were arguing, disputing who was more valiant, who had scored the greatest tally. She hoped there would be no fistfights.

The racket of carousing quieted when two unfamiliar soldiers sought an audience. They were dragging a man between them. All ceased their banter to observe the stranger.

At first Pinna thought the prisoner was crying black tears. On closer inspection, she realized streaks of kohl ran down his rain-wet face. The sight astounded her. The last man she'd seen with eyes rimmed with antimony was a mollis creeping through the back streets of Rome.

An odor of lanolin and wet wool was strong about the captive. Hauled up between the two burly guards he looked a soft, pampered creature. His fringed sheepskin coat was drenched, his fine leather boots sodden, laces trailing. He was clean-shaven, the soft curls of his shoulder-length black hair dripping, his hands as white as a noblewoman's and adorned with gold rings. And yet no patrician lady would wear other than iron jewelry, nor would she paint her fingernails and darken her lashes.

It was obvious he'd been treated roughly: his clothes were in disarray, his top lip swollen, and his cheek bruised. His strange pointed hat was askew, the ties under his chin loosened. And yet there was an air of defiance about him, an aura of a superior condescending to subordinates.

Pinna had seen Etruscans before in Rome. Their sloe eyes and straight nose and brow declared them descendants of a tyrant cast out by her people over a century ago. This one, though, held her attention because of his peculiar almond-shaped eyes. His pupils were large against dark irises, leaving only a rim of white around them. She imagined they could cast a spell. The hair rose on the nape of her neck as his gaze traveled momentarily over her before settling on the consular general.

Both sentries saluted and then one reported. "We caught him trying to pass through a stockade to the north. Our commander said to bring him to you. The priest was driving a cart filled with boxes of scrolls and linen books."

The other soldier brandished a curved staff. "He was carrying this lituus and claims he is a seer. He was overheard talking to a trader about the prodigy at Lake Albanus. He said Veii will not fall until the Romans learn how to mollify the gods. He claimed to know how to do this."

Camillus relaxed in his chair, studying the captive for some time in silence before signaling the soldiers to release him. The man stretched his neck and adjusted an elaborate crescent-shaped fibula fastening his cloak. He seemed unconcerned by the general's scrutiny.

"So you speak Latin, priest?"

"I speak many languages, Furius Camillus." His accent was flawless, his voice deep, as compelling as his gaze. "And the gods speak to me."

"You are an augur then."

"Not just an augur. I am both haruspex and fulgurator."

"Then you are an expert. Expert enough, it seems, to claim you understand the mystery of Lake Albanus."

The Etruscan smoothed one eyebrow. "I may have done. I can't remember."

Camillus tapped his ring, smiling at the man's caginess. The Etruscan fixed his eyes upon this gesture, causing the Roman to cease the movement. Irritated, the general leaned forward. "Not even the Sibylline Books provide an answer to deal with this portent. I think, perhaps, you're just a braggart."

The soothsayer touched his torn lip gingerly. "I'm no boaster. Your augury is primitive."

"Is that so? I took the auspices this morning, which presaged a great victory. And the Veientane dead that litter the ground prove my expertise in determining divine favor."

The prisoner straightened his hat and retied the chin straps. "Feeding hungry chickens puls and being satisfied when they peck at it avidly is hardly a skill."

Pinna blinked. Was he mad? Insulting a consular general? And in the company of his officers? She held her breath, waiting for Camillus to erupt. Her lover, though, was unperturbed. Standing up, he moved to the priest and thrust his face an inch from his. The Etruscan flinched and moved back.

"Tell me, priest, if you're such a great prophet, why were you scurrying in the dark along the northern road? Surely the king needs the services of such a mighty soothsayer. Or are you just a rogue who deserts his city when it is licking its wounds?"

The man fiddled with the golden brooch again, still haughty. "I can assure you, King Kurvenas values my advice. I was traveling to Velzna to consult the Sacred College on his request."

Camillus returned to the repository table and drank some more wine. "It sounds to me that you're just a lowly priest sent to seek advice from his betters." He gestured to the sentries to secure the stranger again. "Take him to the compound and place him with the other prisoners. It will amuse me to keep a holy man as a slave."

At his command all arrogance disappeared from the Etruscan's face. Gulping in air like a landed fish, he struggled against the guards. "Stop. You cannot make me your servant. I am no ordinary cepen. I am Artile Mastarna, high priest of the Temple of Uni and the chief haruspex of Veii."

Pinna gasped and the officers around her broke into chatter. What had been a distraction from their drinking had now become intriguing. Camillus, too, was surprised. He roared at his men to be quiet.

"Artile Mastarna? Brother of the great general? Why, your fame has spread as far as Rome."

The priest drew himself to full height. His eerie gleaming eyes shed their look of fear, his stature once again proud.

Pacing, Camillus examined him. His great rival's sibling was now in his power. A hostage. There was leverage to be gained in such a capture. "Your brother was defeated today. Is that why you fled? Because you fear your city will fall now that his army has been destroyed?"

The soothsayer smoothed his eyebrow. "No, I chose to leave because Mastarna has returned."

Camillus frowned. "So there's enmity between you. Why?"

"You need not know the reason, only that my hatred equals his."

The general circled the Etruscan. Pinna could see him calculating, assessing.

"And you claim to know the required rituals to placate the gods? Appeasement that, if completed correctly, will mean that Veii will fall?"

Smoothing his eyebrow again, once, twice, three times, the seer remained silent, keeping his gaze straight ahead. Camillus leaned close. "How much do you hate your brother?"

The priest's silence continued.

"Enough to want him dead?"

The cat's eyes flickered.

"Enough to help me destroy him?"

Moments passed. The haruspex slowly turned. His voice was mellifluous, conceited again. "Perhaps, Furius Camillus, I might be persuaded."

Artile Mastarna's smile made Pinna shiver. She touched her amulets. She murmured a prayer.

FIFTY-SIX

Veii

Caecilia called for an ewer and a jug of warm water with sandalwood to scent it. The perfume was a comfort, so faint and fragrant compared to the stink of resin.

With the servants' help she cut off Mastarna's drenched tunic and changed the bedding. Then she asked them to leave. She wanted to tend to her husband alone.

It was a shock to see Vel's chest covered with a fine layer of hair. There had been no time for a barber in his haste to return to Veii. She ran her fingers along the raised skin of the cicatrice that slashed his torso, reacquainting herself with its contours. His other scars, too. The geography of battles carved into his flesh. At least their existence reminded her that he had suffered and survived before.

In the mellow light of the candelabras she could see the sun had burned his legs and arms dark enough that bruises barely showed. Yet the olive skin of his abdomen and thighs was dappled. She brushed her lips across the contusions as if such caresses could help.

Squeezing the perfumed water from the dripping sponge, she washed him, taking care not to press too hard on the abrasion where the cuirass had irritated the scar along his hip bone. The wet grain of fabric had rubbed the skin raw. She was gentle, too, as she bathed the grime from his battered face, leaving Arruns to shave the beard on the morrow.

Once she'd scrubbed the black blood from beneath his nails and the whorls of his finger pads, she laid his hand against her cheek, remembering how in lovemaking he would do so. And she thanked Juno that there was heat in his limbs instead of a corpse's coldness; that it was a sheet she drew over him, not a shroud.

She sat beside him when she'd finished. The bed was a rectangle that harbored love and life. Their children had been conceived and born here. It could be a place where death visited also. Only days earlier she had nearly died upon its mattress. She did not want it to be Vel's last resting place either.

She watched the rise and fall of his breath as he lay sleeping. A peaceful rhythm after trauma. His life could have ended today. Attacked by a coward and threatened by her cousin—one with calculated fury, the other with unrestrained rage.

Marcus had told Vel that she was dead to him. She said the words aloud. In the quiet of the room, the shock of their meaning was powerful and deep.

Over the years she'd pondered the effect her leaving might have had on her cousin. She prayed he still loved her even if he detested what she'd done. Now it was clear that forgiveness had been forfeited long ago. Why couldn't he see that Rome had betrayed her? That he had no justification to despise her? That although he was her enemy she'd never desired his demise?

Today they had stared at each other across a battlefield. The distance between them was now measured by more than miles. The loss of him was like a ball of pain. She felt a sob rising in her throat but she stifled her lament. Tears pricked her eyes but she brushed them away with the back of her hand.

The iron bracelet with its Aemilian crest touched her skin. Suddenly anger erupted in her, replacing grief. She wrenched the amulet over her wrist and dropped it to the floor, then kicked it away. Tomorrow she would bury it. It was the last tangible connection to the cousin she'd once known. Marcus had given it to her to shelter her from the evil she might find in Veii. Now she and her family needed protection from him and it would be Rasennan gods who'd provide it.

She remembered the promise she'd been so desperate to extract from Vel, to not attack Rome and restrict himself to defending Veii. Now she felt ashamed she'd been so angry when he'd broken the pledge. For he was right. Romans were like soldier ants, devouring all in their way. She could no longer remain passive, hoping the threat would disappear. The links to her birthplace were those ties that bound her to her cousin. Her love for Marcus had always hindered her from wanting to see Rome fall. Now he wished her dead and she had hardened her heart against him. No longer would she agonize that her kin and the Roman people could be slain.

For Camillus, the wolf, skulked outside her city ready to wreak annihilation. And when he was no longer in office others would follow with the same intent. She knew she was an emblem of sedition and could expect death if they succeeded. So could Mastarna. After today, though, she finally understood that her children would not be spared either. For certain no humanity would be shown to the Veientanes.

Vel's dice box sat on the side table, retrieved from his cloak when the slave boy had collected his master's soiled clothes. Caecilia shook the golden tesserae onto her palm, feeling their worn smoothness.

The dark mastery of Artile over her had ended but there was always the specter of his prescience. Somehow he'd known the result of the throw pointed to Rome, and that she had disobeyed Nortia. Once he'd gulled her into believing she could delay her destiny. And as much as her husband told her she must surrender to fortune, the vestiges of her younger self remained. The hope that she could influence the goddess had never truly left her. It was ingrained in her to chafe against the strands of fate. To try to weave them to her purpose.

Yet Uni, Veii's protectress, had sheltered her city today. The goddess whom she still called Juno sent hail when disaster beckoned. There must have been a reason for this salvation. Had the Veientanes been rescued so that they might smite their enemy? After all, Thefarie was mustering Rasennan forces. Veii could yet march on Rome. And Etruscan kings had ruled there before.

Caecilia traced the symbols on the golden dice with a fingertip. What if her pathway back was via the Veientanes making the Romans their subjects once again? What if her family could pass through the gates of Rome not as captives but as conquerors?

Vel stirred beside her, wakening to pain. Mouth parched, he lay with bloodshot eyes open, disoriented until he saw her. She laid her hand on his forehead, checking for fever.

"Don't fuss." His voice was hoarse.

"I am allowed to worry." She helped him sip some water laced with poppy juice to soothe the pain. "Does it hurt terribly?"

He closed his eyes briefly with the effort of movement before he examined his injured arm. "If I am to be a cripple it might be better if I'd died."

"Don't say such a thing!"

Seeing her stricken face, he reached over to cup her face, tracing the curve of her cheekbone with his thumb. "You are gaunt, Bellatrix. Was the labor very hard?"

"No," she lied. "Although our daughter was a little reluctant to fight her way from the womb."

Vel ran a finger along the birthmark on her neck. "I think, perhaps, that you are not being truthful. I think you have suffered."

Raising his hand to her lips, she kissed his grazed knuckles. "I've forgotten any travail now that we have our healthy child."

"Thank you, Bellatrix, I could have no better wife."

"Nor I a better husband."

He was tiring, shifting his weight to ease the discomfort but finding no relief. Caecilia laid the dice on the bed before propping some pillows behind him. Mastarna gathered them up.

"Ah, I'm glad I did not lose these. They are my luck. They brought you back to me."

Caecilia paused, uncertain if she should confess what the dice had truly determined. But this was not the time. Later, though, she would tell him that she was prepared to stand in the citadel square and declare to all her intention to wage her own war on Rome.

Seeing his weakness, she rose to let him sleep, but he held fast to her hand. "Lie next to me."

Her clothes were stiff with stain and smell, her bodice crusted with what little milk she had, her hair disheveled. "I must bathe first."

"Stay."

Slipping off her ruined shoes, she slid beneath the sheet and curled up beside him, no gap between them. Head resting on his shoulder, she remembered how once she'd lain in her white bridal tunic on their first wedding night, hair still braided, terrified of consummation, loyal only to Rome.

Soothed by the beat of his heart and his scented skin as he slept, she too grew heavy-lidded.

It was nearly dawn, the eastern sky shot with color, the sun's rays bathing the leaves of the grapevine with light. Soon they would be bright with autumn's colors. In winter, when the boughs were bare, Camillus would no longer be a consular general and, by the grace of the gods, Mastarna would be strong again.

Sleep stalking her, Caecilia eased the tesserae from Vel's hand, tightening her fingers around them. Truly a Rasennan. Faithful to Veii. Enemy to Rome.

She had not flouted the goddess.

Nortia brought her back for a reason.

GLOSSARY

Acheron: In Greek mythology, the river of sorrow in the Underworld; in Etruscan religion, the Afterworld or the Beyond, a place to which the dead journeyed over land and sea.

Alabastron: A small flask for perfume or fragrant oils, originally fashioned from alabaster but later made from pottery, metal, or glass.

Antefixes: A stone or ceramic block that covered the end of a tiled ridge on a roof. Antefixes were ornately carved, often with mythological creatures.

Arx: Citadel or fortified high ground within a city.

Aulos: An ancient wind instrument similar to an oboe.

Auspices: Before any decision of state was made, omens were observed and interpreted. This involved watching the flight of birds. To do this one needed *patrician* blood. Only certain magistrates such as a *consul* could take the public auspices, as opposed to the head of the household observing omens for private purposes.

Balteus: A leather shoulder-belt worn diagonally across the body from which a sword was suspended.

Bondsman: A debtor who forfeited his liberty to his creditor to satisfy his debts. He was enslaved until he paid back what he owed.

Boss: A round or conical piece of thick metal jutting from the center of a shield to deflect blows. Bosses were sometimes molded into the shapes of animal's heads or other decorative motifs.

Bucchero: A type of glossy black pottery developed by the Etruscans. The color was produced by reducing the oxygen supply during the firing process.

Bulla: A locket of metal or leather worn to ward off evil spirits. It was removed when a Roman boy reached manhood at fourteen. A Roman girl wore a similar amulet, which was removed on the eve of her wedding. Etruscans wore bullas throughout their lives.

Campus Martius (*Field of Mars*): The level ground between the low-lying flood-prone plain enclosed by a bend of the Tiber River and the slopes of the Quirinal, Capitoline, and Pincian hills. It was dedicated to Mars, the god of war, and was believed to initially belong to an Etruscan king, Tarquinius Superbus. Originally, it was used as a pasture for sheep and horses, but was also used as a military training ground and mustering area. Political assemblies and the elections of magistrates were also held there. As it was located outside the pomerium (sacred boundary) of the city, it was permissible for tombs to be built there.

Cepen: Common word for an Etruscan priest.

Cerate: An unctuous preparation of wax or lard that is sometimes impregnated with resin. The cerate is applied over dressings to ward off infection. Beeswax was often used in ancient times.

Chiton: A long robe worn by both men and women alike in Etruria and Greece. It was similar to the Roman tunic. During the classical period, Etruscan ladies wore linen chitons that clung so tightly to the body their breasts and nipples showed through the material. It was usually worn with a mantle of heavier cloth.

Cista: A small casket, usually cylindrical in shape, used for keeping cosmetics, perfumes, or jewelry.

Cithara/Kithara: An ancient stringed instrument in the lyre family that was played with a plectrum.

Comitium: The open-air area in Rome where the *plebeian* and tribal assemblies met. The *speakers' platform* was located here. The Comitium stood opposite the *Curia* or *Senate House.*

Consul: One of two magistrates with imperium (supreme authority) who held the highest position in the Roman Republic. Both consuls had the right of veto over each other and were entitled to take the public *auspices* that preceded every major action taken on the state's behalf.

Consular general: A military tribune with consular powers. For many years in the early Roman Republic, military tribunes were elected instead of *consuls* because generals were needed on so many war fronts. As imperium (supreme authority) was not granted, *plebeians* could hold the office.

Cuirass/Corselet: Body armor consisting of a breastplate and backplate made from metal, leather, or stiffened linen. A "muscle" cuirass was molded to appear similar to a muscled male torso. In order to protect the thighs and groin, pteruges were worn with a cuirass. Pteruges consisted of flexible strips of layered leather or linen that hung from the waist forming a "kilt." Pteruges could also be attached at the shoulders to protect the upper arms.

Curia (Curia Hostilia): The Senate House in the Roman Forum.

Decurion: One of three knights who led ten men in a *turma.* The senior decurion commanded the *turma* with the other two decurions acting as his deputy.

Defixio: A lead sheet upon which the gods were invoked to either curse or enchant a person. In Rome, defixios were often affixed to the walls of tombs. Under the *Laws of the Twelve Tables* of the early Republic, seeking the destruction of a man through dark magic was subject to capital punishment.

Fascinum: A phallic-shaped amulet worn around the neck. The regenerative power of the phallus was seen as a potent force against the "evil eye."

Fibula/Fibulae: A clasp or brooch used to secure a cloak or worn as an ornament. Simple ones were in the shape of a large safety pin.

Fillet: Bands of wool that a Roman matron would plait into her hair. They were a symbol of a married female Roman citizen, as was the *stola*.

Forum, the: A rectangular plaza in the valley between the Capitoline and Palatine Hills. It was the political and social center of Rome.

Fulgurator: An Etruscan priest skilled in interpreting the will of the gods through analysis of different types of lightning and thunder.

Greaves: Armor that could protect either the shins only or the entire leg to the thigh, depending on the wealth of the soldier.

Haruspex: An Etruscan priest skilled in the art of haruspicy, i.e., dissecting a sacrificial animal's liver for the purpose of divination. A haruspex wore a distinctive hat that twisted to a point. He also wore a sheepskin cloak fastened by a *fibula* at the throat and carried a *lituus* staff.

Honored Way (Cursus Honorum): The method by which a man rose to the supreme office of *consul*; a political ladder whereby a man was elected to certain magistracies in prescribed order and only after reaching a particular age.

Hoplite: A citizen soldier in the heavy infantry who fought in a *phalanx* formation and was recognizable by his round "hoplon" shield. This is a Greek word but is applied to the Roman and Etruscan soldiers to associate them with this type of warfare.

The word "legionary" was not employed until after the Marian reforms to the Roman army.

Imperium: Supreme authority in Rome including command in war, interpretation and execution of the law, and the right to inflict punishment. The ability to take the public *auspices*, which preceded every major action taken on the state's behalf, was granted along with imperium.

Kline: A couch with headrests used in banquets.

Lapis Niger: There is still conjecture among historians as to what constituted the Lapis Niger, or "black stone," in the sanctuary in the *Comitium*. It may refer to a black stone stele inscribed with what is believed to be a dedication to a king. Even in imperial times, various writers disputed the origins of the site, with some claiming it was the spot where King Romulus was murdered. The sanctuary was destroyed during the sacking of Rome by the Gauls in 387 BC. During the Julio-Augustan period, the area was buried under slabs of black marble and this paving also came to be known as the Lapis Niger. The site can still be seen today.

Laws of the Twelve Tables: The legislation that formed the basis of the constitution and customary law (*mos maiorum*) of the Roman Republic. The laws were inscribed on twelve bronze (or ivory) tablets that were displayed in the Forum.

League of the Twelve: Economic and religious confederation of major Etruscan cities. There is conjecture as to exactly which cities formed the League, but I have included those considered most likely to have been included in the League on the map, using their Etruscan names.

Lemur/Lemures: Wandering and vengeful spirits who have been denied proper burial or funeral rites.

Leno: A pimp who ran a brothel (*lupanaria*). Lenos usually kept prostitutes as slaves, although free- and freedwomen were also employed as whores.

Levis/Leves: Skirmishers in the army of the early Roman Republic who were only armed with small, round shields and spears. They were among the poorest of soldiers in the military class structure.

Lictor: In Rome, one of twelve civil servants who protected the kings, and later those magistrates holding imperium (supreme authority). They carried a bundle of rods called the fasces, the symbol of power and authority. *Consuls* were entitled to twelve lictors. The tradition of the lictor and fasces was believed to derive from the Etruscan kings.

Lituus: Crooked staff used by augurs to mark out a ritual space for the purpose of divination.

Lucumo: An Etruscan king who was elected by aristocratic colleges rather than all citizens. He remained in office until his death. However, the exact nature of the Etruscan political power structure and its mechanisms has not yet been determined.

Lupanaria: Literally meaning "wolf den." Brothels were so called because one name for a prostitute was "lupa," or she wolf. There are various explanations for the derivation of the name including the belief that whores were as rapacious as wolves.

Maenad: A priestess who followed the god Dionysus (Greek), Bacchus (Roman), and Fufluns (Etruscan) and was reputed to dance in an ecstatic trance during Dionysian rites, and who wore distinctive clothing such as leopard-skin cloaks.

Mollis/Molles: The pejorative Latin name given to men who were exclusively homosexual rather than bisexual.

Palla: A long, rectangular-shaped cloak worn by Roman women, which could be wrapped around the body and thrown over one shoulder or drawn over the head. It was particularly associated with Roman matrons.

Patera/ae: A shallow dish used to make libations to the gods.

Patrician/s: Wealthy landowners of noble birth who traced their ancestry to the original founders of Rome and claimed to have "divine" blood. They held the highest positions of power during the time of the early Roman Republic.

People's Tribune/s (Tribune of the Plebs): Ten officials elected to protect the rights of *plebeians* as they held the power to veto decrees of the *Senate*, and actions of magistrates. As such they could hinder the levy and funding of troops. It was the only political position a *plebeian* could hold in the early Roman Republic. Their position was sacrosanct and inviolate, and, as such, the death penalty could be inflicted on those who interfered with the exercise of their power.

Phalanx: An infantry battle formation in which eight rows of soldiers held overlapping shields and long spears. As one row fell, the next one took its place. The phalanx formation was originally developed by the Greeks, copied by the Etruscans, and then adopted by the Romans.

Phersu: A masked man who performed blood sacrifices during Etruscan funeral games. He was the precursor to a Roman gladiator.

Plebeian/s: Roman citizens who were not *patricians*. They were denied the right to hold magistracies during the time of the early Roman Republic.

Puls: A boiled wheat porridge that was similar in texture to polenta.

Quern: A hand-operated mill for grinding corn.

Red-figured pottery: A style of pottery developed in Athens that came to replace the earlier form of Corinthian black-figured pottery. The red figures on a black background were produced through a sophisticated three-phase firing process.

Satyr: A male companion of the wine god Dionysus (Greek) or Fufluns (Etruscan), depicted with horse's ears and tail, and sometimes a horse's phallus.

Senate: An advisory council consisting of ex-magistrates but in effect the most powerful governing body in Rome. A senatorial decree (*senatus consultum*) had no formal authority but was generally always made into law.

Senator: A member of the Roman *Senate*. Senators only qualified to be elected if they had previously held office as a magistrate and were wealthy. Senators were entitled to wear a *toga* bordered in purple and a tunic with a broad purple stripe.

Silphion: A plant believed to be of the Ferula genus. It was used in antiquity as a seasoning (laserpicum) but was more famously known for its contraceptive qualities. It was the primary export of the North African city of Cyrene. Due to its efficacy, the plant was so much in demand that it was farmed out and is now extinct.

Sinus: The large fold of material in the front of a *toga* that could be used as a type of pocket.

Speakers' platform: A large curved platform located in the *Comitium* facing the *Curia*. Speakers would address the assemblies there and it was considered a consecrated area. It later came to be known as the Rostra due to the six rams of captured warships (known as rostra) affixed to the platform after the battle of Antium in 338 BC.

Stola: A long, sleeveless, pleated dress worn over a tunic. It was fastened at the shoulders with *fibulae* and worn with two belts, one beneath the breasts and the other around the waist. The stola and woolen hair *fillets* were the symbols of a married female Roman citizen.

Sutler: A civilian merchant who sold supplies to an army in the field.

Sybilline Books: A collection of holy books containing oracular utterances that were consulted by the Roman Senate in times of crisis. These were not prophecies but instead advice as to which expiation rites should be observed in order to avert calamity.

Tebenna: A rounded length of cloth worn by Etruscan men over a *chiton* as a cloak. It was similar in appearance to a *toga* but shorter. The Roman *toga* was derived from this garment.

Tesserae: A game that was usually played with two dice shaken in a cup and then tossed onto a gaming table. Dice were also referred to as tesserae.

Toga: A rounded length of cloth derived from the Etruscan *tebenna* that was draped as a cloak over a tunic. It was the distinctive garment of a male Roman citizen. Magistrates and *senators* were entitled to wear a purple border on their tunics and togas. Prostitutes were required to wear togas as they were not entitled to wear the stola of a respectable Roman matron.

Torque: A necklace of twisted metal open at the front.

Tufa: A form of limestone. The Italian regions of Tuscany and Lazio where the Etruscan cities were located were famous for the tunnels that could be carved out of this soft stone. Tufa could be red, gray, or yellow in color.

Turma/Turmae: A cavalry squadron of thirty men that was split into groups of ten knights, each led by a *decurion*.

Zeri: An opiate elixir. The name is fictitious and based on the Etruscan word for "free" or "serene."

Zilath: Chief magistrate of an Etruscan city with similar authority to a Roman *consul*. He was elected each year by aristocratic colleges rather than all citizens. However, the exact nature of the Etruscan political power structure and its mechanisms has not yet been determined.

AUTHOR'S NOTE

I was inspired to write about the Etruscans after I found a photo of a sixth-century BC sarcophagus upon which a husband and wife were sculpted in a pose of affection. The image of the lovers, known as "The Married Couple," intrigued me. What ancient culture acknowledged women as equals to their husbands? Or exalted marital fidelity with such open sensuality? Discovering the answer led me to the decadent and mystical Etruria, and the war between early Rome and Veii. In my author's note for *The Wedding Shroud* I wrote about the difficulties experienced in researching the Etruscan civilization; I recommend you read it if you are interested to find out more about their origins and religion as well as information on social status and bisexuality in the ancient world. (You can access my author's note via my website, at www.elisabethstorrs.com, together with other pieces of research and photographs on my blog: Triclinium, at www.elisabethstorrs.com/category/blog/triclinium.)

The ancient sources I used to research the siege of Veii were accounts from historians such as Livy, Plutarch, and Dionysius of Halicarnassus. However, problems arose in relying on such commentators due to the fact they were writing centuries after the fall of Etruria with their prejudices firmly entrenched. In essence, what we know about this war is from the viewpoint of the conquerors over the conquered. Nevertheless, the story they tell is compelling. Livy chronicled the events that occurred in each year of the siege, including the lists of the elected military tribunes with consular power (whom I have called "consular generals"). However, as dozens of generals were elected over the ten-year siege, I have pared down the cast by choosing only Genucius and Calvus to represent the plebeians, while highlighting the disastrous feud between the patricians Sergius and Verginius. As for the famous speech exhorting men to fight throughout winter, I have attributed this to Camillus when in fact it was a patrician named Appius Claudius who stirred the common men to fight. I have also condensed the various campaigns and political wrangling across the decade to the last three years of the conflict for the sake of pace and dramatic tension. And, as is the inclination of an historical novelist, I have invented other circumstances to enhance the plot. As for the authenticity of the scenes I describe, I have attempted to be consistent with current historians' views, but ultimately I present my own interpretation of how Etruscans and the early Republican Romans might have lived.

The episode in which the gates were closed on Veientane troops is mentioned only briefly by Livy. As is often the case with this historian, the most appalling events were glossed over in a few lines: "The Veientes, too, suffered heavily, for the gates of the town had been shut to prevent an irruption of the Romans, and many of them were killed outside before they could get through" (*The Early History of Rome*, Book 5.14, translated by A. de Selincourt, Penguin Books, London, 1971, page 357). For those who wish to access Livy's detailed account I recommend reading Book V of *The Early History of Rome*.

The characters who appear in the novel are fictitious, except for those consular generals Livy has mentioned. Indeed, no rendering of the story of Veii can be told without reference to Marcus Furius Camillus. This general (who was appointed dictator five times but was never elected consul) was named the second founder of Rome by the Greek biographer Plutarch due to his incredible political acumen, military innovation, bravery, and charisma. Any other characteristics I may have attributed to him (and the other generals named by Livy) are purely my own invention. This is particularly the case in relation to Camillus's attitude toward supporting the political ambitions of commoners. As such, he was not the lone patrician who was voted in with five plebeian generals. However, given the fact he was elected consular general several times (and later was called upon to lead Rome during various crises), he clearly held the confidence of those voting in the Comitium.

Discovering that Veii and Rome were located a mere twelve miles apart across the Tiber has always captivated me. In essence, just by crossing an expanse of water, you could be transported from the equivalent of the Dark Ages into someplace akin to the Renaissance.

The Etruscans were enlightened and cosmopolitan, and their women were afforded education, high status, and independence. As a result their society was often described as wicked by Greek and Roman historians, whose cultures repressed women and were xenophobic. Etruscan wives dined with their husbands at banquets and drank wine. In such commentators' eyes, this liberal behavior may well have equated with depravity. One infamous account, by an often discredited Greek historian, Theopompus of Chios, claimed that "the women of the Tyrrhenians [Etruscans] are common property." In contrast, their beautiful tomb art portrays devoted and loving husbands and wives. So which version of Etruscan women is correct? Promiscuous or faithful?

Etruscan culture clearly celebrated both marriage and sex. The image of men and women embracing is a constant theme in their tombs, and ranges from being demure, as in the case of "The Married Couple," to strongly erotic (Tomb of the Bulls), and even pornographic (Tomb of the Whippings). The latter illustrations seem to confirm the more prurient view of Etruscan women, but the "symplegma," or sexual embrace, was not always a gratuitous portrayal of abandon but rather an apotropaic symbol invoking the forces of fertility against evil and death.

It is clear from studying this society's art that they celebrated life and followed the religion of Fufluns/Pacha (the Greek Dionysus and Roman Bacchus, whose later cult adherents were famous for indulging in debauchery), which, in its purest form of worship, was a belief in the power of regeneration through the ecstatic merging of the spirit with the god. Interestingly, Etruscan tomb paintings are heavy with Dionysian symbolism when depicting banquets, and their pottery also portrays Bacchanalian scenes. The Pacha Cult was condemned in ancient Greece and Rome because of the opportunity it granted to women and slaves to participate in the rites. This resonates with me in terms of the independence enjoyed by Etruscan women. Accordingly, in my opinion, it may well be possible that their culture condoned female wantonness while also honoring wives and mothers. Certainly, some credence is given by modern historians in regard to illegitimate children, despite the fact it is Theopompus who raised this when he stated "the Tyrrhenians [Etruscans] bring up all the children born not knowing who is the father of each" (fragment from *Histories*, Book 43, of Theopompus of Chios, as quoted by Athenaeus in *The Learned Banquet*, sourced from Sybille Haynes, *Etruscan Civilization*, The J. Paul Getty Trust, Los Angeles, 2000, page 256). From this it can possibly be deduced that noblewomen were wealthy enough to afford to keep the children of extramarital affairs because they could transmit their own status to the children. I have explored this issue in the love affair between Ramutha and Caile, which also was inspired by a favorite theme in Etruscan art of older women embracing youthful lovers. However, I readily accept that my interpretation could be flawed.

The world of Roman women of the early Republic is no less fascinating. As with my research into Etruria, reliable sources were difficult to find to provide a definitive view of this period, and again I was forced to depend on non-contemporaneous sources. Much of what is understood about Roman women in early classical times is often deduced from Roman legislation that was enacted centuries later in the Augustan period. Rome valued monogamy, and the concepts of culpability for adultery and "stuprum" (extramarital sex) were applied when classifying a woman's status. The propriety expected of a Roman matron was the standard by which women were judged. The two ends of the spectrum were the respectable wife versus the dissolute whore. One was lauded as a decent citizen who must be faithful to her husband; the other was so corrupted that she lost all claim to moral or legal rights. The greater the degree of promiscuity, reward for sex, and lack of emotional attachment, the more tainted the woman became. However, given a prostitute was irrevocably stained, she could not be punished for committing adultery. That crime was reserved for a wife alone.

Prostitution was heavily regulated in Rome in the late Republican and imperial times. There is considerable commentary about this period but, alas, no certainty as to the rules relating to the "oldest profession" at the time I set the book. Nevertheless, I have based Pinna's circumstances on the assumption that imperial laws enshrined what had been customary practice throughout Republican times. There is, however, a reference made by the Roman historian Tacitus that an official register of prostitutes was kept "in accordance with a custom which obtained among the early Romans" (Tacitus, *Annals*, ii, 85, as sourced in Otto Keifer, *Sexual Life in Ancient Rome*, Abbey Library, London, 1974, page 60).

There were many different categories of prostitutes, all of whom were known by colorful names. The lupae ("she wolves") who serviced clients in "lupanariae," were reputedly called this because they were as rapacious as wolves. The inspiration for Pinna came from reading about the unregistered "noctiluae" (nightwalkers), who were colloquially known as "night moths," including the "busturiae," who doubled as hired mourners and plied their trade amid the tombs.

A concubine was seen as a mixture between a matron and a harlot. Her status was ambiguous and has been described as "safe and schizophrenic" (Thomas A. J. McGinn, *Concubinage and the Lex Iulia on Adultery*, Vol. 121, Transactions of the American Philological Association, The Johns Hopkins University Press, Baltimore, 1995, page 370). These de facto wives were denied the status of a matron because they had committed stuprum (and, it appears, were not subject to the laws of adultery either), yet they were considered respectable enough to be accepted by society. They were usually slaves or freedwomen, although there is evidence that lower-class freeborn citizens also chose to enter into such relationships. In most instances, concubines were entitled to "divorce" their partners without consent. Often widowers chose de facto wives to avoid complications with the inheritances of their legitimate children when marrying again. Concubines were also commonly taken by young noblemen before the men reached an age to enter political life and were expected to officially wed. And it is true that Camillus was responsible for introducing a bachelor tax because of the tendency of young men to avoid marrying war widows, whose numbers were growing due to the many wars being conducted at this time.

Status was signified through a dress code. Matrons were entitled to wear a stola and fillets in their hair as a symbol of both their married standing and their citizenship. In comparison, a prostitute was singled out by wearing a toga. (Compare this to the garb of Etruscan noblewomen during this period, who wore tight-fitting chitons of the finest material that showed the outline of the breasts and nipples.) (See Larissa Bonfante, *Etruscan Dress*, The Johns Hopkins University Press, Baltimore, 2003, page 39.) I was unable to ascertain whether a freeborn or freed concubine could wear a stola despite the fact she was a citizen. I've assumed the taint of stuprum would preclude such a right. Accordingly, I have deprived Pinna the opportunity, too.

The origins of the Troy Game are obscure. The inspiration for the episode came from the sixth-century BC Tragliatella Vase, which portrays a horseman emerging from a spiral inscribed with the word "Truia." This is considered the earliest depiction of the game. The rite is described in *The Aeneid* by the Roman poet Vergil, as the final event in the funeral games commemorating the death of Anchises, who was the father of the Trojan Aeneas. Vergil alludes to the patterns formed during the initiation exercise as a simulation of the Cretan labyrinth, an escape from which is a triumph of life over death.

The character of the Phersu and his hound are depicted in the Tomb of the Olympic Games and the Tomb of the Augurs at Tarquinia. The equivalent Latin term is "persona" or masked actor. In the murals the Phersu wears a bearded red mask, pointed hat, and short tunic and is torturing a hooded man by letting the dog loose on him. It is a singularly chilling sight. As Etruscan tomb art portrays the events held at funeral games, there is conjecture that the Phersu's role was to conduct a blood sacrifice to placate the anger of the dead while revitalizing the soul of the deceased on the journey to the Beyond. (This rite was echoed in the gladiatorial battles later held at funeral games in Rome.)

As for knowledge of warfare during the early Republic, sources were scarce. Nevertheless, I have attempted to provide as authentic a depiction as possible of military campaigns, as obtained from journal articles about the period. What is of interest is that the

Romans adopted their weaponry and battle formations from the Etruscans (for example, the phalanx). Given there are many readers who are experts on the Roman army, I trust some leeway will be afforded to me for any errors I may have inadvertently made relating to military life.

A bibliography is available on my website (www.elisabethstorrs.com/research.html), but sources I found of particular value in my research included: Sybille Haynes's *Etruscan Civilization* (The J. Paul Getty Trust, Los Angeles, 2000); Eva Cantarella's *Bisexuality in the Ancient World* (Yale University Press, New Haven, 1992); *Etruscans: Eminent Women, Powerful Men*, edited by Patricia S. Lulof and Iefke Van Kampen (W Books, University of Amsterdam, Amsterdam, 2012); Larissa Bonfante and Judith Swaddling's *Etruscan Myths* (The British Museum Press, London, 2006); Larissa Bonfante's *Etruscan Dress* (The Johns Hopkins University Press, Baltimore, 2003); Thomas A. J. McGinn's *Prostitution, Sexuality, and the Law in Ancient Rome* (Oxford University Press, London 1998); *The Oxford Classical Dictionary*, edited by Simon Hornblower, Anthony Spawforth, and Esther Eidinow (Oxford University Press, New York, 2003); *The Religion of the Etruscans*, edited by Nancy De Grummond and Erika Simon (University of Texas Press, Austin, 2006); and Livy's *The Early History of Rome*, translated by A. de Selincourt (Penguin Books, London, 1971).

THE WEDDING SHROUD

If you enjoyed *The Golden Dice*, you might like to read Caecilia's story in *The Wedding Shroud*, the first book in the Tales of Ancient Rome series.

> *"All the drama and sensuality expected of an historical romance, plus a sensitivity to the realities of life in a very different time and world . . ."* Ursula Le Guin

In 406 BC, to seal a tenuous truce, the young Roman Caecilia is wedded to Vel Mastarna, an Etruscan nobleman from Veii. Leaving her militaristic homeland, Caecilia is determined to remain true to Roman virtues while living among the sinful Etruscans. But, despite her best intentions, she is seduced by a culture that offers women education, independence, sexual freedom, and an empowering religion.

Enchanted by Veii but terrified of losing ties to Rome, Caecilia performs rites to delay becoming a mother, thereby postponing true entanglement. Yet as she develops an unexpected love for Mastarna, she's torn between her birthplace and the city in which she now lives. As war looms, Caecilia discovers Fate is not so easy to control, and she must choose where her allegiance lies.

The Golden Dice, the sequel to *The Wedding Shroud*, is the second book in the Tales of Ancient Rome series. The third book, *Call to Juno*, will be published in 2016.

ACKNOWLEDGMENTS

Special thanks and much love to my husband, David, for supporting me in my writing; and to my wonderful sons, Andrew and Lucas, who ground me in my family life. Thanks also to their grandma, Jacqui, to whom I've dedicated this book as well as my parents, Beth and John, who have sadly passed away.

Enormous thanks to the Lake Union team, and to the delightful Jodi Warshaw in particular, who was prepared to offer an opportunity to an Aussie author to reach a wider readership, and to Michelle Hope Anderson, my American copy editor, who has ensured the book is the best it could be.

Many thanks to the patient members of my writing groups: Jacs Vittles, Crisetta MacLeod, Melissa Fagan, Marilyn Harris, Katherine Delaney, and Margaret Rice. And an extra thank-you to Cecilia Rice, with whom I've shared a passion for writing for over twenty years. Also to the wonderful group of authors at HFeBooks, particularly M. Louisa Locke and Rebecca Lochlann. A big thank-you to Catherine Taylor, my Australian copy editor; her enthusiasm for the world of Veii and her astute observations on how to improve my writing make her a delight to work with. Love to

Lisi Schappi for designing my website (www.elisabethstorrs.com) and blog, Triclinium (www.elisabethstorrs.com/category/blog /triclinium); I'm lucky to have such a talented "niece-in-law." Thanks also to Rod Crundwell for composing some wonderful "Etruscan" music to accompany the images. And I'm grateful to Kate Duigan for producing the map. Thanks to Mumtaz Mustafa for designing the beautiful cover, and to Tom Greenwood from Greenwood Studios for doing such a professional job in producing the photo of the beautiful Marcella Wilkinson (who was so generous with her time).

My research into early Republican Rome was greatly assisted by Lea Beness and Tom Hilliard from Macquarie University. And I'm extremely grateful to the esteemed Etruscologist Iefke Van Kampen, for giving me a tour of the excavations on the Piazza D'Armi and Portonnacio D'Apollo at Veii. It is a day that I'll always remember. Thanks also to Isa and Daniele from Artemide Guide for making my tour of Etruria so enjoyable. Through them, I was able to gain access to the necropolises at Tarquinia and Ceverteri and finally see the tombs and funerary art that have inspired so many episodes within my books. And I cannot forget the lovely Anne Clare, who not only guided me around the ruins at Cortona but also was kind enough to send me photos from Museo Archeologico Nazionale at Chiusi (including one of a wedding shroud) after all my research photos were stolen with my wallet, passport, and phone on a train between Camogli and Genova! Finally, many thanks as well to all those not mentioned who have supported, encouraged, and given valuable advice over the course of the writing of this book.

ABOUT THE AUTHOR

Elisabeth Storrs has long held an interest in the history, myths, and legends of the ancient world. She is an Australian author and graduated from the University of Sydney in Arts Law, having studied Classics. She lives with her husband and two sons in Sydney, Australia, and over the years has worked as a solicitor, corporate lawyer, and governance consultant. She is a director of the NSW Writers' Centre and one of the founders of the Historical Novel Society Australasia.

The Golden Dice, the sequel to *The Wedding Shroud*, is the second novel in the Tales of Ancient Rome series set in Ancient Rome and Etruria. The third volume, *Call to Juno*, is currently being written.

The Wedding Shroud and *The Golden Dice* were judged runners-up in the international 2012 and 2013 Sharp Writ Book Awards for General Fiction respectively. *The Golden Dice* was also named as one of the top memorable reads of 2013 by Sarah Johnson, the reviews editor of the *Historical Novels Review*.

Recently, Elisabeth has written "Dying for Rome: Lucretia's Tale," the first short story in her collection *Short Tales of Ancient Rome*, in which she retells the history and legends of Rome from a fresh perspective.

Elisabeth would love you to connect with her on Facebook (www.facebook/pages/Elisabeth-Storrs), Twitter (www.twitter.com /elisabethstorrs), or via her blog, Triclinium (www.elisabethstorrs .com/category/blog/triclinium). And you are welcome to visit her website (www.elisabethstorrs.com) for more information on her books and to sign up to her newsletter.

Word of mouth is crucial for any author to succeed, therefore, if you enjoyed *The Golden Dice*, please consider writing a review at the point of purchase. A line or two can make a big difference and is much appreciated.

21206350R00294

Printed in Great Britain
by Amazon